Murder
in
Winnetka

By
S.C. Pemberton

Pittsburgh, PA

ISBN 1-56315-251-7

Paperback Fiction
© Copyright 2000 S.C. Pemberton
All rights reserved
First Printing—2000
Library of Congress #99-65316

Request for information should be addressed to:

SterlingHouse Publisher Inc.
The Sterling Building
440 Friday Road
Pittsburgh, PA 15209
www.sterlinghousepublisher.com

Cover design: Dan Paterno, Paterno Group Graphics, Chicago, IL
Typesetting: Kathleen M. Gall

Excerpts from "A Streetcar Named Desire" by Tennessee Williams,
Copyright 1947. Reprinted by permission of
New Directions Publishing Corp.

"A Streetcar Named Desire" Chicago Tribune Review by
Richard Christiansen, written for the Northlight Theatre Company,
Skokie, IL., 1996.

Printed in Canada

This book is dedicated with love to *Vernon Cravero*, my hero, my dad.
Thanks for the wings and the flying lessons, Captain!

And to *David*, my lifetime partner, because it never quite occurred to him that I couldn't.
For hugs, hot tea, indulgence and adventure. Thanks for the wild flight, darling!

To my family, who supported and loved me and taught me lessons ... Grazie!

Melissa, my daughter and best friend, who, like Meri, has everything I admire: beauty, brilliance,
talent and charm. Thanks for sharing your wonderful husband, ***Randy Van Popering***, and for
the most beautiful babies, ***Trevor and Nina***. And, thanks for the book of instructions.

Gregg, my son and the rising star, who combines all the genius and sensitivity of an artist with
intelligence, courage, good looks and good humor. Thanks for bringing music into my life.

Jacqueline LaPorte Cravero, my guardian angel, who taught me to love the written word.
Thanks for the roots and for believing in me.

John Pemberton, who loved and supported me like a daughter. Thanks for the Chicago history.

Gary Cravero, *my brother.* Thanks for being the inspiration behind my dedicated
"Do- you-feel-lucky-punk?" detective. And for the gift of your family, ***Terry, Geoffry and Jason***.

Rick Cravero. Thanks for sharing the experiences that allowed me a window into Tony's world.

Debby, Robert, Elizabeth and Max Graham. Thanks for sharing your blessings with me.

To those who've been the wind beneath my wings ... Salute!

Ginny Weissman, who gave me the gifts when I needed them most, her talent, experience
and eagle-eye. Thanks for sharing your roller coaster ride!

To all the wonderful women who've blessed my life with friendship ... Capisce?

Haley Butin, who survived the bumps along with me.
Thanks, for your sounding-board, your shoulder, and for the laughter.

Gaia Tossing. Thanks for your master-mind encouragement.

Susan Downing, the classiest lady around.

Joanne Clay Cure, who's seen it all with me. Thanks for the memories.

Sondra Healy. Thanks for your inspiration and encouragement.

Debby Pemberton and *Joyce Cravero.* Thanks for blending family and friendship.

Grazie to my teachers throughout the years, the muses whose words haunted and inspired me.
Most especially, *Julia Cameron*. Thanks for the gift.

Unity of Chicago and Reverend Ed Townley. Thanks for the road home.

My publisher, **Cynthia Sterling** and editor, **Annick Rouzier**. Thanks for believing in my work.

To the *Winnetka Police Force*: Thanks for being there when you're needed.

And *The Village of Winnetka*: Thank you for your friendships and allowing me to share
your special sense of community with the world.

There must be more to life than having everything.

—*Maurice Sendak*

The first thing is character ... before money or anything else. Money cannot buy it.

—*J. Pierpont Morgan*

A little bit added to what you've already got gives you a whole lot more.

—*P. G. Wodehouse*

PART ONE

DAY ONE
MONDAY, NOVEMBER 18 • 8:30 AM CST

THE BODY was already in a state of rigor mortis when the police detective entered the sprawling Tudor mansion. Even in a village of opulence, like Winnetka, this home was awe-inspiring, majestically standing atop a ragged bluff, lording over an angry, gray Lake Michigan. As he stood in the stone foyer, Detective Charles O'Brien thought of King Arthur's castle. "God, all that's missing is the damn moat!"

Two uniformed officers were talking in hushed voices. Detective O'Brien cleared his throat, perpetually hoarse from too many years of abusing it. "So what do we know here?"

His brusque manner broke the reverie abruptly. Startled, they nodded to the burly O'Brien. The male officer spoke first. "The body was found by the maid at about eight this morning. No one else was home. She called the station at" he checked his notes, "8:06. We arrived five minutes later, cordoned off the area and checked for identification."

"Do we know who he is?" O'Brien asked.

"That's where it really gets strange, sir. According to his ID, the man is Tony Romano." The officer waited while the detective processed the information.

"Holy Shit! You're kidding? What the hell's Tony "The Roman Rooster" Romano doing in Winnetka? Where are the Chamberlains? How long's he been dead?"

The officer locked eyes with his partner before continuing. "The coroner's up there now. My guess? About two days. It's not pretty, sir. Gunshot. He's got no face."

It was mid-November and thirty-three degrees outside, but O'Brien mopped his broadening brow. The overly warm house and the unmistakable smell of death, combined with the acid in O'Brien's churning gut, produced a wave of nausea he fought to control. It wouldn't be long before an onslaught of press descended on the village in hordes.

"They will have a field day with this," O'Brien thought. "Prominent Winnetka Attorney Sought in Slaying of Chicago Mob Boss!" He could write the headline himself.

"So, where are the Chamberlains?" O'Brien steeled himself.

The officer continued to read from his notes. "According to the maid, who's in the kitchen recovering from a bout of the heaves, they're in North Carolina. She says the family's been there for about a week. She also says she has no idea why this man was in the house, especially when the family's gone."

His partner, a slightly-built woman, finally spoke, "No sign of break-in, no sign of a car, other than the Chamberlain's. The house is alarmed, but it's off. Couple of our guys ready to talk to the neighbors when you say so."

O'Brien walked from the entry, larger than his whole apartment, into the kitchen. After ten years on the small, suburban force, he was still struck at the extravagance wealth afforded.

The kitchen was about twenty-five by thirty feet and a composite of stainless steel, gray granite, and black and white tiles. The morning sun reflected off the expanse of water outside the window, intensifying the gleam.

O'Brien's thoughts turned momentarily to his own mother, struggling with large, black, iron pots over an old gas stove in a small walk-up. The apartment he grew up in was not far from here, geographically, but a world away. His mother's loving face was replaced by the one she wore the last time he saw her, the day he buried her, just a few months ago. He shook away his personal tragedy and concentrated on the one at hand.

The maid sat at a large tile-topped table in an alcove across the kitchen. She looked almost child-like in an over-sized, upholstered chair, her thin legs barely touching the floor.

"Excuse me, Miss ..." O'Brien searched for a name.

"Marina Janchevski." She volunteered. O'Brien noted the accent was Polish or Russian.

"Marina, could you tell me what happened? Take your time." He sat down opposite the shaking woman. She couldn't have been more than thirty.

"I come weekdays to clean house, make meals, take care of family. I have key and turn off alarm. Family in North Carolina since last week."

O'Brien made notes as Marina took a sip of tea. "Was the alarm on when you came in this morning?"

"No. I thought maybe I forgot to turn on when I was here Friday. Then, I look around for sign of robber. Things look okay, but I notice funny smell. First I think maybe toilet back-up. It happen before. House is old."

O'Brien looked around at the kitchen. His confusion registered with the maid, and Marina quickly added, "Not old inside. Family always building. House is old but new inside."

"Go on," O'Brien encouraged.

"I go upstairs and open door to the Mister's study. Then I see him," she trailed off and shuddered with the mental picture. O'Brien knew from experience that the image would remain forever.

"I call 911 and wait outside for police." She paused. "I'm sorry. That's all. Will you call family?"

"Do you have a number for them?" O'Brien turned a page in his notebook.

"On the desk." Marina pointed to a built-in desk area complete with personal computer and color TV. A three by five card was neatly printed with a number. He rewrote it and called one of the uniforms.

"Harrison. Have this checked out before I call, and see who it belongs to. I'm not calling blind." The man scribbled in his notes and gave O'Brien a half salute as he walked away.

"Can't put it off any longer, guess I'll have to climb those stairs now." Detective O'Brien braced himself for a mental picture of his own. God, he hated this part of the job.

CHARLIE O'BRIEN left the Chicago force after twenty years. Twenty long, hard years of faceless bodies and senseless shootings and even more nonsensical politics. Twenty years on a big-city force had left him divorced, cynical, and deaf in one ear.

He took his retirement and tried his hand at hobbies and daytime TV. He ate dinners in a neighborhood tavern and drank beers with the locals. He was bored and drying up. When his old friend and police academy partner left the Winnetka force for a cushy job in the private sector ("It's all my connections, Charlie.") O'Brien drove up to the North Shore and found himself a new job at forty three: detective on the Winnetka force. That was ten years ago.

Welcome to the fabled North Shore of Chicago, he thought, the gem of the Chicago suburbs.

Keeping the peace of the affluent proved to be a relatively quiet assignment. Mostly traffic, DUI's, and, of course, burglary—if you're going to steal, might as well steal the stuff worth having. That is, until the twentieth century caught up to the rich and insulated.

O'Brien couldn't exactly call it a crime-wave, but this would make the third big, high-profile murder Winnetka had suffered in ten years. This one, like the two preceding, would capture the public's attention, make the cover of *People*, and invite everyone from local rag reporters to Ted Koppel to speculate.

No time to think about the past, time to concentrate. As he began the long climb to the second level, he unconsciously counted the stairs, something he'd done since he'd been a kid. Charlie counted the forty steps up to his childhood third-floor flat every time he made the ascent. This humble palace boasted thirty steps a flight, and he was winded before reaching the study.

Officers had yellow-taped the thick, Chinese carpet. Dark, dried blood had soaked through the inches of hand-pulled, cream-colored wool to the polished oak floor beneath, leaving behind an obscene stain. O'Brien covered his nose and mouth with his handkerchief. The body of Tony Romano lay sprawled across an antique, cherry desk. What had been his face was now spattered against the wall behind him. The gore left a Picasso pattern dripping down the silk wallcovering. It disappeared behind the hutch, reappearing on the baseboard molding. A gun, looked like a .44 caliber, lay on top of the desk along with an empty file folder. The coroner, Fred Wilkes, walked up behind O'Brien.

"What'd ya think, Fred?" Wilkes, like the detective, had been retired. He was once a noted North Shore surgeon who also found the golden years tarnished. He now acted as coroner the few times he was needed in Winnetka and the New Trier communities.

Fred rubbed his, as yet, unshaven face and pulled at his bottom lip. "I'd say he's been dead about two days. Happened sometime Saturday. I'll know more after the autopsy. Cause of death is pretty obvious. Why and who are your problem, thank God. I've got the forensic boys at bay; I wanted you to see the scene before anyone touched anything. My guess, though, is that it had to be one of those, whatchacallit, 'mushroom' bullets. Took the front of the head and face clean off. Whoever did it really wanted him dead."

"Whatever happened to Saturday Night Specials?" Charlie smiled wryly, and Fred shrugged.

O'Brien really wanted a cigarette. It was mornings like this when he wished he still smoked. Every time he had the craving, he thought of his mother those last few weeks, dying of lung cancer. It didn't help the addictive desire, but the anger overpowered the urge. He pulled a roll of mints from his jacket and flipped two out with his thumb, offering one to Fred. "Is there any coffee? I could sure use a cup," O'Brien asked, happy to have one last vice to savor.

Fred took the mint and nodded. "Why don't I go down to the kitchen and see if the maid can draw me a map. I'll hang around until the lab boys are done, if you don't mind."

O'Brien patted Wilke's thin shoulder. "Thanks, Fred, I'd appreciate that." He really missed knowing his dad. Most of the days went by without Charlie O'Brien reminiscing. It was this kind of tragedy that stirred him up. Maybe, he rationalized, it was easier to get through these things if he just let his mind walk away now and then. It was then that the present intruded rudely, deleting any more personal thoughts.

An officer's loud, insistent voice: "I'm sorry, you can't go up there yet."

"*Chicago Sun-Times*. Let me through."

"Detective O'Brien, could you come down here, please?" the officer more demanded than asked.

"What's the trouble?" O'Brien shouted down.

"Caught the call on the police band." The reporter was already halfway to the top.

"You can't come up—forensics hasn't finished." The lab people took their cue and began the climb, pushing the reporter aside. The reporter joined the group and followed, only to be stopped by O'Brien as he reached the landing.

"Aw, come on O'Brien, you owe me, I made you a star." The newsman was referring to the publicity the detective had received during the last big murder investigation. It was unwanted and unwarranted.

"Yeah, big debt. C'mon, cooperate nicely and I won't have to ask the officer to escort you down." The reporter attempted to see around O'Brien into the study but the detective's ample girth made that rather difficult. Reluctantly he backed down the first few stairs, then turned and walked to the bottom.

"It's begun, sir." O'Brien looked out the leaded-glass window at the end of the landing. Television crews were setting up shop on the stretch of brown lawn. He could see their words turn to clouds that hung, like the cartoon balloons, over their heads. Each group, trying to out-maneuver the other for vantage points in the gray, morning cold.

"What a curious world," O'Brien mused, remembering Alice's *Looking Glass* world, "We seem to have a beheaded a subject. But why and who?" O'Brien the philosopher.

DAY ONE
MONDAY, NOVEMBER 18 • 10:00 AM

BY MID-MORNING all the department people had completed their jobs. The body was photographed, worked over, and, like yesterday's garbage, unceremoniously placed in a large, black plastic bag, ready for transport to the hospital morgue where the autopsy would take place.

"What a strange way for a mobster like Romano to end up," O'Brien reflected, "here in a North Shore mansion where he would have been as welcome as the proverbial plague. This is truly one for the books—and I'm sure there will be more than one when we're finished with this case," he added.

O'Brien spoke briefly with the maid again before asking one of the officers to drive her home, to the Russian section in Skokie. He made a personal bet that she, along with a rather large family, shared a space not as sizeable as the kitchen she was paid to clean. He also guessed she made more in a day than she had in the old country in a month or more. "God bless America," he mumbled sincerely under his breath.

Additional officers were canvassing the neighbors, which wasn't easy. Most of the homes were isolated by the sheer expanse of surrounding property.

Brick and stone made them all insulated and soundproof. North Shore attitude made them inviolate. No moat or fence could protect them from the cruelties of the outside world, and now they would shield themselves with silence.

O'Brien could see people gathering behind the yellow tape running from tree to tree. Tony Orlando once dubbed the yellow ribbon as a symbol for "Welcome Home," but yellow *tape* had an entirely different connotation. The TV news minions were trying to interview the bystanders, mostly to no avail.

It was time to place a call to the Chamberlains. The kitchen, considering its sanitized look, felt remarkably comfortable. O'Brien sat in the over-stuffed chair and sipped a second cup of coffee without tasting it. He studied a photo of Meridith Chamberlain with her two children. Lucky for them, they had their mother's blonde coloring and Nordic features. The three were all smiling into the camera against the backdrop of a cloudless, blue sky. "Their mama's good looks and their daddy's money," O'Brien thought. Her husband, eyes shaded, stood behind them, staring into the distance.

Jonathan Chamberlain was old-line and blue blood. His father, Franklin, represented Illinois in Congress, and his deceased grandfather was once lieutenant governor of the state. The Chamberlains' reputation was as solid as the Lake Michigan bluff their estate overlooked.

O'Brien, being a big fan of black and white movies, thought that Meridith "Meri" Whitney Chamberlain was a dead-ringer for Grace Kelly, one of the detective's favorite leading ladies. If truth be told, Charlie was a fan of most anything that preceded the Johnson administration. His younger colleagues would probably say *Princess Di*, and that, in itself, made him feel older than dirt. And like Winnetka's own royalty, Mrs. Chamberlain was often photographed presiding over half the charity events on the North Shore.

The Whitney name, in and of itself, was a household word. They manufactured and marketed an eclectic group of foods including catsup, mustard, cheeses, sauces, packaged dinners, cookies, and gourmet coffees. Whitney Foods had recently been purchased by the Carolina Tobacco Company in the cigarette manufacturer's attempt to diversify. The tobacco people were investing their considerable assets into products outside the reach of the legal claims. O'Brien thought that suing a cigarette manufacturer after you got sick from using their product was rather like suing a boxer who beat you up after you picked a fight.

The Whitney family, and more specifically, Meridith Whitney Chamberlain, the direct heiress and largest stockholder, had her net worth multiplied considerably after the buy out.

O'Brien set the photo down and considered the corpse. Tony Romano, the reputed mob boss of Chicago, boasted a lineage every bit as pedigreed as the Chamberlains', but in rather disparate circles. Tony's father was the man closest to Jimmy Hoffa. In point of fact, his father had disappeared with the Teamster leader. He was a grand-nephew of Chicago's most colorful don, Alphonse Capone himself. It was rumored that Romano had been hand-picked by the impeccable grand-old-man-of-the-mob, John Gotti. Tony had also proven his qualifications by disposing of any and all pretenders to the title. Not personally, O'Brien was certain. Romano never got his manicured hands dirty.

Fortunately for the city, he did not wield the power of some of his predecessors. Unfortunately for the city, new factions were gaining control. The Asians, the African-Americans, the Puerto Ricans, the Mexicans, and even the Russians were encroaching on the Italians. Thanks to the industrious Chinese, heroin had made a remarkable resurgence and was easier to obtain than ever before. In spite of the international competition, Tony Romano was, in O'Brien's book, a formidable felon. Dead he could understand, but it made no sense for him to be found dead in the home of one of Chicago's most esteemed and wealthy corporate attorneys.

The detective couldn't see it, but Tony's reputation with the ladies was even more impressive. He was photographed with irrefutable beauties and ladies of ill-repute, noteworthy women, and streetwise girls. His Italian ancestors had bequeathed him a shock of dark, wavy hair, a deep clefted-chin, and, somewhere along the line, a wayward wanderer had passed down the bluest eyes a Romano had ever sported. Tony's nickname, "The Roman Rooster" was apt. It referred not only to his public prowess with the ladies but his penchant for perfection and meticulous dress.

O'Brien laughed out loud. "Here was a thug who prided himself on custom- made designer suits. Man, would he be mortified knowing his was ending up in a garbage bag!" To Detective O'Brien, that was a fitting finale.

SITTING BY the kitchen phone while his people finished their investigations, O'Brien dialed the number and took a deep breath. After a series of rings, the phone was answered by a husky female voice, "Yes?"

"Mrs. Chamberlain, my name is Detective O'Brien of the Winnetka Police Force. Is your husband with you?"

"Oh, my God! Is anything wrong?" There was immediate distress in her voice.

"Please, Mrs. Chamberlain. May I speak with your husband?" O'Brien wanted to verify the husband's whereabouts before he relinquished any information.

"Jonathan Chamberlain here. What's the trouble, Officer."

"Detective, Mr. Chamberlain. I'm at your home now. I'll get right to the point. It seems your maid came in this morning and discovered, well, sir, she found the dead body of a Mr. Tony Romano in your study."

"Who? What the hell are you talking about? Are my children all right?"

"Your children? Aren't they with you?" The alarm went off in O'Brien's brain. The maid hadn't mentioned the children!

"No, they're staying with friends in Winnetka. Let me check, and I'll call you back immediately."

"Sir! Wait. Give me the names and addresses, and my men will check on them as well."

"Meri, hand me that book," Chamberlain was talking to his wife. "Here it is. My daughter, Chelsea, she's ten, is with the Easton's at 110 Heatherhill Lane. My son, Hunter, fourteen, is at the McBride's. 1090 Erie Court. Are you at my house?"

"Yes, sir. We'll check and call you back immediately." Before he finished, the connection was broken.

"Harrison? Have a man check on the Chamberlain kids at each of these addresses as fast as they can. Don't alarm the kids, and make sure they know their parents are okay. They'll hear about this on the news soon, and I don't want them coming to this house. Oh, and keep the whereabouts of the kids from the press. Alert the folks they're staying with. In fact, leave an officer at each house, and have them keep this quiet. As quiet as possible in this town."

Harrison left quickly with Officer Patricia O'Donald in tow. O'Brien then called the station to get the phone numbers. He hadn't wanted to impede Chamberlain any more than he had; he understood the man needed to hear his kids' voices. Once O'Brien had the numbers, he dialed. The first number was busy. He tried the second. "Mrs. Easton. This is Detective O'Brien. Is Chelsea Chamberlain with you?"

"No, I've taken her to school. Is everything okay?" Calls from the police did not bring good news. O'Brien tried to explain the situation as succinctly as possible. As he talked to Mrs. Easton he heard the officers arrive. He admonished himself for not remembering it was a school day. He called the station back and asked the dispatcher to reach Harrison and O'Donald and have them check at the schools. Discreetly. Despite the wealth, Winnetka still had a small town mentality, and this news would travel like electricity on a raw, wet wire.

There were few things money could not buy, the detective thought. Remembering the lifeless corpse recently removed from the premises, he added, "But peace of mind will not come cheap for the Chamberlains anymore."

The walkie-talkie on his waistband crackled alive. "Harrison here, sir. Bad news. Neither child is in school. No one seems to have seen them since they were dropped off. The son was brought by bus, and the kids remember seeing him get off but nothing else." O'Brien began to chew his lower lip. He took notes with a shaking hand.

"The daughter was dropped off by car, driven by Brooke Easton. Mrs. Easton said she saw her go into the school. The girl's not there now." Harrison trailed off.

"Oh, God." O'Brien rubbed his now-throbbing temples. "I'll meet you at the station in five. Batten down the hatches, Harrison, it's a whole new ballgame.

We'll need to put together a task force ASAP. I'll call the Chamberlains."

This time the call was picked up on the first ring. "Jonathan Chamberlain," boomed the voice on the other end.

"Mr. Chamberlain, Detective O'Brien."

"I know, Detective," Chamberlain cut him off, "I called, too. My wife's already packing, and I've called for the company jet so we won't be hung up with the commercial flights. We should be home in three or four hours. Please, O'Brien, do everything you can. I don't know what the hell is going on, but all that matters are my children. Please." The final note in the man's voice was desperation.

"Yes, sir. Every man in our force and the entire New Trier community will be working on this within the hour. You have my word." The phone clicked off without any further communication.

Charlie O'Brien felt a migraine strike, and, from experience, he knew he would not be a hundred percent with one of these monster headaches. Thank God they now had a pill to control the pain. Digging into his pocket he came up with the tiny cellophane packet that held the miracle tablet. He popped it into his mouth and washed it down by holding his head under the sink faucet. He splashed the cold water over his face and neck then shook like a dog.

"Okay, Charlie," he addressed himself in the mirror finish on the toaster, "let's bust this one open."

DAY ONE • EARLIER
MONDAY, NOVEMBER 18 • 8:10 AM

NO ONE NOTICED a long, black limousine pull up to the school that Monday morning. New Trier High School stood, since the turn of the century, tall, stately and red-bricked, against the backdrop of Winnetka. New Trier was ranked as one of the top public schools in America, due in part to the huge salaries paid to administrators and teachers. Over four thousand young people trooped into the building daily, dressed in clothing apparently purchased at a local Salvation Army store. "Shabby chic" the fashion editors called the look made famous by grunge rockers. If clothes spoke volumes about who people professed to be, these kids screamed, "I am not my parents!"

The back door of the limo opened just as Hunter Chamberlain stepped off the bus. "Hunter? Hunter Chamberlain?" A voice from the back seat. The young man turned and nodded.

"Your grandfather has had an accident, and your father sent the car to pick you up and take you to the airport for Washington. Get in."

The blonde boy's face reflected alarm. He got in without a backward glance or a word to his friends, who didn't notice he hadn't kept up with their pace.

WITHIN MINUTES, a young woman, anonymous in the crowd of other mothers-of-the-morning, waited at the front entrance to the elementary school. An attractive woman with sun streaks in her long hair, dressed like the others, in gray running attire, waited to approach the girl until her friends were slightly ahead and the car pool driver had turned around the circle.

"Chelsea? Your mom sent me to pick you up. Your grandfather's very ill, and she and your father are on their way to the hospital in Washington. You and your brother are going to fly there to meet them. I'm supposed to take you to the airport."

Chelsea was wary and stood silent. The woman continued in a gentle voice, "I work with your mother at the North Lake Community House. She's already called the school, and they know you're going with me. My name is Laura." The woman held out her hand.

Chelsea wasn't sure. Something told her to go to the office and see if her mother had really called. She was remembering all the warnings from mom and her teachers. She backed off. A hired guard sat, not ten feet away. His presence was a result of the shootings at the school in May of 1987. Another mother was coaxing him to take a forgotten lunch bag to a classroom, and he was busy explaining why he could not leave his post.

The woman in the gray jogging suit never faltered. "It's okay. We can go check at the office if you want. Don't you remember me from your mother's theatre group? Your grandfather is very sick, and we may not have much time. Your brother's already in the car."

Chelsea could see Hunter's face as the window was quickly lowered, then raised. She took the woman's hand and walked to the waiting limo. None of the children hurrying into the building or the mothers delivering last-minute instructions took note.

It happened that fast, that easy, that unremarkable.

DAY ONE
MONDAY, NOVEMBER 18 • 11:00 AM

THE STATION was already on alert. Every man and woman on the force had been called in and now waited in the large conference room. Most of them had been through at least one of these crisis meetings. The police chief was the newest man on the force, having been hired less than a year ago though a nation-wide search. Fortunately, he was a good man, unburdened with ego.

"Okay. Here's what we know," O'Brien began. "At approximately eight o'clock this morning the Chamberlain's maid, one Marina Janchevski, found the dead body of reputed mob boss, Tony Romano. Upon notifying the Chamberlains, who are in Raleigh, North Carolina, we discovered the Chamberlain children had been left with family friends: the daughter, Chelsea, ten, with the Chester Easton's on Meadowbrook; the son, Hunter, fourteen, with the Stephen McBride's on Erie. They were each taken to their respective schools, the daughter by a car pool driven by Brooke Easton, the son to New Trier by school bus. Both were seen leaving the vehicles. Neither arrived. As of this moment they are missing, and we must consider kidnapping." Their was an audible gasp from the room. O'Brien looked around the room and saw pencils poised and all eyes on him. This was new and devastating information.

Until this moment, the demise of a Tony Romano was not necessarily bad news. Except for the unfortunate choice of his departure, the Winnetka police were not on full alert. Now, two of their children were missing, and the force knew what that meant to them—and the entire community.

Chief Atkinson walked over next to O'Brien. O'Brien had filled him in on the case. The chief placed his hand on the detective's shoulder as he spoke. "I've put together a plan of action and called in the Wilmette, Northfield, Glencoe and Kenilworth departments. We'll be holding a taskforce meeting at noon. The Chamberlains should be here by this afternoon. I received a call from Jonathan Chamberlain's law firm, and someone from there will join us. Congressman Chamberlain is also arriving today and wants to be on this. The press conference is scheduled for four. Questions?"

From the back, a woman's voice: "Sir, are we to assume all other duties are to be on hold?"

"Those of you with specific duties should continue until further notice. But I don't think we have any really pressing cases in the queue. Anything but the community's personal safety will be put on hold until further notice."

The chief looked to O'Brien, but the detective was quiet. He was grateful that the tablet he swallowed earlier was working. He was also grateful the captain had appropriated the duty of addressing the squad.

"I know that most of you were here for either the Laurie Dann case or the Bishop/Langert murders, so you know what we're in for with the media. High profile cases translate to tabloid reporting. I don't have to remind you that *No Comment* is the only thing you say. Refer any and all press to me only. If no one else has questions, I'll see you all again at noon. Lunch will be brought in." The silence was punctuated by chairs scraping the tile floor.

O'Brien knew that the chief's request concerning the press had nothing to do with conceit; he was a low-key guy who dreaded the media's assault. It had taken over six months and virtually hundreds of interviews to find Russell Atkinson. Brought in from a similar Connecticut community, the Winnetka Village Board felt he understood their kind of citizenry.

Many of those living within the twenty square miles of Winnetka were listed in *Forbes*. But unlike celebrities, Winnetkans abhorred publicity or notoriety. Residents were professionals and recognizable faces. Some inherited recognizable names, many inherited sizeable fortunes.

Atkinson was accustomed to dealing with monied people and the board liked that. Russell was affable and well liked, but when he took charge he commanded respect and exuded authority. He was raising his own three boys with the same strong ethic. Standing over six feet four, his days of playing college football at Princeton left him with a thick neck and matching arms. His waist was fast catching up to his chest, due in part to the fact that life was good.

Life could get real bad real fast, if Winnetka's new chief of police didn't find the Chamberlain children.

"HOW IN THE HELL can two kids as old as the Chamberlains' disappear?" O'Brien was pacing as one of the patrol officers set out the deli platter. The room was filling up with personnel from the New Trier area.

New Trier Township consisted of five neighboring, but independently run villages. Each village employed their own boards and kept separate police and fire departments, but they shared resources and cooperated for the larger good. The Township high school and the combined voting block wielded an incredible amount of prestige and power.

As newcomers arrived, the dialogue centered around the disappearance of the children. The media, gathered like circled wagons, was pressing for information on the murdered gangster, unaware of the kidnapping. Keeping them at bay had become a full-time assignment for several officers. The four o'clock press conference would give the Chamberlain family time to participate.

"If we could get started," Chief Atkinson began, "Time is of the essence." The room grew quiet as the chief reviewed the points. "A fact sheet is being passed around with the names and addresses of those involved at this time." Papers were shuffled and circulated. "Please note that Detective O'Brien, who heads up the Task Force, and I have assigned duties. No rosters will be posted. We want to keep the details as confidential as possible until we know just what the kidnappers want.

"I repeat my previous admonition to all of you. There is to be no—I repeat, *no*—contact with the press. I cannot stress this enough. Two children's lives may be at stake, and I don't want to see a repeat of what has happened here in the past. There will be no stars as a result of this horrific crime. Do I make myself perfectly clear? Any name I see quoted is grounds for immediate dismissal. I have the cooperation of every village police captain on this, I assure you." Those gathered nodded assent.

"Please, help yourself to lunch fixings while you assemble into the teams assigned. Detective O'Brien and I will be around to meet with each group. Good luck and," he hesitated, "God bless."

"Chief Atkinson, I hate to interrupt, but you have an urgent call." It was the on-duty dispatcher, a large woman, tightly upholstered into her uniform.

"Atkinson, here." He was hoping to hear from the officers installing a trace and a caller ID monitor on the phones at the Chamberlain house.

"Chief Atkinson, I'm Chief Investigator Sam Driscoll—FBI. I got a call from Congressman Chamberlain concerning the disappearance of his grandchildren. I'll be flying in with the congressman on a private jet, and the local agents will meet us there. The Vice President has been informed and has given us his total support to do whatever is necessary to bring them home safely. He feels so adamant he is willing to fly there if necessary."

Atkinson knew the FBI would be coming into the picture, with a kidnapping. But the White House! Then he remembered how much backing, and financial assistance, the Presidential ticket had gotten from the Chamberlain's during the last election. "I'll look forward to your help. All we want is to have those kids returned unharmed. I take it you also know about Tony Romano? We found his body at the Chamberlain home this morning. Very dead."

"I do. Any connection yet?"

"No, sir. My men are at the house now, working on the phones. No calls yet. Should we postpone the press conference until you arrive?"

"By all means. No information goes out until we okay it. See you this afternoon."

Atkinson hung up the phone. "O'Brien?" he said quietly, "That was the FBI." They both winced.

Chief Atkinson and Detective O'Brien made the rounds in the conference room, meeting with assigned teams, all with the objective of finding the two missing children or the murderer of noted Chicago mob boss, Romano. As each group completed their briefing, they left quickly. A unit was headed to each of the schools to make a comprehensive list of the children's friends. Families of the children's companions must be considered. In the two previous, high-profile, murder cases Winnetka had investigated, the perpetrators were local residents. All aspects must be regarded carefully.

AS SHERIDAN ROAD winds its way north, it curved along Lake Michigan like a giant dollar sign. Homes become grander and more exclusive, hugging the water like a fortress against the invasion of city sins. Living on the North Shore is like membership in a private club, except some members tend to forget the source of their initiation fee. The older the money, the more amnesic people were concerning its origin. The longer one belonged to the club, the more insulated they became against the real world.

Winnetka was incorporated in 1850 as a suburban enclave for some of Chicago's monied power brokers. It was located on Lake Michigan, for optimum pleasure, and along the railroad, for utmost convenience. The name of the Village comes from an Indian word meaning "Beautiful Land." A man named Pecker incorporated Winnetka and wanted to name the village "Peckertown." Residents today can thank his wife for vetoing his wish.

From that time until the present, there have only been eight murders: In 1884, out-of-town robbers killed two people. In 1957 a drifter wounded a patrolman but then turned the gun to his own head, killing himself.

On May 20, 1988, Nicholas Corwin, age seven, was killed in Hubbard Woods School by a .357 Magnum when Laurie Wassermann Dann, a thirty two year old woman suffering from severe mental illness went on a murderous rampage. Brave, little Nicky threw himself in front of a classmate when the crazed woman aimed. Ms. Dann wounded six other classmates and, after fleeing the school to a nearby home, shot a 20 year old college student who tried to talk her out of the weapon. He crawled down a long driveway to the waiting arms of paramedics as she held the gun to her own head, ending her sad life.

On April 8, 1990, a young Winnetka couple, Richard Langert, thirty two, and his beautiful wife, Nancy Bishop Langert, twenty seven, were gunned down in their Winnetka townhouse. She was expecting their first baby. Their bodies were found by Nancy's father in the basement the next morning. Richard had been tied up and shot in the back of the head. Nancy died trying to escape on the steps, holding her bleeding abdomen. After almost a year of intense and futile investigation covering every conceivable aspect from the mafia to the IRA, the gunman proved to be a sixteen-year-old New Trier High School student, David Biro. Biro was turned in by his classmate after he bragged about aspiring to be a "professional hitman." The evidence he harbored in his room proved irrefutable, including the gun, a glass cutter and a glove that matched one found at the scene. Biro was convicted of three murders, including the unborn child.

In both cases, the common denominator proved to be parental arrogance; "not-my-child" denial. David Biro and Laurie Wasserman Dann had both been institutionalized for mental illness that included deviant acts of violence. Both fathers had signed their children out of custodial care, overriding the objections voiced by doctors. Both fathers were sued; the Wasserman's by Nicky Corwin's family, the Biro's by Nancy's family, the Bishops. And in each case, the plaintiffs prevailed.

Winnetka Police Chief Herbert Timm became the self-proclaimed authority on the high-profile crimes committed during his tenure, and retired to the lucrative speakers circuit.

DAY ONE
MONDAY, NOVEMBER 18 • 3:00 PM

JONATHAN AND Meridith Chamberlain arrived at the station. Detective O'Brien had seen her picture often enough to recognize her immediately. Her perfect face was marred by overt concern. Slight smudges appeared under her large, green eyes and a furrow was deepening between her arched brows. Her oversized sweater made her seem thinner than O'Brien thought, and he was embarrassed to notice. Her honey-blonde hair was tied back with a ribbon.

Jonathan Chamberlain was, by contrast, all business. Armed with a voluminous notebook, cellular phone and beeper he was ready to work. His beige, wool slacks were perfectly creased, his graying-at-the-temples hair was sprayed into obedience, and his cashmere navy blazer was without a speck.

One of the officers was bringing coffee when sirens broke the neighborhood quiet—freezing them where they stood. O'Brien went to the window and watched as a limousine and a dark blue Chevrolet both pulled across the lawn without concern. Four blue-suited men rushed out of each of the Chevy's doors and stood at attention while the back door of the limo was opened by the driver. A familiar figure emerged. Congressman Franklin Chamberlain was a portly man but carried himself with the dignity years of esteem brought. His mane of white hair blew back from his round, ruddy face in the cold, November wind. He bent into it and made his way into the station house followed by the four men O'Brien knew to be FBI.

O'Brien had to suppress a smile despite the circumstances. The men all wore the obligatory sunglasses that Hollywood associated with Federal Agents. They were right out of Central Casting. The detective shook off the smirk and motioned for the captain.

"Congressman Chamberlain, I hope you had a good flight? I'm Police Chief Russell Atkinson, and this is the man in charge of the case, Detective Charles O'Brien." They clasped hands.

The Congressman looked at his son and daughter-in-law. "Any news?" They shook their heads. Tears appeared on Meridith's cheeks. O'Brien noticed that it was the older man who put his arms around the distraught mother while her husband remained passive.

A tall, well-dressed man stood and walked over to the Chamberlains and was instantly recognized by Jonathan. "Hello, Bob." He turned to the others. "This is one of my partners, Robert Crowley." They shook hands all around.

"Let's get down to business and see what's been done and where we go from here," Jonathan addressed the group. He seated himself at the head of the veneer table. The FBI men all took out their identification and displayed it to O'Brien who made a note of their names in his notebook and introduced them to those in attendance.

The Congressman and Meridith sat on either side of Jonathan. Coffee was brought in, and ceramic cups were placed in front of the Chamberlains. The chief began, "We know very little at this moment. The teams we've assigned to interview, are still out. A press conference, originally scheduled for four," he looked at his watch, "has been rescheduled for six. The Chamberlain's and the Congressman's phones are now tapped and equipped with caller ID. No calls have come through—except for reporters." He addressed Jonathan, "Have you heard anything?"

"No, Chief," Jonathan stated. "We've been traveling most of the day but no notes, no calls. The body of this ..." he reached for a name.

"Tony Romano," Atkinson finished. "Body's been removed from your home. Nothing appears to have been stolen or damaged." He searched Jonathan's face for a sign, "Except for the damage to your study—where the murder was committed."

Meridith shuttered and closed her eyes against the picture. The Congressman cleared his throat to speak, "Do we know why this man was in my son's home, Chief?" Stress was taking its toll on the older man.

"No, sir. The gun he was killed with was found on the desk. The lab is checking for fingerprints. We have pieces to the puzzle, but at this time we can't seem to make them fit. Anything you might be able to tell us would help."

"We'll be taking over the case from here, Chief," Agent Sam Driscoll interjected. "Kidnapping is a Federal offense."

"I understand that, Agent Driscoll," the chief rose as he spoke. "However, murder is still my jurisdiction, and, for the good of the children, I suggest we all work together. Time is of the essence, and my people are familiar with the community. Things will work better if there is cooperation instead of antagonism." O'Brien watched his chief, he was good.

The Congressman spoke with ultimate authority. "I agree. If it takes a Presidential order, I *will* have all of you working together. All I want is the safe return of my grandchildren. Nothing else matters, certainly not egos. I have lived in Winnetka all of my life, and I know how dedicated these men and women are. I trust them. This is a joint effort. Have I made myself perfectly clear?"

"Thank you for your input, sir. I'm sure we will all work together towards that end." The agent put a period at the end of the statement. "I have received a request that we keep Vice President, Henry Boyer, apprised of our progress at all times."

"I think we can handle that," Atkinson assured the agent.

"Excuse me, and I'll find out where the units are and call them in for an update." O'Brien left the room. While the dispatcher called, he stepped outside. The Detective closed his eyes and took a deep breath of the refrigerated air. It was dark now, and he wondered where and how the children were. They were frightened, he knew. He prayed they were unharmed.

Several police vehicles were parking in the lot. Officers were hurrying towards the lights of the station house. O'Brien watched as one of the men inhaled the last of a cigarette and flicked the small torch across the asphalt. O'Brien took one last drag of his mental cigarette and headed back inside.

"What do we know that we didn't this morning?" O'Brien questioned the arriving officer.

"Adams with Unit One, sir. We were assigned to the boy, Hunter." At the mention of his name, Meridith gasped. The officers all turned their attention to the woman at the end of the table. Adams coughed nervously and continued, "Well, we've been to New Trier and to the McBride's. We have a list of his friends and we've talked to most of them. Nothing we can hang our hats on; they're all stunned. Funny thing is, none of the kids on the bus remember seeing him leave the grounds. We're going to do a background check on the families, you know, run them through the computer to see what comes up."

"Our computers can do that faster and more thoroughly, if I may have the list." Agent Driscoll's manner had done an about face after the Congressman's dressing down. The officer looked at O'Brien.

"It's okay, Adams. This is Federal Agent Driscoll, and his team, Sanders, Gurley, and Wolnick. They'll be assisting us and," he looked across the table at his own teams "we're all cooperating on this investigation. As the Congressman stated earlier, nothing matters except the safe return of the Chamberlain children."

"I'm in accord with Detective O'Brien," the captain gave his blessing. The air seemed a bit warmer.

"How about Unit Two?"

"Harrison. We can report about the same. Chelsea Chamberlain was a very good student, and the teachers there are obviously quite concerned. We haven't interviewed the students yet, given their ages. The principal thought a counselor should be present when they're told, and that's planned for tomorrow. We've made cursory phone calls but nothing more. We'll supply our list to you, Driscoll."

"Let's work backwards on the Romano thing. Maybe we can find a link. This is where your guys can really help, Driscoll. I take it you already have a file?"

The agent hefted a large, leather bag on the table. He unzipped it and pulled out a thick folder, handing the contents to one of his men who separated it into piles. Driscoll spoke, "Gary Sanders has been on the case for over a year. We've had a tail on Romano since he became the Chicago Don. He was young for the job, but tough enough. We've taken the liberty of copying our background information. There are five copies of what we know, and what we suspect, about one Anthony Vincent Romano. We already have a team from the Organized Crime Division working on the names you'll see here. Sanders, what can you add?"

Gary Sanders cleared his throat and began, "Romano was involved in many activities, but mainly he was into money laundering through, what appears to be, legitimate businesses. Our man Tony, was a real social climber. It seems he liked the lifestyle of the rich and famous." The remark was obviously directed to the Chamberlains.

"My only business is my law firm, Davidson, McMahon, Crowley, Chamberlain and Dillon. We represent *Fortune 500* companies exclusively." Chamberlain was noticeably angry.

Atkinson was again called on to use his powers of diplomacy. "Please, Mr. Chamberlain, we understand how your family feels and we sympathize with you. But, as an attorney, you must realize we have to investigate every avenue as quickly as possible, for your children's sake."

"Jonathan, please." It was first time Meridith had spoken. Her voice was husky and lilting at the same time. She commanded a presence, and all eyes were on her when she continued. "This is the most difficult thing we've ever had to go through. All I want is to have Hunter and Chelsea home safely." Meredith pleaded, "Please, Jonathan, do whatever it takes."

The elder Chamberlain patted Meri's hand and Jonathan looked contrite. "Sorry. Bob and I will take you through our client list and disclose whatever we can, legally, to see if there is any connection there. Other than that, I don't know how I can help." Jonathan rubbed his reddened eyes. O'Brien noticed a slight flicker cross Crowley's face.

"Could each of you," the chief addressed the family, "make a list of your associates. Anyone and everyone you can think of. Sometimes the connection is obscure, but the picture becomes clearer as we understand the motive. In this case, the perpetrators must want something from one of you. Congressman, are you involved with anything that might be at all connected to organized crime?"

The Congressman visibly searched his memory. As one of the senior and most respected members of the House of Representatives, Franklin Chamberlain sat on the prestigious Ways and Means Committee. It was their responsibility to dole out the money, approve the budgets and sanction expenses. In a town like Washington, where power is fueled by the almighty dollar, there is no greater prerogative.

"I could not begin to recount all the bills that are sitting on my plate at this moment. However, there is a piece of legislation that concerns organized crime. I will have my executive assistant run a computer printout." The Congressman hesitated. "I'm sure that the confidentiality of the information is secure. It cannot be released to the press."

Driscoll and his men nodded, like so many ceramic dolls, all in unison. O'Brien wondered what kind of training they really received in Quantico. He was further ruminating on the fact that the US government was supposed to be of, by and for the people. Why shouldn't the bills be released to the press?

Atkinson dismissed most of the units, and, as the room cleared, O'Brien offered more coffee. Meredith met his eyes for the first time, and he was stunned by how clear and green they were. He shook his head to break the stare he found himself locked in and admonished himself for his carnal feelings.

"Captain, we appreciate the importance of the information you need, but can we do some of this background work later this evening? I think we should form a game plan concerning the press conference and the news of my children's disappearance. Since no one has received any ransom calls or notes, I don't know what to make of the whole thing." Jonathan Chamberlain had once again taken control.

"You're right. Agent Driscoll, what do you propose? You're the expert in these cases."

Driscoll spoke with matched authority. "It has been our experience that if no contact has been made by now, the kidnappers may be panicked. A plea from the parents stating that there will be no retribution may bring them out into the open. Also, getting the kids' pictures out in the media may bring some witnesses. I don't think we have a choice. If the mob is involved, who knows? In the old days, these guys had a sort of 'code'—they never touched wives or kids. But now, things are different. " He trailed off and shrugged his shoulders.

"Well, that makes me feel a hell of lot better!" Chamberlain's temper flared. Cups clattered as his fist banged the table.

O'Brien ignored the attitude. God only knew what he would do if he found himself in Chamberlain's shoes. He might have been tempted to punch the agent instead of the table at such an insensitive remark.

"Look, let's put our heads together and, like Mr. Chamberlain suggested, come up with a plan." O'Brien the referee. "I think that Mrs. Chamberlain should be the one to make the plea," O'Brien continued, "Certainly the mother will elicit more sympathy from everyone, the kidnappers, the public, and, perhaps, even the press."

Meridith nodded. The Congressman stood and walked over to where she was seated. She looked up into his face as he spoke, "You up to the task, Meri?"

She smiled wanly. "Of course, Franklin. I'd give my life for them. I'll do whatever it takes to get them back safely."

DAY ONE
MONDAY, NOVEMBER 18 • 6:00 PM

THE PRESS was in a state of frenzy. Darkness and bitter November cold had turned them into an hysterical mob. Their lights lit up the sky, and flashing cameras punctuated the little darkness that remained. Microphone booms were held above the mass by extended poles that jabbed and bobbed to catch a sound bite.

To accommodate the crowd, Atkinson asked the Fire Chief to remove the engines from their garaged space, turning it into a make-shift conference area. Mikes were placed at intervals in front of a lectern. When the Chamberlains were escorted to the podium, the noise level rose to frenzied pitch.

"Congressman, is Romano's death linked to the hearings on organized crime? Or the Organized Crime Bill in your committee?"

"Chamberlain, how are you connected to the Chicago mob?"

"Meridith, is Tony Romano a friend of yours?"

The questions were hurled at a fevered pace so that one could not be distinguished from the other. Flashes popped, cameras rolled, people pushed and yelled. The journalistic corp, like sharks, was experiencing a feeding frenzy.

"Ladies and gentlemen. May I please have your attention and your cooperation?" The chief waited for some semblance of quiet before he continued. "We have a statement to make, and I must insist on your complete cooperation. It's most imperative that, after I make my statement, you allow Mrs. Chamberlain to make hers without any questions." Shushing turned to quiet.

"At approximately nine o'clock this morning, the Chamberlain's maid, Marina Janchevski, found the body of reputed mob boss Tony Romano. Upon notifying Mr. and Mrs. Chamberlain, in North Carolina on business, we discovered the Chamberlain children—a daughter, Chelsea, age ten, and a son, Hunter, fourteen, were being cared for by family friends here in Winnetka.

"This morning, they were each taken to their respective schools, the daughter by a car pool, the son by bus. Both were seen leaving the vehicles. Neither arrived at their schools. They are missing, and we assume they have been kidnapped, although no communication has been made."

The noise of the throng, despite the admonitions, rose to a fevered pitch. Questions were thrown at the captain so furiously that the cacophony climbed to a steady roar. Camera flashes created instantaneous star bursts. Microphones were shoved at the podium creating piercing feedback. All order was lost.

O'Brien stepped next to the chief of police and, wedging his index and pinky fingers in his mouth, took a breath and whistled his old Cubs salute into the mike. The effect was earsplitting! The mob quieted.

O'Brien spoke. "Hey, we need your help. Nothing can be accomplished like this. Let's remember what's at stake here. Like the Chief said, we need your help."

Atkinson continued, "We have put together a task force made up of the New Trier Township Police Departments. The FBI is working with us. Mrs. Chamberlain will now make a statement which should be quoted directly. We ask all of you to allow her to finish without interruption. Are we all in accord?"

O'Brien reached for Meridith's arm and gently guided her to the microphones. She took a deep breath, moistened her lips, and began in her unique voice.

"As you have just been told, my children, Hunter and Chelsea, are missing. We have received no ransom demands. We are mystified as to why they were taken. I have been assured by Captain Atkinson that neither his task force nor the FBI will take any action if the children are returned safely and unharmed." She looked into the cameras. Her eyes glistened, and a tear made its way down her cheek. "Please, if you have my children—or you know something about their disappearance or whereabouts—*Please* call 1-800-446-7000. My family is offering a reward of a million dollars for their safe return—no questions asked."

At the mention of the reward, O'Brien and Atkinson came to attention. The Chief looked at O'Brien, but O'Brien shrugged. The Chamberlain men, father and son, stood stoic. "Hunter, Chelsea, if you can hear Mother, please be strong, and remember we all love you and are praying for your safe return. May the Lord guide those who hold you or know of your whereabouts. May they hear our prayers and do the right thing. God bless you both, and all of us, and God give us strength and guidance." A silent amen from the crowd punctuated her last word. O'Brien escorted the Chamberlain family away before the reverence broke, and the mood changed.

The chief stayed at the podium to tell the media that copies of the release were available. He then quickly closed the large garage door to the noise and lights.

Driscoll assumed the role of the bad guy. "Why the hell weren't we told of the reward before the press conference? Man, that came from nowhere!"

Jonathan Chamberlain answered matter-of-factly, "Because Meridith came up with it on the spot. But no amount of money is too much to have my children safely returned. If money is what they want, money is what they'll get." His remark rendered silence.

O'Brien broke it. "Look, we're all beat. It's been an incredibly long day for everyone. Mr. and Mrs. Chamberlain, Congressman, why don't you go on home . We'll have a long day tomorrow. The chief and I, and Driscoll's team still have a long night ahead of us. Please be assured we will not rest until your children are back here safely."

Franklin picked up, "Jonathan, you and Meri come back to my house. Chief, I trust you will call my private number if there is any news?" O'Brien had forgotten the Congressman kept his residence in Winnetka. The house was a landmark along the lake shore.

"Of course, sir, but, I'd like to make a suggestion. The kidnappers will probably try and contact the Chamberlains at their home. If it's at all possible, I think they should stay there. We already have a team in place. You'll be safe, and you can call the station at any time. Please try to get some rest. I don't mean to alarm you unnecessarily, but we have no idea of what's ahead."

"Thank you for all you've done. The detective is right, I need to be at home." Meridith shook the hand of everyone before taking her father-in-law's arm. He walked with his son and the host of escorts to a waiting car, parked discreetly in back of the station.

Driscoll informed the chief that his team would be going back downtown to work on the computers there and work with the bureau's profiling expert. "They'll be in touch if they come up with anything. I'll be staying here in Winnetka to help coordinate our efforts." Driscoll retreated to a desk and phone that had been set up for him.

O'Brien waited until he and the Chief were alone. "Let's get something to eat. We need to talk."

ATKINSON AND O'BRIEN sat unnoticed in the back of Lenny's Deli in the northern-most area of Winnetka, Hubbard Woods. Over hot, juicy sandwiches and real egg-creams, the two poured over the reports given to them by the investigating units and the FBI.

"This is interesting," O'Brien observed through a mouthful of corned beef. "It seems that Jonathan Chamberlain is not as flush as he appears. Bank records show that he has taken large amounts of cash out of CDs and investments. It doesn't appear here or ..." he shuffled through the papers, "... anywhere that the monies were reinvested. I can't find a record of where they did go."

The chief stopped chewing. "Really. Let's give all this file to the FBI accounting division and see what they come up with. They'll have an easier time cutting through the red tape the bankers will roll out. What else?"

"According to one of the interviews with Ms. Brooke Easton, the mother of the family where Chelsea was staying and who drove the car pool, Meridith was not happy in her marriage." Now O'Brien paused mid-chew. He picked up his napkin and wiped, first his mouth, then his hands, which he suddenly found to be moist.

"She goes on to say that Mrs. Chamberlain had gone so far as to talk with her concerning an attorney." O'Brien checked his watch. "It's just nine, Captain. How about we talk to Mrs. Easton in person?"

The chief grabbed one last bite, took a swipe with his napkin and threw a twenty dollar bill on the table. "It should be interesting. Let's go."

DAY ONE
MONDAY, NOVEMBER 18 • 10:20 PM EST

THE PRESIDENT of the United States sat on the second floor of the White House, ensconced in his personal living quarters. He rubbed his eyes and walked over to the windows that looked out on Pennsylvania Avenue. Tourists still lingered at the iron fencing, staring up at their leader's residence.

"Shit," he whispered, "sometimes I feel more like a prisoner than the President." Tonight was cold and crystal clear, with stars so bright they seemed poised to drop like remnants of fireworks, sprinkled for a moment, in the sky. He would have enjoyed a walk, but that entailed Secret Service and, oh hell, it was just too damn much trouble.

His private line rang, startling him out of regret. "Yes," he answered.

"Sorry to bother you so late, sir, but it's me, Boyer. Can we talk for a few minutes?"

The President looked at his watch. "A little late, isn't it, Hank? Can it wait?"

Boyer paused. "I'd like you to know before it hits the papers in the morning. You need to be prepared."

The President sighed deeply. "Okay, come on up." While he waited for his vice president to arrive, he imagined the worst. That way, whatever Boyer hit him with was a relief. Most second chairs were merely figureheads, but the President and Henry Boyer had been friends since their days as freshman Congressional Reps. He was grateful for that.

Boyer knocked softly, then walked in to the large living room. The President was sitting on one of the two sofas, sipping his evening brandy.

"Mr. President, Franklin Chamberlain's grandchildren have been kidnapped in Winnetka."

"Oh, my God!" the President stood up. "Do we have details?"

"No. I got a call from the Congressman early this afternoon and told him he had your complete support. I called the FBI Director to let him know you would be on his ass about this. I didn't want to disturb you during your meeting with those Arabs. Then I had a meeting with the speaker about the OCB. Things look good if we can get it out of Chamberlain's committee."

The Organized Crime Bill was the President's baby. He had campaigned against drugs and street crime, but he felt the only way to really combat the problem was to go the source, The Organization.

"This incident may actually help us get the bill through," the President told Boyer, sitting on the edge of his massive desk. "Chamberlain's our holdout. He leans to the left when it comes to Constitutional Rights, and he thinks the bill is uncompromising—gives the courts and the law enforcement too much power. After this, he may back off, and we'll get the OCB through before the Christmas recess. You know what they say, Mr. President, a conservative is a liberal that's been mugged." He attempted a weak laugh that ended in a cough as he caught the President's frown.

The President finished his drink and set the glass down with a flourish. Boyer stood, his dark brows knitted, a look of concern on his face.

"Something wrong, Hank?"

"No, sir. It's just that, well, to be perfectly honest, Chamberlain may be right about this piece of legislation."

"Damn it, you know how I feel about this!" he slapped his hand on the table.

"Yes, sir. Sorry, I'm with you all the way." He turned to leave.

"Oh, by the way, the Chamberlain kids. What's the story?"

Boyer turned back. "Two kids, boy about fourteen, girl a little younger, disappeared from their schools this morning. So far, no note or no ransom demands." Boyer looked away, thinking. "Funny thing, though, big-time Chicago mob boss, Tony Romano, was found dead in the parent's house this morning."

"Jesus Christ! Is it connected?" He now had the President's undivided attention.

"They don't know. Family says not. The Congressman flew out with the Feds in tow. Papers will have a field day with this, though."

Remembering the Chamberlain's contributions, the President asked, "Will this come back to bite us in the ass?"

"I hope not, sir, I certainly hope not. If there is a problem, it's with the Congressman's son, not Franklin."

The President took a deep breath. "Okay then, keep me posted, Hank. You'll stay on top of it?"

"Yes, sir. Good night." Boyer left the room and walked down to the basement of the White House.

He locked the door and picked up his phone which he knew was clear. "I just told the President," he said into the receiver. "And he thinks this will help his bill pass." A pause. "I don't know. We'll have to wait and see."

DAY ONE
MONDAY, NOVEMBER 18 • 9:15 PM CST

THE EASTON'S red-brick home overlooked the eighth hole of the Winnetka golf course. Gravel crunched under the car's tires as the two police investigators drove up to the white columns of the porch. Wind howled as the sensor-timed lights illuminated their path.

The doorbell chimed, and the door was opened tentatively by a paunchy, balding man in his early forties. He looked over the top of his wire-rimmed glasses.

"Yes?"

"Sorry to bother you so late. Mr. Easton?" An affirmative nod. "I'm Police Chief Russell Atkinson, and this is Detective O'Brien. We would like to talk with you and your wife concerning the Chamberlain matter. May we come in?" Both men were holding their badges up to the light.

He opened the door to an expansive marble foyer. The living room, to the right, was furnished in silk draperies and traditional, floral print sofas and chairs, all arranged around a large fireplace. An ebony grand piano held a glorious flower arrangement and brass-framed photos.

To the left of the entry, a dining room table of polished cherry dominated the room. It accommodated twelve matching chairs covered in a deep green damask. Chester Easton called for his wife.

Brooke Easton came down the stairs wearing a baggy knit sweater over tight, pink leggings. Athletic socks were crumpled around her ankles. Her short, ash-streaked hair was swept back from her aristocratic face. Even with no make-up at this hour, Brooke Easton was a very striking woman.

She saw the lawmen standing with her husband before she turned on the landing. Her complexion turned ashen.

"Any news?" Her voice cracked with apprehension.

"No, m'am, we just have a few more questions, if you don't mind," O'Brien said politely, embarrassed to be sounding like Sergeant Friday.

Mrs. Easton reached the bottom of the stairs. "Please, let's go into the family room. I don't want to frighten the children anymore than they are." She motioned them to follow.

The family room was furnished more casually, in soft leather. The two officers sat on the edge of their respective seats and pulled out notebooks.

The chief began, "Mrs. Easton, you told the officer this afternoon that you didn't think Mrs. Chamberlain was happy in her marriage. Can you elaborate?"

"Well," she began and looked towards her husband. Chet Easton was not pleased with her revelation.

"Brooke, I don't think you should be spreading these kinds of rumors."

Before his wife could respond, Atkinson interjected. "Mr. Easton, we understand your reluctance, but even something seemingly insignificant could be important later on. Please allow your wife to continue, and, Mrs. Easton, be as candid as possible. I assure you, anything you tell us will remain in confidence. I am not a big believer in trial-by-press or the sensationalism we see in high-profile cases."

Brooke seemed convinced, but Chet Easton kept his arms folded and watched his wife intently as she spoke. "Meri and I are good friends, and I wouldn't want to say anything that would hurt her or her family. I do know, though, that she was worried about money lately, and that Jonathan was not sleeping at home on a regular basis. She was spending a lot of time at the North Lake Community House—she's on the board there and also involved in the Little Theatre Group, The North Lake Players. She's a very good actress, you know."

The officers exchanged looks before continuing, "Is there anyone you might suggest we talk with that would know more about their personal relationship or their finances?"

The woman looked to the husband before answering. She shook her head but both men had a strong feeling that Brooke Easton knew more than she said.

"Your daughter, Elyse, she's Chelsea best friend?" O'Brien looked at his notes.

"Yes, they are together so much they're beginning to look like sisters." Brooke's smile turned to a sad grimace.

"Thank you very much for your time. Again, we're sorry to bother you so late. If you think of anything, please call on my private number." Atkinson handed his card to the lady.

Once in the car, the chief asked, "So, what are you thinking?"

"I'm thinking there may have been real trouble in paradise before this morning. I'll be anxious to see what Chamberlain has to say concerning his finances. Romano's involvement with money laundering and loan sharking may not be such a stretch after all."

DAY TWO
TUESDAY, NOVEMBER 19 • 12:35 AM

THE STATION HOUSE was usually quiet at this hour on other nights, but on this particular night, all the overhead lights were lit and desks were manned by officers. O'Brien and Atkinson sat across from one another sketching out scenarios. "Let's just say that Chamberlain had gone to Romano for a quick fix," O'Brien ventured. "But that he couldn't pay the vigorish. Suppose they go after the kids as collateral?"

The chief spoke slowly, "But then why was Romano murdered in the home? That's the part that makes no sense." O'Brien had to agree. If they could just make that puzzle part fit, they might have a real clue.

"How about this," O'Brien began to weave the story, "Chamberlain contacts Romano through a friend-of-a-friend. He's an attorney and attorneys have connections. He needs money. Bad investments, another woman, whatever. When he can't pay it back with the interest the mob tacks on, he's threatened.

"So, he high-tails it out of town for a while and ensconces his kids with trusted friends. When Romano figures out where he's hiding, he contacts Chamberlain and threatens him. Chamberlain hires somebody to take out the boss while his out-of-town alibi is good. What do you think?"

"Too easy," Driscoll's interruption startled the two. "Once again, where are the kids? That's where the scenario falls apart." The agent snapped his pencil in two. "Damn. I guess if it was easy, everyone would be a cop, huh?"

O'Brien smiled sadly. "Or there wouldn't be any crime. Then we'd all be out of a job. I thought you might have given up for the night."

"Naw. Just taking a little cat-nap on what you laughingly call a sofa in the lounge. I thought you rich cops in the 'burbs had good stuff." He walked to the coffee pot, grabbing a paper cup.

The Chief rubbed his temples. "Coffee's cold."

"Yeah, you've had too much anyway. Anything new?" O'Brien asked.

"One thing I came across. We got the printout from the Congressman's aide. It seems the funding for the OCB, the Organized Crime Bill, is sitting on his desk waiting for his committee's approval. There could be a connection." Driscoll tasted the coffee then gave up the idea.

"Have you talked to the Congressman about it?" O'Brien asked.

"Not yet, but we will first thing. No one's tried to contact either home, though. I can't understand that. Why snatch the kids?" Driscoll's question went unanswered.

"Look," Atkinson said as he stood, "it's late, and we're all beat. Everything we have so far is being processed through computer. The night shift is working on all possible avenues, and we'll have more information by morning. Let's get a few hours shut-eye, so we won't be basket cases tomorrow."

O'Brien's legs were stiff, and his back screamed for mercy. He rubbed his neck to loosen the sore muscles, praying the migraine wouldn't return. "Where're you staying, Driscoll?" O'Brien asked the agent.

Driscoll shrugged. "My team is booked at the Doubletree, but I'd feel better if you could find a bunk here for me in case anything pops. You're five minutes away if you're needed, but at least I'd be here."

"There's some decent beds in the fire department annex dorms, I'll call over there and tell them to find you accommodations. They also have a pretty good kitchen." The chief was pulling on his wool coat, "Oh, and Driscoll, thanks for the cooperation; it will make all our lives easier." The agent waved at him as he walked to get his briefcase.

"O'Brien, go home. That's where I'm going. The dispatcher will call us if anything breaks. I'll need you one hundred and ten percent tomorrow. Early."

DAY TWO
TUESDAY, NOVEMBER 19 • 3:20 AM

O'BRIEN WOKE with a gasp. Despite the November temperature and the small crack left in the bedroom window, Charlie O'Brien was drenched in sweat. He tried desperately to recall the nightmare that frightened him awake. His body ached for sleep, but he knew from experience, it wouldn't come easily. He got up and walked into the small kitchen in his third-floor condo. The cloud cover turned the night to black ink—no stars, no moon, no street lamp light from this window. "Where are those kids?" O'Brien asked the emptiness.

Photos of the Chamberlain children were on all the newscasts. Intermittent bulletins continued throughout the evening broadcast schedule. The usual crank calls were coming in and were checked out but nothing tangible resulted. O'Brien called the station dispatcher. "Anything new?"

"Go to bed, O'Brien. You know I would have called you if there was. The chief will have your head if you fall asleep at your desk tomorrow. And the rest of us will have your butt if you're in a rotten mood because you haven't slept." The night dispatcher, Georgia Headen, clicked off.

O'Brien opened the nearly empty fridge and took a long drink of V8 juice out of the bottle. The joys of living alone. He pushed his body back in the old recliner and closed his eyes. "Listen to your gut," his mother always told him. It rumbled indignantly at the assault of the spiced tomato drink. O'Brien replayed the scenes he had witnessed between Meridith and Jonathan Chamberlain. Something was wrong—the Chamberlains' were not in sync.

He kept remembering her green eyes. They looked so intently at everyone—but Jonathan. "Something more is going on here. Lovely lady, I want to find your children for you, but I'm going to need some help." He fell asleep praying for assistance from a much higher power.

PART TWO

THREE MONTHS EARLIER
SUNDAY, AUGUST 25 • 5:00 PM CST

IT HAD BEEN an unusually cool and bright summer. Meridith Chamberlain sat on the brick patio outside the North Lake Country Club's grill, sipping her favorite concoction of rum and lemonade over crushed ice with a sprig of mint. The bartender called it a "Merry Meri" and made it only for her.

Jonathan was finishing up his game, and she watched him walk to the eighteenth green along with his law partner, Bob Crowley. Bob's boyish slouch was in direct contrast to Jonathan's aligned, upright posture. Bob smiled easily, flashing dimples and perfect white teeth that, in turn, set-off a Town & Country tan. He wore the latest European styles including silks and gabardines with just the right nonchalance. Jonathan, on the other hand, was always starched and creased in oxford and wool. Meri stood and saw him miss a long putt. Although he laughed amiably, she knew he would be in a foul mood through dinner. Bob made an easy putt, and the two picked up their balls and walked toward the club, followed by their young caddies.

"Hello, Meri," Bob said as he kissed her cheek in greeting. "I see you started without us." He was referring to her glass.

"Call it a prelude." She smiled with wary eyes. She was not fond of Jonathan's partner, and they all knew it. Bob was all the catalyst Jonathan needed to find trouble. Bob was a dangerous combination: divorced, charming and rich. In his early forties, he was still youthful enough to play the single game, and he often encouraged Jonathan to meet *clients* after-hours. Bob wanted a playmate and Jonathan was more than happy to oblige.

"Are you joining us for dinner?" Bob asked, as if it were his party.

"I thought I'd stay. Is anyone joining you?" she inquired pointedly.

"A young lady, yes." Bob's eyes glittered with the knowledge he could still strike a nerve with the imperturbable princess of cool.

By the time the trio entered the refrigerated air of the dining room, the sun was streaking a red blush across the sky. It was going to be a beautiful summer night. Jonathan was on his third straight Dewars. It was going to a killer of an evening. They made polite small talk but Bob was distracted, his gray eyes anxiously watching the door for his evening's companion.

The hostess walked across the dark wood floor towards the Chamberlain's table, leading a young woman. Heads turned in her direction as they passed. The tall blonde was wearing a most inappropriate outfit. In a sea of Navy blazers, khaki slacks and summer dresses, the young woman wore a sheer, iridescent lime dress that billowed over her nude body! Actually, underneath she was wearing the skimpiest flesh-colored shorts Meri had ever seen, and the matching top barely covered her unbridled breasts that swayed with her every step. As she arrived at their table, the room went silent.

"Well, hello, beautiful!" Bob stood and hugged his guest. "This is Selina," he announced. Her skin glowed from the summer sun, and her pouting mouth sported bright pink lipstick that she quickly transferred to Bob's cheek.

Meridith recovered her voice, "Hello. I'm Meri Chamberlain. My husband, Jonathan." Jonathan's jaw dropped as his eyes scanned the length of their new dinner companion.

"Wow. Bob said you were gorgeous, but he didn't say you were down-right delicious!" Jonathan jumped to his feet and hugged the woman tightly.

"Down, boy," Bob teased and seated her as the conversation in the room returned to normal. Meri knew what the talk was about. She caught the eyes of her friends as they stole glances from time to time.

What Meridith couldn't have known was that during dinner, the woman slipped off her sandal and was rubbing the inside of Jonathan's leg with her toe, much to the delight of surrounding patrons, who knew all-too-well what was happening. Jonathan was getting progressively more drunk and more obvious in his attention to the lady Selina.

Selina had a most distracting habit of running her tongue across her mouth and lowering her eyes just enough to peek through her lashes. And she giggled!

Coffee was offered as the bus boy cleared the table. "I'll have a brandy," Jonathan informed the waiter. Meridith winced.

Bob ran his hand down Selina's back and she shivered with delight. "I don't know about you, old man, but this lady and I still have the evening ahead of us. I'm going to take every advantage of one of the last summer nights with one of the world's most beautiful women." Selina rewarded his compliment by puckering her lips and blowing a kiss across the table.

"We're going home, too," Meridith announced.

"Never get married." Jonathan looked at Selina. "It's a fuckin' ball 'n' chain," he was slurring. His voice was louder than necessary, and, with the use of the expletive, several nearby women glared.

"It's been an ..." Meri searched for the right word. "... experience." She stood. "Jonathan, I'll have the valet get the car and meet you out front. Good night." As she walked away, she could feel the icy stare of his eyes on her back. "Tonight will be a nightmare," she predicted.

They rode home in silence. Meridith drove, and Jonathan was slumped down in the passenger seat. Meridith was hoping he had consumed enough alcohol to stay asleep, but, as the car pulled into the garage he sat up straight.

"You bitch," he hissed in her ear. "Don't ever embarrass me like that again." Meridith refused to be baited. She opened the door and tried to get out, but Jonathan was holding her arm tightly.

"Jonathan, you're hurting me. Let go." She jerked away and managed to get out of the car. He was surprisingly fast and arrived at the door into the house before his wife.

"Get out of my way," she demanded.

"You embarrassed me, you fuckin' bitch. Don't ever do that again." His tone was menacing. She knew better than to argue with him when he was drunk and in this mood. Meridith stood her ground and waited.

"Say something!" he demanded.

"Jonathan, please, not now. Let me pass."

The slap came from the dark and surprised her. The left side of her face was stinging, and her neck was wrenched from the force of his hand. She staggered but remained standing. Before he could strike again, she retreated to the back of the garage. The Mercedes sedan left little room in the garage. She bumped her ankle on the end of the fender. "Jonathan, stop it. I mean it, I will not tolerate this. "

The lights went out, and in the blackness, she could hear him laughing softly. It was a menacing sound, but it gave her a clue to his whereabouts. Then there was quiet. All she could hear were footsteps. She tried to lift the garage door but knew it wouldn't budge. She opened the car's rear door to reach the electric eye opener, but as soon as she reached across the seat, she knew it was a fatal mistake.

Jonathan pushed her face down across the bench seat and began tearing at her dress.

"Don't, Jonathan, stop!" Meri tried to fight him, but in this vulnerable position, it was a lost cause. Meri tried to turn over, which would allow her more leverage, but the strength of her captor was overpowering.

Chamberlain pushed the material of her dress out of his way and ripped aside her panties. While holding her face against the leather of the car's seat, he managed to unzip his slacks and free himself of the restraints of his own underwear. Despite the excitement his brutality had aroused, he found his member limp and uncooperative. Now he was furious.

"This is your fault, bitch. You don't turn me on anymore. Do you hear me?"

He slapped at her bare bottom in the hopes of stimulating himself. Nothing. Meridith was crying, but her sobs were being chocked off by Jonathan's suffocating hold on her.

"You're pathetic. I know you want it, baby." As she turned her face to him, he hit her again. The pain seared Meri, and she bolted back with a newfound force. The shock of her reaction caught Jonathan off guard, and he fell back, hitting his head against the open car door. She used the distraction to free herself from underneath the attacker and slid out the driver's side door.

Scrambling across the garage she hurried inside and ran the length of the kitchen to the stairs that led to the safety of her room. Once inside, she locked the door. Meridith needed to check on the children; Hunter had been left in charge and Chelsea had her friend, Elyse Easton, staying over. Jonathan had been sleeping in his den, and Meri was more than relieved. She waited until she heard the door slam before tip-toeing down the hall. The kids slept soundly.

STANDING BEFORE the bathroom mirror, Meri examined the swelling on her cheek. It was going to bruise, even with the cold cloth she applied, and her neck was stiff. As she dabbed stinging iodine to the small cut on her cheek, the bottle dropped from her fingers and bright crimson liquid spilled over her bare toes. "Damn," Meri muttered as she stepped into the steamy shower.

Meridith focused. An inner strength began to emerge as she allowed the water to pummel her angry body. She looked down at her stained feet and was startled. A shiver coursed through her. Suddenly, like summer lightning, she began to reclaim herself, and she laughed out loud. "If this is a sign," she told the ceiling, "I understand." That moment the healing began.

As she dried her body, she toweled the steam off her mirror. Facing herself once again, she didn't see the bruised face but the brave one she'd known since childhood. Meridith held up her ruby-red foot and heard herself repeat with conviction, "You've had the power all the time." And with those words she started down the road back.

MONDAY, AUGUST 26 • 9:00 AM

THE NEXT MORNING, Meridith sat on her deck overlooking Lake Michigan, talking with Brooke Easton and sipping iced cappuccino. Brooke was indulging in shortbread cookies. "You're right, Meri. Even the dark glasses and make-up aren't going to hide that bruise. How will you ever explain that at rehearsal tonight?" Brooke asked her friend between cookie bites.

"I don't know. How about a missed tennis ball? Everyone knows I'm a klutzy athlete." The thought of Meri's shortcoming made Brooke smile. The waves crashed against the bluff as a strong breeze off the lake swept Meri's hair back and she pulled her sweater tighter. Their days outside were numbered.

"Meri, you have to do something. I know you and Jonathan have been fighting, but this!" She winced as she examined the offended eye. "He's never gone this far before! You don't have to put up with this, you're a knock-out." They both laughed at Brooke's unintentional pun. "Besides, even if you were god-awful-ugly, you're rich!"

Meri hugged her friend as they shared laughter. "Brooke, you're right, but, then you're always right!" Brooke winked. "The biggest problem I have is that Jonathan knows every attorney in town. No one will want to represent me against him."

"He may know every attorney in Chicago, but that doesn't mean they all *like* him. You know that lawyer who represented Ellen Thomas last year, Barry Ellison? She had him over for a dinner party, you know, always invite an unattached man to a party! Well, when I mentioned you and I were working on the hospital ball committee together, he asked if I knew Jonathan." She paused for effect.

"It turns out ..." she lowered her voice to a conspiratorial whisper, "... that he went to school with Jonathan, at Northwestern, and your man used some rather dirty tricks, as well as his family name, to win a seat on the moot court, you know, the law school equivalent of the debate team. Anyway, after all these years, it still sticks in Barry's craw. He didn't elaborate, but I got the feeling he would love the opportunity to whip his ass for real, given half a chance."

"Really?" Meri took off her sunglasses and gave her full attention to Brooke.

"Really. Anyway, I'll call Ellen and get his number for you. If you call her, it will be grist for the rumor mill."

Brooke checked the Rolex she always wore on her right arm, a little hint of nonconformism. "Got to run, Meri, and pick up the kids. Sailing lessons at ten. When I die, I want to come back as my own children. What a life!" She pecked at Meri's cheek. "And, next time, kick the bastard in his balls!" With that Brooke Easton trotted across the wooden deck and around the house.

MERI WATCHED the morning sunlight bounce off the water of Lake Michigan. The lake was a creature of multiple personalities. The strong winds that swept across it from Canada churned up its sandy bottom, and it reflected a barren taupe gray in Winter. The schizophrenic summer turned it turquoise and almost inviting, but still too chilly for Meri. The children loved sailing, and the lake always accommodated them, whipping their vessels at speeds that made Meri nervous. Still this was her favorite spot. Measured against the lake's vastness she sometimes felt insignificant. But today, Meri felt empowered. She silently told Brooke not to worry; there would be no next time.

Chelsea broke her mother's meditation with a call from the sun porch, "Mom!" Meri turned and seemed to see her daughter more clearly than she had for a long time.

Chelsea had gotten taller and her blonde hair, pulled tight in a pony tail, brought her face into focus. She was losing her little girl look and turning into a beautiful, young lady.

This revelation made Meri both happy and sad.

"Mom, what happened to your face? Your eye!" Chelsea's bright face clouded over.

"Nothing, honey. I caught it on the car door last night. It's nothing, really." She attempted nonchalance as she replaced her glasses.

"Mom, you don't have to pretend. Hunter and I know about Dad's temper. I know he's my dad and all, but, Mom, I don't think you should allow him to hit you." Chelsea sat down next to her mother. "If you ever wanted him to leave, we would be all right with that. I know that sounds terrible to say about my own dad, but, Mom, you don't deserve to be with someone who treats you like this."

Meri was overcome. She stood up and walked over to Chelsea. Her daughter's big, green eyes invited a hug. Basking in her daughter's courage, Meri's spirit continued its power-surge, as they watched the ricochet of sunlight off the water.

MONDAY, AUGUST 26 • EVENING

JONATHAN DIDN'T RETURN home for dinner that night. Meridith took the children for burgers and shakes before dropping them off at their destinations: Hunter to the movies with Scott McBride; Chelsea to the Easton's.

Meri arrived at the Community House for rehearsal. She was playing Blanche DuBois in Tennessee Williams' *A Streetcar Named Desire*. The part of the tortured beauty was anything but a stretch for her but, to her fellow actors of the North Lake Players, Meridith Chamberlain had it all. No one suspected what her real life was like.

"Before the jokes begin," Meri announced to the group, "I have a black eye. It seems I zigged when I should have zagged on the tennis court, and my opponent won—when my eye failed to return the ball in bounds." She tried to smile.

"Yeah, right. Come on, Meri, 'fess up. The other guy is worse, right?" The Director, Paul Winston, walked over to assess the damage.

Meri's smile widened at his teasing, and he bent down and kissed the swollen cheek gently. The actor playing opposite Meri raised his eyebrows but said nothing. Paul was a charming flirt, and his reputation was often a topic of conversation.

The North Lake Players' productions were as good as any in downtown Chicago. Many of the actors and technicians were people who had studied theatre or dabbled professionally but found that traditional avenues afforded a better living. Their love of the stage, however, endured. It was because they were consummate actors that they were successful at their chosen careers.

Despite the proficiency of the Players and the respect they earned in the spotlight, an aura of infamy surrounded them offstage. Rumors of affairs among the actors were not always unfounded.

"Let's begin, shall we?" Paul clapped his hands and announced, "We still need work on the scene between Stanley and Blanche. Can we start there?"

Meri picked up her script and turned to the scene where Stanley rapes her. She closed her eyes, and the scene between her and Jonathan replayed itself. She shuddered.

"Paul, could we work on that later? That's a little heavy tonight."

"Meri, it's called *acting*. Come on, you won't be able to make a speech to the audience opening night. Use what you're feeling—make it work for you." Paul was insistent.

Joe Stevenson was already center stage. He walked into the wings where his wife, Gillian, stood, holding a copy of the script. Gillian said something to Joe but he ignored her.

Meri looked at the Director, "Where do you want us to begin?"

"Page 128. Pick it up with the operator speech."

Meridith took a deep breath. She held a phone to her ear and began, changing her own voice to one with just a hint of a southern accent. "Operator! Operator! Never mind long-distance. Get Western Union. Western Union!" She paused then began more excitedly in her throaty voice, "Yes! Take down this message! 'In desperate, desperate circumstance! Help me! Caught in a trap—' Oh!"

Joe, playing Stanley, opened the door on the set and emerged to the center of the stage grinning menacingly.

"You left the phone off the hook." He also used a Southern inflection. He crossed the stage and replaced the receiver on its hook.

"Let me—let me get by you!"

Stanley: Get by me! Sure. Go ahead. *He moved back.*

Blanche: You—you stand over there!

Stanley: You got plenty of room to walk by me now. *His grin grew wider, his eyes taunted.*

Blanche: Not with you there! But I've got to get out somehow!

Stanley: You think I'll interfere with you? *His laughter upped the ante.*

Meri's transformation into Blanche was complete. She turned, confused. Stanley took a step toward her and bit his tongue which was protruding between his lips. He delivered his next line softly. "Come to think of it—maybe you wouldn't be so bad to—interfere with."

Blanche: Stay back! Don't you come toward me another step or I'll—

Stanley: What?

Blanche: Some awful thing will happen! It will!

Stanley: What are you putting on now? *Stanley took another step.*

Blanche reached for a bottle placed on a table, smashed it on the table and faced him, clutching the broken top.

Stanley: What did you do that for?

Blanche: So I could twist the broken end in your face!

Stanley: I bet you would do that!

Blanche: I would! I will if you—

Stanley: Oh! so you want some rough-house! All right, let's have some rough-house! *He lunged towards her and overturned the table. She cried out and struck at him with the bottle top, but he caught her wrist.* Tiger—tiger! Drop the bottle top! Drop it! We've had this date with each other from the beginning!

Blanche moaned. The bottle top fell. She sunk to her knees. Stanley picked up her inert figure and carried her to the bed. As the stage lights began to dim, Meri started to cry.

"That's great, guys, really, really great!" Paul shouted as the house lights came up. But Meri found she couldn't stop the tears. Her sobs racked her whole body. Joe stood helplessly staring down at his co-star lying on the stage set bed.

The cast and crew were silent. Meri was lost in her own pain, the line between acting and real life blurred.

After a few interminable minutes, Lanie Flowers stepped out on stage.

"Okay, everybody, Paul said to take a break. Let's give Meri one. This is a tough part, and she's a hell of an actress—I think she deserves a big hand!" Lanie began to clap loudly. A few joined in, half-heartedly. Meri lifted her head and looked around, incredibly embarrassed.

"Sorry, Joe, Paul. Sorry, guys. I don't know what got into me. I've been reaching down so far into my psyche for this part, I guess it got the best of me."

"No apologies for a great performance. If you can give us that opening night, the critics will *come!*" Paul's bawdy reference brought Meri out of her melancholy. "Let's work with Stella and Stanley. Meri take the rest of the night off, get some rest. I'm sure your battle on the tennis court took a lot out of you, too. See you Tuesday." He turned his attention to the actress playing Stella.

Meri wasn't sure if his reference to tennis was sarcastic or not, but she chose to ignore it. She picked up her tote bag and took out a bottle of Evian. She was drinking deeply when Lanie came up behind her.

"Want to talk about it?"

Meri jumped, spilling the water down the front of her sweater.

"Sorry, I didn't mean to startle you."

Lanie was a person you wished were a sister. She was caring, funny and there when you needed a friend. Her pretty face sat atop an upholstered, but very huggable, body.

"It's not your fault." Meri touched her friend's shoulder. "And, thanks, Lanie, for coming to my rescue."

"Come on, Meri, truth. What's with the eye?" Lanie looked right through her.

"It's nothing, Lanie, really. How are the costumes coming?" Meri's attempt to change the subject was rather transparent.

"Nice try." Lanie let her off the hook. "Paul wants the show to look authentic 1940s so I'm off to the resale shops tomorrow. Want to come?"

"Thanks, but I can't. Maybe next time?" Meri allowed herself to be hugged. "See you Tuesday, Lanie."

"You will call me if you need anything?"

She was genuine, and Meri promised. Gathering her things she left quickly. The chilly air was an omen that the summer's softness was surrendering. Meri slipped on her jacket and decided to take a walk before returning home. She wasn't sure if Jonathan would be home yet and she wanted to avoid a confrontation.

THE NORTH Lake Community House had been the center of activity for almost a century. It was a stately institution of solid stone that housed the North Lake Church, scouts, a day care center and senior programs. It offered the citizenry classes in everything from aerobics to zen. It felt warm and welcoming. Meridith Chamberlain walked around the grounds, admiring the plantings that the Women's Board oversaw every spring. The flowers, now in full bloom, were straining against the cool wind. She wondered if they sensed their own, impending finale.

Meri hugged her jacket tighter and walked across to the Congregational Church. She climbed the steps and recalled standing right here for so many important moments in her life. "I remember standing here with Mama every Sunday," she said aloud. "Oh, Mama, you were always there when I needed you, and now, I feel so lost." Meri sat down on the church steps.

MERIDITH'S MOTHER, Barbara Whitney was a bright, loving woman. Brought up in a time when woman were schooled by the right colleges and sororities tutored gentility, Barbara wanted more for her own daughter: she wanted her husband to bring Meridith into the business. Meri was smart, quick and good with people.

She remembered her mother's face the day she told her she was going to major in Theatre at Northwestern—Meri wanted to become an actress. Then she met Jonathan and wanted to become a wife. "How you saw through Jonathan." She had to smile, remembering her mother's admonitions. "Oh, Mama. Now I understand what you were trying to teach me—to be my own person."

Meridith sat on the church steps for a long while. She could recall Christmas services, singing with the choir and her father's loud, strong voice singing slightly off-key. It made her so proud to walk down the aisle with him. She remembered another walk down the aisle with father—towards the altar to meet Jonathan. They had so many hopes, so many dreams—the handsome young couple with all the promise. Meridith laughed at herself even while the tears were still wet on her face. "Like the North Shore woman who wears designer clothing and torn underwear," she mused. "Razzle without dazzle. We look so damn good no one would suspect."

Having no son of his own, Stuart Whitney had hoped that Jonathan would join the food conglomerate, and one day assume the title of president. Jonathan had no such ambition. He was never comfortable with the corporate constraints or the fact that Stuart wanted him to learn the business from the ground up. Jonathan felt he had no such dues to pay. When Stuart Whitney relinquished the role of CEO, handing the reins to a hand-picked heir, he finally felt he could afford to some personal time.

Meri remembered vividly the moment she heard the news: their small private plane had crashed over the mountains in Denver. Both her parents were killed instantly, never knowing their grandchildren-to-be.

Meridith closed her eyes and, sitting outside the chapel, once again renewed her sense of power. Recalling her character, Blanche, she realized she was a victim because she allowed herself to be one. "I understand, Mama. Thank you." Meridith smiled up at the stars knowing that she would be a victim no more.

MERI DECIDED to pick up Chelsea rather than wait for Brooke to deliver her. Hunter would be driven home in time for his ten o'clock curfew. When mother and daughter arrived, they found Jonathan sitting by the solarium window in the kitchen. Meri was relieved to see he was drinking iced tea and eating a sandwich.

He spoke first, addressing Chelsea, "Hello, Princess, have a good day?"

"It was great, Dad. Elyse and I found out we're going to be in the same class, Mrs. Willard, she's nice. We watched all Winnetka movies! *Home Alone* and *Ferris Bueller*— we recognized a lot of the places."

"That's great, Chel. Go on upstairs and get ready for bed. I have to talk to Mom." He gave her a hug. She looked right into her mother's soul with eyes that reflected the older woman's. "Remember our talk. I love you." She disappeared up the back staircase.
Jonathan turned to look at Meri.

"Jonathan, I am too tired to fight."

"Me, too, Meri. Please, we need to talk." Something in his voice was different. She responded to her nickname, which he seldom used, and sat across from him. Jonathan walked across the tile floor, his expensive shoes making a clipped tap, and poured two cups of coffee. He topped hers with skim milk and set them down. "Meri, I've had some bad news." She steeled herself. He searched his cup avoiding her penetrating eyes. "You know I've been playing the Commodities Market. I sold short in the soy bean market, on the advice of that damn Trogdon, our so-called broker. He thought it was going to be a banner summer for the farmers, and it turned out to be a rotten year.

"The bottom line is, I lost. I mean, I lost big. Close to a mill."

Meridith sat, watching his face intently. The enormity of his news took a minute to register. "You mean, a million *dollars*" she asked incredulously.

He shook his head in affirmation but his eyes never left his coffee cup.

"What are you going to do?"

"Me? Don't you mean *us?*" Jonathan stood up, spilling his coffee. Aren't we in this together?"

"No. Jonathan you used my money and lost before. I'm not bailing you out this time." Her voice was hard.

"We could lose everything! I only have another twenty-four hours to clear the deficit in my account. They'll take the house or seize our bank account to make up the margin call." He was bordering on hysterics.

"No, Jonathan. You're wrong. The house belonged to my parents. It's mine in entirety, protected by a land trust. My trust fund is in my name with the children as beneficiaries. The Whitney stock and its dividends are also in my name, alone. My father was very specific in his will. It made me angry at the time, that he didn't trust you enough to leave everything in joint tenancy, but now, I understand."

It took Jonathan only a minute to recover from his contrite posture to the angry man she had been expecting.

"Illinois is a community property state. Half of everything is mine, anyway." He was smug now.

"Sorry, Jonathan, you've gotten some bad advice. Anything I received through inheritance remains mine and does not become part of our community property. The Whitney attorneys have assured me that this is the law in Illinois." Meridith tried to sound firm, but her resolve was giving way to Jonathan's menacing stance over her. She tried to stand up and had to push her chair backwards to allow herself enough room to do so.

"You're not walking away from this thing that easy!" Jonathan grabbed at his wife, and she and the heavy chair fell back.

"Jonathan, don't touch me! I mean it!" Meridith was awkwardly attempting to right herself when the French door from the deck opened.

"Leave her alone, Dad!" Hunter demanded.

Jonathan jumped back and tried to smile. "It's not what you think, Hunter, I was only trying to help your mother up." He reached out his hand to Meridith. But Hunter pushed around him and gently lifted his mother.

"Go away, Dad. Leave us alone." Meridith felt a surge of pride. It took great courage for Hunter to stand up to his father. Jonathan glared at the two sets of green eyes defying him. He abruptly walked out of the room.

They listened to Jonathan's footsteps grow quieter as he crossed the foyer, and then they disappeared as he left the house.

Hugging her son, Meri was aware that he, too, had grown taller. They were both growing up faster than she had realized. He wriggled out of her arms and self-consciously kissed her cheek before bolting upstairs. She walked to the window, thinking about the fragile bonds that tie families together and how easily they could fray and break. With each wave that crashed against the bluff, her resolve grew stronger.

TUESDAY, AUGUST 27 · MORNING

BROOKE EASTON had given Meridith the attorney's number. Meri dialed with a surprisingly steady hand. "Mr. Ellison, please, this is Meridith Whitney Chamberlain," she heard her voice as if it came from another source. Jonathan had not returned home last night, and he was still among the missing today.

"Mrs. Chamberlain! Barry Ellison here. What may I do for you?" His voice was reassuring and strong.

"Mr. Ellison, you helped a friend of mine, Ellen Thomas. She speaks very highly of you, and I was wondering if we might meet. I have a very personal matter I need to discuss, and I am in need of legal advice." Meridith was sure that the information she had received from the Whitney attorneys was correct, but there was a great deal of money at stake, as well as her children's future. She remembered how long and hard her father had worked to make a million dollars and how easily Jonathan could lose it.

"Certainly. Let me see. How about tomorrow? We could meet at my office around noon." He was intrigued.

"Yes, that would work out fine. Thank you."

"I'm at Thirty-three North Dearborn, Fortieth Floor. I look forward to meeting with you tomorrow, Mrs. Chamberlain, and I hope I will be able to help."

"I'm sure you will. Thank you again. Good bye." She hung up.

WHILE MERIDITH was making her appointment with the attorney, Jonathan Chamberlain was also making a date with destiny.

"Look, Bob, I know this is not the way the firm likes to handle financial matters; but I need help, and I need it fast!" Jonathan was trying desperately to convince Robert Crowley to lend him over eight hundred thousand dollars from the partnership fund.

"No can do, Jon, old man," Bob shook his head. "How in the hell could this happen? Never mind, I don't want to know. What about Meridith? The Whitney stock is worth a fortune, and she owns a huge block since they sold out to Carolina Tobacco."

"Yeah, and it's all in her name, and she's holding out." Jonathan searched his cabinet for the bottle of Glenlivit he kept there. Pouring it straight into a coffee cup, he gulped it. "That's how I got into this mess. I've been playing the market in the hopes of accumulating enough money of my own to leave her. I'm fucking sick of her holding the purse strings, Bob. It's been a nightmare."

"That certainly won't help." Bob watched him down the scotch. He bit his lower lip, frowned, and paused. "Look, I hate to do this, but—."

"But what? Don't hold out on me if you have an idea," Jonathan prodded.

"I have a friend who has a client that may be able to help you with a short- term loan. But it's risky. The guy has a real shady reputation. Supposedly mob connections. What the hell am I doing? Never mind. Forget I ever said that."

Bob started to walk out of Jonathan's office.

"Wait! Look, Bob, I'll do anything. Meridith and I only have a couple hundred thousand in our joint account. Everything else is in her name. I can't ask my father, either. He doesn't have that kind of liquidity. They'll go after me, even my share of the partnership. You've got to help me." Bob was sickened by Jonathan's pathetic plea.

"Okay, it's your funeral, buddy. The lawyer's name is Silverman, Joel Silverman. He's got an office on Taylor Street, in the Italian section. Tell him you're one of my partners. The rest is up to you." Bob closed the door to Jonathan's office as he left.

Robert Crowley walked directly to the office of the firm's senior partner, MacKenzie Davidson. The older man was sitting behind his leather-top desk gazing out at Chicago's jagged skyline. He swiveled to face the door as Bob entered.

MacKenzie, "Mac," still had a full head of wavy hair at sixty five. The dark, fiery red hair that had once been his trademark had now faded to the color of summer straw. His aqua eyes were shining, and he always looked like he had just heard the punch line of a great story, ready to break into a broad smile. Mac made clients and colleagues alike feel good about themselves. It was no wonder he was a success.

"Problem?" Mac asked.

"I hope not, but maybe. I think we need to have Chamberlain's billing practices checked. He's got some real financial worries, and I'm concerned about how the firm will handle any repercussions. Better safe than sorry."

Mac frowned and rubbed his eyes. He took a deep breath before he spoke. "I'm unhappy it has come to this, but I'm not surprised. I've heard some rumblings about how wildly he has been playing the market. I spoke with him a few weeks ago, but he assured me that Meridith was backing him. Call accounting. Have them check out all our records and accounts. Quietly. Keep this between us, no need to stir up trouble if nothing's wrong."

Bob nodded and left.

THE CALL to Joel Silverman, Esquire, had gone through to the man, himself. "No secretary," Jonathan noted.

Silverman was caught off-guard when Chamberlain introduced himself. It was not everyday he received a call from one of Chicago's uncrowned royalty. He sat back in his swivel chair and put his shoes on his worn desk, admiring the shine of the Italian leather.

"What can I do for you, *Jonathan*?" The use of Chamberlain's first name made him flinch—and Silverman smile.

"Look, Silverman, I'll get right to the point. My partner, Robert Crowley, suggested you might be able to put me in touch with someone who could offer me a short-term loan. I seem to have over-extended myself in the Commodity Market."

Silverman was unwrapping a large, deep brown Cuban cigar and enjoying the aroma while the other attorney continued.

"I need about eight hundred for a few weeks." He was sure he could convince Meridith into making the loan good by then.

"Eight hundred *large*?" Silverman's eyebrows rose. He said nothing, but his mind was reeling. "Why in the hell would a man of Chamberlain's wealth need to borrow that kind of cash with the interest he would have to pay?" he thought.

"Yes, but it would be short-term. Can you help?"

"I'll call my client, and we'll be back to you within the hour. Your number?" Silverman scratched out a downtown exchange and hung up. Before dialing again, he lit the cigar he had been fondling and sucked deeply, relishing the first good smoke of the day.

"This could prove to be a very interesting arrangement! Mr. Chamberlain, you may have just found yourself a new partner, another legitimate businessman," he announced to himself as he punched the buttons on his phone.

TUESDAY, AUGUST 27 • AFTERNOON

THE WHEELS were in motion: the law firm of Davidson, McMahon, Crowley, Chamberlain and Dillon had been discretely invaded by an outside accounting firm of as many last names. When partners Shane Dillon and Ryan McMahon walked into Mac's office, they were told the independent audit was at the request of their own accounting department, who needed the figures for a tax audit. It seemed to satisfy their concern, and no mention was made to any of the associates.

JONATHAN CHAMBERLAIN'S partnership came as a direct result of his father's Washington position. Jonathan had not graduated a member of the "Law Review," in the upper ten percent of Northwestern's Law School. Nor did he have an outstanding record during his tenure as an associate. However, the prestige of having the son of one of the country's reigning elder statesmen as a partner was an opportunity MacKenzie Davidson had seized. Chamberlain's name on the letterhead was worth splitting the yearly profits.

Then, an unexpected bonus: Chamberlain became the firm's leading rain-maker. Whitney Foods sold out to Carolina Tobacco and hired Davidson, et al to handle the Chicago food division. Jonathan's marriage connection now reaped the benefit of over a million dollars a year in billings.

While several hundred thousand dollars annually was more money than most people ever earn, to a man like Jonathan Chamberlain it was never enough.

Meridith had been schooled in money-management by bankers and attorneys who were used to guarding their clients' capital like a mother tiger surrounded by jackals. The credo they lived by was simple: *NEVER TOUCH THE PRINCIPAL.*

Granted, the Whitney's vast portfolio threw off over half a million dollars in dividends and interest, most of it was reinvested, and always in safe and sheltered ventures. Meridith met with her investment team each month, but always alone.

It galled Jonathan that she would not allow him to become a trustee of her portfolio or even to attend the meetings with her. Her father's influence.

AS CHAMBERLAIN sat as his desk waiting for a phone call, he remembered George Whitney, and the sour stomach he had been experiencing migrated to his throat. He fumbled through his desk for an antacid and washed it down with scotch. The ring of the phone made him jump and the acid burned more steadily.

"Chamberlain." He hoped his voice sounded calmer than he felt.

"Mr. Chamberlain. I'm so pleased to be speaking with you." The deep baritone voice on the other end was not what Jonathan expected. It was cultured and clipped and polite. "I'm a client of Joel Silverman's, and he told me you might be in need of my services."

"I'm sorry. You are—?" Jonathan was trying to put a face on the disembodied voice.

"I apologize, I should have introduced myself, but I'd rather do that in person. Might we meet? I understand time is of the essence, so I would suggest we do so today. How about The Greenhouse, on the twelfth floor of the Ritz Carleton, by the fountain, in, say, one hour?"

Jonathan checked his watch. Even that made the bile rise in protest—the timepiece had been a gift from his wife. "Yeah, one hour. How will I know you?"

"I'll know you." The phone resumed the drone of the dial tone.

TUESDAY, AUGUST 27 • 1:00 PM

THE RITZ CARLETON was one of Chicago's five-star hotels. It was adjacent to the Magnificent Mile's landmark Water Tower Place, seventy two floors of shops, hotel rooms and expensive condominiums. Across the street, the John Hancock building rose to the impressive height of ninety-nine stories.

As the elevator opened to the twelfth floor, Chamberlain stepped out on the expanse of marble. A lavish fountain spilled into a surrounding bath, as bronze egrets poised to fly through the overhead skylight. The echo spray of cascading water drowned out the ambient noise of conversation. Jonathan understood the significance of the meeting place: taping the conversation would be impossible.

The Greenhouse was aptly named. An entire wall of glass allowed sunlight to flood the tastefully decorated salon. Queen Anne chairs, upholstered in soft, floral prints, were grouped into conversation areas around carved cherry tables. The sumptuous ambiance afforded privacy and a sense of drawing-room comfort.

Jonathan scanned the room for a lone man. The maitre d' caught his eye and motioned for Jonathan to follow. He seated him near the silent grand piano. The waiter took his order and disappeared. As Jonathan watched, a figure walked across the polished floor toward him. The man was impeccably dressed in a deep olive, gaberdine suit, obviously custom-fitted to his broad-shouldered, narrow-waisted form. His soft, raw-silk shirt was unbuttoned at the throat and a few stray chest hairs snaked their way to freedom. His gait was confident, defiant. He was, in a word, elegant.

What struck Jonathan most about the man approaching was his incredible sense of confidence. From his abundance of dark, wavy hair that fell across his tanned face to the cleft in his strong chin, the man commanded attention. And he got it. As the maitre d' scurried to escort him to Jonathan's table, heads turned in his direction, and women smiled coyly. Jonathan rose to greet the outstretched manicured hand that was offered.

"Mr. Chamberlain?" It was the voice from the phone. "Tony Romano." Jonathan kept his face blank even as the name registered. Big time headlines. Jonathan remembered an episode of *Investigative Reports* by Bill Kurtis. The man wasn't just connected, he was *the* connection. Once seated, Romano nodded and the piano began to play Gershwin via computer tapes. Additional noise but no musician seated close enough to overhear.

"So, tell me, Mr. Chamberlain, what seems to be the problem?" Romano sat back and placed his left foot across his right leg, displaying a soft, woven leather, Italian moccasin. Jonathan recalled something a colleague said, "It isn't the shoes, it's the way a man walks in them."

As Romano lit up a tiny, thin, brown cigar, not much bigger than a cigarette, a martini appeared before him. Jonathan couldn't remember the man ordering. It sat untouched.

"Mr. Romano, I don't know how much you know about my circumstances, so I'll get right to the point. It seems I have over-extended myself in the commodities market. My damn broker, Arthur Trogdon, told me sell soy beans short. Well, it was a shit year, and, to make a long story short, I need about eight hundred thousand by tomorrow afternoon." Chamberlain finished his scotch in one gulp and motioned for the waiter to bring another. Romano sat back, seemingly uninterested, watching the smoke curling towards the ceiling. Neither man spoke.

When the waiter brought Jonathan's second drink and it disappeared, Romano picked up his stemmed glass and held it up to the light, removing the pierced olive.

"Alcohol is a dangerous drug. It numbs the mind. It is important to feel life, to get involved with living. How will we enjoy the highs if we don't experience the lows?" He smiled before downing the drink in one swallow. Romano uncrossed his legs and sat forward in his chair. His face was so close that Jonathan could smell the expensive cologne, Acqua di Selva. His piercing, ice-blue eyes bored into Jonathan's watering, brown orbs. "Mr. Chamberlain, why come to me? Your wife is a wealthy woman."

"My wife is an avaricious bitch." Chamberlain stated the fact. "The money is her family's, and, well, she and I are not getting along at the moment."

Romano thought about Chamberlain's comment. He twirled the cigar in his fingers, took another drag, and then spoke quietly. "Mr. Chamberlain, my people are not in the banking business. Our interest rates are not controlled by the Fed. In fact, Mr. Greenspan looks like a fairy godfather compared to us." He smiled at the analogy.

"What are the terms?" Chamberlain's mouth was dry, and his palms were getting damp.

"We give you eight today, you give us back ten in thirty days. Fair enough?"

Romano stubbed out his cigar to emphasize the point.

Chamberlain's stomach flopped, and the acid theme played an encore in time with Gershwin's *Rhapsody in Blue*.

"That's—that's two hundred thousand interest for one month!" His hands were shaking, and he could feel the sweat melt down his chest, and plaster his shirt to his back.

"That's the terms. Take it or leave it." Romano rose. "You know my number, Mr. Chamberlain. If I don't hear from you by this evening, we'll both pretend this meeting never took place."

Jonathan thought about approaching Meridith again. Damn her, and damn her money. If he took Romano's money, he would pay off the shortage at the brokerage firm then tell

Meridith she could have a divorce if he could have a decent settlement. Surely it would be worth several million to her. He would be in a much better bargaining position after he was out from under this pressure. "Okay, Mr. Romano, you've got a deal. When can I get the money?"

"Patience is a virtue, Mr. Chamberlain, and one that would be prudent for you to practice. Remember, we do not deal in checks or contracts. The money will be on your desk within the hour. We expect payment in kind. Cash only." Romano extended his hand for the second time. "Thank you for the drink, sir, it has been my pleasure." With that, he turned and walked away.

Jonathan was still shaking as he sat down and signaled another drink. He had an hour to kill, and he certainly wasn't ready to return to the office. Besides, he had to calm his agitation.

TUESDAY, AUGUST 27 • 3:00 PM

THE HEAD of the accounting firm, Arthur Trilloby, was a balding, doughy man. Davidson noted that, in another time and place, the accountant would have been wearing green eyeshades and arm garters.

"Mr. Davidson, I have some rather disconcerting news," he began.

"Get to the point," MacKenzie prodded.

"All the partner and associate records are in order—except for Mr. Chamberlain's. According to his own log records, which we took from his computer, he has been billing over a hundred hours a week to Carolina Tobacco. We can only verify thirty hours submitted to the accounting department for client billing. And the same thirty hours are accounted for in revenues." The CPA allowed his words to trail off.

Davidson sighed deeply. "Damn." He ran his hands through his wavy hair. "If you could have your report ready for me as soon as possible, I would appreciate it. Could you give me a ball park estimate of how much money is unaccounted for?"

"Roughly? It seems the practice has been going on for at least eight months now. He has reported about thirty accountable hours to the firm. The remaining seventy hours don't show up in the firm's billings. If you're asking for my own hypothesis, I think he's opened up another bank account somewhere. As a partner, he could do that. Then he bills Carolina Tobacco directly for the additional hours and deposits those funds to the bogus account."

"Could he do that? I mean, that easily?"

"Sure, if the checks are made out to the firm. It has happened before, in fact, right here in Chicago. I would suggest we double-check all his expense requests, too."

"Work with the accounting department. Have your theory checked out. Print out his billing log and have the accounting department at CT give you copies of all invoices they received during this past year. Tell them we've had a computer shut-down or something, and we need it to put the program back together. Obviously, time and discretion are of the utmost importance. Let's find out what's happened by tomorrow. Thank you for all your cooperation and discretion."

As Trilloby left, Davidson buzzed his secretary. "Get Crowley here—now."

TUESDAY, AUGUST 27 • 3:30 PM

THE MESSENGER delivered the heavy carton to the receptionist. It was marked:
PERSONAL AND CONFIDENTIAL.
TO BE OPENED ONLY BY J. CHAMBERLAIN.
The package was left on Jonathan's cluttered desk.

When Chamberlain returned and found the box, he locked the door. Opening it carefully, he discovered one hundred and sixty neatly wrapped bundles of one hundred dollar bills. Each bundle contained fifty bills. No note.

Jonathan laid the bundles across his desk and touched each one fondly. He placed them back in their container before calling his broker.

He tried calling Bob to thank him for the connection but was told by the secretary that Mr. Crowley was in a meeting with Mac.

"No message. I'll catch him tomorrow," Jonathan told her and was out the door before she could answer.

TUESDAY, AUGUST 27 • 6:00 PM

JONATHAN ARRIVED home in great spirits. He found Marina alone in a kitchen that smelled like old-world cooking and new-world clean. "Hello, Mister. You have good day?"

"Yes, a great day, Marina! Where are my wife and children?" He handed her a bouquet of soft, lavender roses, Meri's favorite.

"Oh, how beautiful! I put them in water. Misses down by the beach with kids."

Jonathan stepped out on the deck and saw Meri standing by the edge of the gently rolling waves, watching Hunter and Chelsea navigate their small Sunfish. Her silhouette against the cascading sunset was still lithe and shapely.

"Maybe we could still salvage something and get back on track," Jonathan thought, remembering the passion they once felt.

"Meri!" He called to her over the wind. She turned and looked up at the house. Even in the twilight, Jonathan could see her frown.

"Then again, maybe not."

Most nights they ate in the solarium of the kitchen as the dining room was too formal for family. Tonight's dinner was strained. The children tried to make conversation, but Meridith spoke directly to them, avoiding all conversation with her husband. Both children had plans for the evening.

"Do you have rehearsal tonight?" Jonathan asked after they'd gone.

"No, tomorrow, but I'm very tired, and thought I would just take a long, hot bath and go to bed with my script. Lines to learn, you know." She never looked directly at him. He did notice that her eye was bruised, even though she artfully used make-up to conceal the purple and gray. He winced.

"Meri, I didn't want you to worry about the money for the broker. I've taken care of it."

"And how did you manage that?" He now had her attention.

"I got a loan from a friend."

"How will you repay it?" She was thinking about her appointment with Barry Ellison. She would feel better knowing her money was protected from his abuses.

"I'll cover it. It's my problem." He tried to dismiss her concern and change the subject. "Did you notice the flowers?" The arrangement had been placed in the foyer.

"Thank you, they match my eye." She was referring to their unique purple color.

"Damn you, Meridith. You just can't let anything go, can you?"

"I don't want to fight with you, Jonathan." She walked out of the room. He sat there while Marina cleared the dishes.

"I go after cleaning dishes, Mister. Is okay? My husband pick me up. We take kids to beach to see music tonight." There was an outdoor concert at the Gillson Beach in Wilmette.

"How nice. Have a good time." Jonathan was thinking about a simpler life as he emptied his amber tea into the sink, refilling the glass with golden liquid scotch.

Stepping out on the deck he toasted the star-studded night. "It just doesn't get any better than this." Jonathan walked down the bluff to where his family had stood just an hour before. He sat down in the sand, still wearing his suit slacks, downed his drink, and cried softly.

WEDNESDAY, AUGUST 28 • NOON

THIRTY-THREE NORTH Dearborn was across the street from The Daley Center, Chicago's courthouse, named after the Grand Ol' Man of Chicago Politics, Richard J. Daley.

Meridith Chamberlain walked through the revolving door and rode the elevator up. After introducing herself to Mr. Ellison's secretary, Ms. Scanlon, she was ushered into the attorney's office.

Barry Ellison was tall, lanky, sandy-haired and affable. He had hazel eyes that met Meridith's in an honest, curious way. His tanned face was slightly creased across his brow, and deep crinkles emphasized a smile that flashed easily and often.

Meri thought, "At twenty, you have the face God gave you, at forty you have the face you deserve." Barry Ellison was a man who enjoyed life.

Meridith wore a pastel pink, linen sheath and just a hint of rose blush that made her summer skin glow.

"Mrs. Chamberlain, how nice to meet you. I've long been an admirer but pictures don't do you justice. Please, sit down. Would you like coffee?"

"No, thank you." She was suddenly very self-conscious. "I really don't know where to begin."

"Let's start with lunch, then. I've reserved a table at Nick's Fish Market. It's just a block or so from here. Would you mind walking? It's still summer outside, last time I looked." He smiled—or had he ever stopped?

"That sounds nice." She returned his smile and stood.

"We're going to lunch, Ms. Scanlon." Ellison held the door for Meri. The secretary appraised Meridith over the tops of her half-glasses. Behind her back, the secretary raised her eyebrows and whistled softly.

Meridith and the attorney walked down the steps to Nick's, one floor below ground. It was dark with atmosphere and the savory smells of fresh seafood. Ellison removed his sunglasses as his eyes adjusted to the soft lighting.

He was not one to encourage courthouse gossip, and he recognized a number of familiar faces at the bar so he ushered his new client to a corner table, with her back to the door. They ordered wine and made small talk.

"Mr. Ellison—" she began.

"Barry, please," he cut in.

"Barry. I'm sure you're wondering why I need your services." Her eyes begged the question.

"I wish it were because you enjoy my company, but I know there must be a reason you need my professional advice." His face was open and easy to talk to.

"Ellen Thomas speaks very highly of you."

"So you said. On the phone."

"Oh, yes. As you may know, my family left me a great deal of money. They worked hard to earn it and to protect it and me. I'm seriously considering—" she took a deep breath, "—divorce. I need your advice before I do anything imprudent."

"What about your own attorneys?"

"They're corporate, you know. And, besides, my husband is a partner in the firm that represents Whitney Foods and Carolina Tobacco. That's part of my problem.

"The firm that has been with my family, the Whitney attorneys, are rather old and stodgy. I don't think they'd be too good in a courtroom brawl. And that's what I'm expecting. I need someone who understands the divorce and inheritance laws. Jonathan has made a mess of his own personal finances, and I don't trust him. I'll be candid. I understand there was no love lost between the two of you and I need someone who's not afraid to take him on. Jonathan is not going to give up this kind of money easily, without a fight."

"Well, Mrs. Chamberlain, that's quite an agenda you've set." Barry took a long gulp, finishing the last of his wine.

"Meri, please." The waiter appeared to refill their glasses.

Barry held his up and offered a toast, "Here's to winners, Meri Chamberlain."

"I'll drink to that!" Meri's wink made the attorney's heart beat faster, but he reminded himself this was business. Barry was beaming. Not only was his luncheon companion a bright, beautiful lady, but he would finally be able to even the score with that egotistical ass, Jonathan Chamberlain. And for much higher stakes than a seat on the moot court!

There were so many things he needed to know and much research that needed to be done. It could all wait until they returned to the office.

"Please do not discuss the divorce with Jonathan, we don't want to tip our hand. I understand that will be difficult," Barry reminded her, "but it is very important."

Before the afternoon was over, Meridith had given her newly hired attorney most of the information he needed. What she had not disclosed to her lawyer was the fact that Jonathan was mentally and, more recently, physically abusive, but she felt she had the strength she needed to deal with it. That knowledge gave her power.

Ellison found it difficult to keep his mind on the matters at hand. When she held out her hand to say good-bye, he took her small hand in both of his and held on just a moment too long. After Meridith left his office, Barry could still smell the lingering fragrance of her perfume.

MONDAY, SEPTEMBER 2 • LABOR DAY

THE COUNTRY CLUB was festive, enjoying the last official weekend of summer. Tomorrow the pool would close, and school would open. The sun cooperated, but the air was crisper, signaling the officially authorized arrival of autumn.

The children were at the swimming pool. Hunter was standing at the diving board, encouraging another boy who seemed to have lost his nerve, to jump. Chelsea and Elyse were slathering oil on their budding bodies encouraging a last-minute revival of their summer tans. They were all trying to ignore the goose bumps. Meridith sat alone on the patio overlooking the golf greens.

"Something to drink, Mrs. Chamberlain?" the waitress asked.

"Yes, some hot coffee. Lace it with Frangelica, please."

THE NORTH LAKE Country Club had occupied these sixty prime acres for over one hundred and twenty-five years. The original club house had been rebuilt several times but always in the same architectural mode: English Tudor.

Anglophilia probably began right after the first rag-tag group of refugees staked out Plymouth Rock. The sons and daughters of the Mayflower crew solemnly swear their ancestors were lords rather than looters, duchesses not dishwashers, less felon than royal forefather. The lamentable irony is that revisionist history becomes more fictional with every generation. Those who rewrite history are destined to delete it.

AS MERIDITH sipped her coffee she spotted Brooke Easton walking with several women, all clad in golfing attire. The group was moving briskly, and Meri was glad she was wearing her over-sized sunglasses. Even though make-up now concealed her bruise, the afternoon sun was merciless. These women would love a new topic to gossip about in the locker room, and Meri didn't relish becoming the target of their barbs.

"Hey, Meri! We missed you on the course today," Brooke shouted.

"Thank you but I'm just enjoying the day."

Brooke noticed Meri adjusted her glasses. "Are you staying for the party tonight?" Brooke asked, hanging back as the other women smiled and walked on. "Are you all right? I've been so worried."

"I'm fine, really. But I met with Barry Ellison, and he's terrific. He advised me to say nothing until everything is in order, so, please don't say anything, even to Chet."

"Old Chet is the soul of discretion, but I know what you mean about this group. Wow, they would just love to have this scoop! Do you think you'll stay for dinner?"

"I need to see how Jonathan fared on the course." She lowered her glasses. "How will my eye fare?"

Brooke surveyed the damage. "A little more foundation should do. What do you think Jonathan will do when you tell him?"

Meridith shrugged. "I'll cross that bridge then." Meri looked at her friend. "Brooke, thanks for being here."

"Hey, you're the reason I gave up daytime soaps!" Brooke always made Meri smile.

"You're the reason I'm giving up my melodramatic life," she volleyed back. "I want to grow up and be Brooke Easton!" Arm-in-arm they headed to the clubhouse.

BOTH OF Chamberlain children were happy to pursue their plans for the last night of summer vacation. Hunter went to the first freshman dance of the year at New Trier, and Chelsea left with Elyse and her *au pair'*, a Swedish woman.

Meridith sat at the communal dressing table brushing her wind-damaged hair, watching the others prance about the locker room, chattering and dressing for dinner. What is this new thing, she asked herself, of grown women dressing like boys in baggy khakis? It was so unattractive. She dubbed them *The Mom Squad*, as they compared car-pool schedules, making play-dates. They brandished their gray hair like a badge of honor. They should be ticketed by Clairol, Meri thought, because they were much prettier than they allowed themselves to be.

Meri was tickled with her role as Fashion Police and continued her patrol. She gave another group the coveted title, *Society Matrons*; women who suffer from Designer Deficiency Syndrome—tasteful but predictable. She issued a citation for Navy blazers.

Then there were the designing women: *The Diva's*, over-dressed and self-gratified. The Diva spends her life in salons, spas and sessions having convinced her husband she couldn't possibly, not even for a day, exist without the assistance of a host of hired helpers. She ticketed them for failing to have a purpose.

She checked her watch, mentally admonished herself for being so judgmental, tossed aside her imaginary ticket book, and adjoined court for the dining room.

Meridith steeled herself. She saw Jonathan across the Red Room with a group of men. As she approached, Jonathan smiled. She was relieved to see him holding a bottle of Evian.

"Meri, you look beautiful this evening. But when doesn't she?" one of the men commented.

"Jonathan, you lucky dog! Your wife has to be the best looking woman in the club," another one remarked. Meri returned his warm smile. "Not to mention, the richest!" he continued with a jab to Jonathan's arm. Meri winced.

"Yeah, that's me, Mr. Lucky." His mirthless laugh sent a shiver through Meri.

"Are you cold, Meridith?" the older gentlemen asked gallantly.

"A little." She rubbed her arms. "It's getting to be that time again."

"There are only two seasons in Chicago: winter and *under construction!*" He offered the old joke to polite laughter.

"But, just think, if Chicago had better weather, everyone would live here," Meridith remarked with a smile.

"Not to change this fascinating subject, but did you see the size of those new club heads in the pro shop?" another member of the quartet asked, downing his drink.

"Wasn't it Einstein who said *size is relative?*" the older man remarked.

"Naw, I think it was Mae West," the first retorted, surpressing a satisfied smirk. The men all chuckled as the dinner bell rang.

AFTER AN awkwardly polite and overly long dinner, Jonathan and Meridith drove home in silence.

"Jonathan, are you all right?" she finally asked as they pulled into the garage.

"Fine, Meri, fine. It's been a long week, and I'm very tired." Neither spoke as they entered the house and retreated to their separate rooms.

MONDAY, SEPTEMBER 16

IT TOOK ALMOST TWO WEEKS for the law firm to ready the ammunition. It was Pearl Harbor when they dropped the bomb at their monthly Partners' Meeting in the board room.

As Jonathan entered it was obvious this wasn't going to be the usual what-are-the-numbers council. He was the last one seated and the faces of his partners were shrouded and grave. No one met his eyes.

"Hey, what gives?" he asked.

"Jonathan, no use beating around the bush," Mac began. "We've asked an outside CPA firm to audit our accounting and billing records, and there are some major discrepancies in yours. Would you care to try to explain and rectify this while it is still just among us?"

Chamberlain sat dumb-founded. "Where had this come from?" he thought. "What the hell was going on?"

"I'm not sure what you're talking about," Jonathan played for time.

"I think you do know. You have been very guarded, almost solicitous, concerning the Whitney Foods account. We all appreciated this, all-in-the-family and that sort of thing. But, according to your computer logs, you have been billing them almost a hundred hours a week, and the accounting department can only justify thirty hours in revenues. Also, your expense account statements seem to be four times that of any other partner."

All eyes were now focused on Chamberlain. Jonathan gulped for air. The room seemed to be closing in on him. His chest was tight, and his stomach churned acid that was burning right through to his dampening shirt. He stammered but found he couldn't complete a sentence. No one else spoke.

"Look," he began, "that money wasn't the firm's anyway. I gave the firm the revenues from the actual work I did. The other monies, well, they were really mine, anyway. I mean, they were Meridith's, she owns the company. So, I took a little from Whitney Foods' vast wealth, going around my wife. There's really no crime here. The same with the expense account. Whitney paid those, too. I didn't take any of the firm's money or anything out of your pockets."

His explanation was delivered in a strange voice. Jonathan could hear his words, but he was experiencing some sort of out-of-body trip. He was standing over the table and watching himself. He felt like he was being sucked down a drain, swirling around. The room was become fuzzy, and he was losing focus.

Jonathan stood, shaking. He gestured, but his hand seemed disconnected from his arm and flailed wildly. He couldn't feel it. The partners reared back as his hand waved in their faces, unsure as to what he would do or even what they should do.

"Jonathan, let's get hold of ourselves, shall we?" Davidson was trying to regain a sense of control.

"Mac, I—I—" Chamberlain grabbed at chest and thudded down on top of the polished conference table spilling water glasses as he fell.

"Call 911, quick! Oh, my God!"

TUESDAY, SEPTEMBER 17

AS JONATHAN regained consciousness, his first thought was: I'm dead. Meridith, his father, Hunter and Chelsea all stood around his bed staring down. As he began remembering the last few minutes of consciousness, he could only hope he had left this world.

"Jonathan? Jon, can you hear me?" It was Meri's voice, but raspier and sad.

"Daddy?" Chelsea.

"Dad?" Hunter.

He still didn't answer, but his eyes were focusing more clearly now.

"Jonathan? Can you hear me, son?" Definitely Franklin's.

"Yes, father," Jonathan answered automatically. But his throat burned, and his mouth was so dry his lips cracked as he moved them. He could feel Meri's hand on his face and feel Chelsea rest her head against his chest. Then he tried to move. Wires everywhere. Wires connected to beeping machines.

"Don't move, Jonathan, don't try to talk. You had a mild heart attack, but you're going to be fine," his father was reassuring.

"How did I ever let this happen?" he thought.

"You're going to be just fine," Meri repeated.

"If only she knew," his mind said. He listened to the rhythmic beeping of the machines monitoring his weakened heart. He prayed it would stop.

WEDNESDAY, SEPTEMBER 18 • MORNING

NORTHWESTERN MEMORIAL Hospital, in the heart of downtown Chicago, was a city unto itself. One of the country's foremost teaching and research hospitals, it attracted the brightest and the best. Occupying a multitude of high-rises along the lake shore, they were all connected by underground, heated tunnels and gleaming, glass walkways towering three stories over the city's traffic and busy intersections. Jonathan Chamberlain was in good hands.

As the wires were removed from Jonathan's unprotesting body, the doctors assured Meridith that he was recovering. To Meridith, though, he seemed to have lost his fight.

"Jonathan? How are you feeling this morning?" Meri asked softly. His eyes fluttered, took a moment to focus on her face, then closed again. "Can I get you anything?" She noticed the tray was untouched.

A nurse entered the private room Jonathan had been taken to after leaving intensive care. "Mrs. Chamberlain?" Meridith nodded. "This is for you."

Meri took the pink slip and read: *"Meridith. We need to speak at your convenience. It is most imperative that we talk privately. MacKenzie Davidson."*

"That's odd," Meri thought as she slipped it in her pocket. "If Mac were worried about Jonathan, why not speak with me here?" A foreboding chill ran down her spine. Meri walked past the busy nurses' station unnoticed. She found a pay phone where she could speak without being overheard and placed the call to MacKenzie. They had been instant friends since the day they met, and, since the loss of her father, Mac now filled a familial role.

The secretary who answered asked about Jonathan, then put her through. Mac answered immediately.

"Meri! How good to hear your voice. I talked with the doctors, and I understand Jonathan is going to be fine. That's good news. Really good. How are *you* doing?"

"A little shaken, but I'm fine, too, thank you." A pause. "Mac, you and I are not the sort to skirt the issue. I got your message, and I'm hoping that I read something into it that you did not intend. Is there a problem?"

Mac took a deep breath. "Meridith, is it possible we might meet and talk in person?"

"Is it that bad, Mac?" Meri's mind was searching for a clue.

"Yes, I'm afraid it is. It has to do with how Jonathan has handled the Whitney Foods corporate account. Look, I really hadn't wanted to get into it like this, over the phone. Please, can we meet somewhere and talk? How about the Union League Club in one hour?"

"All right. I'll be there just as soon as I can."

"I'll meet you in the main dining room. And, Meri, I'm sorry to burden you with this after what's happened, but I think the heart thing was a result of this coming out in the open."

"I understand, Mac. See you in an hour or so. Good bye." Meridith hung up the phone and discovered her hand was shaking.

THE UNION LEAGUE CLUB was once an exclusive, male-dominated bastion of big business and back-room politics. Unobtrusively located in the heart of the LaSalle finance district, it offers its private members a place to dine, exercise, meet-and-greet, or even spend a few nights in small, tastefully appointed rooms. It has recently offered memberships to women.

The doorman smiled widely at Meridith Chamberlain as she entered the revolving doors. Mac was waiting for her in the darkly marbled lobby. He stood as she approached.

"Meridith, how good to see you." He kissed her cheek. She returned it with a genuine hug. "I've made reservations upstairs."

The dining room occupied an entire floor but was most impressive because the ceiling extended up three levels of open space. The expanse of walls was paneled in dark mahogany and accented by expertly hand-craved moldings. Heavy draperies adorned tall windows that separated its members from the outside noise and inconveniences. The overall impression was one of the grandeur of a bygone era, elegance recreated for the upwardly mobile of today.

The maitre d' took her suede, mink-lined trench coat, sincerely appreciating Meridith's understated style. She was wearing an elegant gray pants suit over a blue cashmere sweater. A scarf depicting Monet's "Water Lilies" was tossed across her shoulder.

Meridith ordered a glass of Chablis and Mac ordered a J&B on the rocks.
They talked about Jonathan's health and his prognosis, each attempting to remain polite as the drinks were served.

"Meri," he began after a healthy slug, "I know these past few days have been difficult and, believe me, I think the world of you. If I didn't have to—"

"Mac," she interrupted, "let me make this easier for both of us. I know how you feel about Jonathan and me. When given the choice between good news and bad news, please, cut to the chase."

"Okay." He finished his drink. "Jonathan asked Robert Crowley to approach the partners for a rather large loan—eight hundred thousand. He said he made a bad judgment call in the commodities market."

"I know about that, go on."

"Well, Bob came to me. Something about his conversation with Jonathan set off an alarm. I don't know what tipped him off, but, just to be safe, we brought in an outside auditor. The news was not good. It seems Jonathan was billing Whitney Foods thirty hours a week, and those revenues were deposited to the firm's account. But he was billing them an additional seventy hours, and those monies were deposited to another account he opened in the firm's name."

Meridith searched the older man's face for reassurance. "There's no mistake?"

"Unfortunately, no. There's also some major discrepancies in his expense vouchers." Mac signaled the waiter who appeared instantly.

"I'll have a glass of Chablis. Meridith?"

She looked down at her glass, still untouched. "Nothing, thank you."

Meri was fighting to keep the tears at bay. Her throat felt as though a knot was tightening around it, making swallowing almost impossible.

"What are you going to do, Mac?"

"The figure we're looking at right now is close to seven hundred thousand."

"Mac, you've got to be joking!" Meridith asked incredulously.

Mac just shook his head. They were both quiet as the waiter picked up Mac's empty glass and replaced it.

"Geez, I hate this, Meri. Especially now. I am truly sorry."

"Why? You certainly didn't do anything." Meridith tried to swallow her wine. "No wonder his heart failed. Between this and the deal with the market going south, he must have been at a total loss. Poor Jonathan."

"How can you say that, Meri! My god, the man stole from you and your company, he cheated his own law firm, he gambled money that wasn't his!"

Meridith bit her lower lip and tried to smile. "Mac, you and I will never understand a man like Jonathan. He always wanted more than he had. Even when he had everything, he was willing to gamble it all for the sake of just a little more. I don't know, maybe he didn't feel he deserved everything he did have so he shot craps with it."

"You're a hell of a lot more understanding that I would be. Meri, I know this is none of my business, but—well, to put it bluntly, Jonathan is not, in my opinion, a very good husband. How can you put up with this?"

"I don't know, Mac." She was deciding whether to confide in Mac about her meeting with Barry Ellison when the waiter returned.

"Are you dining with us this afternoon, Mr. Davidson?" the waiter asked.

"Meri, you really need to eat something." Addressing the waiter, he asked, "How's the soup today?"

"Let me bring you some bookbinders, it's made with fresh snapper, accompanied by an array of small sandwiches?" He looked to Mac for approval.

"That sounds perfect."

While Mac was ordering, Meridith was busy formulating a plan. She had decided against divulging the pending divorce to Mac, instead she opened with: "Mac, how long can we keep Jonathan's indiscretion—" Mac raised his eyebrows but Meri continued, "from becoming a scandal for the firm and for him personally?"

"No one at Whitney or Carolina Tobacco has noticed the over-billing. I'm sure with the new acquisition, the high legal fees were virtually hidden. He covered his bases pretty well. I would imagine we could keep this between the firm and you and Jonathan for quite a while. What do you have in mind?"

Meridith locked her eyes on his. "I promise to keep the firm out of the line of fire. Eventually, I will make sure the monies are returned to Whitney Foods, but, for now, I would like to handle this myself."

"What about Jonathan?"

"Jonathan will take an extended leave of absence, explained by his heart attack. After six months or so, and some therapy—which you will insist on—he might be able to return to the firm. You and the other partners can make that determination after he has had the opportunity to recover, both physically and psychologically."

Mac sipped his wine, appraising the woman that sat across from him. "I can't speak for the entire firm, but it's something to consider. No one wishes to see this go public. The scandal would ruin the firm and Jonathan might risk criminal prosecution, even if you made the money good."

"You and I both know the firm will abide by your recommendation." Meri's emerald eyes pleaded with Mac.

"I'll talk to them. Meri, are you sure this is what you want to do? That's a hell of a lot of money. Of course, when it comes right down to it, it's not the money, it's the principle."

"I know. But some things come with a high price tag." Whenever people say it's about the principle, it's always about the money, Meridith thought, but said aloud, "Oh, by the way, Mac, is there anything left in the account he opened?"

"We don't know. He may have had the money transferred off-shore, even to a Swiss account."

"Just thought I'd ask." Meridith doubted it. She finished her wine as the waiter set bowls of steaming, red fish chowder down. "And one more request, Mac. You let me tell Jonathan about our deal."

"*Bon appetit,*" he saluted her with his spoon. "You're a better person than I, Miss Meri, yes, m'am, a better person." She rewarded his compliment with a sad smile. "I only wish you had someone who appreciated and deserved you.

WEDNESDAY, SEPTEMBER 18 • EVENING

BY THE TIME Meridith returned home she ached. The strain of these last few days was catching up to her. Meri had asked Marina to stay with the children. Hunter and Chelsea protested vehemently, but secretly, they were glad to have her smiling face as a constant in their lives—and her cookies surely didn't hurt.

The kitchen emanated pork roast and chocolate. Meridith felt simultaneously happy and sad. Houses should smell inviting when you enter, she thought, they should be *homes* for happy families.

Meri's mother had loved to cook and to entertain. Even when her father hired help, Meri knew she would find her mother in the kitchen. "After all, George," Barbara Whitney often reminded her husband, "many of the famous Whitney Food recipes were originally mine! Who knows what I'll come up with, left to my own devices."

Guests in the Whitney home were treated like family and family members were favored, like honored guests. Meri's heart was heavy as she entered the grand, black and white kitchen, so different from the bright yellow it had been when she was a child. The same room, yet so dissimilar now.

"Misses," she was greeted by Marina, "how are you?" Meridith helped Marina with her English, and Meri was so pleased, not only by her progress with the language but with Marina's warmth and kindness.

"I'm okay, Marina, thank you. Something smells wonderful." Meri opened the top of the double oven. The blast of hot air that escaped carried with it the delight of garlic, sweet potatoes and pork. "Mmm. Marina, you are a magician. I didn't think I was hungry until now." She grabbed a cookie cooling on the counter. It was warm and the chocolate melted down her chin.

"Shouldn't eat before dinner, Mom," Chelsea scolded, smiling. But she knew chocolate was her mother's vice, and it was fun to catch her in such an uncharacteristic moment. "How's Dad?"

"He's better, honey."

"When are they letting him out?" she asked.

"It depends. Probably next week sometime." Meri knew it would depend on Jonathan's cooperation, and, right now, he wasn't trying very hard at all.

"Call me when it's ready." She kissed her mother and walked up the back stairs to her room.

The meal was as delicious as it smelled. Meri asked Marina to join them at the kitchen table, and all four ate with total abandon. It was the first time Meri remembered eating a family meal since Jonathan's illness. The children even sat at the table long after the cookies were devoured and talked with their mother while Marina did the dishes. They had just disappeared up the stairs when the door chime startled the two women.

Marina looked at Meri who shrugged. Marina went to the foyer and opened the large oak door. Meri could hear voices, Marina's, then a man's deep resonance. She wiped her hands on her napkin and followed the sound of the exchange.

As she entered the light of the foyer, she saw a tall, dark haired, unfamiliar man.

"Yes, may I help you?" She might have been frightened by the sight of a stranger at this hour, but something about him made her curious instead of anxious.

"Mrs. Chamberlain?" He walked in.

"I'm Meridith Chamberlain. And you are?"

He extended his hand. "Tony Romano." The name did not strike a cord of recognition with her. "I'm a friend of your husbands. May I come in?"

Marina looked to Meri for permission. The man was ruggedly handsome, but something about him was slightly ominous. Even so, Meridith sensed no danger.

"Please, come in to library." She gestured to a dark room off the foyer. Marina was hesitant. "It's all right, Marina, I'll call you if I need anything," Meri told her, and she walked back to the kitchen.

The library was just that. Cherry paneled walls were lined with books: novels, biographies, art books, children's stories, plays, leather-bound books containing photographs Meri cherished, cookbooks handed down by Meri's mother, and even some of Jonathan's law books. This library was not for show. It harbored books people read and valued.

Tony was not impressed by wealth. He surrounded himself with people who made big money. He was impressed by class, though, and this woman was the genuine article.

"Please, Mr. Romano, sit down. May I get you anything? Coffee, a drink, perhaps?"

"No, thank you." He surveyed the furnishings and chose a large, burgundy club chair to seat himself. Meridith leaned against the small writing desk and folded her arms.

"What may I do for you, Mr. Romano?" Her tone was curt. She was having second thoughts about inviting this stranger into her home just because he said was Jonathan's friend. She searched her memory for a clue.

"Tony, please, Mrs. Chamberlain." He waited, but she made no attempt to correct herself. He continued, "Your husband and I have a recent business relationship." He pulled a small, brown cigar out of his jacket. "Do you mind if I smoke?"

"I'd rather you didn't, please." He nodded and continued to play with the cigar, but never unwrapped the cellophane.

"Your husband and I met a few weeks ago through a mutual business connection. I was hoping this matter would be concluded without anyone becoming involved, but, when I heard Jonathan had a heart attack, I became concerned. How is he doing?"

"He's doing better but not great, I'm afraid." Meridith watched the man intently for a clue. While there was something menacing about him, she was, nevertheless, intrigued. "Mr. Romano, I must be blunt. I have no idea who you are or what you're talking about. Could you please elaborate?"

Tony took a deep breath, "Mrs. Chamberlain, I'll get right to the point. Jonathan came to me for money. He needed it, and I loaned it to him. It's as simple as that. He promised to repay me by the end of this month. Right now, there's no problem, but, under the circumstances, I just wanted to make you aware of our arrangement."

Romano stood up, placed the cigar back in his jacket and thrust his hands into his pants pockets. He faced Meridith squarely on.

Meridith stood now and folded her arms across her chest. She had taken the clip out of her hair after dinner, and it fell softly around her face, leaving her looking innocent and vulnerable. Tony saw this but saw, too, a woman of great strength and quiet character. She was very different than the people he usually dealt with.

"And just how much money are we talking about, Mr. Romano?"

"An even mill." His flashing blue eyes never left hers. Meridith did not flinch. She would have made a hell of a poker player.

"I take it you mean a million dollars?" In talking about money, people who had it rarely said the word *dollars*.

"A million dollars," he repeated.

"I see." Now she sat. Meridith was glad she was wearing slacks that covered her shaking knees. She folded her hands in her lap to quiet and conceal their trembling.

Tony did, however, notice her loss of composure. While he might have reveled in his one-upmanship with anyone else, he felt angry at Chamberlain for allowing this to happen to this particular woman and at himself for causing her apparent anguish.

"When was my husband supposed to have this money to you, Mr. Romano?" Before this morning, Meridith might have questioned the amount or even the fact that Jonathan owed this man anything. But, now, she was resigned to the reality that her husband was leading a life she knew nothing about. She remembered Jonathan telling her he had taken care of his problem. Her doubt faded.

"By the end of the month."

"You'll have your money, Mr. Romano." Meridith stood, signaling this meeting had come to an end. "How will I contact you?"

Tony produced a card. "You can reach me at this number any time." She took it from his hand. The card was imprinted with raised, gold lettering. His name and number, nothing else.

"Thank you." She escorted him to the front door.

"Mrs. Chamberlain, I know I have no right to say this, but I'm sorry you had to get mixed up in this. If there is anything you need, please call me." His voice was sincere.

"That's very kind of you," she forced a slight smile, but her eyes remained sad. "Good night."

"Good night." The door closed behind him. Meridith watched through the small, leaded-glass portal in the oak door. She might have cried, but, after today, there were no more tears.

MERIDITH'S TRIPS to the hospital were perfunctory. She had convinced Franklin to return to Washington. He had postponed several important committee meetings and was anxious about falling behind in his schedule. Meridith promised to call if there was any change.

Now she had to deal with Romano.

Jonathan's convalescence and his physical test results continued to improve, while his mood and his attitude remained somber and uncooperative. Meridith debated whether to talk with him about the money, and she reveled in the fact that she held not only the upper hand, but all the aces. This could go any way she played it. She was, indeed, proving to be an excellent cardshark.

When the doctors told Meri they were releasing Jonathan, she made up her mind to lay out the cards.

"Jonathan, how are you feeling?" Meridith greeted him brightly. His face had taken on a chalky pallor under the shadow of several week's worth of dark beard.

"I'm all right." He turned his head away.

"Have you eaten?"

"Just juice. I'd kill for a cup of Marina's coffee."

"I'll be right back." Her wink made Jonathan smile. She returned with a large, steaming cup of rich, decaf coffee, and the wry smile returned to Jonathan's face, if only for a minute. After a few sips, some of the color seemed to be returning to his face.

"Meri, we need to talk," he began. "But first, let me shower and shave. I can't even face myself like this." Meridith heard the shower run and walked into the hall.

She was lost in thought gazing out the high windows when his voice startled her, "Is this a little better?" Jonathan wore the velour robe she had brought earlier. His dark hair was wet, but combed neatly and his own good looks were returning, despite the hospital lights.

"Well, where do we begin?" He searched her face for an answer.

"Your father showed me a spot where we can talk privately, not to mention the ambiance nicer. Come with me." Meridith led Jonathan to a rooftop patio.

"The sun feels good," Jonathan said as he held his face to the sky, eyes closed. "I wasn't sure I'd feel it on my face again."

"You had us all a little scared," she admitted. "The doctors say you'll be fine, but you have to watch yourself. And no stress." Meri watched for a reaction.

"Yeah, that's easy for them to say." Silence.

"Jonathan, I know." Meri kept her eyes on Jonathan's upturned face.

"You know what?" Now he opened his eyes and stared at her, curious.

"Everything."

"What the hell are you talking about? *What* do you know?" A sharpness returned to his voice.

"About the money from Romano and about the law firm billings. Is there anything else?" Meri's voice remained controlled. Jonathan sunk back in his chair.

"Is there any money left—from the other accounts you set up?"

He shook his head and sighed before asking, "What are you going to do?" He couldn't look at her.

"I can make it all good." She made the statement without any emotion.

Jonathan sat very still—stunned—before stating, "But that's close two million dollars!"

"I know, but it can be handled."

Jonathan was incredulous. "Meri, does this mean you'll give me the money?"

"Jonathan, I know you've been seriously ill, but I have one thing to say: If you ever lay a hand on me, ever again, I will see that you pay dearly for it." Her eyes flashed, and there was an intensity that Jonathan had never witnessed. He felt contrite.

"Meri, I'm so sorry. Really I am. This past week has given me time to think. A near-death experience can do that." He tried to smile. "Do you think there is still a chance you and I can work things out?" He bit his lip.

"Jonathan, my plan was to ask you for a divorce in exchange for paying off on your debts." He jolted back, as if physically punched.

"No, Meri. Please," he begged. His voice seemed disconnected. "Let me show you I've changed." He was valiantly trying to control the contortions his face was making.

"Under the circumstances, and for the children's sake, I'll wait and see." Meridith was drained. "Let's go back inside. Jonathan, I need for you to be well. I know our talk didn't help, but I thought I should tell you now. This is a great deal of money, and it will take some time to get it together. Everything I have is invested, and I can't withdraw that kind of money without some resistance from my people. But the children really need to know their father, and you need to know them."

"Meri, I love you," he offered.

"In your own way, I'm sure you do. But no promises." She stood up. Jonathan was shaking. Meridith searched inside for a wheelchair and found one folded against the wall. She pushed it to where Jonathan was sitting.

"I don't need that thing," he grimaced.

"Please, just sit down, and let me take you back. No relapses." Suddenly he looked older and vulnerable. He sat wearily in the canvas seat and allowed himself to be pushed into the elevator and then his room. They were silent during the trip.

"Will you come tomorrow?" Jonathan asked as he slipped back into bed.

"I'll bring the children. It's Saturday, maybe we'll bring you home with us." Meri tried to sound bright, but her voice remained flat.

"Home." Jonathan repeated. "I'd like that, Meri. I'd like that a lot."

MERI DROVE home along Lake Shore Drive. The sun danced off the Lake Michigan water. Tiny crystals of light refracted from every peak, taunting Meri's dark mood, defying her to smile. Meri never tired of watching the water ballet.

She acquiesced to the siren seduction of the lake, opening her sunroof and windows. She turned up the radio and allowed the wind to whip her hair in time to the old rhythms of *Blood, Sweat and Tears*, as she weaved along the ribbon of highway that hugged the water, heading toward Sheridan Road and home.

MERIDITH walked into the house as Marina was putting on her coat to leave. "Mister doing better?" Marina asked earnestly.

"Yes, thank you. He may even be home this weekend."

"That good news, Misses. You need me here? I come back if you need me."

"That's so nice of you, Marina, thank you. Mr. Chamberlain did say he missed your coffee." Marina smiled brightly. "I'll call you and let you know if we'll need you. Have a nice night." Meri searched the kitchen desk for Tony Romano's card. She picked it up and ran her finger across the raised lettering before dialing.

"Mr. Romano's residence. May I say who's calling?" The voice was a woman's. Could there be a Mrs. Romano, Meri wondered.

"Meridith Chamberlain." There was a pause at the other end. "Mrs. Jonathan Chamberlain."

"One moment, please." After a minute, Meri heard a click.

"Tony Romano. Mrs. Chamberlain, how nice to hear from you." The deep resonance of his voice startled Meri.

She got directly to the point, "Mr. Romano, you and I have some business to conclude. When may we meet?"

"There is a restaurant on Taylor Street, Rosebud. Do you know it?"

"No, but I'll find it. What time?"

"Tonight? Is eight o'clock good for you?"

Meridith looked at the glass clock, it was four thirty now. "Eight o'clock at the Rosebud on Taylor. Mr. Romano, I take it you don't want a check? How about a wire transfer?"

"No, that won't work. Tonight, we will discuss repayment. I look forward to seeing you, Mrs. Chamberlain. I'm sorry it has to be under these circumstances."

"It couldn't be any other way, Mr. Romano. Good bye." As Meridith poured herself a cup of coffee, she discovered her hand was shaking. She walked out on the patio and breathed deep, allowing the chill off the lake to cool her burning cheeks. Mug in hand, she walked down to the beach and suddenly found herself sipping warm coffee in cold Lake Michigan water.

"Hey, daydreamer! Can anyone join the party?" Brooke was running down the steps, as fast as the incline would allow. Still dressed in tennis attire, Brooke was the quintessence of the North Shore. She was, without trying, what all other woman aspired to be: beautiful without being intimidating, bright without being condescending, and rich without being pretentious. When she reached the water's edge she was breathless.

"Have you heard?" she asked, but continued without waiting for an answer. "Gillian Stevenson found her husband in their bed with another woman! And guess who the woman was?" Meridith shook her head and shrugged.

"Terri White! Her so-called *best friend*! Can you believe it!"

Meridith's eyes widened. "Brooke, don't even say that!"

"Its true! Lanie Flowers was driving the car pool and went to drop the Stevenson kids off when it happened. She was right there—in the middle of it! When she dropped Chelsea and Elyse off at my house, she was so shook up I asked her to come in and calm down. She's been at my house with the scoop for the past hour. Can you believe it! She said Gillian was supposed to be at a meeting at the North Lake House, but it was canceled. Gillian came home and found Joe and Terri in her own bed—naked as the day they were born!"

"What did she do?" Meri couldn't believe what she was hearing. Joe seemed like such a straight-arrow guy, quiet, shy."

"Well, Gillian really is a lady. She told Joe to get dressed and Terri to get the hell out of her house. But when the kids came in, she grabbed them and ran to the car, where Lanie was. Lanie wanted Gillian to come home with her, but Gillian just put the kids in Lanie's car and drove off in her Jag."

"My God!"

"Say, isn't Joe in the play with you? Did you have a clue?"

"Nothing. He's always been a perfect gentleman. Gillian and Terri are both on the theatre board, and they've co-chaired a hundred projects together. I just can't believe it." The tide was coming in, and Meri now stood knee-high in cold water.

"Meri! You're getting soaking wet. Let's go in the house, it's getting cold." Meridith laughed when she realized how far she had walked into the surf.

When the two women reached the house, Meri asked Brooke to wait while she changed.

"Can't, honey. Chet and I take the kids out on Fridays, it's family night. Speaking of that, I'm supposed to ask you if Chelsea can go with us tonight. Bowling of all things. Kids' choice." Brooke rolled her eyes in mock resignation, but Meri knew she secretly loved the game, as disreputable as it was.

"That would be wonderful. Jonathan is scheduled to come home tomorrow or Sunday, and I have a few things to do before he gets here."

"How rude of me not to ask! How is he doing?"

"He's much better, thank you. Let me get some things for Chelsea."

Chelsea's room was decorated in raspberry, Laura Ashley print. She had her own fireplace and bathroom, done in matching tiles. Meri packed her overnight bag as the women talked about Terri White and what this would do to all of the children involved. Meri thought about how hurt Gillian had to be and Terri's husband, Ed, a sweetheart of a guy who worked on the North Lake Players' productions.

"Terri is such a mousey little thing. Who would have thought?" Brooke added as she picked up Chelsea's bag. "Well, take care, darling. Don't worry about your progeny, she's in good hands." She kissed Meri lightly and flew down the stairs. Meri was marveling at her energy when the thought occurred to her of how much energy she wasted worrying.

"Shake it off, lady," she told herself. "At least you have the wherewithal to handle any situation. It could be worse."

"Mom!" The changing voice of Hunter hollered up from the bottom of the stairs.

"Hunter!" Meri leaned over the banister. "How nice to see you," she teased.

"Mom, cut it out. How's Dad?"

"Much better. They may let him come home this weekend. Do you want to go to the hospital with me tomorrow?"

"Yeah, I guess. But, tonight, could I go with Scott? His dad will take us to the New Trier-Evanston football game."

Meridith was suddenly envious. Her daughter and son were experiencing the kind of family life she wanted for them—but with other families. A happy family is all she had ever wanted.

"I guess so, Hunter. Will you spend the night with the McBride's?"

"If it's okay, Mom?" He saw the look on his mother's face. "Where is Chelsea, Mom?"

"She's sleeping over at the Easton's."

"Gee, I forgot you'll be here all alone. Do you want me to stay?" She smiled lovingly at her son, wishing she could stay with him. But tonight was the night to solve Jonathan's problems.

"I'm fine, sweetheart. I have something I have to do for Dad. You and Scott have a great time, and we'll spend tomorrow night together." He allowed his mother a short hug before disengaging himself.

"Have to get some things—" He ran up the back stairs.

The boy was too quickly becoming a young man. Pride tinged by sadness. Meridith sighed as she followed his lead up the back stairs.

Once in her room, she sat down on the bed and pulled off the damp slacks and stockings. The master bedroom was decorated in pale yellows and grays. The king-sized, oak, canopy bed was draped in silk, and a gray cashmere down-filled comforter covered it. Meri walked across the plush carpeting into the tiled bath.

A gray, oval tub dominated the center of the room. Undressing as she waited for the water to turn hot, she poured scented oil and stepped gratefully into the sudsy bath, immersing herself completely in the fragrant steam. As the whirlpool kicked in, she closed her eyes and let her mind go blank. Unfortunately, it wouldn't stay clear. Thoughts of Jonathan in the hospital bed, of Tony Romano's disarming, blue eyes, and of her friends and the rumors that would haunt their family.

She thought about life in Winnetka. The sense of community was genuine, but it came with a price. Somewhere along the way, you lost your anonymity. Like other affluent areas— Westport, Grosse Pointe, Marin County, Park Cities—Winnetkans were keenly aware of what everything appraised for and the source of one's funds. There was a financial pecking order in the social structure, and it was akin to swimming with the sharks. After your finances, your personal relationships were fair game for general review. The vintage grapevine was steeped in smugness and the gossip mill would be working overtime tonight, Meridith was sure of that.

When the whirlpool shut off, Meri emptied the tub and dried off. "Now, what does one wear to settle a debt—" she asked out loud. "Is this man a racketeer or a raconteur?" Laughing in spite of herself, she settled on a simple, black Chanel dress.

Bending from the waist, she brushed her hair gingerly, flipping it back as she stood to appraise the effect. A halo of gold surrounded her face, and she smiled into the mirror. Suddenly Meri felt very much like a character in one of her favorite movies, *To Catch A Thief*. She quickly admonished herself for feeling much too capricious. After all, Tony Romano was not Cary Grant, and this certainly was no old movie plot.

As Meridith slid into her car, she checked for a map. Assuring herself of the location of Taylor Street, she drove east on the Edens Expressway. Once through the maze of over-and-under-passes she looked for the green sign that pointed the way to Little Italy, just south of the city.

Meridith drove slowly along busy Taylor Street searching for The Rosebud among the other Italian eateries. The sign appeared over a corner stucco building. A valet took her car, and she entered the restaurant searching for the face of the man she was meeting.

"Welcome to the Rosebud. Do you have a reservation?" An attractive hostess with a heavy accent greeted her.

"I'm here to meet Mr. Romano," she answered.

The hostess came to attention and smiled brightly. "Of course, I should have recognized you from his description. Please, this way." She led her to a small table situated off the noisy, main dining area. There was an authenticity to this favored Italian eatery.

Tony watched as Meridith approached, marveling at the way she glided across the floor, oblivious to the heads turning in her direction. He stood and smiled. She did not return the greeting.

"You look lovely tonight, Mrs. Chamberlain." Meridith only nodded. She allowed the host to pull out her chair and seated herself before speaking.

"The restaurant is charming, Mr. Romano." Meridith rehearsed this scene on the drive down, but now felt herself lost in the atmosphere. Tony's startling, blue eyes were captivating. He was wearing a charcoal suit and deep blue, silk shirt, unbuttoned at the neck. Although he never wore a tie, he did sport a silk handkerchief tucked in his breast pocket.

"Please, may I call you Meridith? Just for tonight I'd like to pretend there is no *Mister* Chamberlain." His intense stare made her nervous, and she found herself blushing—and embarrassed to be doing so.

"Meridith is fine."

"Then, may I ask you to call me Tony? Whenever a beautiful woman calls me Mr. Romano, I look over my shoulder for my father." He was smiling. It was contagious. The waiter appeared with a bottle of red wine. Tony inspected the label, *Tessera Merlot*, and nodded. Sipping the small amount that was poured in his glass, he knitted his eyebrows then smiled widely. "That's perfect, Giuseppe, thank you."

The waiter beamed as he filled Meri's glass and then Tony's. "What's good tonight?"

"Everything is good, Mr. Romano, but since they knew you was coming, the chef he made your favorite, saltimbocca."

"That's great." Tony looked to Meridith. "Will you trust me?" She raised her eyebrows. "To order for you." She smiled again, and Tony noticed a small dimple on either side of her mouth. "We're in your hands," he told the pleased waiter who instantly disappeared.

The music, the wine, the candles, the happy people around her exhilarated Meri, and she almost forgot why she was meeting a man named *Tony Romano*. The stage was set, and like any good actress, she became the heroine, transforming into the part.

The food was marvelous! And so much of it. The salad was crisp and filled with olives, ripe tomatoes and biting peppers. The rich soup was aromatic, and the fish course came wrapped in brown paper that, when punctured by the waiter, revealed perfectly seasoned and perfectly delicious red snapper. Champagne sorbet arrived, cleansing their palate for the main course. The saltimbocca, thin escallops of veal wrapped around Parma ham and a sage leaf, was sauteed and served over handmade pasta in a light cream sauce.

Just when Meridith thought she couldn't put another bite in her mouth, the waiter brought a rich teriamisu, soaked in espresso and kaluha, along with a steaming cappuccino.

"Oh, I can't move," she confessed.

"Don't. That was my plan."

Her plan had been to have dinner and settle the debt. Now she found herself drawn out, talking about things she and Jonathan never discussed: her love of the theatre, what her plans had been, her hopes for her children. Everything but her marriage and Jonathan.

"So, you are an actress?" he asked her.

"Well, I once had great aspirations, you know, Broadway, big time. But that was before I had a family. Now, I'm happy doing little theatre. I'm in rehearsals now for *A Streetcar Named Desire*. Do you know the play?"

"The Tennessee Williams classic? Of course. You're playing Blanche DuBois." It was a statement.

"How did you know?"

"Because you are like the character: beautiful, vulnerable, a woman of grace from another era."

She was at a loss! Not only did he know the play, he was familiar with its nuances. "I must know more about this side of you," she insisted. "Tell me, Tony, what is your favorite play?"

"Let me see," he thought. "I love the real classics—Shakespeare, Ibsen, Shaw, and those dark Russian dramatists!" He laughed at himself.

"Okay, quiz—name your favorite Shakespearean play," she challenged. He fascinated her.

"Mmm. I love the intrigue of *Hamlet* and *MacBeth* but I'm a romantic at heart." He paused with closed eyes. "*Romeo and Juliet.*"

"Star-crossed lovers ..." She added, the impact of that statement startling her. She recovered by picking up her wine glass.

Tony had a hard time reconciling this lovely woman with Jonathan Chamberlain, the man he'd met at Ritz just weeks earlier. He pulled a cigar from his jacket pocket and was about to liberate it from the metal tube when he held it up to her. "Do you mind?" he asked politely.

"Usually I would, but tonight? When in Rome—go ahead." She marveled at her abandon.

"That's the spirit." He winked as he punctured the end with a small silver pick. He lit the small cigar with a gold lighter and sat back, crossing his foot over his knee. "Sometimes I think Italians invented food, they so thoroughly enjoy it. I'm happy to see you enjoyed yourself. I was worried you wouldn't, Meridith."

She watched his expression. This man was so different than the men she knew. He seemed so much more alive and intense; his passion for life was contagious. He poured the last of the wine and then held his glass close to hers.

"Now and then it is a joy to have one's table red with wine and roses."

"I'm impressed," Meri admitted as she tipped her glass.

"I'd like to take credit but it was a quote from Oscar Wilde."

"And well read," she teased.

"Catholic schools. DePaul University. They still know how to teach—and to discipline. That's the only way to get kids to learn. Those nuns never heard of students' rights." They both laughed. "Once, I wanted to be a teacher."

"What changed your mind?"

"My father died." She watched his jaw clench. His charisma was enveloping. While she was unaware of his reputation, she realized the kind of man he had to be, considering the situation. But Meridith couldn't remember the last time she felt reckless or daring, if ever. Tonight she could be someone else.

"You may call me Meri," she simply stated. Tony smiled broadly.

"*Merry* suits you, you make people happy. Do you know you actually sparkle?" She beamed. She loved the way Tony really listened to her and the provocative way he looked at her made her feel like a woman again.

"Tell me, Miss Meri, what is *your* favorite play?"

She was thoughtful. "Obviously, I love Williams' work. The characters are so poignant, they seem to speak to me."

"Are you telling me you're sad?" he asked.

"No, but maybe a little too intense. I love the line from *The Glass Menagerie* when Laura tells her gentleman caller she has 'pleurisies,' and he thinks she says 'blue roses.'" She found herself staring deeply into the black pool in the widening center of his blue eyes and quickly changed the subject. "And, speaking of roses, I love the new hybrid rose. It's blue-lavender, and it reminds me of Laura. Those are the kind of plays I love to perform but they're not always the kind of plays audiences like to see!" she laughed.

"It amazes me that a hundred thousand people will show up to watch a football game, even if the teams aren't good, yet if a few hundred people come to a wonderful play or concert, the performers are thrilled," Tony said.

This was a man of many surprises. The waiter appeared with another bottle of wonderful vintage wine, and Tony continued, "You know my forefathers probably sat in the Coliseum cheering for the lions, or were eaten by one," they both laughed, "and when I watch the fans at a sporting event, I realize we haven't come a real long way, baby—only the uniforms change." He sipped, never taking his eyes off her.

It had to be the wine, she was so warm. She slid off her jacket. The man across the table reached out and placed his hand on top of hers. The warmth quickly spread. Oh, my God, Meri thought, what is happening? "I'll be right back," she promised, and retreated to the ladies room.

She faced herself in the mirror, and the flushed reflection mocked her. Her hair took on a life of its own, curling softly around her damp skin. Her lips were fuller, and her eyes heavy-lidded. "Meri, snap out of it!" she demanded. A woman walked in and stared at her curiously. Meri smiled meekly and stepped inside the stall. She waited until the woman left before coming out. The same new face remained in the mirror. Meri powdered its nose and applied lipstick to the pouty mouth. She found this refection appealing and smiled. It smiled back, knowingly. She shook the head full of blonde hair, causing it to swell proudly and walked out.

As Tony watched Meridith return to his table, he sensed the change, too. The reserved, icy lady who glided towards him several hours earlier had morphed into a seductive woman. The black dress accentuated her body as she floated over the room. The heads not only turned but stared, enviously. Tony felt as though his heart would burst.

He first considered the seduction of Meridith Chamberlain when he met her at the Winnetka estate. Her high-and-mighty attitude intrigued him; her frosty reserve challenged his ego. And, it would certainly piss off that ass of a husband! But, now, he was feeling something entirely different. Jesus, he thought, could I actually have a heart?

The table had been cleared and two snifters were filled with warm brandy. Meri sipped hers without question. Tony's sharp features were now fuzzy around the edges. What was she doing?

Tony was careful not to break the delicate mood. He pulled his chair around the small table. He was so close he could smell the delicate fragrance of her hair. Her eyes were intensely green and, from here, he could count the flecks of gold that floated in them.

"Tell me, Miss Meri, what goes on behind those emerald eyes?"

"You are a very different kind of man."

"Different good or different bad?"

"Just different. As Tennessee might say, 'It's been a long, hot summer!'"

She laughed at her joke. "And, I'm being someone other myself."

"I like who you are." His mouth was so near she could see the shadow forecasting his facial hair. She was fascinated by his eyelashes, so black in contrast to his royal blue eyes, as they waved to her when he smiled.

His lips brushed hers lightly. She could taste the brandy on his mouth, and the sweet cigar smell that lingered. The intake of her breath pulled him closer and he kissed her so gently she sighed.

"Please. We shouldn't do this," she said softly but didn't move away.

"Why not?"

"I'm married. And you?" She sat still.

"No." He didn't elaborate. "Meri, are you happy?" He watched her face intently.

She sat back and squinted, searching for the answer. "I've never really thought it was that simple," she shrugged,"but that doesn't make this right."

"Right?" he laughed. "And you always have to do what's *right*? Why don't you do what makes you *happy*?"

Meridith thought about this for a long time. Maybe a minute. "What makes me happy? I don't think I know what that is."

"Perhaps that's why you don't do it. Do you have to be back soon?"

"No." Meri was about to explain but stopped herself.

"You have trusted me so far, and I haven't disappointed you. Will you trust me a while longer?" She had been foolish to come here tonight. No one even knew where she! She should have confided in Brooke at least. This was absurd!

"Yes." He held out his hand, and she placed hers in it. He helped her up, and she took her jacket and purse, placed her arm through his, and walked obliviously to a waiting car, silencing the gawking diners in her wake.

"I'll have you and your car driven home safely, later." He whispered something to the driver of the car, and they were whisked away. Meridith leaned her head back and allowed herself the luxury of this fantasy.

As the door was opened she recognized Lake Point Towers, the round, black condominium building closest to the lakefront. An elevator took them up sixty stories and opened directly to the foyer of Tony's apartment. It occupied an entire floor and boasted a one-hundred-and-eighty-degree view of the lake and an alternative semi-circle view of the twinkling city skyline. It stole her breath!

Meri walked through the living room, marveling at the panorama. Navy Pier jutted into the black water of the lake, lighting up the sky with its carnival atmosphere. The ferris wheel glittered as it looped around, offering its occupants the cityscape as a favor.

Tony retreated to the bar in the den. The slow strains of Miles Davis' alto sax saturated the room. Meri turned to discover her host opening a bottle of *Perrier-Jouëts*, champagne.

"I really shouldn't," she chided out loud.

"And you always do what you should, don't you, Miss Meri?" He teased as he handed her the, already frosting, tall flute.

"Mmm-umm," she replied as she sipped the cold, fizzing bubbles.

"Here's to what's right and to what *feels* right." He touched his glass to hers, and the crystal chimed.

Tony watched her walk to window. He knew he could have her. She was so vulnerable, and he had a knack with women. But Meridith was different. He didn't want her to regret this tomorrow. On the other hand, he rationalized, he could take her home now, and she might never see him again, anyway.

Tony came up behind her and pulled her close to him. She leaned back into his strong body, feeling safe in his arms. He took her glass and set it down, turning her around to face him. She encircled his neck, pulling him towards her.

There is always that singular moment before a first kiss when the anticipation is so powerful it electrifies. As their mouths melted together they felt a surge so strong a moan escaped. A bolt of lightening lit up the black sky announcing the rain that suddenly washed against the window, pounding in unison with their hearts.

Tony's lips never left Meri's as he lifted her off the floor and carried her, unprotesting, to his bedroom. He gently placed her in the middle of the large bed. She watched as he quickly unbuttoned his shirt. His chest was tan through a mat of dark hair, a single gold chain lay nestled against it. He unzipped his pants and stepped out of them, folding them neatly across a wooden valet stand. Meri smiled.

His underwear was silk and abbreviated. She could see he was aroused, but he didn't remove them. Instead he pulled her to a sitting position and reached around to unzip her dress. The dress slipped down, exposing a black lace bra barely covering her swelling breasts. He kissed her cleavage and unhooked the bra. He expected her to be beautiful, but he hadn't expected her body to be so magnificent!

Meri's tan faded to white around her high, firm breasts. Her nipples were bright pink and hard, begging to be kissed. Tony surrendered to their request.

After a moment, Meri pushed him away and stood up. Her dress fell to the floor and Tony's laugh startled her.

"You're wearing my fantasy!" he exclaimed.

Meri smiled, but in the dark, she was blushing again. "I find a garter belt cooler and more comfortable than panty hose," she explained, but Tony was delighted.

"Come over here." He had backed away for a better look and sat down in an overstuffed wing chair. He wanted to watch her walk across the room like that. She acquiesced, coming slowly to him. "My God, you are incredible!" He couldn't remember wanting a woman as badly as he did at this moment. She knew it, too.

When she stood directly in front of him, she bent over and unhooked the fastener that held the black silk stockings. He reached out to touch her, but she backed away.

"Can't touch until I'm ready," she teased.

"I'm ready." He watched in fascination as she turned over the lacy edging and slid the stockings down her long legs. She was still wearing the black lace garter belt when he scooped her up and laid her gently down on the bed. Usually he was careful of the expensive silk spread, but, tonight, the only thought he had was to possess this woman totally.

When he entered her wet, warm body, they both cried out. It was only a few minutes before he collapsed against her, drenched in sweet sweat. He smiled, knowing this was just the prelude.

SATURDAY, SEPTEMBER 28
THE BRIGHT LIGHT OF DAY

AS THE SUN ROSE over the lake, spreading a rosy glow across the sleeping water, Meri stirred. She opened her eyes in the strange room, remembering the night before. Each time they had made love, it had been more passionate, more uninhibited, more liberating. By the time sleep overpowered them, they knew each other's bodies intimately.

The reality was as jarring as the bright morning light, and Meridith felt a sense of shame. Her body felt sticky and sore. She turned over to find the bed empty and scooted out of it, grabbing the wrinkled sheet to wrap herself, and searched for a bathroom. The first door she opened was a large, walk-in closet filled with men's clothes. She saw herself in the full-length mirror, gasped, then quickly closed the door.

A second door proved to be the bathroom. This was no ordinary room! Gray Italian marble set off the huge Jacuzzi tub. The shower stall was glass, and all the fixtures were plated in fourteen carat gold.

Meridith wasn't impressed by the decor—she was stunned by her behavior. Whether it was the alcohol or the events of the past few months, this was completely out of character for her. She locked the door and turned on the shower. After allowing the hot water to beat sense into her head, she cried.

The knock on the door startled her. Would Tony Romano use this against her? She really didn't know very much about the man whose bed—and body—she shared last night. What had come over her?

"Meri? Are you all right? Want some coffee?" His voice through the door.

"I'll be out in a minute," she called back. She found shampoo and washed her hair and soaped her whole body. She recoiled at her body's betrayal. She turned off the water and stepped out to find a velour robe and thick terry towels on a heated rack. She tied the robe around herself and looked in the mirror, pulling a comb through her hair.

Meri took a deep breath before opening the door to the bedroom to face her opponent, feeling like the robed boxer entering the ring.

"Well, good morning, sleepyhead," he smiled at her, holding a steaming mug of coffee out as a lure. She accepted it, smiling sheepishly in spite of herself.

"What time is it?" she asked.

"Ten thirty."

"Oh, my God, I'm supposed to take the children to see Jonathan today. They may release him." She was panicked. The children would worry if they came home and didn't find her.

"Call the children, and tell them something has come up you have to take care of. Call the hospital, and tell them you can't take Jonathan home until tomorrow. They'd love to add one more day to their bill, and it won't hurt him."

"I can't do that," she protested.

"Why not? I need to be with you today. I know what you're thinking, and I can't let you go this way."

"How do you know what I'm thinking?" she asked defiantly.

"Meridith Whitney Chamberlain, I've searched for you my whole life. I want to know everything about you. You are different from any woman I've ever known, and you make me want to be different than I am. Does that make sense?"

"No. But, then nothing about this has made sense."

"Call them." It was a statement not a request.

Meri took her coffee and went in the den to make the calls. The children were happy to spend the day with their friends instead of making a trip to the hospital. Jonathan was disappointed and insisted on knowing what she was doing. She told him the truth: She was squaring away his debt with Tony Romano.

He simply said "Oh."

She promised to be there tomorrow and would have everything ready for his trip home.

"Meri, I love you," Jonathan ventured.

"See you tomorrow, Jonathan," she replied and replaced the phone.

When she looked up Tony was standing in the doorway. "See, that wasn't hard, was it?"

"Yes and no," she replied honestly. "But you were right about one thing, we can't leave it like this. By the way, the coffee is delicious. It's my vice, you know."

"If you think the coffee is good, wait until you taste breakfast," he said crooking his finger to invite her into the kitchen.

"You can cook, too?"

She sat, once again, across from this man, this Tony Romano, and ate.

"For a lithe woman, you sure can put it away," he marveled watching her devour the omelet he'd made.

"Mmm," was all she answered.

"Do you know how young you look all scrubbed with your hair wet and brushed back like that?" She shook her head. "About twelve." She smiled broadly, chewing on an English muffin. "That makes me feel like a pervert," he laughed. "But, of course, last night you looked a little different."

At the mention of 'last night,' she pushed back her plate and looked at him. "Okay, what happened last night?"

"You don't remember?" He wasn't sure if she was kidding or really hadn't remembered one of the best nights of his life.

"Of course I remember *that* part. What I'm asking is *how* did it happen? And I'm not going to blame it on the wine."

"Thank God for that. I thought it was me, or rather, something that happened between us."

"What did happen, Tony?" She was serious.

"Meri, from the first moment I saw you standing in the entry of your house, something happened to me. I knew I had to have you, but I never thought I had a chance in hell. Do you believe in kismet?"

"As in *it was meant to happen?*"

"Something like that. It's as if I've known you in another life."

"That's deja vu."

"All over again," he kidded.

"How can this be happening?"

"Meri, I can't explain how I feel, I only know I need you more than life itself. I can't make sense of it, either. I watched you sleep last night, and I wanted to climb inside you."

"You did." She lowered her eyes remembering the total abandon.

"That's part of it. Making love to you is like walking barefoot across your soul. I need to possess you." She sat up straighter, startled by the word *possess*.

"Maybe *possess* it not the right way to say it. I want to give you me in return." He stood up and walked over to the window facing the city. "God, I can't believe I'm talking like this. Meri," he turned to face her, "I've never told a woman I loved her before. I know this is hard to understand. Hell, it's hard for me to understand, and I'm saying it! Come here."

Meri stood up and walked over to his side. He tugged at the tie holding the robe together, and it fell open. He put his arms around her body and held her close. He was wearing a cotton sweater and jeans, but she could feel his body respond.

She lifted her face to his, and he kissed her forehead. "There is so much you need to know about my life before we can go further. Do you want to?"

"I think so."

"You can't think, you have to know." She nodded yes. "Meri, I love you more than you can ever know."

"Make love to me?" she asked. The robe dropped to the floor.

MAKING LOVE in the daylight was different. They were both aware that with each kiss, each caress, each climax, there was commitment. Their love-making wasn't as intense as it had been in the dark, but it was more satisfying because it filled an emptiness they'd experienced for so long. Tony was gentle, coaxing Meri to peaks she'd never scaled. It was a delicious morning.

After it was finally over, they held on to one another tightly but were quiet.

Tony broke the silence, "Hey, you with that sappy look on your face, how about something to drink?"

"Water, water!" She licked her lips in mock misery.

"I can do better than that," he promised as he disengaged himself.

"Nothing with alcohol," Meri warned.

"Would I do that to you?" he asked looking innocent.

"Why not, you've done everything else!" They both laughed. Tony returned with a tray holding two frosted mugs filled with ice and club soda. She gulped it greedily while the ice crackled.

"Let's get dressed and go for a ride."

"Tony, what do I wear? My black dress from last night?"

"Your black dress is downstairs being cleaned. I called Chanel, I noticed the label, and had them send over these." He placed a large shopping bag on the bed.

"Are you kidding?" She opened the bag to find a pair of white, sueded- denim jeans, canvas tennis shoes, and a deep green cashmere sweater. A soft windbreaker and scarf were included as well as a new undergarments. "What—how? How did you know my size?"

"Are you kidding?" he winked. She blushed again.

"Do you do that often?" he asked.

"No, before last night I can't remember the last time. You embarrass me."

"Really? I can't remember a girl who got embarrassed, let alone blushed about it. It's endearing." She frowned. "No, really, it is."

Meri grabbed the bag and walked to the bathroom. "Thank you for the clothes. I love the green sweater."

"I thought, with your eyes, it's got to be your color." She didn't want to think about the other women Tony had known, but he obviously had very good taste. "You must have had something particular in mind when you ordered this particular ensemble, what kind of ride are we going on?"

Tony took her hand and pulled her to the window. He pointed to Monroe Harbor where sailboats were maneuvering with billowed canvas out into the bluer center of the lake.

"My boat. Lake Michigan. Let's go, we're missing out on one of the last warm days." He smacked her bottom playfully. Meridith turned in anger.

"Tony, don't ever do that again—not even in jest."

"What?" he asked seriously.

"Hit me."

"I'm sorry, Meri, honest I am. I would never hurt you, and I would kill anyone who did." He looked so shocked and so contrite Meridith sensed his sincerity.

As she closed the bathroom door, Tony sat on the edge of the bed trying to make sense out of what just happened. He went over the conversation in his head, and it suddenly dawned on him.

"Son of a bitch." A chill went through his body.

MERI WAS SO INTRIGUED by the man who took her arm she never noticed the two men who followed them. The same men had watched them intently throughout dinner. These were Tony Romano's boys.

The two well-dressed men who trailed their boss were also being followed. The man who shadowed them was not as expensively dressed. He was the FBI agent, Gary Sanders, permanently assigned to follow the Chicago kingpin. He was well aware that Tony's boys knew they were being tracked, but all the king's players continued the game.

Growing up in Winnetka, Meridith was used to monied people. In this day and age, however, Winnetkans rarely relied on servants. Indeed, good help was hard to find. But not for Tony Romano. Whenever and wherever he turned, there was someone waiting on him.

A limo took them to the Monroe Harbor where a craft much too large to be called a mere boat was purring in anticipation. Her door was opened by the driver. Tony slid across the seat and searched for the car following his. His eyes met theirs and, in silent communication, told them there was no need to board the yacht. One of the men gave a half-salute and rested against the hood of the dark blue Lincoln. Sanders sat across the parking lot and spoke into a small cellular phone.

FOR THE RICH, the fact that their fortunes are public knowledge has always made safety a concern, but most people cherish their freedom as much as their security.

Freedom was a relative term for Tony Romano. He planned to spend a few hours with Meridith Chamberlain in a place where he could be certain no one would be eavesdropping.

Meri wrinkled her nose. "It smells like fall." He smiled at her. The driver of the limo reached inside and pulled out a pair of dark, designer sunglasses and handed them to Meri without a word.

"Thank you," she said as she looked curiously at Tony. He just nodded at the driver. The city had a November closing deadline for the marinas, and most of the berths were empty. The few remaining crafts took advantage of this glorious Saturday. The halyards clanked a song of welcome as Tony took her hand, and they walked down the pier to board the sleek sixty-foot cruiser.

Meri smiled when she saw the name painted on the aft, *CAPISCE*. She stepped below and surveyed the interior. The windows were tinted, so it took a moment for her eyes to adjust as she pushed the sunglasses to the top of her head.

The salon was decorated in deep caramel, leather sofas were built into the dark paneled walls and a bar dominated the starboard. Matching bucket chairs swiveled at the stern awaiting their captain.

"Wow, some boat," Meri marveled. "Wait, I know, it's not a *boat*, it's a *yacht*," she corrected herself, smiling coyly.

"No, it's just my boat." He seemed nonchalant, almost embarrassed by indulgence and excesses. "It's one of the few places where I have complete privacy." Meridith was reminded of just who and what the man was and shivered involuntarily.

"Something to drink, sir?" the yacht's captain asked.

"Coffee?" he asked, noting her chill.

"That would be lovely." Up until last night, it was her biggest vice.

"How about some Italian coffee?" he offered. The captain disappeared.

"Italian coffee?" she asked.

"Espresso, Tuaca and steamed milk. We go the Irish one better."

"Was there a question?" He looked at her so innocently she wanted to hug him. Meri wanted so much to trust this man, but she sensed danger. Was she trading one bad situation for another?

The captain reappeared with two crystal mugs filled with fragrant coffee overflowing with whipped cream.

"I thought you said milk, this looks fattening," Meri said as she removed one of the mugs and brought it to her mouth. "It tastes fattening—but wonderful!" Tony reached out and wiped a bit of cream off the corner of her mouth.

"We've worked off enough calories to indulge," he countered. Meri took his hand and placed the finger with the whipped cream in her mouth and sucked gently. Tony closed his eyes in ecstasy. When he opened them she was smiling coyly. "For a real lady, you have the potential to be a Jezebel, do you know that?" He kissed her mouth, still swollen from the previous night.

Tony took her hand and led her to the ship's stern. She could see Buckingham Fountain against the backdrop of the architectural outline and, as they moved into the lake, watched the unique cityscape fade away. Neither spoke until the horizon was flat and the coffee cold.

Meridith traced his chiseled profile and felt his jaw work in concentration. His nose had the tiniest bump across the bridge and the cleft in his chin was so deep she wondered how he shaved. It was obvious that someone in his ancestral linage had posed for Michelangelo, she thought, smiling to herself.

The wind was colder as the ship headed towards the Michigan border. Meri tied the scarf around her hair.

"Meri, do you know what I do?" he finally asked without looking at her.

"More or less." Actually, it was less.

Tony paced the stern of the ship. The small cigar he had tried to light kept going out in the wind, so he tossed it into the foaming wake. There was a grace about the man, a panache that belied a bad man. As the ship continued its journey across the wide expanse of sapphire water, Meri steeled herself for his answer.

He took a deep breath. "My family has been involved with money-making businesses since they came to this country around the turn of the century. Sometimes these enterprises were outside the law, sometimes they just skirted it." Meridith remained very still.

"Look, I wouldn't tell you things now if I didn't have an ulterior motive. I want you to know, up front, who Tony Romano is." He turned to face her squarely on. He had to speak louder because the wind stole his words. "I'm going to say this only once and only here." His paranoia was contagious.

"I am a student of history. My people go back thousands of years, to Roman soldiers, or even Caesar himself, who knows? But one thing is for sure—they fought for everything they had. Once, the Roman Empire ruled the entire civilized world. Think about it, Meredith, they robbed and even killed for everything they had. History is nothing more than a compilation of wars and battlefields. That's part of our heritage, our history, something to be proud of. It was this quest for power that propelled civilization, drove evolution.

"Your people came from Europe to escape laws they didn't like, and they made new ones. Laws are all man-made. Hell, only Moses really knows if God gave him those Commandments or he chiseled them in stone to keep his people in line."

Meri was entranced by the man's rhetoric as he continued: "Dostoyevsky said, 'Even if there is no God man would have invented him.' Do you know why? To keep order. I have my own laws, I make them."

Meridith was spellbound. Tony's fervor and intensity was mesmerizing as he proceeded, "My people have their fingers in many pies. Politics, the police, retail, wholesale, transportation—the world runs on money. Money moves everything.

"You think that your company, Whitney Foods, is exempt? We own stock. You wonder why the tobacco industry continues to flourish even though everyone knows how dangerous smoking is? We make it happen. The government continues to subsidize tobacco farmers because our politicians make it happen.

"The entertainment business? We make stars, and we break them. A hundred million dollars to make a movie? Where do people think that kind of money comes from? And if we want our stars to light up in a movie, they do, and we sell more cigars or cigarettes or god-damn chew if we want to.

"We make music and we make the musicians. It costs millions of dollars to set up a recording studio, more to put together a decent band and promote them. Where do people think an simple artist could come up that kind of bankroll? They need us, then we own them.

"We've elected politicians. From aldermen to presidents. And we've broken the sons-of-bitches when they didn't listen. Are you with me?" He was on a mission, trying to convince her of an evil force that sounded as alien as any fable. Meridith grasped the railing on the boat as much to stop her hands from shaking as for support. She nodded, but she didn't understand. Still, Tony went on, "Yeah, we sold liquor when the law said it was illegal. We ran numbers and houses of prostitution, both victimless crimes. We were into, what the Feds called, the White Rackets. Then, the South Americans and the Asians smelled profit and got involved in drugs. My Organization didn't want to get mixed up in drugs. But the younger ones said it was the only way to compete. There were big internal wars. Older members were killed off."

Tony stopped for a moment to assess her reaction. Meridith stood quietly listening. Like an evangelist at a revival, Tony continued. "All Italians want to be the boss, the man with the power. The whole New York Organization split up during the power struggles, and, as a result, they lost all their power. Chicago had to be protected from all the new factions. So they brought in new blood." He stopped to look at her. She was frozen to the railing, staring intently at him. Then he took her shoulders in his hands and faced her squarely on. "Me, Tony Romano."

Her face searched his. The blue in his eyes blazed almost black as he held on to her and continued. "My father, Vincenzo, was Jimmy Hoffa's right hand. You don't hear much about him, but he was murdered with the Teamster boss. I may not know where my father's bones lie, but I know where all the other bodies are buried."

Tony continued to weave the narrative. "My family tree? Yours may have come over on the friggin' Mayflower but mine probably owned it. My godfather, as in holding me over the baptism bowl, was Tony Acardo. And my great-uncle was, you won't believe it, Al Capone." Tony waited for that to sink in. "I was chosen for this job by John Gotti after Carlo Gambino was killed. The reason I run the Chicago Organization is that I take nothing from nobody. If it wasn't for us, the Colombians, the Chinese, the Puerto Ricans, and the Blacks would take Chicago from people like the Whitneys and the Chamberlains and turn it into a friggin' jungle and rub your noses in their victory. Thanks to the Asian drug lords, heroin is the new drug of choice. You think this country is run by white-bread officials that the people elect? That's because that's what we want you think. We're the hired guns. The real threat isn't organized crime, it's *disorganized* crime. If the government ever eliminated the Organization, anarchy would prevail."

Now Tony turned to her. "And because there will always be someone who wants a shot at the boss, two men follow me at all times to make sure I'm protected. An FBI agent follows them, noting all my activities. That's how I live."

When he was finished he took another deep breath and sagged down into one of the secured chairs.

"My world is filled with danger and violence, I have no right to ask anyone, let alone a woman like you, to share it. The women I've known were either window-dressing or whores. I've never known anyone like you, Meri. You have an option now—you can write me a check and I'll take you back home and you can forget you ever knew me. Or you can get to know the man I'd like to be—with you."

Meridith had forgotten about the money, but Tony's reference was as chilling a reality-check as the cold spray from the lake. She was ashamed and confused. Even if she decided to get to know him, what could they possibly have together? She had children to think about, and a position in the community, and a company. Let alone a husband. Even though she had spoken to an attorney, she was still very married. And who could predict what he would do when his ego was threatened?

Tony watched her mind working. He knew what she was thinking. "Excuse me, I'll be right back," he said quietly and walked into the salon. Before he returned, Meridith could feel the ship turn about. When she saw him again, his face was dark and closed to her. "I'll take you back now. The captain has made lunch. Are you hungry?" She shook her head no but they walked into the main salon.

The captain had spread out a feast, but they politely picked at the large shrimps and cold salmon. Meri spread caviar on a piece of dark rye and offered it to Tony. He shook his head.

She broke the tension. "Tony, I appreciate your honesty. Everything you say may well be the truth, as you know it, but I have a difficult time reconciling what you've said with what I believe. And I have obligations that make me who I am."

Meri toyed with her napkin and continued, "When my parents were killed—" Tony raised his eyebrows in a question. "— in a plane crash, I felt so alone. Jonathan and I do not have a happy or even a good marriage, but I do have two children whom I love more than life. Without a good father, I owe them a happy home. I'm in no position to make any commitments to anyone, let alone someone I've known less than twenty four hours."

Until that moment she hadn't really thought about a commitment to Tony. The whole idea of changing her life dramatically was absurd. Tony walked to the bar, poured himself a brandy, and threw it back. "What now?"

"I don't know the man who runs the *Chicago Organization*, as you call it. I only know an intelligent, incredibly loving man who treats me like a princess and makes me feel more alive than I have in a long time. Tony," she looked into his sad face, "I've spent my entire life insulated in a private world. Tasting a different kind of life may be the spice I need. I feel like I've been sleeping-walking, and, suddenly I woke up to find you." His eyes connected with hers.

"Last night you asked me if I always did what I should and what was right. Maybe a part of me feels that I deserve a little indulgence, or maybe I'm still reeling from all the wine, but—" Tony looked expectantly into her face, flushed from the sun and wind, waiting for the inevitable. "I don't want to stop seeing you."

The relief he felt couldn't be measured. He wanted to hug her and kiss her and tell her how thankful he was, but he remained passive and seated.

"Tony, couldn't we take it a little slower, just enjoy what we have found in each other? For now. Do we have to think about the tomorrows? I couldn't make promises regardless of who you are."

"I always get what I want," he teased.

"Yes, but do you always want what you get?" Her mimic dispelled the tension. Tony pulled her up and searched her face before kissing her deeply.

He called the captain on the boat's intercom and told him, once again, to turn the boat around, and drop anchor when they were more than three miles offshore.

"Is there a significance in *three miles*?" Meridith asked.

"International waters," he looked smug.

"In Lake Michigan?" They laughed together for the first time that morning.

MERIDITH HAD never before bitten into forbidden fruit. The experience was totally electric. Tony lit a fire in her soul, and now every fiber of her being was rejoicing in the blaze.

The Captain's Quarters were located in the bow. Although everything on a ship is secured to accommodate movement, the room was the ultimate in luxury and extravagance. The walls were oak-paneled and polished to an almost-reflective brilliance, subdued by royal blue furnishings. Meri whistled as she entered the cabin. The water splashed against the porthole and the ship rocked, causing her fall against Tony. He caught her in his arms.

He undressed her standing up, kissing every part of her body as he uncovered it. She was surprised at how her body responded to his touch. She had not been with many men before she met Jonathan and none since. Sex with Jonathan had been unsatisfying. He was as selfish in that aspect as he was in life.

Meri wanted to return some of the pleasure Tony had given her. She gently pushed him into one of the captain's chairs and straddled him. She began kissing his face, his eyes, his ears, his neck and finally his mouth. She worked her way down his chest, flicking her tongue against his rock-hard nipples. He moaned as she moved backward and continued her journey down.

When she pulled at the elastic of his underwear he sprang forward. She placed her mouth around him, and it was all he could do to contain his passion. He pulled her up and lifted her off the floor and placed her on his bed.

Tony made love to her slowly, to the rhythmic rocking of the boat, until she cried out his name over and over in a gratified chant. Then they fell asleep wrapped tightly together. When Meri awoke, she found Tony sitting on the edge of bed, dressed. He was staring intently at her face.

"Don't you ever close your eyes?" she asked sleepily.

"It's a luxury I rarely indulge in. Even then, I sleep like a cat, awake at the slightest sound. Comes with the territory. When do you have to be back?"

She looked out the porthole to find the sun deep in the western sky. "What time is it?"

"Four thirty." She sat up and looked sadly at Tony.

"I should be home soon, my children will worry." She laughed softly at the weak joke. He pulled her to her feet and kissed her again.

"You can use the shower in here." He handed her a mug of rich, black coffee. "We'll be back at the harbor in a half an hour. My car is waiting. You'll be home before six. Is that okay?"

She nodded as she sipped. "You're going to spoil me."

"That's the plan."

"You admit then that you do have a plan?" she asked.

He frowned.

She pulled at the corner of his mouth with her finger. "I'm teasing. I haven't seen you smile all day."

"When I was smiling, your eyes were closed," he retorted. She blushed.

"There you go again!" Now he was smiling broadly.

"Whatever it takes." She sauntered naked into the ship's head.

AS THE SHIP headed back to Monroe Harbor, Meridith and Tony witnessed the sun's valiant effort to stay afloat. It sat on the edge of the horizon, between the water and the sky, gasping golden red rays into the blue sky before succumbing to Poseidon's beckoning. Neither of them spoke but held to the each other and the day.

Finally Tony broke the silence. "Meri, did you understand what I told you earlier?"

"You mean about the Chicago Organization?"

"Yeah, about who I am."

"Tony, you hit me with your own version of *The Godfather*. It is very difficult to believe that you guys control *everything*. I still believe in America and that the power of its people."

He looked skeptical.

"I do! I believe in the Constitution, in the justice system and in private enterprise. Besides, don't the papers keep quoting you guys as saying there is no such thing as the *Mafia*!"

Tony looked into her open and innocent face. He kissed the tip of her nose and smiled sadly. "You sound like a Girl Scout. You believe in whatever you please, my darling Meri, and I will respect it."

"Tony," she was serious, "do you believe in God?"

He squinted his eyes in concentration. "I believe in a higher power. Even though I went

84

to Catholic schools, I don't believe there's an old man in white robes with a big book of what's right and wrong. I'm not arrogant enough to believe that my whole life is planned out. I think this higher power gave man, or woman—" he smiled at Meri, "—an intellect, a free will and a right to claim our own destiny. We are responsible for our decisions."

"Do you think the things your *Organization* does are right?"

Tony hugged Meri and laughed out loud. "My sweet, wonderful Meri. That is a question for another day. So we finish our heavy discussion with what's right once again. I only know you feel so right in my arms. When I tell you I love you, I know that feels right. I'm hedonistic. Anything this good could not be wrong. *Capisce!*"

"*Capisce!*" she nodded her head against his chest. She stayed wrapped in his embrace until the ship docked against the wooden berth. They watched from the bridge of the ship as night fell and marveled as the skyline spilled its reflection across the black water.

SUNDAY, SEPTEMBER 29 • 10:00 AM

MERIDITH AND the children arrived at the hospital to find Jonathan dressed and waiting. His mood was as somber as the day.

The trip home was uneventful but seemed excruciatingly longer than usual. The children listened to their personal headsets while Meridith drove and Jonathan stared out the window. The sunny, Indian Summer Saturday had abruptly turned into a cold, rainy, gray fall Sunday. Leaves pirouetted from the sidewalks into the gutters, clogging them, creating large puddles at every intersection.

Once they were alone in the kitchen Jonathan asked, "So, I assume you've taken care of everything, in the usual, efficient Meridith Whitney manner?" She presumed he was talking about the issue of his debts.

"I'm working on it," she told him.

"What the hell does that mean *you're working on it*?"

"What do you want me to say, Jonathan?" She began filling the coffeepot.

"What did Mac say? Do I still have a job? And how, may I ask, did you contact and meet Romano? What was that all about?"

At the mention of Tony's name, Meridith turned a deep crimson. "I told you that Mr. Romano came to the house right after you were taken to the hospital. He said he didn't want me involved but, under the circumstances, he thought he should protect his interest." She was at the sink with her back to him.

"So? What did you do, just write him a damned check?"

She faced him. "No, Jonathan. First off, I knew that you had covered the Commodity

Market short-sell somehow, and that was for over eight hundred thousand. When Mr. Romano told me you owed him a million by the end of the month, I figured that was how you got the money. When we talked in the hospital and I knew for sure that was the case, I came home and called Mr. Romano. We met last night and we had dinner. He told me to write a check to his attorney, Joel Silverman.

"And, as for your law firm, Mac said your partnership would remain intact as long as you took some time off to recover. As to when and to whom the money is returned, you and I need to talk." She refrained from talking to him about the divorce in his frame of mind.

"I called here Friday night, late, and there was no answer. I called all day Saturday. Where the hell were you?"

"I met Mr. Romano at an Italian restaurant, had dinner and came home. I was tired, I guess I didn't hear the phone. Saturday I ran errands, picked up the kids and took them to dinner. When I heard your messages, I was in no mood to fight with you. I knew I'd see you today, what's the difference?" She hated this.

"The difference is that my wife is meeting the biggest hoodlum in Chicago, and I can't get hold of her. I've just had a heart attack and I'm not supposed to ask or worry? What the hell is wrong with you? And, by the way, are you giving him a check?"

"Mr. Romano was a perfect gentleman. And, as for him being a *hoodlum*, you're the one who chose to do business with him; I was left to conclude it. The same way I'm going to conclude this conversation. And as for handling things, I'm very glad you're home to handle some of them yourself."

"You don't sound like you're glad I'm home."

"I'm glad you're well." That was honest. He watched her walk up the back stairs and knew something about her was very different.

SUNDAY, SEPTEMBER 29 • EVENING

AS MERIDITH prepared for rehearsal, she wondered what would happen if Joe Stevenson were replaced. The show was scheduled to open in three weeks.

Meri looked in on Hunter, working on his computer, and Chelsea, reading. She gave them each a kiss and reminded them: "Lights out at ten." Driving to the North Lake House she silently thanked the Lord for giving her such wonderful children and promised herself there would be more joy in their lives very soon.

The theatre was bright with rehearsal lights. Small groups congregated, talking anxiously. When Paul Winston, the Director, saw Meri he sidestepped through the aisles to reach her. "Meri, how are you?" She had missed rehearsals during Jonathan's hospital stay. "How's Jonathan?"

"He's good, thank you for asking. I'm ready to go."

"Have you heard about Joe and Gillian?" She just nodded. "Well, we had understudies working for both of you. It was awful. You both are perfect in your roles. I talked to Joe. He wants to do the part, but he was worried that you might not want to work with him."

"Why wouldn't I?"

"Well," he paused, "you do have the reputation for being rather straight and, you know, sorta' judgmental. I hope I haven't offended you."

"No, but I hadn't realized." Meri blushed, thinking about Tony. Paul took it has a sign he had offended her.

"I'm sorry, Meri, I didn't mean to hurt your feelings. Damn. Open mouth, insert foot. That's me."

"No, no, that's not it all, Paul. Where's Joe? Let me talk to him, and we'll be ready to go in a few minutes."

"Great! That's what I was hoping to hear. We've still got three weeks, and, with a few extra rehearsals, we'll be ready to knock 'em dead." He hugged her enthusiastically and called out, "Okay! We're ready to begin. Let's start with scene five." He turned to Meri, "You and Joe be ready in ten?"

She nodded and found her stage-mate sitting in the lobby reading his script. "Stan - leee!" She mocked the well-known reading of "Stella" his character was noted for. He looked up and smiled broadly.

"You heard, huh?" She nodded. "What an ass I've made of myself. I don't know how it happened, Meri. One minute I was talking to Terri and the next we were in bed together, and Gillian walks in. God, I've made a mess of things." He looked like he wanted to cry. "Word must have traveled like lightning through *this* town. If you sneeze on Elm Street they bless you on Sheridan Road!"

"Look, Joe, you can do one of two things now: Hang your head and slink out of town or get down on your knees and apologize to Gillian; promise you'll make it up to her if it takes the rest of your lives. And, and this is important here—hold your head up, look 'em in the eye and get on with your life." Joe's jaw was grinding. "Where is Gillian now?" Meri asked.

"She's at home. I've been staying with my folks in Evanston. I tried to talk to her, but she won't speak to me. Maybe you could talk to her, Meri. She respects you." Meri thought she was the last person who should be giving advice—or maybe the first.

"I'd be happy to do whatever I can. Are you ready to go on? I haven't looked at my script much, so I may be a little rusty."

"You not know your lines? Give me a break." He put his arm around Meri's shoulder. "Let's give 'em the show they came for. And, Meri? Thanks for the support." They walked back into the auditorium.

Paul saw them walking arm-in-arm and was elated.

"Okay, that scene is going well. I've got notes, but I'll save them. Let's begin with scene one and see how far we can get tonight. I won't stop you, don't stop yourselves, stay in character, and keep going. Everyone ready? Lights up."

Meri watched as Joe Stevenson turned into the crudely sensual Stanley Kowalski and bellowed, "Hey, there! Stella baby!" She knew he would be fine. Becoming another person made it easier sometimes.

MONDAY, SEPTEMBER 30 • MORNING

"MR. ELLISON'S OFFICE."

"This is Mrs. Chamberlain. Is he in?"

"One moment please." An orchestral version of a Beatles hit.

"Hello! I was wondering if I would hear from you again." His voice sounded earnest.

"Yes, it's been a few weeks, hasn't it. Jonathan was in the hospital, you know. He had a mild heart attack."

"I heard. I take it he's better?"

"Yes, I brought him home yesterday. But, Barry, I still want to proceed with the divorce. I haven't told him yet, in so many words, but he knows I've now come to the end of my rope. Have you researched the inheritance laws?"

"I have quite a bit of information to go over with you, and I would like your permission to talk to the attorneys who drew up your parents' wills and administer the trust. Is that possible?"

"Yes, I'll speak with them. In the meantime, I wanted you to know what was happening and to thank you so much for everything. I really appreciate knowing I have you in my corner."

"It's my privilege, Meridith. I'll look forward to talking to you real soon. Call me if you need anything. Anything at all." The sincerity was very real.

"Thank you again, Barry. Bye."

He sat there, holding the phone receiver in his hand listening to the dial tone, wishing he had an excuse to see her sooner rather than later.

MONDAY, SEPTEMBER 30 • MORNING

"SO WHAT THE HELL you doin' with Chamberlain's wife?" Dolf asked Tony insolently. Dolf was short for Adolpho Cashiano, a man much too coarse for the polished full name. Dolf was much more fitting considering his corpulent frame and brash manner. He had flown in from Las Vegas to talk about the future of the gambling ships proliferating throughout the Midwest along the myriad of waterways.

"Why is that any of your business?" Tony answered with his own question. He was furious that word of his relationship with Meridith had gotten out and mentally made a note to find out exactly who had been the bearer of the news, but he outwardly remained cool and composed.

"Why? Because he owes the Organization an even mill *and*, also, because his ol' man holds the purse strings on the congress *who*, I might remind you, are trying to pass a bill that would try and curtail our business dealings." Dolf attempted to deliver his diatribe with a dramatic flair, all in a single breath. He did not succeed. The buttons down the front of his polyester shirt strained to hold the cloth together. There was a stain, presumably coffee, that patterned permanent blotches down the front, drawing even more attention to the size of his bulging belly.

"I find Meridith Chamberlain an attractive and charming woman, that's all there is to that. She is meeting me on Wednesday at Silverman's office to square away the debt, right on time." Tony's mind was racing. This was the first he had heard of Chamberlain's old man having that kind of power. What the hell was going on?

"Hey, Tony, you old rooster. Can't you leave a single woman unlaid by you. Do you have to fuck 'em all before you die?" Dolf's crude remark, punctuated by the obscenities, made Tony's skin crawl.

Tony sprang from his chair. "Dolf, if you can't keep a civil tongue, get the hell out of my house. No one talks to me like that. No one." He grabbed Dolf by his dirty shirt and held it tight under the fat man's chins. The look in Tony's eyes made the larger man back off.

"Hey, hey, Tony, calm down. I'm just kiddin'. Really, no harm meant." The two body guards appeared from nowhere.

"Trouble, boss?" the taller man asked.

"I don't know. Dolf, do we have trouble here?" Tony released his shirt and shoved him back into the sofa—it skidded a few inches on the bare wood floors.

"No. No, trouble, boys. Tony and me was just having a difference of opinion. I see it his way now. No problem." Dolf's knees were wobbly when he tried to stand, and his heart was pounding. God damn, Dolf thought, I have to take off some of this weight before my heart attacks me. "Mind if I use your john?" He walked down the hall before anyone answered.

"Okay, boss?" the same man asked.

"Yeah, yeah. That son of a bitch pissed me off." Tony walked over to the two men and faced them squarely on, his anger still evident. "Two questions: who else, other than the two of you, knew about my seeing Meridith Chamberlain, and who did you two talk to?"

The two men avoided eye contact. They knew anything they said could mean their lives. "I haven't talked to anyone about anything, let alone the broad, I mean, the lady. Really boss. I don't know who else knew." The other man nodded in agreement.

"Me, neither. Nothing. I said nothing. I know better," Frankie assured him. Tony searched their faces for a sign. His gut confirmed their story.

"Okay, I believe you. But stay close until this maniac is out of here."

"But, boss," the shorter man continued, "you were at the Rosebud with her, and there's a lot of people watching you there. I seen lots of people poking each other when the two of youse left. She made quite a exit that night on your arm. Neither of youse was watching the crowd like me and Frankie was. They was noticin', all right."

"Thanks, Julie. You're right, a lot of the guys were there on Friday night, and any one of them could have put two and two together. After all, my companion has had her picture in the paper almost as much as I have. Well, I should have thought that one through. My first mistake, the Rosebud. Why don't you guys go on in the kitchen and fix yourselves something."

"Hey, Ton-ny, that's quite an outhouse you have here!" Dolf had returned. "What a layout here. I thought my place in Vegas was nice, but I ain't got no view like this!" He whistled to express his appreciation for the penthouse.

"Look, Dolf, I've got another appointment after yours, so let's get down to business, shall we?'"

"Sure, Tony, sure." He noticed the two body guards pulling provisions from the shiny, black, glass refrigerator. "What say we have a bite while we talk?" Dolf kept walking towards the kitchen without waiting for an answer.

"Help yourself, Dolf, I have a phone call to make and, I'll be right with you."

Dolf's head was deep in the refrigerator when he answered, "Yeah, go right ahead."

Tony walked into his den and closed the door. There he unscrewed the mouthpiece, checking for his scrambler before dialing. The phone was answered by a single word: "Clear?"

"Yeah, I'm clear here. I need to ask a question? Dolf Cashiano is here. Said he was coming in to talk about the gambling boats. Instead, he hits me with something about the Chamberlain loan and the guy's old man, a Congressman, having the purse strings to fund the OCB. What's all that about?"

"Aw, shit. That turd can't keep anything to himself. We were going to talk to you about that in Silverman's office, where we know we're clear. Hold off on taking the money from the guy's wife. I don't care what else you do with her, just don't make any promises. And don't take the money. We have another way, a better way, to have him pay us off. Tony, this couldn't have worked out better for the Organization. You must have a sixth sense. Everything you touch turns to gold. Pure gold." The line went dead.

WEDNESDAY, OCTOBER 2

MERIDITH HAD not heard from Tony since Saturday night. Today was the day she was to meet him at Joel Silverman's office.

"Jonathan, I have a meeting this morning for the hospital ball committee."

"Do you have to go? They can certainly get along without you for one meeting." Jonathan was pouting.

"You'll be fine. Marina is here, and I'll be home in a few hours." His face stayed clouded, but he said nothing.

Meridith dressed carefully. She decided on a plum jacket with matching slacks and a soft pink sweater. But just before walking out the door, she ran back upstairs and changed the pants for a short, matching skirt and pulled the pins out of her French-twisted hair and brushed it out. Standing in front of the mirror she smiled. Satisfied she slipped into the garage before Jonathan noticed. She left him staring at an inane talk show.

JOEL SILVERMAN'S office was located in the loop. But unlike the large, multi-named firms, his office was a sole-proprietorship. He didn't need anyone to share his business. His only business was the Organization.

Meridith was scheduled to arrive at eleven. Romano had been with Silverman since eight. Tony had been dreading this meeting. He knew, only too well, what the outcome would be. He was right. His people wanted Congressman Chamberlain to table the Organized Crime Bill until after the November elections. With a few more of their own in Washington, they could kill the bill in committee. Tony had no problem with the plan—if only Meridith weren't involved.

He was opening a cigar when the secretary announced her. "I'll leave it to you to handle the lady," Silverman offered politely. "Are we ready for her?" Tony nodded. "Send Mrs. Chamberlain in," he told the intercom.

When Meri entered the room, Tony and Silverman both rose. Tony felt slightly dizzy, and his heart pounded as she came towards him, her perfume meeting him head on. She held out her hand, he took it wanting to hold all of her. Instead, he shook it cordially. "Mrs. Chamberlain, good to see you again."

Meridith felt his strong hand around hers and a chill went through her. She ached to feel his mouth. "Mr. Romano," she turned to the attorney, "Mr. Silverman?" They released hands, and she took the chair next to Tony's, across from the desk.

The secretary brought in a silver tray. "I see we have refreshments," Silverman offered. "Why don't we move to where we're more comfortable?"

The group reseated themselves in blood-red leather, wing chairs arranged around a marble table. The secretary stayed to pour rich, Italian coffee into china cups then retreated without saying a word.

Meridith broke the silence: "Mr. Silverman, I'm here to settle my husband's debt. How do we begin?"

Tony began, "Meri, now that Jonathan is out of danger, we would like to deal directly with him."

"Jonathan has no money. You'll have to *deal* with me if you want your money." Meridith suddenly lost the child-like venerability. Her face showed no emotion, but her eyes flickered with a different fire.

Silverman realized there was more going on than a discussion about money. He spoke up. "We may have a way Mr. Chamberlain can, shall we say, work off his debt. But we need to speak directly with him." Meridith's blood ran cold. The chill of excitement she experienced earlier quickly turned to fear. What in the hell could they possibly want from Jonathan?

"Do not mistake my good manners for stupidity, Mr. Silverman. My husband is in no condition to work, he was just released from the hospital on Sunday. He is in therapy to rebuild his heart, and a shock now could kill him."

"This isn't strenuous work, Mrs. Chamberlain. It requires only a few phone calls. It will be his decision." Silverman rose, his coffee untouched. "If you'll excuse me, I have a few calls of my own to make." He left the room.

Meridith waited until the door closed. "What is going on, Tony? What do they want of Jonathan?"

Tony was quiet, but his mind raced. Should he confide in Meri? He wanted to trust her, but he knew she had strong convictions. "Jonathan has connections, Meri. We need him to make a few introductions, that's all, I swear, nothing dangerous. You know I wouldn't stand for anything that would put you or your family in jeopardy."

Meridith held his eyes for a long time before she spoke. "Tony, I want to believe you with all my heart. But, believe this: I would never allow Jonathan to do anything that would put him or my children at risk. I may not be in love with him now, but he is the father of my children—and they mean more to me than my own life. If I felt, for one minute that you have used me to get to him or to further your own purposes, you will have more to fear from me than anyone else on this earth."

Her resolve and courage stunned him, and Tony plummeted deeper into the black hole he was free falling through. He had never met a woman like this. Why did it have to be under these circumstances? If there is a God, he thought, perhaps this was the punishment for the life he lived, the ultimate irony, his own private hell. "I understand what you are saying, Meri, and I respect it. May I take you to lunch?"

An hour ago she would have been delighted. Now she simply said, "No, thank you, I have to get back." He stood, shook his head and, once again, held out his hand.

"I understand. Will I see you again?" His heart stopped, he held his breath in anticipation.

"I don't know, Tony. I really don't know. I'll have Jonathan call Mr. Silverman this afternoon. I may accompany him to any future meetings." She faced him. "You may think you own the civilized world, Mr. Romano, but you will never own my family. Good bye." As she picked up her purse Tony noticed her hands were shaking. She walked out of the room without looking back.

When the door closed behind her he said softly, "Good bye, Meri."

MERIDITH WAS still shaking as she drove home. Her car weaved through the traffic as her temper flared. Then the anger melted to tears of humiliation, spilling down her cheeks, escaping from under her sunglasses. When she was a block from home she realized she couldn't walk into the house in this state.

Instead, she pulled her car into the deserted Tower Road Beach parking lot. Meridith removed her heels and felt the cold sand through her stockings. Lake Michigan was a fresh water reservoir, but today it smelled salty and fishy. Seagulls swooped and screamed in search of a midday meal, and a lone sail silhouetted the gray sky.

Meridith could distinguish the rooftop of her own house. She leaned back against the rock bluff and watched the white crests of water foam against the sand. Her tears were hot as they slid down her cold face. She tried to sort out her feelings, but the fury she felt was all mixed up with pain; the outrage and indignation with shame and humiliation.

Meridith stayed on the beach for over an hour before the cold wind drove her back to her car. She surveyed herself in the car mirror: her hair was disheveled, her make-up gone, her stockings run. "Oh, lord, how will I ever get past Jonathan?"

"Where the hell have you been? It's four o'clock!" Jonathan met Meridith at the door.

"Jonathan, calm down. Let me change my clothes. We have to talk. Will you make coffee and meet me in the kitchen?" She walked upstairs before he could answer.

When she returned, Jonathan was seated at the kitchen table. Two mugs sat, steaming. "So? What's the story?" Jonathan, in character, went right to the bottom line.

"Jonathan, I talked to Joel Silverman today."

"I thought you were going to the hospital ball meeting," Jonathan interrupted.

"I did, but I got a call from Mr. Silverman to meet him at his office," Meridith lied. "I didn't want to upset you, and I thought I could handle it."

"And?" Jonathan coerced.

"Tony Romano was there when I arrived." Meri's face reddened at the mention of his name. Needing a moment to compose herself, she got up and walked to the counter, searching for the milk. Jonathan was quiet, waiting for the other shoe to drop. "I was prepared to have the money wire-transferred to Mr. Silverman, but then they said they didn't want my money. When I asked them why, Mr. Silverman said they wanted to speak with you. They said there were some things you could do for them in lieu of repaying the loan."

"What things?" Jonathan asked suspiciously.

"I asked the same question," Meri answered, toying with her spoon. "They were very vague. I got angry and told them you wouldn't do anything that would endanger your safety or our family." Jonathan was pleased by her protective tone and the use of *our family*.

"And they said?"

"Just that they wanted to meet with you. I reminded them about your health and told them that I would probably be present at any meeting, but Silverman said he would call you to set it up. Then I left." Jonathan sat back in his chair appraising his wife. Something had changed, even her tone of voice was different. She rose from the table. "When you get the call, we'll decide what to do. In the meantime, don't talk to me unless you can do it civilly. I told you, Jonathan, things will be different." She grabbed her mug and took it upstairs with her, leaving an astonished Jonathan alone at the table.

THURSDAY, OCTOBER 3

REHEARSALS WENT WELL that night. Talk among the North Lake Players continued to focus on the Stevensons and the Whites. Terri had moved to her parents' house in Wisconsin, and Gillian had allowed Joe to move back with the family.

Meri was tired as left that evening. As she walked alone through the dark parking lot she was conscious of the moonless quiet and the eerie hush. The deep green of her car blended into the blackness. She failed to notice the dark, low-slung sports car parked a few spaces from hers. As she took the keys from her bag a voice startled her.

"Meri? I need to talk to you." A muffled scream stuck in her throat.

"It's me, Tony. Meri, please let me talk to you." She could hardly hear him over the pounding of her heart.

"Oh, my God, Tony, you scared me to death." Her shaking hand was still holding the key.

"Here, let me help you." He guided the key into the lock and opened the door. "Slide over, I'll drive." She inched across to the passenger side, and Tony jumped in and started the engine. Before she could object, he drove the three blocks to the deserted beach. He parked the car under a low-hanging tree and turned it off. They sat in silence for several very long minutes.

"I don't know where to begin," he said simply.

"Tony, please, there is no beginning, only an end."

"Are you always that poetic?" he teased.

"Poetic justice, I'd say," she caught his mood.

"Meri, can I do one thing?" Without waiting for an answer, he reached across and cupped her face in his hands. He looked deeply into her eyes and turned his head slightly to one side. When their lips met, her resolve faded. A slow moan escaped as she returned the kiss with a fervor that surprised him.

"Meri, I've missed you more than I could have imagined. You must understand, I had no idea Silverman was going to ask that of you before that morning. The whole thing was put together before anyone talked to me."

"Tony, what are you talking about? Put what together? What is it they want from Jonathan?"

"Meri, listen to me. Jonathan's father, the Congressman, is very powerful and influential. He has a bill in his committee called the Organized Crime Bill. Certain people want it terminated, or at least stalled. Congressman Chamberlain has the power to stop the bill by not funding it. They want Jonathan to talk to his father, that's all."

"What makes you think Jonathan has any power over his father. Franklin is a very ethical, honorable man. He wouldn't impede important legislation just because Jonathan asked him."

"Not even for a million dollar debt?"

"No. I honestly don't believe Franklin could be bought."

"What if Jonathan's life were in danger?"

"What? What are you saying?" Meri backed away from him and, even in the dark, he could see the fear in her face.

"I'm not saying anything, Meri, and I certainly wouldn't hurt Jonathan. But there are people out there who would go to any lengths to keep this bill from becoming law. It will give the FBI more power than they already have and throw the Constitution out of the window. This bill could hurt ordinary people as well as my people."

"I don't believe you."

"Meri, there's so many things I want to tell you, but I don't want to waste our time together giving speeches." He reached to kiss her again, but she opened the door and got out. Tony opened the driver's door and walked around to face her.

"Meri, right now the FBI has the power to seize all your assets if they find the smallest amount of an illegal drug on your premises. Are you aware that over eighty percent of all the people arrested by the DEA are acquitted, but their property is never returned? The government has found a major source of income, and they're not going to give it up. They spend billions of dollars for wire taps, surveillance and witness payoffs, money that could go to much better uses. It's all a game to them."

"Tony, I'm tired and I'm cold and in no mood for one of your good-guys-bad-guys lectures. Please take me back."

He was desperate to convince her. "Do you know who the biggest importer of illegal drugs is?" She shook her head. "Not us, or even the Colombians or the Asians. The CIA. That's right, your own rogue branch of the judicial department."

"Please, Tony, you've got to tell them Jonathan doesn't have that kind of power over his father. I don't know about the bill, or about the CIA or about illegal drugs. I can wire-transfer the money tomorrow. You can't let Jonathan get any more involved than he is."

"I'll try and talk to them. But we need to meet with Jonathan. Silverman will call him in the morning to set up an appointment. Don't come with him. The less they think you know, the better." Tony put his arms around Meri, and she buried her face in his chest.

"I don't understand what's happening, Tony. Suddenly the whole world seems like a bad movie script." He lifted her chin and kissed her cheeks, her forehead, her eyes and, finally, her lips. He tasted the salt as the tears spilled into his mouth. He held her close, wishing with all his might that he could take her away and begin, again, in a new world—a world he could script that had something he could never promise her: a happy ending.

TONY AND Meridith held on to one another for a long while, saying nothing. Finally, Meri spoke quietly, "Tony, I have to go home."

"I know." He rested his chin on the top of her head. He could smell the flowery fragrance of her hair, and he ran his cheek across it. "Meri, I understand that you don't know me at all, but you must know one thing: I have never felt this way about another person in my life. You have affected me in a way I never thought possible."

Meridith took his hands in hers and stepped back. "Tony, you're trying to weave me a tale about a world without heroes. According to you, there are no good guys in white hats, villains in black. Sorry, but I can't buy it."

He kissed the palm of her hand. "Meri, more than anything I would like to be your hero, but the hats people wear today are all shades of gray. You must know, though, there's nothing I wouldn't do for you, nothing."

Her heart wanted to climb inside him, but her head was sending out danger signals. "I've really got to go." He released her hands. She slid into the driver's seat and he into the passenger's. The Mercedes engine roared, and she backed out of the parking lot onto Sheridan Road.

Winnetka was quiet as they pulled up next to Tony's Porsche. Frankie jumped to attention, and the door opened as Tony stepped out. She surveyed the flashy, sapphire blue car and the man waiting for the return of his boss. "What about the FBI? Aren't they supposed to be trailing you?"

Tony smiled wryly. "Twenty-four-seven." She looked puzzled. "All the time. Someday, I'll let you in on a little secret." Meri stared at him, a surprised look punctuated by raised eyebrows. He laughed sadly as he walked around the car.

"When does your play open?" Tony asked through the car window.

"Friday, the eighteenth. We play for four weekends."

"Are you any good?" His heart was hurting, and he made small talk.

"Naw," she shook her head. She lifted her face up and he saw tears twinkle in her eyes. He wanted to bring this woman home with him and never let her out of his sight.

"Any extra tickets? I promise to be one of the good guys and not make trouble."

"Tony, I don't know. We'll see. Remember, Winnetka is a small village and people notice. They also talk." She kissed her own fingers and placed them on Tony's mouth. He held her hand and kissed it back.

"I love you, Meri, I really do." He stood in the deserted parking lot and watched until the taillights of her car faded.

FRIDAY, OCTOBER 4 • 10:00 AM

"I'M MEETING ROMANO and Silverman at two. They're sending a car for me." Jonathan made this pronouncement as Meridith finished buttering waffles for the children's breakfast. At the mention of "sending a car," her heart took a tumble.

Her life was fast becoming a Scorsese movie.

"Can we wait until the children leave, and then we'll talk?" She placed their plates at the table.

"What's there to talk about?" Jonathan took his coffee cup and walked upstairs. Hunter and Chelsea left for school, chattering, toting overflowing backpacks and grumbling about having to wear jackets now.

Meridith steeled herself. "Hello, may I come in?" she asked as she entered the den. Jonathan was at his desk, staring out the window.

"Help yourself."

"What did Silverman say when you talked to him?"

"Nothing except to be at his office at two. And that they'd send a car."

"Jonathan, do you want me to go with you?"

"Why? To hold my hand? Damn it, Meridith, I got into this mess, let me get out of it. They don't want your money. Maybe there's something I can do to square things, if not, maybe being bumped off wouldn't be the worst thing for me now." His melodramatic statement, delivered so dispassionately, frightened Meri.

"Jonathan! Don't even joke about that!" She wanted to tell him about the crime bill in his father's committee, but she couldn't do that without tipping her hand.

"Look, if they'll accept the money, call me and I'll arrange to have it wire-transferred today. Otherwise, please don't do anything that will put you in any deeper than you are."

"Meridith—" He started but trailed off. After an agonizing moment of silence, Meri walked out of the den.

"If you need anything, I'll be down in the sunroom," she stated without turning. His gaze never left the window.

FRIDAY, OCTOBER 4 • 2:00 PM

TONY HAD A DIFFICULT TIME keeping his cool when Chamberlain entered Silverman's office. The shot of brandy he added to his coffee helped to keep Tony's fists from clenching as Jonathan took the seat across from him at the marble table. Silverman spoke first: "Mr. Chamberlain, thank you for joining us this morning. I know you've been through quite an ordeal, and I appreciate the fact that you could be here on such short notice. Would you like something?"

"Nothing, thank you." Tony leaned back in his chair, blew smoke from his tiny Cuban cigar and scrutinized Jonathan through the haze. The hard stare made Jonathan uncomfortable, and he picked up a napkin from the table and wiped his hands. The other two men noted the nervous reaction and exchanged glances. "Could we get down to business? I have an appointment later this afternoon."

"Certainly," Silverman remained charming. "Mr. Chamberlain, your wife has graciously offered to repay your note to Mr. Romano. However," he smiled, "a situation has come to our attention that you may be able to assist us in resolving. Should you cooperate, Mr. Romano will consider your debt paid in full, and you'll never hear from either of us again."

"And this situation is—" Jonathan's heart was pounding, and the sweat beaded across his lip and forehead. He stole a quick look at Romano. The man's glare generated a pounding in his heart, and he looked back at Silverman.

"Quite simple, really. Your father, Congressman Chamberlain heads the House Ways and Means Committee. Good man, your father, I voted for him myself."

"Get to the point." Jonathan felt the back of his shirt go damp. He wished he had asked for something cold, but now was too nervous to reach across the table for the icy pitcher. His hands were shaking badly.

"The point is, Mr. Chamberlain, the Congressman has a bill before his committee, the Organized Crime Bill. Should he decide that the funding for this bill is a little too steep for the American taxpayer, it would make my clients very happy. Possibly, a great majority of the rest of the country, too. This legislation comes with a very high price tag."

Jonathan was stunned. The thought of telling his father anything never quite occurred to him, let alone anything that might have to do with his official duties. "I couldn't do that, and, even if I agreed, my father wouldn't stop a bill because I asked him to!"

"All we ask is that you think about it, Mr. Chamberlain. Killing that bill saves the taxpayer and doesn't hurt anyone. Remember, a million dollars is a lot of money. To anyone." His inference didn't go without meaning to Jonathan. "We're not asking *you* to kill anyone, after all." The lawyer smiled his Cheshire Cat grin. "Just a bill before the committee. A small price to pay, I'd say. Considering." Silverman spoke softly, emphasizing each short sentence. "Perhaps, if nothing else, Mr. Chamberlain, you could convince your father to study it further, perhaps delay the funding until after the election?"

Jonathan looked at Romano. Tony remained silent, indifferent as he reached for his coffee cup. Silverman's voice filled the quiet void: "We've taken up enough of your valuable time, Mr. Chamberlain. The car is waiting for you. Think about our proposition, and let us know. But time is of the essence. Congress takes its holiday break soon, and we would like this matter resolved before then."

"I'll have to think it over. I take it returning the money is not an option at the moment?"

"That's correct, sir. We would like you to do us this small favor, in lieu of repayment." Silverman stood and buzzed his secretary, who appeared instantly. "Please get Mr. Chamberlain's coat and see that he finds the car downstairs, Ms. Gelman." She nodded.

"Just the coat, thank you. I'll find my own way home. We'll be in touch." He rose on shaking knees.

"Oh, I'm sure, Mr. Chamberlain. I'm very sure." Jonathan took his coat and left the room without speaking. His mouth was too dry to find words. He was behind the polished brass of closed elevator doors when Tony picked up the coffee cup and threw it at the wall.

FRIDAY, OCTOBER 4 • 4:30 PM

"HOW DID IT GO?" Meridith was waiting for him in the entry.

"Do you know what they want from me?" he asked, throwing his coat across the round table in the foyer, knocking off the flower arrangement. Before she could answer he continued, "They want me to have my father kill a bill before his committee that would investigate their illegal activities! Can you believe it? That they think I could if I wanted to!"

Meridith picked up the basket and began rearranging the flowers. "Leave those alone, Marina can do that. I need a drink." He went to the bar with Meri at his heels.

"Jonathan, you're not supposed to have liquor with your medication."

"To hell with that. To hell with everything! What do I have to lose?" He poured a tumbler full of Glenlivit and gulped it without taking a breath. "Shit, Meridith, what am I going to do?"

"I don't know, Jonathan, I really don't." She thought of nothing else since the limo had driven away. Now, faced with the certainty of the dilemma, she had no idea what he would do. One thing was for certain. Nothing he could say or do would sway his father. He poured a second drink, and darkness shrouded his face. "You know why we're in this mess, don't you?" She shook her head. "If you had given me the money when I'd asked you for it, none of this would have happened."

He finished the drink and threw the glass across the room. The leaded crystal smashed into shards against the wall. Meridith turned to leave.

"Where do you think you're going, bitch? You fucking, frigid princess. *You* hold the money. *You* own the house. *You* have the trust fund. *You* own the stock." He grabbed her arm in a vice grip.

"Let go of me, Jonathan, I'm warning you—"

"*You're* warning *me*?" He threw his head back and laughed evilly. "As long as I'm breaking the rules, let's break them all. You and I haven't had sex in a long time, princess. I feel like it now." Still holding her arm, he whipped her around and grabbed her face in his other hand.

"Jonathan, please—"

"Jonathan, please," he mimicked her. "Beg a little, Queen Meridith. See what it feels like to have to beg." He twisted her arm and pulled her towards him. He grabbed at her breast with his free hand, hurting her. His mouth was wet and tasted like scotch as it covered hers.

"Let go of me *now*!" Meridith commanded as she pulled her arm free. Her voice remained in control, but she radiated a courage Jonathan recognized. He released his hold.

"Whoa, where's that coming from? You getting lessons from the Mafia these days?"

"Jonathan, never touch me again! I told you I would no longer stand for this abusive behavior. You promised to change, but obviously your promises mean nothing. I told you I would try. Now all bets are off. Somehow, we will make it through this mess you've gotten us in, but plan to move out once this situation is resolved." He watched in astonishment as she walked up the winding staircase. Then he poured himself another stiff drink.

SATURDAY, OCTOBER 4 • 8:30 AM

"I'M LEAVING FOR Washington this afternoon. I called a limo to pick me up. I don't know when I'll be back, if you care." Jonathan stood at the door to the room they had once shared.

"So you're going to talk to your father?"

"Do I have a choice?" Jonathan's complexion was gray, his eyes red. He wore a trench coat and carried a tweed hanging bag.

"I don't know. Are you staying at your father's townhouse?"

"I'll call you. Say good bye to the kids for me."

"I'm sure they're up." She glanced at the clock. Almost nine.

"Their doors are closed. Tell them I should be home by Monday." He turned and walked down the hallway. Meridith sat down on the edge of the bed and closed her eyes. She prayed for courage.

SATURDAY. OCTOBER 4 • 1:00 PM EST

PLANES LANDING at Reagan Washington National must fly along the Potomac River, with all its twists and turns, to abate noise in the Capital. The pilot clicked on the intercom and announced that, to the left, the white spire of the Washington Monument could be seen. The tourists craned their necks. It was a magnificent city, and this fall Saturday was glorious. The trees surrounding the river were brilliant shades of gold, red and yellow. Jonathan's eyes, however, never left his lap. He realized his badly bitten thumb nail was bleeding.

The airport was small for one located in the heart of the nation's capital. Passengers landing at National walked steps to the curb.

"Taxi, mister?" a foreign voice beckoned Jonathan. He slipped in the yellow sedan and was whisked away.

Franklin Chamberlain kept a townhouse in Georgetown. The ride from the airport took only minutes across the Key Bridge. The Iranian driver tried to carry on an insipid conversation about taxes and government, Jonathan ignored him.

Standing outside his father's doorway, Jonathan paused. He had rehearsed a dozen different scenarios to explain why he was in town, unannounced, and why he cared about this crime bill. Nothing made sense.

The townhouse was a block off Wisconsin Avenue, the main thoroughfare through Georgetown, and was situated just steps from the sidewalk. Tourists and residents alike were jostling one another as they paraded down the crowded main street. No one noticed the well-dressed businessman ringing the doorbell of this historic structure.

"Jonathan! What are you doing here? Why didn't you call?" Franklin was both surprised and pleased to see his son standing there looking better than the last time he'd seen him in the hospital.

"Spur of the moment. I was getting in Meridith's way just hanging around the house, so I thought I'd spend some time with my father."

"Come in! Here, let me take your coat." Even though it was a weekend afternoon, Franklin was wearing a starched white shirt and tie. His only concession to casual was a navy, cardigan sweater. "Have you had lunch?"

"No, just a snack on the plane."

"My housekeeper just left, but let me see what I have," Franklin offered.

"I'm not really hungry, Father, but I would have a drink. Scotch, if you have it."

"Should you have alcohol after your heart condition?" Franklin's face showed concern.

"No, but I will anyway." He found the bar and made his own drink, sans ice.

"Jonathan, is there anything wrong?"

"No, Father, really. Just a social visit." He finished the drink quickly. "Would you mind if I had a short nap. I've been traveling since this morning, and I'm still a little shaky."

"Please do. You know where the guest room is. If you need anything, just ask. I'll call my housekeeper to come in if you'd like."

"No, Father, I'm fine. We'll eat out, if you don't mind."

"That would be perfect, I don't do that much anymore. First, get some rest." Jonathan refilled his glass before making his way up the narrow stairs. Once the door was closed to the bedroom, Franklin went into the kitchen to call Meridith.

His call was answered by the machine. He left a short message: "Meridith? Franklin here. Jonathan's just arrived. Please call me as soon as you get in. I need to know what's going on."

SATURDAY, OCTOBER 4 • 7:00 PM EST

THE TWO MEN sat at a quiet table in the back of Clyde's, under a glass ceiling. The restaurant, located along M Street, had been a favorite of Washingtonians for years. Developers in the nation's capital strive to keep the integrity of historic structures. When they built a mall along the traveled street, the exterior kept the secret of a three-story, modern, glass galleria inside, aptly named Georgetown Park. Clyde's original restaurant remained intact: oak bar, solarium, hanging plants and Beltway Insiders.

After they finished a dinner of Maryland crab cakes and corn bread, Franklin sat back and looked his son straight on. "Are you going to tell me now, or will we continue this game of cat and mouse?" No wonder his father wielded such power.

"No games, Father." Jonathan turned to look for their waiter. He really needed a drink.

"I talked to Meridith at the hospital. I know the problems you've had at the firm. Is this about money? I'll help you, you know."

"Damn that woman!" Jonathan fumed mentally. Did his father know about the loan from Romano, too? No, even Meridith wouldn't be that stupid. He wished she'd told him about their conversation. He felt blind-sided.

"Is this about you and Meridith? Are you separated?"

"No, Father, not now, anyway, but don't be surprised if it comes to that. I can't put up with her control anymore. She holds the purse strings, and she never lets me forget it."

"Jonathan, if you need money, I'll be glad to give it you. The house in Winnetka is yours anyway. It must be worth several million by now. It's all paid for. Bought it for less than a hundred thousand back in the sixties. I don't know how people afford it these days."

"Maybe I'll take you up on it, Father, but, for now, I'm all right. Really, this is just a social visit." Jonathan wished he'd known this earlier, but this information could be his salvation. The waiter appeared.

"Anything else, gentlemen?"

"Yes, bring me a double scotch, rocks. Wait, cancel that. I'll have a rusty nail, double, in a very large snifter."

"Jonathan!" The waiter paused and looked at the two men.

"Father, please." Turning to the waiter: "Now."

The man vanished before there was any more argument. Franklin was quiet as the drink appeared. Scotch laced with Drambuie, a lethal concoction. Jonathan took a slug then sat back and smiled. The warm liquor burned its way down to his stomach, leaving a mellow glow behind.

"Father, let's talk about you." He ignored the older man's hard stare. "What major legislation sits waiting for the House's most powerful Congressman to put his John Hancock on?"

"Oh, they always have a new version of the same old thing to fight about. Every generation wants to reinvented the wheel." The elder man smiled sadly.

"I read you've got a new crime bill in your committee. What's that all about? Didn't we just pass a crime bill a few years ago?"

"This one is aimed at the heart of organized crime. It will give the FBI a great deal more power. And money. Local officials will also be allowed more leeway than I feel comfortable with." This the first ray of hope beamed at Jonathan. "Then you're not going to fund it?" He tried to sound disinterested.

"Not the way it stands. I think something needs to be done to fight these Organizations that threaten our way of life, but we also need to keep the Constitution in mind. Many officials may use their power in ways this legislation doesn't intend."

The drinks' effect was nothing compared to the impact of Franklin's statement. The bill may be dead regardless! Jonathan would be off the hook without compromising himself or his father. The world would be a wonderful place, if he pulled this out of the fire. He'd be off the hook.

"So, what now?"

"I'm sending it back to the committee to rewrite. We'll see what they come up with." Franklin was worried about his son's heart and his heavy drinking. He had not spoken to Meridith and was anxious to do so before the night was over. "If you're ready, I'm very tired, it's been a long week."

"Longer than you'll ever know." Jonathan downed the last of his drink and stood up.

"I've got the check, son, let's go."

The two men walked through the bustling crowd: sightseers, panhandlers, college kids, tourists, cruising singles, couples holding hands, bikers, cyclists, baby carriage pushers, all moving slowly along cracked sidewalks, gaping into the storefronts and at each other. Georgetown on Saturday night was the town's main attraction. The locals didn't call it *amateur hour* for nothing.

SUNDAY, OCTOBER 6

MERIDITH WAS DREAMING. She was in a house searching for the door, desperately trying to leave. Someone needed her, but it was so dark she couldn't find her way out. A phone was ringing in her dream. She fought to wake up, but the bell kept chiming. She opened her eyes to find her own telephone ringing.

"Hello?" The clock said seven thirty.

"Meri?" Tony's voice sent her stomach into a cartwheel. "Sorry to call so early, but I wanted to catch you while I've got a clear line." Her head wasn't lucid enough to understand the meaning.

"What's wrong?"

"Nothing. I wanted to take you and your children to my church and to my mother's for Sunday dinner. I promise your children will think we're just old friends. My mother's crazy to meet you. Please come."

Her mind was spinning. Jonathan. Oh, yes, in Washington. What would she tell Hunter and Chelsea? "When? How?"

"River Forest. Drive your car to Silverman's, I'll meet you there, in the underground garage, in two hours. Will that give you enough time?"

"Nine thirty at Silverman's garage. I can't believe I'm doing this ..."

"I can. See you then."

MERIDITH TOLD the children over breakfast she was taking them to meet someone she'd met at the theatre. "He's a producer who may want to shoot a picture in Winnetka." She hated lies but didn't know how to explain this new person in her life. "I met him when he came to the North Lake House, and he asked me to show him around. Now he's repaying the favor by taking us to his church and dinner at his family's house."

Hunter balked. "Do I have to go, Mom? I don't know these people, and I'm sure it will be boring." Nothing could be worse to North Shore children than "boring."

"Yes, you will see how other families live, and you may just enjoy yourself. Please, for me?" He folded his arms in defiance but shrugged.

"All right, but I need to come home early. I have a ton of homework."

"That's the first time I've heard you ask to do homework," Chelsea remarked. "Anyway, *I* want to go. What should I wear, Mom?" Meridith smiled, a woman's first question.

SHE SAW the waiting limousine's door open before her engine died. Tony quickly emerged and ran to her car.

"Is that him, Mom?" Chelsea asked.

"Wow, he hired a limo to pick us up," Hunter tried to appear unimpressed.

"Tony, how nice to see you again," Meridith said sweetly.

"Mrs. Chamberlain, thank you for accepting my invitation. This must be Hunter and, of course, Chelsea. Chelsea, you are as beautiful as your mother." Her daughter beamed.

"Chelsea, Hunter, this is Mr. Romano." His name stuck in her throat. She tried not to look at them for fear of giving herself away. They walked to the car, not daring to touch. Hunter took a seat with his back to the driver and Chelsea sat down beside him. As soon as Meridith was comfortable, Tony sat down next to her, facing the children.

"Hunter, I understand you are a hockey fan."

"Yeah," the young man answered with no enthusiasm.

"See many games?"

Hunter shook his head.

"I have season tickets, maybe we could take in a few? You could bring your friends." He had Hunter's attention. "I thought you might like this, if you should decide to go." Tony picked up a bag resting at his feet and handed it to Hunter. The young man looked quizzically at his mother who only smiled. Inside the package was a black and red Blackhawks jacket.

"Wow, thanks." Hunter took the soft, leather coat with the huge Indian insignia embroidered on the back. As he examined it, lovingly running his hand over the logo, his eyes opened wide. "Mom! Look, it's autographed by the team!" Gold-inked signatures covered the back of the jacket.

"Hunter, that's incredible! Tony, how generous of you."

"Thank you so, so much, Mr. Romano. Wait until the guys see this. It's awesome. Really, really awesome—" His eyes never left the jacket's back as he traced the names with his finger.

"Don't think I've forgotten you, Miss Chamberlain. I know it should be ladies first, but I've saved the best for last." Chelsea lowered her eyes and Tony marveled at the resemblance between mother and daughter. His heart did a quick drum roll. From behind the car's seat Tony pulled a large shopping bag and handed it to the little girl. Meri and Hunter watched anxiously.

Chelsea reached into the golden bag and pulled out a doll wrapped in pink tissue paper. Her face was bright with anticipation as she unwrapped it carefully. The doll looked like a smaller replica of Chelsea herself, complete with the same, blonde hairstyle and emerald eyes.

She even mirrored Chelsea's deep, left dimple. Meri gasped as Chelsea sat frozen in awe.

"Tony, how—?"

"I have a friend who makes dolls. She took a photo of Chelsea and made this, in her own words, her masterpiece. She said she would someday like to meet the young lady with such a beautiful face. Do you like it, Chelsea?" Tony was watching her with such intensity.

"I love her! I have a doll collection, and I'll love her even when I'm too old for dolls."

"You'll never be too old for dolls, look at me," Meri reminded her. They had lovingly collected the dolls together. Chelsea wasn't listening. She was busy combing back the doll's hair and exploring her elaborate outfit.

"You've made quite an impression, Mr. Romano." Meri was amazed at the lengths he had gone to, remembering things she'd told him about the children. "But, how did you get a photo of Chelsea?" Meri was bothered.

"I called the school for a yearbook." She had visions of a stalker with a camera. "How else would I have gotten it?"

"I don't know, but—" She never finished the sentence.

They pulled up in front of a large, Catholic cathedral. "I know you are Episcopalian, but you'll find our mass very close to yours." The children followed her into the church; Hunter, wearing his new jacket, Chelsea, holding her doll.

The irony of the situation did not escape Meridith. Jonathan had not attended church with her for years. Judging by his familiarity with the rituals, Tony rarely missed a Sunday. Meri studied his profile, as she had on the yacht, but, this time, he was deep in prayer.

At the end of the mass, the monsignor made a point to shake Tony's hand and meet the Chamberlain family.

There was hot chocolate and coffee in the car—a little something for the drive to Tony's mother's house. This also delighted the children. "Is it your intention to spoil all of us?" Meri, too, was having a wonderful time.

"Absolutely!" Tony's smile never left his face.

"BELLISIMA!" was all Mrs. Romano could say when she saw Meri and the children. Her silver hair was pulled back and twisted into a figure eight at her neck and her big, brown eyes were moist with tears as she hugged and kissed Tony, Meri and the children. It had been so long since Meridith had experienced this kind of familial love, she found herself blinking back tears. If only her children could have known their grandparents.

Mrs. Romano was a tiny woman whose body showed the strain of supporting enormous bosoms. They meshed together to form a single upholstered mass, dominating her torso from neck to waist. She wore a pink and black, flowered dress with a lace collar and heavy, black shoes. "You all musta be hungry," Mrs. Romano stated as she beckoned them into her dining room. The savory smells of tomato sauce and garlic and fresh bread reminded them they hadn't eaten.

The house itself was built around nineteen twenty. The walls were stucco and decorated with religious paintings and family pictures. Dark beams sectioned off the high ceilings. The doorways were arched and the oak floors covered with patterned Persian rugs. The furniture was large, baroque and well-used. Heavy damask and velvet draperies hung at the windows. The dining table seated twenty. It was the center of all family gatherings. Today the lace tablecloth was topped by the most beautiful bone china Meri had ever seen. A centerpiece of red roses sat between two silver candelabras that held creamy white candles.

"Mrs. Romano, your china is lovely," Meri told her as she held one of the delicate cups up to the light. The elaborate fruit pattern around the edge was trimmed in gold.

"Mama Rosa, please, Meri. I call you Meri, yes?" Her accent was delightful.

Meridith smiled at her. "Of course, call me Meri."

"The dishes came with me from Italy. They belong to *mia madre*, my mother."

"What part of Italy are you from, Mama Rosa?"

"Me? I come from Palermo. You been?"

"I've been to Milan and Florence and Rome. And, of course, Venice. But, unfortunately, always as a tourist. I'd love to spend more time exploring all the little villages and the coast."

"I'd love to go back. Tony's father's family come from Sicily a long time ago. I come here to marry Vincenzo. You must go to Sicily. But, maybe not. A rich, beautiful American, you may have trouble. Ah, you go with Tony, and you have no trouble."

"Mama, what are you saying?" Tony came up behind his mother and hugged her. "Isn't she something, Mama?" Meri blushed.

"You make me embarrass, Antonio, don't do that," Rosa reprimanded her son.

"Aw, I'm sorry, Mama, I'm sorry, Meri," he teased.

"Tell the family supper is ready. Wash your hands." Rosa walked into the kitchen. Meri laughed at the thought that he would have a mother who told him to wash his hands.

"She really is wonderful, Tony," Meri said. "What did you tell her about me, about us?"

"That I love you."

"Tony, you didn't!" Meridith searched the room to see who may have overheard.

"Yes, I did," he looked so innocently smug.

"Did you tell her," she lowered her voice to a whisper, "that I was married?"

"No, because you won't be much longer."

"What does that mean?" Meridith was worried there was an ominous meaning to his statement.

"It means that you and Jonathan will get divorced, and then you won't be."

"Oh."

"*Mange, mange.* Come and eat," Rosa was herding the small gatherings into the dining room. Hunter and Chelsea came into the room with a group of children from the basement.

"Wow, Mom, they have the coolest stuff down there—videos, electronic pinball machines, a pool table and a big screen TV. It's awesome!" Hunter was sold.

The dining room table was quickly populated by dark haired men, quiet women and laughing children. Hunter and Chelsea seemed right at home among the Romano cousins. Tony's place was at the head of the table. He held out a chair for Meri to his right. He seated Mama Rosa at his left, but she kept returning to the kitchen at regular intervals. "Doesn't Mama have help?" Meri whispered to Tony during one of her absences.

"Are you kidding? Believe me, we've tried. She lives to cook for these Sunday dinners. No one's going to steal her thunder. We've got a woman who comes in to clean up later."

Mama Rosa continued dishing the food in proportions that made Meridith swoon, but the plates emptied as fast as she filled them. There were several kinds of pasta covered in Mama's rich, red sauce. Salads, crisp from the garden, dressed with olive oil and biting balsamic vinegar; breads so hot that the butter melted into the yeasty dough before it could be spread; an antipasto of peppers, salami, cheese, olives, calamari and artichokes marinated in spicy oil; sweet melon wrapped in prosciutto. And wine. The most delicious red wine Meri had ever tasted. She couldn't decide if the wine made the food better or vice versa. It didn't matter. It was all a little taste of heaven.

"Georgie, come help me," Mama cried from the kitchen. Georgie and his wife scrambled to help. The man emerged with a huge silver platter holding a roast beef wrapped in a delicate pastry shell.

"Mama, my favorite!" Tony exclaimed as he jumped up and went to hug his mother.

"Hey, it's not everyday my boy comes home with such a beautiful woman," Mama looked to Meri.

"I knew you two would love each other," Tony beamed. Meridith noticed that the wives at the table didn't seem to share Tony's admiration. Meri looked to see if the children had picked up on the remark, but they were playing with a small octopus discovered among the antipasto. Hunter was hopping the dead creature along the table toward his sister who was totally grossed out.

By the time Mama brought out the demitasse cups with espresso and crystal liqueur glasses for sambuco, Meri thought she would burst.

"What's for dessert, Mama?" Tony called to his mother.

"Be quiet, you," she told him as she carried in a platter of cannoli.
The room oohed and awed as she set in down.

The children weren't sure about something filled with cheese for dessert. "*Gelato* for the children in the kitchen," Mama told them. The Romano children rushed from the table.

"What's gella—what she said? Jello?" Chelsea asked.

Tony took her hand. "Italian ice cream. Mama makes it herself, and it's fantastic," he told her. "Bring me back a dish?" She nodded and ran back with the others. "Meri, have a cannoli?"

"I really couldn't. Honestly."

"You'll hurt Mama's feelings. Here, have a bite." He picked one of the tube-shaped pieces of pastry and held it to her mouth. She bit into it and the mascarpone and ricotta cheese spurted out around her mouth and into Tony's lap. One of the woman across from him blurted, "Oh, no!"

"Tony, I'm so sorry," Meridith was very embarrassed.

"Hey, don't worry. It's just slacks. That's why we have dry cleaners." The family had never seen Tony nonchalant about his clothing. He wiped the cheese off with his napkin. "Mama, you still have some of my clothes here?"

"Of course. Enjoy the cannoli, then change," she ordered. Tony leaned over and kissed the sweet dessert off the corner of her mouth. When he laughed, the table sighed. Mama grabbed his cheek, "You're a devil, Antonio, and I love you!" Meri looked around the table at the strange, new faces watching her.

You're a long, long way from Winnetka, Meridith told herself, and it was a happy place to be.

Meridith offered to help in the kitchen after, but Tony had other plans. "We're going for a drive," he whispered to her. While he left to find a car, Meri went down to the basement to see what the children found so fascinating. It was, as Hunter proclaimed, better than the mall arcade.

"Tony is going to show me around, will you be all right here?"

"Sure, Mom, take your time, it's great here," Hunter told her without looking up from his pool shot.

"Where's Chelsea?"

"I'm here, Mom," she yelled across the large room. Meri turned to see her daughter climb out of the playhouse. "Look, there's a TV in the playhouse! And it really works!"

Meri shook her head in wonder. "I'll be back in a while, you both be good," she advised. Neither one acknowledged her.

"Meri! Come on, I've got a car out back." Tony was waiting at the top of the basement steps. He had one of his cousin's cars, a '95 Toyota, running in the alley. As they left by the back door, Tony pulled on a wool cap and sun glasses. He handed Meri a scarf, sunglasses and a wool jacket.

"Are we going incognito?" she laughed.

"Sort of. It never hurts in my line of work." Meri wrapped the scarf around her hair and adjusted the large, dark glasses.

"You look like Jackie Kennedy," Tony appraised her. She lowered the glasses and peered over the top, raising her eyebrows. "God, I love you," he told her as he grabbed Meri's hand and jogged down the steps and into the unobtrusive auto.

As they drove around the city of River Forest, Tony talked about his childhood, growing up "connected."

"Unlike the guy in *Goodfellows*, I never really wanted to be a wiseguy. I was a pretty good student, and, for a while, I thought I'd teach. I love kids."

"I remember. You're great with mine."

"They're pretty terrific, too." He leaned across the console and kissed her.

"So, how did you end up—the boss?"

"El Duce? I was mad as hell when my father disappeared. Then I spent the summer with my uncles in New York. After I got my MBA, the Organization thought I could legitimize their businesses. That's how I got involved initially, giving them advice on how to invest their ill-gotten gain. Then, I found I had a gift for *persuasion*."

"I can certainly attest to that!" She reached over and pinched his arm. His bicep bulged reactively.

"Do you remember the television program *Happy Days*?"

"Sure," Meri was confused about the direction of the conversation.

"Remember the character, 'Fonzie?' He started out as a real hood—motorcycle, black leather jacket, the whole bit. Everyone was so intimidated by him, except, during the entire series, he never hit anyone. But there was always the *threat*. Winkler, himself, is a short guy, about five feet five. His real life persona is the same way—larger-than-life. He *thought* he was in control, therefore, he was. People respond to intimidation. That's the real name of the game."

Meri marveled at his power to captivate. Certainly this was his greatest strength. "You would have made an incredible politician," she announced, "you might even have been President."

"What makes you think I don't have that kind of power?" he asked, seriously.

"I—I don't know, do you?"

"I live in the same circles, play pretty much by the same rules, surrounded by body guards and the FBI. I just try to keep a lower profile, and my spin doctors are not as good."

"Tony, what will happen to Jonathan?" Meri braced for an answer. Now Tony took a minute to shift gears, blind-sided by the abrupt change of subject. "If he keeps the bill from being funded, nothing. If not, you're likely to part with some of the Whitney fortune."

"Will they accept the money then?"

"Probably. They realize Jonathan has only limited influence. They know he's in Washington now, and that's in his favor. Hell, Meri, I promise you the man won't get knocked off." He tried to laugh, but it stuck in his throat. "I wouldn't allow it."

"I'd prefer it if they would just take the money and close the entire matter."

Tony looked into her eyes, searching. They drove several more miles in silence until the car entered the forest preserve. Tony drove through the deserted parking area to a far corner, hidden by the drooping branches of a willow, and turned off the engine.

"Let's walk," he suggested as he came around and opened her door. The trails were covered in fallen, brown leaves, and the ground was soft. Her pumps dug into the moist earth as she gingerly maneuvered the pathway.

"Not my best hiking shoes," she laughed.

"Meri, stop." Tony took her arms and placed them around his own waist. She held her face up to be kissed, and his mouth found hers. They were eager and ravenous, hungry for one another, yet insatiable. His tongue was hot as it caressed her mouth. He pulled his face back slightly, to look at hers, but she gently nipped at his lips. Her tongue darted and teased the corner of his mouth.

"You're a wanton woman, do you know that?"

"And I get whatever I wanton!" She was giggling.

"Ooh, that was really bad. Is this what I'm going to have to put up with?" She buried her face in his windbreaker.

"I thought we weren't going to talk about commitment."

"Who's talking commitment? Excuse me, I was kidding, not asking for your hand." He began working the muscle in his jaw.

"I'm sorry, Tony, really I am. There's nothing I would like more than to pretend we're all one-big-happy-family, but we're a little old to play house. I've seen the repercussion of affairs, and I can't do that to my children. You should see what goes on in Winnetka."

"I've seen it, Meri, everywhere. There is a world outside of Winnetka, you know. Ah, Meri, this is eating me up. I can't sleep, can't eat, everywhere I look I see your face."

"Tony, hold me ..." He kissed her once again.

"God, this is awful," he scowled at the car. "Have you ever made love in the back seat of a Toyota?"

She looked skeptically at Tony, then shrugged.

"Wait, don't answer that, I don't want to know," he was laughing as he tugged her hand back down the path. Her shoes barely sunk into the muddy ground as she raced him back to the parking lot. Her heel caught in the wet earth and, as she bent to free it, her hand brushed a patch of clover.

"Look! This is the first time I've found a four-leaf clover. I thought they were manufactured, I've never seen one growing." She picked it carefully and presented it to him.

"No, it's yours, you found it, you keep it."

"I've had a lifetime of good luck, I want you to have it." He took it from her and, removing his wallet from his back pocket, carefully placed the clover in the billfold.

"If Lady Luck brings me you, it's all I'll ever need." He kissed her, and they walked on to the car. He held the rear door open for her, and she slid over, making room for him. He seemed to fumbling with something in his jacket pocket. Meridith winced, suddenly feeling very self-conscious. As Tony entered the car and closed the door she made herself look at what his hand held. It was a narrow, black velvet, jewelry case.

"Tony, no presents for me. The gifts you gave the children were far too extravagant. I'm truly embarrassed."

"Meri, I can't give you what I'd like, so I'm giving you what I hope you will like. After all, I accepted your gift graciously. The four-leaf clover?" He handed her the box.

"This is symbolic of our whole relationship: I want to say *no* but I'm having too much fun saying *yes*." She opened the box slowly, savoring the moment. "Ooh, Tony, it's beautiful!" Meri removed a bracelet from its satin bed and held it up. Large diamonds were held together by gold threads weaving figure eights between them.

"If a single diamond on your finger represents love and commitment, these diamonds encircle your wrist, multiplied many times, to remind you how much more I love you."

"Tony, I can't accept this!" But even as she spoke the words Meri was wrapping the bauble around her arm. In the fading twilight Tony found the clasp and secured it, kissing the hand it adorned. Tiny goose-bumps appeared on her arm, and Tony kissed each one as he worked his way towards her waiting mouth.

MONDAY, OCTOBER 7

"THAT SON-OF-A-BITCH, Romano. Gotti is locked up in Marion, who gives a shit if he picked that Roman Rooster to run Chicago? I say we take him out and put somebody in there who's got some real balls. More than just for screwing women. I'm telling you he's not a made man."

"Calm down, Masucchi, you're gonna bust a blood vessel. You should see your face, its purple."

"*Mi madonna*, I really want to do him." The fat man pounded his fist into his palm to make the point. The two men sat in the back of La Vita, a small restaurant on Taylor Street, stirring sugar into thick coffee. Masucchi had stuffed his six foot five, three hundred pound plus frame into a suit off the rack that didn't quite fit. He looked uncomfortable and kept tugging at the sleeves. His tie only made it to the middle button on his polyester shirt. Silvio Masucchi had flown in from New York to talk to the man who knew Tony Romano better than anyone, Frank Delvecchio, one of Romano's bodyguards.

"Look, Frankie, the Organization is gettin' fed up with Romano, he's going soft.

Everybody thought the guy was so tough, I mean, he certainly acted the part when he took over. Him with the big college degrees, trying to make everything so legal. The money is gettin' laundered okay, but no new stuff is coming down and now it looks like the Russians are gettin' a real strong-hold in Chicago. That with the Japs and the Chinks and the Spicks ... Well, it don't look good for us bein' on top in Chi-town anymore."

Frankie was grateful for many things, not the least of which was the fact that Romano was a good teacher. Frankie learned fast and well. Now, like his boss, Frankie remained cool in the face of a man he thought belonged in another era. "Look, Masucchi, I think that Tony is looking for a way out himself. He's done a good job. The Organization has a lot of clean money these days, thanks to him. Why not let him walk?"

"You shithead fool! Let him walk where? Right into the arms of that rich broad and who next? The fuckin' Fibbies? How long do you think he'd last straight?" Masucchi slicked back his thinning, greasy hair with his hand before wiping it across his strained sleeve. Frankie winced.

"What makes you think Romano would talk to the Feds? Look, I know him, and one thing he's not, is a rat."

"I want him out. I think I got enough votes lined up to do the job. Are you in with me or not on this?"

Frankie looked into his cup for the answer. Masucchi was an impatient bastard. "Are you in or out?" Masucchi's voice was raised and several heads turned their way.

"I'm with the Organization," Frankie answered quietly. Masucchi seemed happy, and Frankie figured the fat man wasn't bright enough to realize he hadn't gotten an answer.

"I'll tell you one thing, though. If he don't kill this new crime bill, I won't have to line up votes. He'll be one dead *duce*. Look, I gotta lot of calls to make while I'm town. I don't want Romano to know I'm here, but I sure could use your help, I don't know my way around. Call Tony, and tell him you'll be tied up today."

"Sure, Silvi, sure." Frankie's mind was racing. Better that he should keep his eyes and ears open and know what this guy was doing. He was going to be trouble, real trouble. Frankie could feel it.

Masucchi threw a five across the table and they walked out into the gray, Chicago day.

MONDAY, OCTOBER 7 · MORNING

JONATHAN HAD already left Washington for Chicago when Franklin Chamberlain finally reached Meridith. "Tell me, Meridith, how are things between you and Jonathan?" Meri hadn't spoken with her husband since Saturday morning and had no idea what he and his father had talked about. She hesitated.

"Well, to be truthful, Franklin, not so good." His heart hurt. "I told him I would try to work things out if he would change, but that doesn't seem to be happening."

"He arrived here on Saturday very upset, but, by the time he left, he seemed cheered. I hope his visit was helpful."

"I hope so, too, Franklin. So you two had a nice time?" She wondered how Jonathan had handled the situation.

"Very nice. One thing bothered me, though. Meridith, have you noticed that Jonathan is drinking quite heavily? Especially considering what he's just been though."

She was keenly aware. "I'll talk to Jonathan when he returns. And to his doctor. Thank you for your concern, Franklin." Her voice echoed her sincerity.

"Meridith, you know how I feel about you and the children. You are my only family now. Please, no matter what happens, don't shut me out." Now Meri's heart was heavy.

"I promise that will never happen, Franklin. I love you."

"I love you, too, Meri. Call me after you've had a chance to speak with my son, and, please, keep me posted."

"I promise." She took this opportunity to ask, "How are the wheels of Congress turning these days? Are you going to have your desk cleared before the holiday break?"

"Oh, the faces change but there will always be a wrench in the cog of progress." She couldn't decipher if there was a meaning there or not.

"Well, you call me, too, if you need anything. Is that a promise?"

"Meridith, you are a gem; I only wish my son appreciated you. I'm going to ring off, dear. Take care." She had forgotten to ask what time Jonathan left. She wanted to hear Tony's voice but denied herself that small pleasure. She left the house moments before the phone began ringing.

●　●　●

"DAMN, she's not home." Tony folded the cellular phone and replaced it in his pocket. "I got a strange call from Frankie," he told Julie, aka Jules Carboni, his other body guard. "Said he wouldn't be around today."

"That's funny. I talked to him this morning, and he wasn't sick or anything."

"Yeah, funny." Romano squinted into the sky outside his window. He trusted Frankie, but, in this business, trust was a relative term.

"Chamberlain should be back from D.C. today, boss. You want I should go out to Winnetka and pick him up for a talk?"

"No, Julie, he should call Silverman. The less I have to do with the man the better." Julie knew he had been sleeping with Chamberlain's wife and wondered what would happen to the husband once they were through with him. It was not his job to wonder, though, so he changed the subject.

"Hey, boss, how about some lunch. There's a new restaurant, La Vita, wanna try it?"

"No, thanks, Julie. I need to go over the figures Dolf left me with Silverman. I'll be there when, and if, we get a call from Chamberlain. You can go after you've dropped me, if you want."

"No, boss. I shouldn't leave you alone. Even with the lawyer. I'll have something sent over. Are you ready?"

"Let me get a coat." As Tony slipped it on he could still smell Meri's perfume clinging to the shoulder. His stomach lurched. His jaw worked thinking about Jonathan back at the Winnetka house.

SILVERMAN HIT Tony with the news before his coat was hung up. "I heard from Chamberlain. He swears his father is sending the bill back to committee. Says the old man feels the new legislation takes away too many Constitutional Rights. Thank God he's a politician with a conscience. What now?"

"I'm satisfied. We'll call New York and let them know."

"What about the money?" Silverman asked.

"What about it?"

"Nothing. How about I buy lunch? Not much more to do here today."

"Not so fast. I've got the figures from the gambling ships we need to go over. Julie's in the hall. There's a new restaurant he wanted to try out. Tell him to get something and bring it back."

With that, Tony settled in to calculate the Organization's take.

MONDAY, OCTOBER 7 · NOON

"ANYTHING MORE ABOUT my Crime Bill," the President asked the second-in-command, Henry Boyer.

"I talked to several members of Ways and Means today. They say Chamberlain is still digging in his heels. Suggestions?"

The President chewed on the inside of his lip. "Damn. I've got to get this thing to pass before Christmas. Any chance of that?"

"Let me work on it," Boyer offered.

"You're a good man, Hank. Thanks." The President shuffled through the stack of papers littering his desk in the Oval Office and called to his secretary, "Where's my speech, Olivia?"

"I'll get right on it, sir."

"See that you do," he stated as he put his half-glasses on his nose. "And keep on that committee's collective asses, I need that legislation!"

"Yes, sir," Boyer whispered as he left the office.

MONDAY, OCTOBER 7 • AFTERNOON

"SANDERS, HERE. Something's up." FBI Agent Gary Sanders called the Washington office to speak to Sam Driscoll. When he heard the Director's voice at the other end, he continued, "Big Silvio Masucchi just arrived here in Chicago from New York. He met with one of Romano's guys, Frankie Delvecchio, a young man on the move. They seem to be traveling around town making all the obligatory stops. But, and get this, without Romano."

"Where are you now?"

"Outside the Teamster's office, just west of downtown Chicago. I'm telling you, my gut is burning. Something's up."

"Where's Romano now?"

"At his attorney's office in the loop. You know, Joel Silverman."

"Okay, have someone else watch Romano, and you stay with Masucchi. Anything else?"

"Yeah, and again, this is just my ulcer acting up but—well, Romano's been acting real strange. Lost him a couple of times. Heard he's been with some woman. I haven't been able to ID her yet, but her photos gone in the system. Last week he got in his limo and drove to Kenosha and back without leaving the car. Didn't even make a phone call the whole time."

"Who was with him?"

"No one but Julie Carbon, one of his muscles, who drove."

"That is strange. Okay, keep me posted, and we'll step up the taped surveillance. Maybe we can pick up something there."

"Right, but I've got to go. They just came out of the building."

After Sanders signed off, Sam Driscoll sat with the phone in is hand. He dialed the Chicago office and ordered another agent to tail Romano while Sanders stayed on Masucchi. Then he made a note in the computer file before leaving for a lunch with several congressmen on the new Organized Crime Bill.

THURSDAY, OCTOBER 17

FOR TWO WEEKS Meridith had blocked out thoughts of Tony, concentrating only on her play. Rehearsals had taken up her evenings, and the children were busy with school. Jonathan's firm suggested he take the rest of the year off promising to reevaluate his partnership in January. For her, the days were never long enough, for him, they dragged endlessly, ranging from monotony to tedium.

THE STAGE at the North Lake House had been transformed into a weathered two-flat, in the poorer section of New Orleans just after World War II. Iron trellises framed the walls, cut away for the audience. Meridith marveled at how talented people could work with a few boards and set pieces to bring a fictional world to life as she walked unnoticed backstage.

Dress rehearsal was chaotic, but, as stage superstitions go, that insured a great opening. Gillian and Joe seemed to have worked out their problems, and she was again reigning over the confusion backstage as the stage manager.

"Meri, you were terrific!" Paul rushed to hug her.

"Thanks, I guess we pulled another one out of the fire," she offered.

"You and Joe were sensational. Now, if we could only get the crew's act together, we'll have a show." Bedlam continued around them. Someone had splashed wet paint on one of the costumes, Blanche's nightgown, and Gillian was trying to keep the wardrobe designer and the construction foreman from coming to blows. The lighting designer was crawling precariously across the narrow catwalk twenty feet overhead, all the time yelling because someone installed the wrong gel. Hammering punctuated all the heated discussions.

"I'm going on home, Paul, I'm really tired." The final scene was grueling and Meri really needed to unwind.

"Sure, Meri, you go ahead."

"Is this where I find the leading lady?" Meri jumped when she heard the voice.

"Tony! What are you doing here?" Her eyes searched the room. Over fifty people filled the auditorium, all tending to their own personal crises.

"I've stayed away as long as I can. I knew I wouldn't be able to talk to you tomorrow, so I thought I would celebrate your success a night early." He took her bag and walked out the open side door. Meri turned to see Lanie Flowers watching curiously. Meridith waved politely and followed Tony to his idling Porsche.

Tony drove through Winnetka like he lived there. "Where are we going?" she asked as he maneuvered down the quiet streets.

He leaned across and placed his finger to her lips. "Surprise."

"Tony, I can't be too late," she warned.

"I know, Cinderella." The thought of Meri living with Chamberlain made his blood rush, but, for now, Tony remained a patient man. He turned into a small restaurant off Waukegan Road, the Carousel.

"Tony, I can't go in there, people I know eat here."

"It's okay, Meri, trust me." He helped her out of the car and they walked around back.

The owner opened the door and escorted them to a private room where Sinatra music played and candles burned.

"Enjoy, Mr. Romano," the tall man said closing the door. A bottle of wine was open, and a feast filled the oblong table next to a small circular one set for them.

"I understood actresses were famished after rehearsal. *Mange*, my love."

"You sound like Mama," Meri teased.

"First, a toast. Italians are notoriously superstitious, you know. To a fabulous opening night!" He held out a glass to her. She took it and touched it lightly to the rim of his before tasting a glorious, red wine.

"Mmm, delicious!"

"Yes, you are," he touched her cheek. When Meri found she couldn't take another bite, she leaned back from the table and sighed.

"Tony, you make me feel so good in so many ways, but why do I feel like the other shoe is ready to drop?"

"Meri," he began by savoring her name, "I've always been able to fix anything I wanted, to make it go my way. With you, it may not be so easy."

"I've thought a great deal about what you told me on the boat. Even if I buy everything, which I find difficult, how did you end up ..." she trailed off, unable to find a word for Tony's power.

"—the boss," he finished. She nodded. "My father never wanted me to go into the business. I went to DePaul and later to Northwestern, where I received my MBA. Papa was part of the teamsters, and a lot of the things he did really helped the people."

"Go on," Meri urged.

Tony took a deep breath. "I had an older brother, Dennis. Denny and Dad were just alike. Denny was the one groomed for the Organization."

"I didn't know you have a brother." Meri took his hand.

"He was killed." The words hung in the air. "In Vietnam. I was still in high school when it happened. Papa was never the same. Mama didn't come out of her room for months. She was just beginning to recover when my father disappeared with Hoffa. His body was never found, and my mother refused to believe he was dead. I think a little part of her still waits for him to show up for Sunday dinner."

"Were you and your brother close?"

"He was eight years older, so that made it tough. We had different interests, but I idolized him. He was tall and had this great, wavy hair. Back in those days, he combed it back, real high." He smiled at the memory, and Meri smiled with him. "He looked like a cross between Elvis and Rock Hudson."

"Wow, some combination," Meri added, looking at Tony's winsome face.

"Yeah, well, one day he gets a letter from Lyndon Johnson and the next day he's dead. See, that's the thing, Meri." He became earnest and leaned across the table to make her understand. "A man gets elected, like your father-in-law, and he has the power to kill people."

"I don't think it's quite that simple," Meri contradicted.

He became more intense. "No? Think about it. I agree that the two world wars were a matter of survival. But what about all the others? Korea, Vietnam, Desert Storm, Kosovo. Our guys didn't like the way the other guys were running their countries. So we put on uniforms, go over there, and kill them. Some of our guys get killed in the process. We give medals, bury them with honor, and go on. Did any of their deaths change anything in history? No, it was all about power, and the economy, you can bet on that. Did you ever stop and think that we've had a conflict during the term of almost every Democratic President in this century?" He finished his wine, giving Meridith a chance to think about his statement.

"We have. And, those *conflicts* helped the economy. If people fight and die for any cause they believe in, that's okay. *If* they choose to participate. Did the American people ever vote to take part in those conflicts?"

Meridith was very still while Tony poured another glass of wine and took a sip. "That doesn't explain how you got this job," Meri finally said quietly.

"Gotti came to town, right after he took over. There was some talk that he had Carlo Gambino killed. Tony Arcardo was dead. The Spilatro brothers had been killed. He was looking for someone without a reputation or a record and with a brain. I was recruited."

"What do you really do?" She wasn't sure she wanted the answer.

"Look, Meri, the Organization does a lot of things. If you want to know what I do, personally, I'm like the president of a company. I oversee. I don't carry a gun. I give orders, and they're carried out. I make sure the company runs at a profit. I look out for the economy, so to speak. I've tried my damndest to put the money in legitimate enterprises. We pay all our taxes. I've even given a great deal of money to charity and to the arts." Her smile was tolerant. "Of course, I took a lot of heat for it, too." The smile got wider, and she shook her head.

"Tell me, Meridith Whitney Chamberlain, do you know where all *your money* came from?"

Her smile froze and became a frown. "What do you mean?" she asked with more than a hint of agitatation

"I mean, affluence was acquired, somewhere along the line. By robber barons, by thieves, by men who used other men, even by kings stealing from other kings and countries. The Getty's weren't very different from the Gotti's just a few generations ago ..." he trailed the thought into the candle-lit darkness of the restaurant.

Meridith was suddenly very tired. The wine diluted the adrenalin. "I need to get home and get some beauty sleep before tomorrow."

"I'll be there, Meri."

"The party is at my home, afterward. You may stop by, if you'd like."

"Really? What would Jonathan say?"

"I don't really care anymore, Tony. But, for my children's sake, remain cool."

He mocked a hurt expression. "Wasn't I a perfect gentleman?"

"I'm sorry, of course you were." She stood and kissed his cheek. "I still have to go back and retrieve my car."

"Ah, it's past midnight and Cinderella is still a princess!" Tony looked at the gold Piaget on his arm.

"Come on, Black Prince, my chariot awaits." Arm in arm they walked out the back door and around to the Porsche.

FRIDAY, OCTOBER 18

OPENING NIGHT! Butterflies were doing the Riverdance in Meri's stomach. The doorbell chimed.

"I'll get it!" Chelsea yelled.

"Mommy! Mommy!" Meridith looked over the balcony to see an enormous bouquet of deep lavender-blue roses brought into the foyer. She ran down the long flight of twisting stairs, breathless at the bottom.

"Who's it from?"

"Sign here," the boy extended a clipboard. Closing the door, she looked for a card.

"Here it is, Mom," Chelsea handed over the envelope.

"It's from the cast," she lied.

"Wow," Chelsea exclaimed as she accompanied the bouquet into the kitchen with Marina.

The card actually read:

"I understand I should tell you to Break a Leg.
Break all the hearts instead—but mine.
Blue roses and purple shadows echo a blue rendezvous.
This gentleman caller remains in love with you.
Tony."

She slipped it in her pocket. "The food just got delivered for the party, Misses."

"That's wonderful! She kissed Marina on her soft cheek, picked up her bags and fled to the garage.

THE AUDIENCE sat mesmerized as *A Streetcar Named Desire* journeyed through the sad world of New Orleans in the forties. Meridith's portrayal of Blanche DuBois, the haggard and fragile, southern beauty, was chilling. Now, as the play headed towards its cruel climax, they watched Blanche's last grasp at happiness being destroyed. Stanley, Stella's barbarian of a husband, talks Stella into having her sister committed to an asylum. Stanley brutally raped Blanche earlier and now wants the delicate woman out of his house.

The curtain closed to a moment of silence as the audience sat spellbound. But, as it reopened for the curtain-call, the applause was instantaneous and thunderous. Each character appeared from the wings to bravos and cheers. When Joe ran in from stage left, the clamor grew louder. He held out his hand to Meri as the audience jumped to their feet in an ovation she would remember all the days of her life.

As the actors joined hands for their final bow, a uniformed man approached the stage carrying a basket of flowers more at home in the winner's circle of a race track. It dwarfed the carrier.

"Oh, no," Meri whispered as the man handed the basket to her. The cast was shell-shocked. Nothing like this happens at a North Lake Players production.

"Are you kidding?" Joe asked Meri as the curtains closed and the applause died down.

"Hey, look what's back here!" Gillian called out to the cast and crew. Bottles of chilled champagne and boxes of Godiva chocolate lined the dressing room tables.

"Wow! Who did this?" Paul asked over the cheering.

"I don't know. They just materialized during the final scene. This is the way I found it!" Gillian was in shock.

"Well, whoever you are, this one's for you!" Joe toasted as he began filling glasses.

"Hear! Hear!" Gillian joined in, upending her glass.

Meri stood at the entrance to the green room enjoying the moment. As the champagne was passed she saw the label—*Perrier-Jouët*. She knew who was responsible, and she loved him for it. "Some people *have* money, and some people *enjoy* it." She held up her own glass and silently toasted their benefactor.

THE PARTY was in high gear by the time Meridith drove into the garage. Cars lined the streets surrounding her home, and the music could be heard from the curb.

"Here she is!" Greetings of congratulations were shouted over the roar of the party as she made her way through the house. Groups gathered in every room, enjoying the food, the spirits, and the view from the bluff. As she picked up bits of the conversations she heard good comments on the play and theatre talk in general.

"Mommy, you were wonderful!" Chelsea was in the kitchen, nibbling on the dessert tray.

"Thank you, honey. Did you like the show? You weren't upset with some of the scenes, were you?"

"Of course not. I told you before, Mom, I'm not a baby." Meri kissed her and joined her in desecrating the icing off the pastries. They shared a secret laugh.

"Where's Hunter?"

"Upstairs with Scott. They took their food up to play Nintendo."

"Is this what big stars do after opening night?" It was Tony in her kitchen.

She tried to say something, but the cream filling oozed out of the pastry leaving behind the chocolate frosting. He wiped the cream off her mouth with his thumb. "It seems we stood and talked like this before," he smiled and licked it from his hand.

"—And laughed before." She finished the song lyric.

"—But I can't remember where or when. We have another thing in common." Meri surveyed the room. People were absorbed in their own dialogues, no one seemed to notice.

"It's strange to be here," Tony commented.

"Not as strange as having you here," she returned the volley.

"You were absolutely marvelous! I watched you up on stage, and you were transformed into that character. I totally believed you."

"Thank you, that means a lot." She was glowing. "Oh! And thank you so much for the champagne. It was the most incredible moment."

"Who do they think arranged it?"

"An angel, which of course, you are." She wanted to hold him close. "So, you liked the production?"

"Absolutely! I see a lot of theatre downtown and, quite honestly, I wasn't expecting … well, you know, Meri, *but*, it was absolutely wonderful. Very professional. Of course, I wanted to kill that guy during the last scene. Had to keep reminding myself he was only an actor. But when he kissed you, I had to walk out in the lobby." Meri smiled coyly. She couldn't remember Jonathan ever being jealous.

"Speaking of that guy, let me introduce you," Meri interrupted as she saw Joe approaching. "Joe, I'd like you to meet a good friend of mine, Tony Romano. Tony, my fellow thespian, Joe Stevenson."

"I was just telling Meri how much I enjoyed the show," Tony told Joe as he shook his hand. Joe's reticence turned to pride.

"Tony mentioned that he sees a lot of theatre, and he thought we were very *professional*." Meri knew that would bait Joe.

"I'm always surprised when people use the word *professional* to an artist of any kind. You realize that there are no talent tests, and being paid doesn't necessarily make one good?"

For the first time since Meridith had known Tony Romano, he seemed taken aback, but he quickly recovered, "Yes, but do you know the word *amateur* comes from the Latin word, *amor*, meaning *for the love of!*"

"My high school Latin teacher would be ashamed of me for missing that," Joe smiled.

Tony continued, "One of my favorite musicals is *A Chorus Line,* and I was always taken with the song, *'What I Did For Love'.* All I can say is, what you did this evening definitely ranked right up there with any professional production I've ever seen. You obviously love the theatre, and the theatre is very lucky to have you both."

Joe was more than appeased. "Thanks. Look, it was great meeting you, but I've got to get something to eat before I crash. Great party, Meri," and he was off to the buffet table.

"Did you have something to eat?" Meri asked Tony.

"What I'd really like is a glass of wine. Let's try and make our way to the bar." She started to take Tony's hand but stopped short of touching him. As the two inched their way through the crowd, Meridith realized Jonathan was staring. Thinking quickly she took Tony's arm and guided him towards her husband. When Tony caught Jonathan's eye, he stopped abruptly.

"Go on," Meridith urged, "you have to talk to him, otherwise, it will look funny."

"Jonathan," Tony offered his hand.

"I didn't realize you took an interest in theatre, especially out here in the burbs." Jonathan's voice was flat. Meridith recognized the look in his eye and saw the tumbler of scotch in his fist. A small bead of sweat appeared across his upper lip.

"I love all the arts, Mr. Chamberlain, and I quite enjoyed the production this evening. Tennessee Williams is a favorite of mine, and, when your lovely wife mentioned she was starring in *Streetcar,* I made a note to attend. She was gracious enough to ask me to your party when I congratulated her backstage." Jonathan looked from Tony to Meridith but said nothing. He gulped the remainder of the amber liquor and walked away.

"He knows," Meri stated as Jonathan walked out of earshot.

"What now?" he asked. Meri shrugged.

"Meridith Chamberlain! Isn't it enough you get all the plum parts and have the most wonderful home, but do you have to monopolize the party's handsomest man, too?" She was startled by the voice of Lanie Flowers. "Introduce me, and tell me all about him!"

"Lanie, Tony," is all Meri said before he was stolen away by the gregarious woman and reintroduced to the group of women standing in wait. The community theatre attracted a myriad of single and divorced women. Meridith watched with admiration, slightly tinged with envy, as each of the woman attempted to flirt with the eligible, extremely attractive, new man. Several times he caught her eye and gave her an I'd-rather-be-with-you-look, but she just smiled and nodded.

As the party wore down, Meri grew more fatigued. Jonathan disappeared. She was hoping that she would find him asleep in the den.

"Misses, party is almost over. My husband here to pick me up. Okay if I leave?" Marina asked politely.

"Of course! Marina, you did a marvelous job." Meri led the way back to kitchen where she fished a bill out of her purse. She handed it to Marina. "You've done so many extra things lately I want you to have a little bonus. Thank you again, Marina, and have a nice Sunday with your family."

"Thank you, Misses," Marina kissed her cheek. "Oh, and, Misses? Mr. Romano is a real nice man." Meri looked at her maid curiously. "He give me a little something, too. He said to take good care of you and the kids." Marina's husband appeared at the back door, and she picked up her shopping bag, leaving Meri wondering when she would stop being astonished by this new man.

"I have to go, too, Mrs. Chamberlain." It was Tony.

She looked to see who was standing nearby. "You are something, do you know that? Marina just told me that you gave her extra money."

"I want to make sure you and the children are well taken care of."

"And money ensures that?"

"Money ensures *almost* everything," his eyes were teasing her.

"Thank you so much for *everything*," she returned his look. He surveyed the kitchen area then grabbed her arm and pulled her out the back door where they were immediately greeted by the cold wind.

"I've wanted to do this all night," he whispered and then kissed her so deeply she forgot where she was. Suddenly, the back door opened—then slammed shut. Tony, still holding Meri, stared at it.

"Who do you think that was?" Tony asked her.

"I don't know. You'd better go." Meridith's heart was pounding.

"I'm sorry, Meri. I hope I haven't caused any problems. I'll walk around, my car is parked on the street."

"I'll be fine. Do you have the limo waiting?"

"No, my Porsche. Promise me one thing. You'll call if there is any problem?"

"I promise, but I'll be fine. I'm sure it wasn't Jonathan, or he would have created a scene." Tony kissed her lightly and disappeared into the darkness.

THE PARTY ended and Jonathan never reappeared. Meri looked in on her sleeping children and then walked down the hall to her own room. She entered and touched the light switch just as a hand met her face with a loud and painful *smack*. She fell back against the wall, more from surprise than force.

"Jonathan!"

"You two-timing, fucking bitch! How could you?" Meridith knew Jonathan had opened the door.

"Jonathan, please, I never meant for it to happen." She steadied herself. Her mind raced. She didn't want the police here, but how could she diffuse the situation?

"Jonathan, you're in no mood to discuss this calmly. Please, leave me alone, and we'll talk tomorrow." He stood, appraising her with a hate she'd never seen before. "Jonathan?" He walked towards her, slowly. Then, in an instant, he grabbed her shoulders with both hands and shook her.

"You god-damned bitch! I saw Hunter's jacket. He told me about Sunday. How could you involve *my* children?" He shook her again. "The flowers. I'm not blind, I saw the way the two of you looked at each other. Right here in my own house. Pardon me, *your* house." Meridith's fear was growing with each second. "You think you'll divorce me, and I'll walk away. You pay off my debts, and I'll go away. Is that the plan. Did you think I am a fool? That I didn't know what you were planning?

"Well, the shoe is on the other foot now, my little *actress*. Let's see how the court looks at an adulteress wife. I'll get the kids *and* the money. Want to talk deal now?" His grip was so firm, she felt her hands tingling.

"It's not like that! It was just a kiss, that's all." He let go of her arm long enough to free his right hand and smacked her face again—hard. With his left hand still holding on to her, the force of the hit caused her neck to jerk painfully.

"Stop it now! Jonathan!" She tasted a trickle of blood that ran down her mouth where she'd bit her lip. It triggered a strength that came from deep in her psyche. She clinched her fist and right-crossed his jaw, knocking him down.

"You're not worth the effort," he spewed, picking himself off the floor. The revulsion she felt couldn't be measured. He turned his back to her and walked out of the room. She wanted to call Tony, but she knew what he would do. As much as she hated Jonathan, a part of her was terribly frightened by the thought of Tony's wrath. She remembered what he'd told her he'd do to anyone who hurt her. Threat or no threat, there was no doubt in her mind, Tony would kill her husband if he knew.

She stepped into the shower stall and felt the pinpricks of hot water sooth her aching body. Meridith methodically began to plan her own revenge.

SATURDAY, OCTOBER 19

THE MORNING SUN streamed across her face. As Meri threw her arm over her eyes to shut out the light, she felt the pain of her tender jaw. The reality of the night before came flooding back. She walked into the bathroom as the phone rang.

"Hello?"

"Have you seen the *Tribune*?" It was Paul Winston, the Director.

"No, I just woke up." The clock read nine eighteen.

"You won't believe it! Richard Christiansen was there and reviewed the show and, Meri, he loved it! We've never been reviewed by the *Chicago Tribune*! Did you know he was going to be there? Who invited him?"

Meridith was overwhelmed. "Calm down, Paul. Let me read it, and I'll call you back."

"Hurry. I've got to call Joe. I can't believe it. He loved my direction!"

He hung up. Meri shook her head trying to make sense of his call. The *Tribune*? There was only one answer: Tony.

She took a minute to survey her face. A purple bruise was growing along from her left ear to her mouth. Her right hand was sore, but remembering how she'd injured it made her feel much better. Throwing a robe on, she ran downstairs.

Chelsea was watching cartoons with a bowl of cereal. Hunter and Scott had warmed up leftovers from the party.

"Hey, Mom, you were pretty good last night," Hunter confessed.

"Thanks, honey. I hope I didn't embarrass you." She smiled as she poured coffee.

"Naw, I've seen you in plays before."

Meri unfolded the paper, turning to the "Tempo" section. There, on the front page was the headline:

A Sturdy "Streetcar" Still Cranks

That old but still powerful "A Streetcar Named Desire" really rumbles along in a surprising place—The North Lake Community House. Tennessee Williams' drama opened with a high-volume roar. Director Paul Winston gave his standing-room-only audience a faithful, sturdy, sometimes stirring retelling of the story.

Leading lady, Meridith Chamberlain, gave a diaphanous portrait of Blanche DuBois. Amidst the ear-splitting burst of New Orleans jazz and the cranking and groaning of the symbolic streetcar, Blanche appears in a bit of stillness, all in white, wandering unwittingly into the street called Elysian Fields. A few surprise line readings added extra pop to her dialogue.

The review went on to praise the work of her co-star, Joe Stevenson, and the other cast members. It even gave mention to the work of the designers. Meridith reread it a second time. Then the phone started: Joe, then Brooke, then Lanie. Everyone was elated! She walked to her desk looking for scissors when she discovered a sealed envelope taped to the computer screen. She opened it and read:

"Meridith: Obviously, there is nothing left between us. I'm moving to my father's house and will bring the rest of my things later. Bob will represent me, all correspondence should go through him.

I can not stop you from seeing Tony Romano, but keep him away

126

from my children. I don't have to remind you what the consequences could be. Believe me, I will find out. Jonathan."

Meridith sat down and stared at the neat penmanship. The roller coaster ride continued to careen around hidden curves.

SATURDAY, OCTOBER 19

SATURDAY NIGHT'S performance was electric. The cast was so energized by their *downtown review* they were off the charts! By the time they took their last curtain call, Meridith felt like she could sleep for a year. Groups gathered to decide where they were going as Meri headed for her car. "Meri? You're coming with us?"

"Sorry, I'm really tired." She drove home with an ache in her heart. The house had an eerie feeling to it. Chelsea was with Brooke and Hunter was at the McBride's. Meridith set the alarm and went up to a hot bath and bed feeling terribly alone and sad.

MONDAY, OCTOBER 21

"I NEED TO BE totally candid with you." Meridith began as soon as the amenities were dispensed with.

"I'm your lawyer, anything you tell me is privileged." He braced himself for news he wasn't sure he wanted to hear.

"Jonathan may have something to use against me."

"I don't know, Meridith. The inheritance laws are pretty much in your favor, and your corporate attorneys have you well protected."

"Jonathan is going to accuse me of having an affair." Barry was quiet. His heart was beating double-time. He hadn't wanted to know this.

"Illinois is still a No-Fault Divorce State. But if he makes this accusation, and can prove it, it will hurt your custody battle. He'll hold you up for the money using the children as his weapon. Some of the older judges are still archaic in their rulings, despite the women's movement."

Meri sat studying her hands. "What should I do?"

"The fact that he moved out is in your favor. Can he prove anything?" Barry refrained from asking the obvious: was it true?

"Nothing, really. More suspicions and innuendoes."

"Meridith, all I can do is advise you. Be very careful. We're not only talking about millions of dollars but about your safety. Are you sure there's nothing you would like me to do to keep him away from you?"

"I think it would just make it worse."

"Do you want me to begin divorce proceedings?" She nodded. A tear rolled down her face. "Are you all right?"

"I'll be fine." She believed that.

Now he nodded. What an incredible woman, he thought. He wondered just how much of a bastard Jonathan Chamberlain really was. Barry Ellison knew one thing for certain: Chamberlain was a fool, and he would hand Meridith her husband's head before this was over.

FRIDAY, OCTOBER 25

DOLF CASHIANO and Silvio Masucchi, two men of tremendous power and immense girth, sat in the Rosebud Restaurant. Masucchi had spent a week in Chicago lining up his votes and fostering his power base. Now he was back to put his plan into action.

"Can I get you anything else?" the waitress asked incredulously. The men had eaten plate after plate of pasta, veal Parmesan and cheese ravioli.

"What's for dessert?" Dolf asked.

"What would you like? We've got gelato, Italian cheesecake, chocolate cream pie—"

"Tell you what. Bring us a slice of everything, and we'll pick at it while we talk," Masucchi suggested. Dolf nodded. Finally, a man who understood eating. Dolf was sick of the new breed of health nuts, always worried about their weight and cholesterol. These were the same pansies that wanted the Organization to go straight. Fuck 'em.

"Oh, honey, bring us the pot of coffee, too." The woman shook her head as she walked to the kitchen. She hoped these guys tipped as good as they ate.

"So ya ready to leave the bright lights of Vegas and join me here in Chicago if I take over?" Masucchi asked Dolf.

"Yeah, Vegas is great, but there's too much heat, too many eyes watching to make a decent living any more. There's more room to move around here."

Masucchi admired the man's candor. He knew he could speak his mind. "We've got to get Romano out of *El Duce's* seat. He's too soft. I know he's supposed to be connected, but he's never made his bones." The reference was to the fact that Romano had never actually killed anyone. Masucchi continued, "The Russians are moving in fast, and they're mean sons-of-bitches. They'll take over if we're not tougher. We've already lost almost all the drug business. If Romano has his way, we'll be listed on the stock exchange."

"What would you do?" Dolf asked, using his fork to scrape the last of the chocolate off his plate.

"Aw, a few big raids. A few dead bodies floatin' down the Chicago River and we'll have the respect back we deserve. All we have to do is git rid of Romano."

"So, what are we going to do with him? How're you gonna take him out? It won't be easy." Dolf asked, generously pouring sugar into his coffee.

"I wasn't sure until I heard that Chamberlain left his wife. Then it hit me! It's so simple it's almost too easy." Masucchi laughed loudly. He had found the ally he needed in Dolf. The man had no conscience and could be trusted to carry out his plan without going to any of the other people in the Organization. By the time Romano was dead, Masucchi's people would be in control and the new faction would be on their way out.

"Chamberlain never did pay back the mill. He says he talked his father into holding back on the Crime Bill but, who knows. I say we go to him and offer to take out Romano *and* his unfaithful wife for the money. Kill two birds with the same bullet, so to speak."

"Or at least the same gun," Dolf laughed at his own joke. "I get it. We get rid of Romano and get paid to do it. Wow." Masucchi accepted Dolf's appreciation of his plan.

"Then Chamberlain gets his wife's money, and we get him. Pipeline to his old man in Congress and to the Carolina Tobacco Company all in one fell shot. Or maybe two."

"We need to keep him in line. Keep him tied to the murders."

"The guy's straight. I'll wear a wire when we make the deal. Then he's ours."

"That seems too easy." The dessert tray rested on a stand between the two men. Dolf picked up a plate of cheese cake and scraped the tiramisu on top of it. He forked a huge bite into his mouth.

"Sometimes, you've got luck on your side," Masucchi told his partner through a mouthful of whipped cream. He patted his own side, feeling the automatic pistol nestled under his arm.

SATURDAY, OCTOBER 26 • AFTERNOON

SILVIO MASUCCHI and Dolf Cashiano drove up to the Congressman's house just a few miles south of Meridith's, on Sheridan Road. The home was a red brick colonial complete with white Grecian columns bearing the weight of the second story. A brass knocker engraved *Chamberlain* punctuated the oversized front doors.

"Some joint, huh?" Dolf asked Masucchi.

"They say the rich ain't any different from you and me. That's a laugh!" Masucchi lived in Brooklyn, in a small apartment he shared with his girlfriend and her mother.

"Who knows, Silvie, when we take over Chicago, maybe we'll come out and live here on the North Shore. Think dey'd notice a couple a dagos like us in da middle of all dis white Wonder Bread?" His Brooklyn accent made him sound Runyonesque. Masucchi turned off the motor on his rented Lincoln. A weary looking woman opened the front door.

"No salesmen allowed," she told them.

"We ain't salesmen, lady. We're here to see the Congressman's son, Jonathan Chamberlain."

"Do you have an appointment?" She was brandishing a broom like a baseball bat. They got out of the car and approached her.

"No. Tell him two of Tony Romano's associates are here to see him. He'll see us, I guarantee it." She closed the door.

"What if he won't see us?" Dolf asked as the door reopened. Jonathan Chamberlain stood there looking apprehensive.

"Mr. Chamberlain, you don't know us, but we're associates of Tony Romano." Jonathan said nothing, so Masucchi continued, "We think you might be interested in a little proposition we have. Can we talk?"

"We'll talk out back." The men walked around the house to a patio that overlooked a private beach. Here riparian property leveled from steep bluffs to more traditional beach front.

"Wow!" Dolf let out a long wolf-whistle.

"Okay, guys, what's this all about?" Jonathan asked abruptly. Masucchi was enjoying the moment. He knew Jonathan was uncomfortable but was either afraid to ask them to leave or curious.

"Let's get right to the point, Mr. Chamberlain. We know that you and the misses have split, and we know why. Tony Romano." Jonathan winced but remained quiet. "We don't like Romano any more than you do. So, what are we going to do about him?"

"What makes you think I could do anything? Even if I wanted to." Jonathan told the fat men. Leaves cluttered the stone patio, and Dolf kicked at them, childlike. Jonathan's nose was starting to run from the cold, and he pulled a linen handkerchief from his pocket. Masucchi thought that Chamberlain and Romano were poured from the same mold— pansies, both of 'em, scared to get their hands dirty. He'd show them, he'd show them all, he thought.

"How'd you like to have Romano gone?" Masucchi dove in.

"From Chicago?" Jonathan asked.

"From the planet." Masucchi smiled evilly.

"Why ask me? If you want him gone, what does that have to do with me?"

The man wasn't as foolish as Masucchi first thought.

"Because we could arrange an accident that could include a certain married lady. I think that would leave you with all the Whitney money, stock and the kids. We call it Italian divorce. Interested?"

Jonathan's heart beat faster. The chill he was feeling had nothing to do with the temperature. He chewed on the inside of his cheek. For five long minutes the only sound was the wind blowing off the lake, bending the stripped trees, and a dog barking further down the beach.

"I have to think about this," Jonathan finally stated flatly.

"Sure, sure. This is a big decision, and we wouldn't want you to make up your mind in a hurry. You think, and we'll be in touch." Masucchi rose from the sling chair that bent beneath his weight, and the two walked back around to their car.

Jonathan watched them disappear around the house. He leaned against the big tree, staring out at the lake, gnawing on his thumb nail.

"The trap is baited," Masucchi told his sidekick. "All we have to do now is wait for the call."

"You think he'll go for it?"

"No doubt. The man's desperate, and we've given him an easy out."

"But you didn't say nuthin' about the money."

"Too soon. Let him think about it—and want it. Then we hit him with the money. A good salesman makes the customer want the product—bad—before he quotes the price. Never fails."

"But why should he need his wife's money, the guy looks pretty good off hisself. Did'ya see that house." He whistled.

"Did ya ever hear the story about the guy that walks into the bar and sits down next to the gorgeous broad? He asks her if she'd go to bed with him for a million bucks. 'A million dollars?' she asks. He says 'Yeah, a million bucks.' So she smiles and says 'For a million, I guess I would.' The he asks her 'How about for a nickel?' She gets mad and says 'What kinda girl do you think I am?" And he says, 'We already know that, now we're gonna negotiate the price.'"

Dolf laughed out loud at the old joke. "So, what's your point?" he asked.

Masucchi frowned. "The point is, everybody has a price. That's why the Organization is where it is today. There ain't nobody that don't got a price. Chamberlain will think about having all her money and, then, he's ours."

"Have you thought how we're goin' do it?" Dolf liked the way the man's mind worked.

"Not exactly. One of his boys, Frankie Delvecchio, is with me. That'll work for us. But now that I know I can suck in Chamberlain and have some cash, it'll come to me. Hey, you hungry? Let's find a place to eat, that'll help me think."

Dolf was glad he'd hooked up with Masucchi. The man was good. And tough, Dolf liked that. He was tired of pretty boys with manicured nails, afraid to get their hands dirty. It was going to be like the old days once again. He sat back and enjoyed the ride along Lake Shore Drive, watching the city skyline appear and grow larger as they traveled south looking for a good place to eat.

SATURDAY, OCTOBER 26

AS MERIDITH LEFT the theatre, she ached from exhaustion. The performance had gone well and heavy make-up had covered the tender bruises. As she walked, unnoticed, out to her car, she discovered a note slipped discreetly under her windshield wiper. It read: *"Meri, Please meet me at the Carousel. We need to talk. T."* She looked around the parking lot but saw only theatre people gathered in small groups and cars idling.

Secure that the children were asleep and tended by Marina, the car drove itself towards Waukegan Road.

Tony was waiting outside. "Meri! Thank you for meeting me, I know you're tired, but we need to talk. Are you hungry?"

"No, but I do need something to drink."

"First—" As his mouth met hers, she wrapped her arms around his neck and pulled him closer, passionately returning his kiss. She felt his body respond but he pushed her gently away.

"We'd better go in before it's too late," he winked and ignited fireworks in her stomach. Reluctantly, she allowed herself to be escorted into the back room of the Carousel.

"So, what's the scoop?" she teased.

"Seriously, Meri, something's up." The private room was set up with salad, soup bowls filled with steaming minestrone, and hot bread. He never failed to amaze her.

"There are two men, one from New York, the other from Vegas, who are trying to take over Chicago. They've been in town recently, stirring up trouble. Today they went to see Jonathan." He picked up and inspected his wine.

"Why?"

"I don't know. Have you spoken with him?"

"No. How do you know he moved out?" she asked, her glass poised. Tony looked uncomfortable.

"I've had someone watching the house." He saw the look on her face. "Wait. Before you explode, it's for your own safety. And the children's, believe me."

Meridith's pulse raced and she chewed her lower lip. Her anger mixed with anxiety. "Am I not safe?" she asked quietly.

"I don't know, but better to err on the side of caution. Between Jonathan's temper and what is going on inside the Organization ... Meri, they know you and I have been seeing each other."

Oh, my God, what have I done? she asked herself. "So you don't know what they want with Jonathan?"

"I believe they are trying to use my relationship with you to get him to do something. I'll find out, believe me." His jaw was working.

Meri finished her wine, trying to calm her frayed nerves. "What should I do?" she asked.

"Nothing. Let me handle this. I promise you, Meri, you and the children are not in danger. Believe me, I would kill anyone who hurt you."

The scary thing was, she did believe him.

SUNDAY, OCTOBER 28

"IT STINKS, BOSS. What it smells like to me, is a power struggle." Frankie finished his account and sat back. Tony Romano and Frankie Delvecchio were seated in Tony's penthouse. Tony wasn't sure who he could trust these days. Frankie always came across as a standup guy, but then, he couldn't be too careful.

"So, Silvio Masucchi and Dolf Cashiano want Chamberlain to give them a million bucks to have Meridith and me bumped off. Then they take over." Just saying Meri's name in connection with her murder made Tony's blood run cold and his temper burn hot. He walked over to the bar and poured Courvoisier into his coffee. "Want something?" he asked Frankie. Frankie joined him at the bar, hoisting himself onto one of the brass stools, and poured brandy into his cup.

Tony took a Cuban from his locked humidor, carefully unwrapped it and savored the aroma, deep in thought. Frankie remained quiet, watching his boss finger the phallic-shaped stogie. "How're they going to do it?" Tony finally broke the silence.

"I don't think they know, they're waiting to hear from Chamberlain. They don't have the money yet. They just wanted to know if I was in or out, they're testing me—to see if I say anything to you. They're not brain surgeons, these guys. I'll tell you one thing, though. They really want to go back to the days when shoot-outs settled disputes and bloody bodies floated in the river. Talking to them is an experience."

Tony handed the cigar to Frankie who looked overly appreciative. Tony's mouth was too sour to smoke now. "Look," Tony began walking to the window. "Make these guys think you're going along with them. Tell them you hate my guts. See who they've got lined up on their side. I need to know where I stand. Find out as many details as you can, but, whatever you do, Frankie, promise me one thing. If anything happens to me, you'll do whatever you have to do to keep Meridith Chamberlain safe. Go to the feds if you have to." He turned to face his *paesan.*

"Promise me!"

Frankie had never seen his boss like this before. "Sure, boss, sure."

"I'm putting five hundred thou in an off-shore account in the Cayman's, in your name. I'll call the bank and have the account ready for you this afternoon. This is to ensure your loyalty. Make no mistake, Frankie, I'll always take care of you. If you go with these guys, they'll take care of you all right. You'll be one of the floating bodies. They won't leave any witnesses, and they won't let anyone who was once loyal to me live."

Frankie was suddenly very aware of the dangerous waters he treaded. "Maybe," he thought, "I'll just disappear when this shit goes down." Chicago winters were getting to him, and he could live like a king on some island in the Bahamas on the money. Frankie thought that if he could just make it through this, he'd be okay. "Boss, I came to you with this because I wanted to. The money is great, but I'd have done the same thing without it. I promise I'll make sure the lady is safe." Tony stared out the window, watching the fog descend over the skyscrapers.

"All right, Frankie, you did real good." Frankie waited until he was in the hall to light up. Sucking hard on the cigar, his head reeled.

MONDAY, OCTOBER 28

JONATHAN CHAMBERLAIN had not slept or eaten much, despite Margaret's attempt to entice him with food. Franklin's housekeeper wanted to call his doctor but that suggestion was met with an upended glass of Glenfiddich, single malt scotch.

"Congressman, I don't know what to do for him," she told Franklin when he called.

"Thank you for your concern, Margaret, put him on the phone."

"Mr. Chamberlain, it's your father." She walked to the library where he sat, staring out the window.

"Tell him I can't talk right now, Margaret."

"But sir—"

"Tell him, Margaret!" She backed quickly out of the room.

"He won't speak with you, Congressman, and, I don't know what to do."

"I'll call Meridith and his doctor. Don't worry, everything will be fine." As he hung up, he wished that he believed that. Just as Margaret hung up the phone, it rang again.

"I wanna speak to Jonathan Chamberlain." The voice was insistent.

"He's not talking calls right now. Would you like to leave a message?"

"He'll talk to me. Tell him it's Masu—Tell him it's the guy he spoke with on Saturday. He'll know"

"Mr. Chamberlain?"

"I don't want to talk to anyone."

"I know, sir, and I tried to tell him, but he said you would want to talk to him."

"Him? Who?" Jonathan was annoyed.

"The man who was here on Saturday. I didn't catch his name." Jonathan dropped his glass, spilling what little scotch was left.

"I'll take it in here," Jonathan told her, ignoring the spill. He grabbed the cordless phone.

"Yes, sir." Margaret didn't like this and made a note to tell the Congressman.

"Chamberlain," Jonathan barked into the receiver.

"Hello, Jonathan." Masucchi was savoring the moment. "Have you had a chance to think about our—offer?"

"I don't want to talk on the phone? Where can we meet?"

Masucchi was not a big fan of technology, either. "There's a gentleman's health club in Cicero, we can meet in the steam room. The name of the place is Jack's Gym, right off Cicero Avenue. Think you can find the place?"

"I'll find it. When?"

"Wednesday, eight o'clock. Place is pretty empty by then. And, Chamberlain, no tricks, no wires, no cops. This is just a hypothetical discussion we're having. Understood?"

"I understand. Jack's Gym, in Cicero on Wednesday night." He hung up.

"Margaret, I'm going to lie down for a while. No calls."

"Yes, sir." Margaret watched him climb the winding staircase. His face was ashen and dark circles punctuated his lifeless eyes. "Dear Lord, help him," she prayed as his door shut out the world.

WEDNESDAY, OCTOBER 30

JACK'S GYM smelled like a high school locker room: sweat, dirty socks, mildew. The odor assaulted Jonathan as he entered the arena area. Two black men were sparring in trunks and helmets, a small rivet of blood ran from one's mouth. He didn't seem to notice. Onlookers shouted. Most of the exercise equipment went unused at this hour. He could smell strong chlorine, there must be an indoor pool.

"Help ya, buddy?" A squat man asked him. Jonathan's expensive trench coat labeled him an outsider.

"I'm supposed to meet someone in the steam room." The little guy, dressed in a sweat shirt with the gym's name across it, scrunched his face in skepticism.

"Steam room is through those doors, through the massage room, then turn left." He shrugged at a young black man who had ceased pummeling the punching bag to stare at Jonathan. Chamberlain walked through the double doors and stopped abruptly. There, in the massage room, lying on the table, naked under a sheet, was the immense form of Masucchi. He was being rubbed-down by a man almost as large, dressed in a "Jack's Gym" tee shirt.

"Hey, Chamberlain, we'll meet here." Jonathan looked around. Dolf was seated nearby finishing a sandwich.

"I thought you said—" he didn't finish the sentence. Jonathan wasn't worried about being overheard because he didn't plan to say anything that could later be used against him. I might be desperate, he thought, but I should have learned something from fucking law school.

"Take off your coat, have a massage." Masucchi offered.

"No, thanks," Jonathan said flatly as he slipped off the heavy coat.

"That wasn't a suggestion." Masucchi ordered. The masseuse turned, folded his massive arms across his chest, and waited while Jonathan unbuttoned his shirt. When he was stripped down to his underwear, he stated, "I'm leaving these on."

"Suit yourself," Masucchi answered. Jonathan climbed on the narrow table and uttered an "oomph" as the man began his intense rubdown.

"You're really tense," the masseuse commented.

"Maybe we can help," Masucchi began, sitting up on the table next to Chamberlain's, with the sheet barely covering his lap. His breasts hung like an old woman's, resting on the folds of his massive belly. The hair on his chest was graying and curly, like used steel wool. Sweat poured from Masucchi's many chins and he wiped his face on the sheet. As the burly man began his assault on Jonathan, his muscles tensed against the man's hands.

Masucchi spoke, "Romano, that fucking bastard, is as big a pain-in-the-ass to us as he is to you. That's why we can help one another. Dolf," he shouted to his friend, "bring a beer, I'm hotter than hell. You want something?" Jonathan mumbled a *no*.

"We would like to make Romano disappear. The trouble is, we need a little dough to get the job done right." At the mention of money, Jonathan's stomach knotted as tightly as his shoulder muscles. He sat upright.

"Look, let's get something straight. I don't have any money, and I'm not going to pay to have your problems taken care of. So, if that's your angle, we can end this fiasco right now."

"Take it easy, Chamberlain, you're much too tense. Let the man finish, you'll feel better."

"No thanks. I've had enough! This meeting is finished." He jumped from the table, but the masseuse blocked his path.

Dolf was on his feet. "The meeting is over when I damn well say it's over, Chamberlain, so just take it easy." Crumbs fell from his generous lap as he waited for word from the large, naked man on the table.

"Listen you fuckin' prick." Masucchi punched his sausage-sized finger into Chamberlain's chest. "We know you have no money. It's all your wife's or your father's dough. But we know if your old lady divorces you, you get nothing. Which, according to the word is on the street, she *is* going to do. So, we're doing you a favor. If she and her new lover happen to suffer a little—accident, you get everything—the kids, the house, the money, the stocks. That's what we're offering you."

Masucchi stopped talking long enough to wipe under his arms. "Once the money is yours, we'd just like to be remembered."

Jonathan's temper was now overshadowed by fear. He grabbed Masucchi's sweat-drenched rubbery arm. "Don't ever touch me again, you son of a bitch. I understand the proposition. I understood it yesterday. I kept this meeting to see if you were sent by Romano or the cops. I'm not going to be set up again." Jonathan grabbed his clothes in his fist and turned to Masucchi. "I'm not ready to make this decision. Call me in a week."

Once through the door, he stepped into his pants and shoes, threw his shirt on and reached his arms into his coat, forgoing buttons. He felt his car keys in the pocket and fled through the arena to the outside world. His car, parked at the curb, had a bright orange parking ticket tucked under the wiper. Swearing, he unlocked the door, slid in and squealed the tires speeding away. He breathed deeply to rid his head of the stench.

"So, what now?" Dolf asked, handing Masucchi a cold beer.

"We wait. I'm telling you, he's ours," the fat man told him as he greedily sucked on the brown bottle. "Patience, my man, and we'll have it all."

FRIDAY, NOVEMBER 8

THE WEEKS passed tortuously slow for Jonathan. What little sleep he managed to steal was tormented by nightmares. He kept remembering the early years with Meridith: the feel of her skin, the sound of her laughter, the murmurs of her love-making. He couldn't pinpoint exactly when it had gone wrong or why, only that it had.

"Hello?" He heard the throaty lilt of her voice through the receiver.

"Meri?"

"Jonathan? How are you." Franklin's call had worried her, but she refused to play nursemaid anymore.

"I've been better," he honestly admitted. "How are the children?"

"They're fine. I told them you were staying at Franklin's for a while. They know more than we'd like to think." A long pause.

"Look, Meridith, may I see you? We need to talk."

"I don't know, Jonathan. All our talks seem to end up in an argument, and I really don't need that. This is the last weekend of my show. Maybe Sunday?"

"How's your show going?"

"Great. Did you see the review in the Trib?" I even got an invitation to audition for Steppenwolf Theatre."

"I'm impressed. Maybe I'll come tonight, if you don't mind." There was a pause on the other end. Jonathan felt his pulse race. "May we could go for a drink afterward?"

"No. But I will have a late supper with you. No alcohol."

"All right," he smiled. "How about that little seafood place in Highwood?"

"That would be nice. I'll meet you after the show." Maybe there was still something worth salvaging.

"And, Meri, break a leg." She was surprised he remembered that expression. "Thanks."

JONATHAN WATCHED the production with feelings ranging from pride to remorse and regret. He winced watching Meridith's face during the rape scene. He was glad when the final curtain closed and quickly walked outside and breathed the cool into his tight lungs. His heart swelled when he saw Meri emerge from the side door of the theatre.

"You were terrific," he told her honestly. "I'd forgotten how good you really are."

She smiled and slid into the open car door.

The ride to Highwood, about twenty minutes north along Sheridan Road, was a pretty one. Dinner at the small, dimly lit restaurant was pleasant. Meri asked about his trip to Washington and his father.

"D.C. is so beautiful at the change of seasons. We'll have to take the children this spring. They haven't been in a while and my father loves to show them around."

"And show them off," Meri added.

"And show them off," he agreed. Maybe there was hope. Maybe he could dismiss those thugs and get his life back to where it was just a few months ago. Maybe.

"Jonathan, I need to go, I'm tired. I have one more performance."

"Sure, honey." Maybe his life was returning to normal.

AS THE WINDING road curved into Winnetka, Jonathan asked, "Should I just take you home, or do you want to pick up your car?" What he really wanted to know was—could he come home?

"I'd better get it, I'll need it tomorrow." Jonathan understood the answer. He drove into the parking lot and pulled up next to her lone car. "Meri?" His question hung in the air. "Thank you for seeing me," he broke the silence.

"And, Jonathan, thanks for trying."

"Tell the children I—I love them." He had such a hard time with that word.

"I will. Good night." He sat there until she was safely out of sight.

"They're going to get rid of Romano with or without me, then my troubles will be over. I'll just tell them to get lost and leave me—and Meridith—alone." Just saying that lifted the load from his shoulders. Jonathan drove back to this father's house whistling.

SATURDAY, NOVEMBER 9

THE FINAL CURTAIN CALL ended with tears and hugs. The cast and crew stood behind the closed, red velvet curtain, savoring the last moment of the show. Crowds of well-wishers joined them in congratulations.

Gillian was doing her best to begin the strike, the tearing down of the set, so they could adjourn to the closing night party. "Here, you take this," she handed a drill to Joe, "And begin the strike!" The noise of the reverse drill removing screws from the set pieces that made up the Kowalski's seedy apartment drove the well-wishers away. Meri began to pack up. Even the adrenalin from her performance was waning. The fatigue was overwhelming. As the fantasy world on the stage disappeared, she was overcome with sadness.

Actors experience this inevitable let-down at the end of every production. Perhaps its all part of the neurosis known as theatre.

THE PARTY WAS as expected—happily sad. It was held at Paul's house, a large Victorian he had lovingly remodeled himself. After gorging on a buffet table laid out like a Roman feast, the party assembled in the great room to watch the crew perform a silly satire on the production they called *"A Street Walker Lit My Fire."*

The festivities were still going strong when Meridith quietly left. She drove home listening to the haunting voice of Ella Fitzgerald sing "The Man I Love." As the garage door groaned open, Meri saw the large, dark blue limo's lights loom behind her. A shiver of adrenaline raced through her as she gunned the engine and pulled into the garage. Tony emerged in her rear view mirror, and she fought to breathe again. "You're always scaring me—stop it!" But his arms were around her before she could finish her reprimand.

"I've been waiting for hours. I was worried." He was serious.

"We always have a party closing night. It's hard to let go, and people hang around forever."

"Meri, we've got to talk. May I come in?"

She opened the door and quietly climbed the back stairs to the bedroom wing. Both children were sleeping soundly. When she returned to the kitchen Tony was making coffee.

"Coffee? Even for me this is a strange hour for that!"

"Italians always drink coffee when they talk. It's either this or spaghetti."

"How about if I make us hot chocolate?" she suggested. "Chocolate is my other weakness, especially when a show closes."

"I'll remember that," he promised. Her heart lurched. "I've missed you so much, Meri." They hadn't spoken in over a week. Meridith brought the steaming mugs of chocolate milk into the library where Tony lit the fire. Sitting on the sofa, he held her face gently, and she sighed.

"Meri, why couldn't I have met you years ago? Do you realize we were at Northwestern at the same time?"

"Obviously not in same circles," she teased.

Tony bristled. "Then I guess we wouldn't have met." She pulled him back to her.

"I was joking. Honestly, Tony, of all the things I am, I'm not a snob!"

"Meri, we are what we are. And that's what I've come to talk to you about." He was so solemn, it scared her.

"Honey, what's the matter?" She held her breath.

He stood up and walked to the fire. "Some people want to take over Chicago."

"Let them! Then you can get out of the Organization, and we can live happily ever after."

"You don't turn in your resignation to the Organization. The only way they can take over is to take me out." He inflamed the burning logs with the poker.

"That's crazy! Why?" She went to his side.

"Because, that's the way it is."

"Can't you talk to them?"

"It's not like that, Meri, believe me."

"Change it. You said you make the rules." She was challenging him with his own words.

"My darling, innocent Meri." Tony took her in his arms, "I think I may have a plan, but I can't talk about it. In the meantime, if anything happens to me, please understand I tried. And, Meri," he pulled her so close to him that she could see the fire reflect in his eyes, "Please know how much I love you." In that instant, he kissed her soul.

Meri locked the library door. For hours she and Tony made love, seeking passionately to become part of one another and shut out the world. As the fire died and the sun stole away the night, they held on tightly, crying soft, silent tears of joy and pain and longing and frustration.

TONY LEFT quietly before the sun rose. The limo, parked discreetly down the street, flashed its lights when he appeared. Meri watched, with a heavy heart, as Tony disappeared down the drive.

SUNDAY, NOVEMBER 10

"DID YOU see the paper this morning?" The ringing phone brought Tony out of a heavy sleep.

"Who is this?" he asked as he found the clock. Ten thirty.

"It's Gravani. Are you still sleeping? It's almost noon. Who's the broad?" Gravani was Tony's counterpart in New York.

"Yeah, late night and none of your damned business. What's in the paper?"

"The Ways and Means Committee sent the Organized Crime Bill to Congress. Sorrento is so fucking mad he can't talk. I thought you had that whole thing under control."

"Shit. Hold on." Tony went into the living room where the paper was lying on the counter, next to the brewed coffee. He opened the heavy Sunday edition to the front page.

CONGRESS AIMS DIRECT HIT AT ORGANIZED CRIME the headline screamed. Even reading it made Tony's head hurt.

He picked up the kitchen extension. "Georgie, can I call you back?"

"Sure. Hey, man, if you need anything, call." George Gravani knew there were going to be repercussions.

Fucking Chamberlain, Tony swore.

•   •   •

"DID YOU see the goddamn paper?" Masucchi asked Dolf over the phone.

"No. Why?" Dolf swallowed the jelly donut he was chewing.

"*Madone*, Chamberlain fucked up—royally. The Crime Bill will pass. Heads are gonna roll. We might not have to do this ourself, after all." An evil laugh.

"Things couldn't be workin' out better," Dolf told his new *paesan*.

"You got that fuckin' right. I'm gonna see Sorrento today. Talk to you later." The phone went dead.

•   •   •

JONATHAN SLEPT through the night for the first time in weeks. He walked into the kitchen to find Margaret cooking. "Are you hungry, sir?" she asked hopefully.

"Starved, Margaret, starved."

"Oh, good. I've made French toast with the egg-substitute." She handed him coffee with the paper.

"It's a wonderful world, Margaret," he told her as he opened it to the front page. "Oh, my God!" he gasped, dropping the hot cup.

"What is it, Mister Chamberlain?"

He stared at the headline then read down the first column:

The powerful House Ways and Means Committee, lead by veteran Illinois Congressman Franklin Chamberlain, sent the controversial Organized Crime Bill to Congress late yesterday afternoon. Working in an overtime session at the request of the President, Chamberlain said "I personally felt the bill needed additional work in committee, however, the President made me a believer."

According to informed sources, the President asked that the OCB go before the full House for a vote prior to the holiday recess. "This powerful legislation would give law enforcement authorities the leverage they need to break the back of organized crime," the President said. "I feel confident of its passage."

Jonathan threw the paper across the room without reading further. "I've got to talk to my father. And my wife," he muttered and fled upstairs. Margaret picked up the paper and read through it. She couldn't imagine why he was so upset.

• • •

THE CHILDREN were still asleep when Meridith went down to the kitchen. She was grinding beans for coffee as she unwrapped Sunday's *Tribune*.

"Oh, no! Dear God ..." Her hands trembled as she read the headline. The phone rang and answered immediately.

"Meridith! Did you see the paper?" Jonathan's voice quivered.

"Just now. What happened?"

"I don't know. I called my father, but his housekeeper said he's at church. Can I come over?"

"Of course." He hung up. With a shaky finger, she punched Tony's number.

"Yeah?" Tony answered abruptly.

"Tony? It's Meridith. Have you read the paper?"

A deep sign, "Yeah."

"What does this mean?"

"I don't know. I tried to call New York, but they're not taking my call. Not a good sign." Meri focused on his face, drawing it in her head.

"What should I do, Tony? Can I give them the money now?"

"I don't know, sit tight. And, please, be careful." There was a pause. "I'm going to New York today to see if I can talk to him in person."

"Will I see you again?" Her heart was hurting.

"I—I really don't know. Meri, why don't you take the kids and leave town for a while?"

"It's that bad?" The words caught in her throat.

"Listen, I've got an idea. I'll have one of my guys come by and pick up a check from you. I'll take it with me to show good faith on Jonathan's part. Maybe if they get the money—who knows? After all, a million dollars isn't chump change."

"All right." She thought for a minute, "It's Sunday and I'll have to call the bank in the morning to have the money transferred. Who do you want me to make it out to?"

"Leave it blank." Another pause. "Meri, I love you."

"I love you, too, Tony. Please take care of yourself."

"Meri? Do you believe in reincarnation?"

The abrupt change in direction threw her. "What?"

"I think I've loved you in a past life, and I will love you in the next. Just wait for me next time, okay?" He laughed sadly.

"Okay. How will I know you?" She was trying to match his forced nonchalance.

"I'll probably weigh three hundred pounds and drool, but I'll know you. You'll always be the most beautiful woman God ever created, inside and out. I love you. Good bye." He hung up before she could answer. She was crying when the doorbell chimed.

"Meridith? My God!" Jonathan entered and grabbed her tightly, holding her for dear life. "You've been crying!" He wiped her tears.

"Come inside." She led him to the kitchen. "Tony called." A cloud descended over Jonathan's face. "He said he would have someone come by for a check, and he would take it to New York and try to salvage this."

"Are you going to give him the money?"

"Of course. Jonathan, do you think they'll hurt you?"

"No." There was no conviction in his voice.

"Are you still seeing Romano?" Jonathan made a big deal out of fixing some coffee, avoiding her eyes.

"Not any more." She could say this with a certain amount of honesty.
"But I don't want to talk about that now." That seemed to satisfy him.

"So, what then?"

"I was thinking." She stopped and turned to face him. "We need to go to North Carolina to work out things between the company and the law firm. I talked to the corporate attorneys, they haven't been told of the over-billing errors yet. I told Mac I'd take care of it." Jonathan sat down in one of the chairs and studied his thumb nail.

Meridith continued, "I think if we go together we'll have more credibility. Getting you out of town right now sounds like a good idea. Hunter can stay with Scott's family, I'm sure, and I know Brooke will watch Chelsea at her house."

"I'll call the airlines. Tonight?" he asked. She nodded agreement. "Don't you think the children should go with us?" he looked worried.

"Ordinarily I'd feel better if they were with us, but right now I think they may be safer with our friends. We may be a target wherever we are." She shivered at the thought. Jonathan busied himself dialing to mask his own chill.

• PART THREE •

DAY ONE
MONDAY, NOVEMBER 18 • 0:00 AM

TONY WAS DEAD. The plane trip took less than three hours, but it seemed an eternity to Meridith. As sad as she wanted to feel, she was terrified for her children. Where were they? Were they hurt? Were they—? She couldn't bring herself to even think it. The small, private plane dropped, and Meri's stomach turned over. "Excuse me," she told Jonathan. She barely made it to the bathroom before vomiting.

"Are you all right?" Jonathan asked her when she returned. Her face was white, her eyes were circled with worry.

"No."

"Meri, do you think Romano has anything to do with the children?"

"No, Jonathan, I don't. I'm not sure it isn't the Organization, but I know if Tony had anything to say, he wouldn't have involved the children."

"Do you have an idea who killed him?" She couldn't speak. She shook her head, and it liberated tears. Jonathan looked away. It galled him to think the tears were for that hoodlum. But at least he was dead.

"You handled the lawyers at Carolina Tobacco well," he told her, trying to change the subject.

"It's ironic," she answered, "that no one even questions a legal bill, especially at the corporate level. They were so excited when they heard that there were billing errors and they were going to get money back, I'd thought that guy, Fleishman, would wet himself." Ordinarily, Jonathan would have smiled at her uncharacteristic, off-color humor, but he just nodded. Jonathan handed Meridith a bottle of Evian. They traveled in silence. He wondered how to get hold of those two thugs he'd met with at Jack's Gym. They could have taken the children for ransom. He was debating what to tell the authorities when the pilot announced the landing.

First he had to talk to a lawyer he could trust, probably Bob, then figure out what to do. Maybe he could find the children and redeem himself with Meridith.

A car was waiting at Palwaukee, the small private airport just west of Winnetka. They arrived at the police station to face a barrage of media—cameras, mikes, and lights—and questions hurled at them like buckshot. They were escorted through the babel and maze of flashing bulbs into the sanctity of the station. Meridith thought of the celebrities and criminals assaulted by the media but never expected to be at the center of controversy. Life was turning her world upside- down, like a kaleidoscope, altering reality into a nightmare. When would she ever wake up, she wondered.

DAY ONE
MONDAY, NOVEMBER 18 • 8:00 PM CST

"JONATHAN, YOU DIDN'T tell them anything about knowing ... Tony Romano or your problems." Meridith couldn't say Tony's name without shuddering. The press pack followed their car down Sheridan Road as they returned home.

"I know. I have to talk to Bob Crowley and tell him the whole story first. I can't make matters worse by implicating us. Meridith, do you know if your check was cashed?" Meri had not spoken to Tony since they left for Carolina. As each day went by she was more certain she would never talk to him again. The driver who picked up her check said nothing more than thank you.

"I'll call the bank first thing in the morning. Jonathan, if I tell the police tonight, they can check immediately."

"Wait."

"But the children! I really don't care what happens to me, it's only money. What's the worst thing they can do? We borrowed money and returned it. But if, by waiting, something happens to the children—I could never forgive myself." She began to cry again. "I don't think I could even go on."

"Let me call Bob and see what he thinks." The car pulled into the steep, winding driveway through the crowd of flashing cameras. Police barricades kept them from standing too close to the house. Meri stood inside the garage facing the door. She couldn't go into the house where Tony died. And to see the children's things!

"Oh, God," she said aloud, "please give me strength." The kitchen was occupied by a team of police people and FBI agents. The coffee pot was half-empty and brown stains surrounded the machine. Cups were everywhere, take-out food bags and a pizza carton littered the countertops, half-eaten sandwiches cluttered the table. Meridith stood frozen.

"Mrs. Chamberlain, come in." It was Harrison, Detective O'Brien's right hand man. "I'm sorry we've left your place such a mess, but with people here so long, it's hard to keep it clean."

"That's the least of our worries," she assured him.

"Can I get you something?" he asked her politely.

"No, thank you." Her stomach churned.

"Mrs. Chamberlain? You know what my wife likes when she's not feeling well? A cup of tea. Would you allow me?"

"That would be nice, Officer Harrison." He searched for tea bags as Meri went up the back stairs. The front stairs were cordoned off by bright yellow, crime scene tape. Forensic people had dusted the room for prints, leaving white powder residue everywhere. The Chinese carpet and the cherry desk bore the macabre silhouette of Tony's body in taped outline. The silk wallpaper was scarred by the imprint of his life's blood. The room was a surreal museum of death.

The room Jonathan lived in was now the room Tony died in. Meri shivered as she walked by the children's rooms. Sobs choked her burning throat. "Please, help me get through this," she prayed. "Please keep my children safe."

Suddenly, she felt self-indulgent and selfish. The last month of her life she'd thought mostly of her own wants and needs. "I'm so sorry." Somehow, this must be retribution for her infidelity, she thought. The pain of her grief was so real it racked her soul and clenched her stomach. Her whole body shook with sobs.

Meri sat down on the edge of her bed, trying to regain control.

"Mrs. Chamberlain?" It was Harrison. He walked in with a tray holding a pot of tea and a cup. He poured and handed it to her. Meri's hand was shaking so badly she spilled it bringing it to her mouth.

"Call me if you need anything." The officer turned into the hall but before the door closed Meri heard, "I'm sorry, m'am, you can't come up here." She listened.

"Tell Mrs. Chamberlain it's Brooke, Brooke Easton."

Meridith called to her friend, "Brooke! Oh, my God, Brooke!" They met each other with an embrace. Brooke broke into tears as they clung to one another, holding tight for consolation. The policeman quietly walked away.

Once the women were alone, Brooke took Meri's hand. "Meri! What the hell is going on? Do you have any idea of what happened here?"

"Brooke, Tony Romano—" she shivered again but continued, "—Tony and I were ... lovers."

"Oh, my God, Meri, does Jonathan know?" Meri nodded, sipping the cooling tea. "You don't think Jonathan could have—?" Brooke couldn't finish the question.

"Oh God, no! He's been with me at the Carolina Tobacco offices. At least I don't think so ..." Meridith went to the fireplace, "Brooke, help me light this thing, I'm freezing."

"Sit down, Meri, and let me do it," Brooke gently pushed her friend into the chaise before turning on the gas to light the logs. Once an even flame was glowing, Brooke handed Meri a refilled tea cup and sat across from her in the rocking chair.

WHEN SHE FINISHED the story, Brooke sat, staring at her friend. "And all this time you said nothing to me?" Meri shook her head then stood up and rubbed her aching neck. She warmed her hands in front of the fire.

"Do you have an idea where the children are or who has them?" The tears resurfaced. "Meri, you have to tell the police! They'll find out, and then it will look bad for you."

"But all that means nothing now. All I want is to have my children back." Brooke held her friend until the sobs stopped. She led her to the bed, pulled back the comforter, and coaxed her to lie down.

"I'll be right back," Brooke promised. She returned with Dr. Fred Wilkes, retired family physician and friend.

"Meri? I'm going to give you a sedative, all right?" he asked as he was readying the syringe.

"I need to be awake if anyone calls or there's news," Meridith protested.

"I'll be here, Meri. I'll wake you, I promise." Brooke nodded at the doctor injecting Meridith's arm. She didn't flinch. Brooke and Dr. Wilkes sat with her until her breathing was steady and she was asleep.

They tip-toed out of the room leaving Meridith alone with her nightmares.

DAY TWO
TUESDAY, NOVEMBER 19 • 6:00 AM

DETECTIVE CHARLES O'BRIEN never went back to sleep after being awakened at three o'clock by a chilling nightmare. After an hour of tossing and tangling himself in sheets, he showered and dressed. Driving to the station was a solitary experience. The streets, illuminated by lamps, were still. The large homes loomed ghostly, lit only by scattered lights.

The Winnetka Police Station was already in gear. News vans had camped out all night, hoping for a break. O'Brien walked through the frosty air into the warmth of the station house. He was met by the graveyard dispatcher, "Mornin' Detective."

"Anything new?"

"You mean since you called a half hour ago? No. I heard that FBI agent, Driscoll, moving around here a while ago."

"Thanks," O'Brien answered, as he walked through the locked door.

Pouring himself a cup of bitter coffee, he saw Driscoll sitting at the conference table, a sheaf of papers spread before him.

"You're up early," Driscoll greeted him.

"Yeah. Anything?" O'Brien took a chair next to Driscoll.

"I'm not sure. I had a chance to go through the reports from Agent Sanders. Jonathan Chamberlain met with Romano at the Ritz-Carleton bar on Tuesday, August 27. They were together for the better part of an hour. According to the report, our man couldn't make out the conversation, but it was definitely Chamberlain and Romano.

"Here, look at this. On Wednesday, September 18, Romano's Lincoln limousine was followed to the Chamberlain home. It was eight o'clock. He was inside less than hour. Hardly a social visit. And, on Friday, October 5, Chamberlain was seen going into Romano's attorney's office, while Romano was also there. Attorney is a guy named Joel Silverman. His only client is the Organization."

"So, there is a connection?" O'Brien asked pointedly.

"Seems that way."

"And Chamberlain lied when he was asked, outright, if he knew Tony Romano."

"That's the way it's going down."

"I'm going back to the Chamberlain's. Want to come?"

Driscoll looked at his watch, "It's not quite six."

"If they were your kids, would you be asleep?" O'Brien was already gathering up the notes. Driscoll buttoned the top button of his wrinkled, white shirt and grabbed his tie.

THEY RANG the doorbell, listening to it reverberate throughout the cavernous house.

"Some place," Driscoll noted as he surveyed the property.

"You haven't been here?" O'Brien asked. Driscoll shook his head as the large, oak door opened. "Just a humble place to hang your skivvies," O'Brien cracked wisely. Driscoll whistled softly as he entered the foyer.

"Welcome to Winnetka," the detective whispered to the FBI agent.

The officers who greeted them were part of the larger New Trier Task Force. O'Brien and Driscoll flashed their ID and walked into the cluttered kitchen.

"Where are the Chamberlains?" O'Brien asked the female officer.

"Still upstairs. Dr. Wilkes gave Mrs. Chamberlain a sedative around ten last night. Her friend, Brooke Easton, slept in her room. The husband slept in his son's room, but he's been up and down all night."

"No calls?" Driscoll asked the agent sitting at the table where a recorder had been set up.

"A few friends. Chamberlain put in a call to one of his law partners, Robert Crowley. Guy said he would be here today. Otherwise ..." the agent shrugged.

O'Brien was ready to climb the stairs when Jonathan appeared. "News?" he asked anxiously.

"No. Just a few questions for you, Mr. Chamberlain." Jonathan blanched.

"You'll have to wait until my attorney arrives." He turned and disappeared back up the stairs.

O'Brien turned to Driscoll. "I guess that answers that."

• • •

THE TWO CHICAGO PAPERS arrived before dawn each day on the broad front porch of the Congressman's beachfront home. Margaret brought the papers in the house and removed them from the plastic wrappers. This morning, a brown envelope fell out of the *Sun-Times* package. She lifted it up to inspect it. In large black letters across the front of the eight by ten envelope was printed: *To be opened by the Honorable Franklin Chamberlain, Congressman. ONLY.*

"Congressman!" Margaret ran up the stairs faster than she thought possible. "Congressman!" Franklin hadn't slept at all and was already dressing when he heard her calling. Keeping his heart in check he dropped the tie he was holding and hurried to meet her.

"Margaret, what is it?" She handed him the envelope.

"This was in with the newspaper—*Sun-Times.*" She shoved the envelope at him.

"Did you touch it?"

"Of course I touched it. I'm holding it, aren't I?"

"I'm sorry." He took it from her, very carefully handling it by the corner of the package. A Winnetka policeman was stationed in his library. "Call the officer," he asked Margaret.

"I'm here, sir, I heard Margaret. What is it?" Franklin held the brown envelope.

"Margaret opened the *Sun-Times*, and this fell out." The officer withdrew a rubber glove from his pocket and pulled it on. He carefully took the flat, brown package from the Congressman's trembling hand. He placed the innocuous, but, now menacing item on the bureau. "Let me call the chief." The call was patched through to O'Brien who was at the Congressman's house in less than five minutes. O'Brien and Driscoll donned the obligatory rubber gloves.

"We'll take this to the station before we open it," he stated.

"Wait!" Franklin declared. "What if they're watching the house, and the enclosed instructions told me not to call the authorities. They'll know I've called you." The law enforcement people exchanged looks. He was right.

After a moment O'Brien announced, "Okay, here's the plan. Driscoll and I will leave. The officer will stay with you. I'll wrap the envelope in plastic wrap, to protect its integrity for the forensic people, and put it under my coat. No one will see that it left the house."

"That's no good," Franklin protested. "How will I know what it says? What if the instructions ask that I do something immediately?" Once again, the Congressman's mind was working faster than the so-called authorities.

"Okay, what do you propose?" Driscoll asked Franklin.

"You and O'Brien leave, like you suggested. Immediately. I will open the package carefully, using your latex gloves."

"I can't let you do that, Congressman. What if it's a letter bomb?" The five people gathered in the foyer froze.

"Call the bomb squad and your forensic people, O'Brien," Driscoll ordered.

"No, please!" Franklin could envision the lights and sirens. "Let's go with O'Brien's plan. Leave quietly and take the envelope with you, under your coat. I'll stay here. Call me with the instructions. Whoever wrote the note, if they're watching the house, will think its still here, if I don't go with you."

Driscoll looked to O'Brien with raised eyebrows. "All right, but let's do it now. If it is a letter bomb on a timer, every minute counts," O'Brien said. "Margaret, get me some plastic wrap." She was back in seconds.

"Here you go, sir." She was flushed and shaking. O'Brien tore off a generous sheet and carefully wrapped the envelope. He held it next to his heart, beating so hard he was afraid it would come through his shirt. He pulled another sheet of plastic off the roll and wrapped it around his chest to hold the package tight.

With his jacket on he whispered, "Let's get this show on the road—"
The Congressman watched them leave, barely breathing, as O'Brien yelled loudly, "And Congressman, we'll be back to interview you later, after you've had a chance to get dressed. Thanks for your time," as he slid into the passenger side of the police car. "You drive." Driscoll started the engine and carefully backed onto Sheridan Road.

"Don't use the radio, too easily monitored," O'Brien told him. "We'll be there in a second, anyway."

The two men walked casually into the station. Once behind closed doors, Driscoll helped him remove his heavy jacket and found scissors to cut the plastic wrap from his body.

"Call the chief," O'Brien told Harrison, who was just signing in. "Then call the bomb squad and forensics. Tell them all to arrive quietly. We may be watched." The brown envelope was now lying innocently in the middle of the conference table. "And everybody, get the hell out of the room until we make sure it won't explode! Quietly!"

IT TOOK ALMOST twenty minutes for the FBI forensic force to arrive, while the bomb squad waited impatiently. The time seemed interminable for the Congressman who sat, phone in hand. The FBI arrived with a new, laser x-ray machine. By passing the envelope under its beam, they determined no plastic explosives were used.

"That's something," O'Brien commented.

"Your tax dollars at work," Driscoll answered. "It's fantastic, but it cost a small fortune. Its being used experimentally in some of the larger airports to inspect luggage."

"I'll feel better when they all have it," O'Brien told him.

"Then the terrorists will figure out a new way to blow us all to kingdom come. They always seem to be one step ahead."

"They have more money. They also don't need an act of Congress for funding." O'Brien the philosopher, again.

"Let's open it, and see what it holds," the chief stated, cutting short the political forum. Now the forensic people began. They dusted for prints, finding only a few, O'Brien was betting on Margaret's. With a small, razor-like scalpel they sliced it open and slid a single page from the envelope, dusting it and passing it under a high-powered black light.

"No prints," one of the men told his audience.

"Damn," O'Brien uttered. "Read it," he ordered.

The man read aloud:

> *Dear Congressman Chamberlain:*
>
> *Your grandchildren are safe and unharmed. Your son, Jonathan, guaranteed you would table the Organized Crime Bill indefinitely. We are sorry you didn't comply. The House vote on this unconstitutional legislation is scheduled for Friday. You MUST make certain that the OCB does NOT pass. If you are able to garner the votes necessary, your grandchildren will be returned to their home Friday evening.*
>
> *We will not discuss their fate should you fail and the bill passes. Or you go to the media. We will be watching the news.*
>
> *A PARTY OF CONCERNED AMERICANS*

"Oh, my God!" Chief Atkinson exclaimed. "What now?"

"Call the Congressman," O'Brien ordered. "Never mind, I'll go there. They said nothing about the cops, and now we know why—our hands are as tied as his."

O'Brien grabbed his coat and the chief matched his stride to the car.

The Congressman read the note and his body sagged into a nearby chair. He held his head and cried. Atkinson and O'Brien could do nothing but watch uncomfortably. "Does my son know?" he finally asked.

"No, sir, we came directly here."

"I want to talk to him myself." The ire in the elder man's voice made even the weathered detective cringe.

As they walked to the police car, O'Brien whispered to Atkinson, "I'm glad I'm not in his son's shoes right now, in more ways than one. Poor bastard." The thought of Meridith Chamberlain's pain seared through his tough, old, policeman's heart.

DAY TWO
TUESDAY, NOVEMBER 19 • 8:00 AM

FRANKLIN CHAMBERLAIN ignored the questions shouted at him by reporters. He opened the front door without knocking, and the officer in the entry sprang to attention. "It's okay, he's Congressman Chamberlain," O'Brien assured him as they walked into the kitchen.

Jonathan Chamberlain was seated at the table. He stood when he saw his father. "Good morning," he addressed him, as well as O'Brien, Driscoll and Chief Atkinson. Then, quickly, "You've heard something?"

"Yes, Jonathan, we have."

"The children, they're okay?" He steeled himself.

"We received a note. It said the children are safe—"

"What do they want, money?" Jonathan interrupted.

"—Let me finish," Franklin ordered. "When Margaret brought in the papers, a note was included with the *Sun-Times*. I called the police, and they opened the envelope, fearing it might be a letter-bomb." Jonathan shuddered. "Fortunately, it was not. But it did state that you had promised that I would table the Organized Crime Bill indefinitely. Is that true?"

"Father, I ..." he looked at each of the law officers. "I ..." he stammered.

"They are now asking that I find a way to amass enough votes to defeat the bill when it goes before the full House. Jonathan, who are these people?"

Jonathan had wanted Bob Crowley present before he spoke to the police, but now he was at a loss. "Father, I will speak to you, privately, but I can't talk in front of them."

"Jonathan! We're talking about your children—my grandchildren. Their very lives are at stake! How dare you consider your legal position at a time like this. You tell them everything you know! I will not have my grandchildren used as a pawn and the congressional system manipulated by thugs." The rage in the older man's face was uncontrolled. His neck muscles banded so tightly that his face contorted from the tension.

Meridith was awake when she heard the shouting downstairs. Brooke had fallen asleep on the chaise in front of the fire, and Meri was careful not to wake her. With a pounding heart, she grabbed her bathrobe and, still barefoot, ran down the backstairs.

As she turned on the landing, she saw Franklin, his face inflamed bright red, standing over Jonathan. The police officers were standing behind the Congressman.

"What's happened? Franklin, what is going on?" All faces turned to her in unison. "Have you heard anything? The children, are they all right?" She held on to the bannister, steadying herself for news.

"I received a note from the kidnappers this morning. They say the children are unharmed, so far, and will be returned on Friday—if I cooperate."

"How much money do they want?"

"They don't want money, Meridith, they want me to stop the Organized Crime Bill from passing on Friday." Meri knew. She sat down on the steps, feeling like she'd taken a blow to her gut.

"Jonathan, you've got to tell them. Everything. If you don't, I will."

O'Brien looked to the chief.

"Tell us what, Meridith," Franklin asked. She rose, feeling disembodied, floating down the stairs. The room spun in a surreal pattern of lights. Meri sat down in one of the overstuffed chairs. She stared out the window, seeing a seagull swoop down and glide over the choppy water. "Meridith, please, you've got to tell the officers everything you can. Anything that will help the children." Franklin was pleading.

"Jonathan, will you tell them or will I?" She never looked at him.

When he spoke, Jonathan's voice sounded flat. He began his oratory, "Last summer I got in trouble, financially, by selling short in the Market. Meridith said she wouldn't give me the money." She could feel Jonathan's eyes on her. "So I talked to one of my partners, Bob Crowley. He told me to call a friend of his, Joel Silverman, for a short-term loan. Turns out Romano was the *client* with money. Before I could pay it back, Romano tells me that it will be forgiven if my father tables the Crime Bill. I can pretty much guess why, considering." Driscoll was mesmerized as Jonathan continued to unravel the web that was woven last summer.

"While I was in Washington, my father tells me that he doesn't like the bill, the way it's written, and is going to send it back to committee. I don't say anything, I figure my troubles are over. And, that's pretty much it, until we got the call from Detective O'Brien." When he finished, the Congressman sat down heavily, shaking his head. Meridith was listening. He left out quite a bit, not the least of which was her relationship with Tony, but she added nothing.

"So, other than Joel Silverman and Tony Romano, you spoke to no one? You have no other names to give us?"

A debate continued in his head: Should he tell them about the two guys at the gym? He didn't even know their names! What was he going to say—two guys show up at my house and offer to knock off my wife and her lover, a known gangster? So, I meet them at a flea-bag gym in Cicero, get a massage and tell them to call me in a week? Nice try. "No." He said in reply.

"Get Silverman in here, pronto." Driscoll was talking to O'Brien.

O'Brien was at the phone when Driscoll stopped him, "Wait. I'll have one of my men pick him up. They're downtown already, and Sanders knows where his office is. We'll also need to talk to this Bob Crowley."

"Is there anything else you think would help us, Mrs. Chamberlain?" O'Brien asked. She shook her head, her uncombed hair emphasized the *no*.

"Mr. Chamberlain, if you know anything that might help us find your children, please call me," Chief Atkinson pleaded. He nodded toward the door and O'Brien obliged.

"Thanks again for your help, Congressman. We have a little more to go on now. Would you like a ride back home?" O'Brien, the good cop.

"No. I'm going to stay and talk with my family. Thank *you* for all your help."

O'Brien and Atkinson walked into a day that was growing colder.

"What do you think?" .

"Curiouser and curiouser," O'Brien answered. "The lady knows more than she's saying. And, Chamberlain definitely gave a nice little *Reader's Digest* version in front of the good Congressman."

"Yeah, my take exactly. What now, Sherlock?" the Chief asked O'Brien.

"Well, let's let J. Edgar do some of our dirty work. I'd like to go back to the station and read through some of those reports. Maybe we'll find something our agent friend missed. Or failed to share."

"I wonder what the Congressman will do if we can't find the kids before Friday?" the chief queried.

"I don't know. Your grandchildren on one hand, the United States Congress on the other. A lot of those elected officials have sold out for a lot less."

"Sad commentary, ain't it?" the chief patted the detective's shoulder.

"So, we've got less than seventy hours to find the kids?" O'Brien said as he reached in his pocket for his cigarettes. He found only a half pack of Lifesavers. He took one out and offered the package to Atkinson.

"No thanks, I'm trying to cut back," the chief told him. "But I will spring for breakfast. Lenny's?"

"Big spender. Let's pick up the file first, we'll take it with us. Some of that crap may be easier to stomach with a decent cup of coffee. And let's move fast, before the G-man decides to join us."

"Have the younger Chamberlain tailed if he leaves the house," Atkinson stated.

"Good thought. I guess that's why you get the big bucks," O'Brien razzed the chief. Then the reporters started to shout.

"No comment," Atkinson said as he climbed into the car.

"See, there you go again, earning the big bucks," O'Brien laughed as they drove through the geometrically-multiplying, media mass.

FBI SPECIAL AGENT Samuel L. Driscoll felt he was finally making some headway. He'd have this case cracked before Friday and be back in Washington before Thanksgiving. The President wanted to be kept personally informed. This would be a big feather in Driscoll's cap and a giant step toward a White House assignment. God, he was going to love traveling with the top guy. All the state dinners, executive privileges, perks. Things were going great. This would be wrapped up in a few days.

"Sanders, pick up Joel Silverman, and pick up a Mr. Robert Crowley, he's with Chamberlain's law firm. Bring them down to the Winnetka Station ASAP."

"Did we catch a break?"

"I think so. I'll fill you in when you get here, but I want these guys, yesterday. Got it?" He hung up. Driscoll searched the downstairs for O'Brien and Atkinson. Their car was gone. Damn. One thing he really hated was smart-ass local cops. He wished they'd just step back and let a professional handle these cases. He'd have to really read that new OCB bill everyone was talking about. Hopefully, it put the power where it belonged. And more money wouldn't hurt the bureau, either. When this was over, he and the Congressman would have a long chat. A good friend in the House would be a nice little bonus.

Wow, he'd love to be a fly on the wall when the Chamberlains let loose. There was more going on here than they were telling. He'd talk to Sanders about putting a bug here in the kitchen and another one in the bedroom.

BROOKE CAME DOWNSTAIRS, still dressed in the sweater and slacks she arrived in last night. "Meri, how are you? Why didn't you wake me?"

"I didn't think you got much sleep, and I felt bad. Thank you for last night."

"Don't be silly, I love you. Any news?"

"Franklin received a ransom note." Brooke gasped. "The good news is that the children are all right and they don't want money. The bad news is that they want Franklin to have the Organized Crime Bill defeated on Friday."

"What?" Brooke turned to the Congressman.

"That's it in a nutshell," Franklin admitted.

"What are you going to do?" Brooke asked, incredulous.

"Good question. What are we going to do?" he addressed Jonathan.

Jonathan grabbed a coat. "I have to go out. I'll be back later."

"But Jonathan, we need to talk!" Franklin tried to stop him.

"Not now, Father, I may know someone who knows something."

"Tell the police. Let them handle this before you make more of a mess. Or the children get hurt." But the garage door was grinding and the engine gunning before the Congressman finished speaking.

JACK'S GYM was closed even though it was almost ten. A heavy chain was wrapped around the handles to the doors and secured with a padlock. Chamberlain banged on the metal door and yelled, "Anyone in there?"

The same squat man who directed him last week appeared through the small window in the door. "What's your problem?" His voice was muffled through the glass.

"Open up. I need to talk to you!" The little man turned away. "Wait! Chamberlain held up a twenty dollar bill to the window. He heard nothing for a minute when a side door opened.

"In here," he was told. "Whadda ya want?" The man was rubbing thick sleep from his eyes as Chamberlain entered the gym. The smell was more offensive than it had been when populated.

"Look," he began, fishing more money from his pocket. "I've got money. It's yours if you can answer my questions correctly."

"I know you ain't no cop. Your shoes are too nice. Whadda ya want to know?"

"I met with two guys here last week. Both big and fat. One was getting a massage while I was here. Who are they, and where can I find them?" Squatman thought a moment, scratching his crotch absently. He hawked and spit, and Jonathan fought an internal shiver as the little man eyed the bills greedily. Jonathan fanned them closer to his face, smelling the man's foul breath.

The little man could no longer ignore the temptation of the money. "They ain't from around here. Masucchi, the guy on the table, is from New York. Silvio Masucchi." He pulled two twenties from Chamberlain's fan of bills.

"There's more money in it for you. Go on."

"Listen, you didn't hear this from me. Those guys are mean, butt-ugly mean." Jonathan thrust the money in his face, and he went on. "Other guy, one that's always stuffin' his face, he's Dolf something. Don't remember his last name, but he's from Vegas. Fucker's always braggin' 'bout his connections. That's all I know."

"Think. It's important. They may have my kids. How would I find them?"

Squatman looked at Chamberlain hard. "Say, wait a minute. You're the guy on TV. I saw it on the news. From Winnetka. Your kids have been kidnapped. My God!"

Chamberlain grabbed him by his smelly sweatshirt, "Listen you shit-head. There's a million dollar reward in it for you if I find them unharmed. For a million bucks you could own this whole fucking town. You find out who and where they are, and it's yours." Squat man's eyes widened to the size of ping-pong balls. Chamberlain could see the red veins crossed through them. Sweat popped out on his forehead.

"Yes sir! Yes sir! I'll find them. Where can I reach you?"

"You can't." Jonathan did not want him calling the house phones where everyone was listening. "I'll call you at three o'clock today. Say nothing to anyone else. Remember, lives may depend on you. Understand?"

"Yes sir! Three o'clock. I'll be here.

"By the way, what's your name?"

"Jack, Jack Handy. And I'll find out, you can count on it!"

Chamberlain dropped the sweatshirt and walked out the open door. As his car pulled back onto Cicero Avenue, he did not notice the dark blue Chevy parked across the street. Two plain-clothes officers were calling in to O'Brien.

"He just left, Detective. Should I tail him or talk to the guy he just left?"

"Stay with him. I'll send someone over to follow-up. Jack's Gym on Cicero Avenue. Good work, keep me posted."

"HE JUST left a place called Jack's Gym in Cicero," O'Brien reported to Atkinson as they were seated in their usual back booth. "Like I was saying, *curiouser and curiouser*. You want to go over there, or should I send someone?"

"Bring the file, we're on our way. This I've got to see for myself." Atkinson threw bills on the table as O'Brien blew a kiss to his favorite waitress who returned it with a broad smile. The radio crackled, "Chief, Harrison needs to talk with you. Says he's got something that can't wait."

"Put him through. Harrison, what is it?"

"Chief! O'Donald and I just left the house of a woman named Lanie Flowers. She said she met Tony Romano at a party given by, get this, *Mrs.* Chamberlain! After opening night at the community theatre. She said he and the Misses seemed to be 'good friends,' as she put it. She also said Romano was 'charming.' Nice lady, Mrs. Flowers, very concerned about the kids. Said they call her Aunt Lanie. Thought you'd want to know this before the debriefing this afternoon."

"You're right, Harrison. Thanks, keep me posted." The radio was quiet.

The thought that Meridith Chamberlain was more and more involved bothered O'Brien. I don't know why I should care, he thought, but damn, I do. He wanted her unsullied, hoping against hope that she would emerge unscathed.

THE DOOR TO JACK'S GYM was opened for the second time that morning but this time for two officers, brandishing badges. "I'm Chief Atkinson, this is Detective O'Brien, from the Winnetka Police."

"A little out of your league here, ain't you?"

"We're investigating the kidnapping of two children, the Chamberlain's, and the murder of Tony Romano. We'd like to talk to you." The chief was polite. The Squatman wasn't fast enough on his feet to hide his surprise concerning Romano's murder. Obviously, he didn't listen to the news thoroughly.

"I don't know nothin' about no murder. How would I know about that?"

"You got any ID?" the Chief asked.

"Yeah, my wallet's in my room, upstairs. I'm Jack Handy. It's my gym."

"Jonathan Chamberlain was just here. What did he want?"

"I don't know no Chamberlain."

O'Brien, the bad cop, broke in, "Listen, punk, we *know* Chamberlain was just here and we *know* you talked to him. What we need to know from you is what he said and what you told him?" Handy was silent. O'Brien shoved his finger into the guy, backing him against the wall. "You can talk to us now or we'll turn you over to the fuckin' Feds who ain't as accommodating as us nice folks from Winnetka. What's your choice?"

Handy made a quick decision. "Chamberlain was here last week with two guys from out of town. He wanted to know where he could find them. I told him I didn't know. He left." O'Brien ambushed Squatman, grabbing his arm and twisting it behind him. Then he shoved his hand into Handy's grimy pocket and pulled out a wad of twenties.

"Awful lot of cash to be carrying around these parts, wouldn't you say, Chief. Hey, wait, what's this! They look counterfeit to me. Let's run him in."

"Get your coat and your wallet, Handy, you're coming with us." Atkinson insisted.

"I can't. I've got—things to do."

"Either come clean or your 'things' will have to fucking wait while we book you for counterfeiting—a Federal offense, right Chief?" O'Brien still had Handy's arm in a vice grip behind him. The defenseless man was struggling to right himself, in obvious pain. O'Brien held his breath against the assault of the man's odor.

Handy thought a long minute. "Do I get the reward even if you guys find the kids?" The Chief and O'Brien stared at Squatman, then exchanged glances.

"If your information leads us to the kids, you get the reward," Atkinson assured him.

"Can we get something to eat? It was a bad night last night."

"I'll buy you the biggest breakfast in town if you have information for us," O'Brien told him, releasing his grip. "Get your coat."

THEY ENTERED one of the many Greek family diners in the area. The Chief and O'Brien nursed strong coffee watching Handy consume the overcooked, under-seasoned food. After the little man shoveled in more food than O'Brien ate in a day, he wiped the last of bits of egg with a corner of toast and popped into his mouth. He was finally ready to talk. O'Brien ignored the yolk that clung to the corner of his sagging, beard-stubbled mouth.

"Last week these two thugs from outta town come inta my place like they own the joint, pushin' people around, givin' orders. Big guy, name's Masucchi, Silvio Masucchi, acts like a big shit. Says he's gonna run Chicago, and, if I play my cards right, he'll turn my gym into one of those fancy health clubs. Like I need that."

"Go on," the chief prodded.

"Anyway, his buddy, another fat slob—" Handy squinted his eyes trying his memory, "—his name's Dolf something. I been tryin' to think of his last name but it's some Italian name, ends with an o. Anyway, the two of 'em meet up with this Chamberlain guy, who comes in, fancy coat, expensive shoes, 'bout a week ago. He gets a rub-down and leaves. That's all I know. Until this morning, Chamberlain comes in, banging on my door, waving twenties around, and tells me if I can give him these fellas names, and where he can find them, I get the reward for his kids. Is it really a million bucks?"

"*If* we find them unharmed." O'Brien's mind was reeling. Now the thing was coming together. A few puzzle pieces, if not meshing, now looked like they might fit somewhere.

"Oh, wait, the other guy, Dolf. What the hell kinda name is Dolf anyway?" Handy was trying hard to be one of the guys. "This Dolf guy, says he's from Vegas. Says if I'm ever that way, he'll show me a real good time. Says he's connected. Still looks like an fuckin' asshole to me. Oh, sorry, officers."

"We are familiar with those words in Winnetka, too, Handy," O'Brien appeased.

"Anyway, thanks for the grub." Handy wiped his mouth.

"One more thing," O'Brien looked right into Handy's eyes, "Tony Romano, he ever come into your place?"

"Romano in my gym? No way. I didn't know him *personally*."

"Handy, if you hear anything, you'll call, okay?"

"Sure, sure. Thanks again. You Winnetka cops got a lot more class than the Chicago cops, I got to say."

"I used to be a Chicago cop, Handy." O'Brien watched his reaction.

"Well, you sure moved up."

O'Brien laughed. "Anything more you can think of, you call." He handed his card across the battered table.

"One thing. Chamberlain said he would call me at three to see what I found out. Whadda want I should do?"

The chief spoke, "Tell him you're still working on it. You've got our card if you do find out anything. But, we need to know first, remember that. These guys are not screwing around, and there are two kids' lives at stake."

O'Brien added, "Thanks again for your cooperation." For the second time that morning, Atkinson threw bills on a table. The officers walked out, leaving Jack Handy polishing off the remaining food.

"WE HAVE to run these guys through the computers, and we'll have to let Driscoll in, " Atkinson said as he perused the FBI files. O'Brien drove.

"I know. And he's going to be pissed as hell when he finds out we followed up without him." O'Brien had no love lost for Feds.

"I'll handle Driscoll. You want to talk to Mrs. Chamberlain? I think she's ready to spill but not in front of the husband."

"Sure." O'Brien was not looking forward to grilling the lady.

"Hey, look at this! On Monday, October 7, Sanders called Driscoll to report that, get this, Silvio Masucchi was in town. Driscoll called another agent to follow Romano while Sanders stayed with Masucchi. Masucchi is connected in New York, but a big trouble-maker. He had Romano's boy, Frankie Delvecchio, with him all day."

O'Brien whistled appreciatively. "Every now and then you get a break!" The chief was skimming through the reports, his eyes scanning for the name again. "Bingo! On Saturday, October 26, three weeks ago, Masucchi and—here it is!—*Adolpho Cashiano* rented a car and drove to Winnetka to the Congressman's house! Find out if the Honorable Rep was in town that day, Charlie. We're cooking with gas, now."

The chief dog-eared the pages he'd found as they pulled into the station's lot. Reporters still circled the area like vultures anticipating a massacre.

DAY TWO
TUESDAY, NOVEMBER 19 • NOON

"DAMN YOU GUYS! You shouldn't have taken off without me." Driscoll banged the table for emphasis.

"Calm down. Listen, Sam, you've already read these reports, we just wanted to catch up over breakfast. We got the call on the radio and followed up. We're giving you everything we uncovered," the chief stated in a reassuring tone.

"Hey, you said time is of the essence, Driscoll, we were just trying to make the most of it," O'Brien added.

Although not appeased, the agent lowered his voice. "All right, give me the names, and we'll run 'em. Wherever these bastards are, my guys will have them in custody within the hour." While the chief had Driscoll reigned in and occupied, O'Brien signaled he was going back to the Chamberlains. Atkinson gave him a half-salute as the detective exited the back door.

"I NEED to speak to Mrs. Chamberlain," O'Brien told Mrs. Easton. Brooke had just returned, having gone home to quickly shower, change, and make sure her children were safely delivered to school. Paranoia was running rampant through the village.

"It might be better if you talked to her upstairs," Brooke suggested as she disappeared. That suited the detective fine.

"Please, come up," Brooke called down. "Meri, I'm here if you need anything," she reminded Meri before leaving.

Meridith was standing in front of the fire. "Hello, Detective O'Brien."

"Mrs. Chamberlain. Thanks for seeing me. I know how you must feel, but you might know more than you think, anything that may help us find your children." He stayed focused on the kids.

"Please, sit down, Detective." He chose the rocker.

"Mrs. Chamberlain, I'm gonna be straight with you. When Officer Harrison interviewed your friends he met with—" He check his notes. "—Mrs. Lanie Flowers. She told him she met Tony Romano at your home. He was attending a party you gave after a play."

Meri searched her hands for the right answer. "That's true." She was quiet. "Detective, you're being very kind. I'm going to be honest with you, too. I would like to ask for your confidentiality, but I know that may not be possible. I just ask that you are careful about what you share with the press until after my children are returned."

"Of course, Mrs. Chamberlain. Believe me, if we could screen the media, we'd all be happier. I'm not your priest, so I can't give you absolution, but I will tell you I'm not going to hold a press conference, either."

"Thank you. Coffee?" He nodded and watched her gather her thoughts as she poured two cups. She spoke as she walked to the window, "Jonathan and I do not have what people would call a good marriage. Oh, I'm not making excuses for myself, Detective, I'm just trying to explain how this happened.

"Jonathan lost a great deal of money in the market. I refused to bail him out again. I thought I could make a deal: the money in exchange for an amicable divorce." She stopped to sip her coffee. "My family left me the only heir to Whitney Foods. I didn't want to see their money squandered. It should go to my children. Well, patience is not a virtue Jonathan enjoys. Before we had an opportunity to work things out, he went to Tony Romano." Her voice quivered when she said his name. O'Brien knew.

It took her a minute to find her composure. "Jonathan had also gotten involved in another—situation. He handles the Whitney Food account at his firm. He had been over-billing Carolina Tobacco Company, who bought us out this year. The law firm found out and insisted he return the money."

"How much money are we talking about, Mrs. Chamberlain?"

She flinched. "About two million dollars between the two issues."

O'Brien fought to maintain his objectivity. "Go on."

"It was during a meeting with the firm's partners that he suffered his heart attack." No wonder, O'Brien thought. "I told him I would make the money good with Carolina Tobacco. That's why we were in Raleigh. But long before that, Mr. Romano came to the house to talk about the debt owed to him, right after Jonathan's illness. That's how we met."

O'Brien thought about the lady's vulnerability and how that son-of-a-bitch had taken advantage of her. He remembered the mobster's face splattered against the wall and felt avenged.

"Well, Detective, Mr. Romano and I became ... very good friends. Yes, he came to a performance at the theatre and to the party afterward. That was the night Jonathan found out about us and moved to his father's house, here in Winnetka."

"Did you pay back the money to Romano?" O'Brien set his coffee cup down. Meridith walked back to the chaise.

"Not then. That's when it really got strange. Tony told me that people in New York wanted Jonathan to ask his father to table the Crime Bill. Jonathan told you the truth about flying to Washington and his father telling him the legislation was going back to committee. Honestly, Detective, we thought everything was going to be okay." She paused, "Then we saw the paper, a week ago Sunday. The committee gave the bill funding, and it was going to a vote before the full House immediately. Then it all hit the fan."

"Did you talk to Romano after that?"

"Yes. He said he was going to New York to work it out. I gave him a check for the million dollars. Rather, I gave the check to a man Tony sent to pick it up. I never heard from him again."

"You have no idea what he was doing in your home this weekend when he was killed?" She shook her head then grabbed a tissue and wiped her face. "Mrs. Chamberlain, was your husband with you at all times in North Carolina?"

"Yes." Her face showed concern.

"There's no chance he came back here without you knowing it?"

"Detective, you don't think Jonathan could have . . ." She couldn't finish the sentence.

"I don't think anything right now, I'm just asking questions. Do you know if the check was cashed?"

"I called the bank this morning. It was cashed. Last Wednesday."

"Can I have the name of your bank? I'd like to see who endorsed it. Who was it made out to?"

"It was blank."

"Let me get this straight. You gave a blank check for a million dollars to a man who showed up at your door?" Meri chewed her bottom lip and shrugged. My God, O'Brien thought, this guy was one hell of a salesman, or cocksman, as his nickname implied.

"Mrs. Chamberlain, did you ever meet or hear the names of a Silvio Masucchi or Adolpho Cashiano? She thought then shook her head no. "Romano or your husband never mentioned them?"

"No. Who are they, Detective?"

"We're not sure right now, but they met with your husband, maybe on more than one occasion. About what, we don't know."

"I do know that Tony was worried. He said there were some men in town who wanted to take over Chicago. He never told me their names. I don't know if these were the same men or not, but he said some men from out of town met with Jonathan."

That added up. He refrained from asking when Romano told her this bit of information, he could only guess.

"What may I do to help?" she asked.

"I'd like your permission to go over your bank records and your husband's, too."

"Certainly. And—" She took out a pen and paper from the carved desk in the corner, "—this is the name of my accountant. I'll tell him to cooperate in every way."

"Thank you. And, Mrs. Chamberlain, I appreciate your candor. I'll do whatever I can to keep it out of the papers."

"Thank you, Detective. And, please, call me Meridith." She smiled sadly. "Detective, in the vein of honesty we've opened, what are the chances my children will be returned safely?"

"I honestly don't know, Meridith. I wish I did. We're not dealing with run-of-the-mill-kidnapping-for-money. We're dealing with a sophisticated Organization who wants something more valuable than money—a Congressional vote. Perhaps they realize how valuable these children are, and we'll have them back before the weekend. I'm praying with you."

"Thank you for that. You'll keep me informed?"

"Certainly. Take care, Mrs. Chamberlain. Meridith." He walked down the front stairs, passing the den where Romano was murdered. You son-of-a-bitch, he thought once again, you got what you deserved.

"I SHOULD HAVE been there when you interviewed the wife!" Agent Driscoll was on the rampage.

"Look, I think I got more out of her one-on-one than if we'd brought her here with an audience. We got the information, what more do you want?" O'Brien kept his voice even.

"Are you sure you got everything? Women like that know how to play men. Look at what she did with Romano." Driscoll was a bastard, O'Brien thought, and he ignored the remark. O'Brien hadn't taken notes during the interview; he was more interested in reading her than writing. Now he needed to get his impressions down.

"Give me a minute to get my gather my thoughts," he barked at Driscoll. "Five minutes. Okay?"

"Sure, Detective, ask for my permission now," the agent's sarcasm registered. O'Brien felt the migraine returning and swallowed the miracle pill before sitting down with a yellow pad.

"Damn, he muttered, "money don't buy smarts!"

O'BRIEN OPENED THE ANTE. "All right, this is how it's looking," he began. The core group was gathered. "It all seems to have begun in late August." O'Brien looked at his pad.

"Today, a new wrinkle showed up in the old face of intrigue—" He smiled as he began to share.

"You found something *new* out this morning?" Driscoll asked, his face reddening.

"This very morning." He upped the ante.

"When were you going to tell me?" Driscoll shouted.

"I'm telling you now."

Driscoll scowled but sat down. "Okay," O'Brien took a sip of water, and, one-by-one, he assembled the puzzle pieces he'd been gathering.

"But here's where it gets complicated," O'Brien paused. Now he had to disclose Meridith's secret. He felt badly. But as he'd told her, he wasn't a priest and he had to find her kids. "Romano comes out to talk to Mrs. Chamberlain while her husband's in the hospital. He wants to make sure his bases are covered if the old man croaks." O'Brien winced. "They become romantically involved."

"What?!" Driscoll's voice rose again. "Holy shit!"

O'Brien started to make excuses for her but stopped himself. "It gets worse. Chamberlain found out. He moves out, to his father's house down the street. I need to know some dates here." Harrison, O'Donald and Sanders began writing. "When was Chamberlain in and out of which hospital? And when did he move into his fathers and when was the

Congressman here in town during the last month?" Thank God the pill was working, O'Brien thought as he continued. "Also, is there any way Chamberlain could have returned from North Carolina over the weekend, killed Romano, and gotten back to Raleigh without the wife knowing? Check." He looked at his notes again. "Chief, you want to fill them in on the meeting with Jack Handy?"

Atkinson took the floor. "I take it you have all seen and read the ransom note?" Heads bobbed. "We had Jonathan Chamberlain followed. He went to a broken-down gym in Cicero, Jack's. A little out of character. So Detective O'Brien and I talk with the owner, one Jack Handy. Jack's a foul little man but a wealth of information. Seems like Jonathan Chamberlain met with two very connected wiseguys, Silvio Masucchi, visiting from the Big Apple, and Adolpho Cashiano, aka Dolf, Vegas' best."

Agent Gary Sanders looked up from his notes, the chief caught his eye. "Right, Sanders, you tailed him and one of Romano's men."

Sanders piped up, "I called you about that, Sam, remember? They went into the Teamster office on Ashland Avenue. He came back to town later and—it's in my notes—went with this Cashiano guy out to the Congressman's in Winnetka." Sander's excitement was contagious.

"Right," O'Brien finished, "on Saturday, October 26, the two men rented a car and met with Jonathan Chamberlain."

Driscoll figured it out. "Word on the street is they're trying to take over Chicago. It would make sense that they enlisted Chamberlain, who, by now, knew his wife was having an affair with the mob boss. They were probably planning to take Romano out anyway, but asked Chamberlain for money to do the dirty deed." Finally, thought O'Brien, we've given him enough clues.

"I've asked Mrs. Chamberlain for permission to go over their bank records. O'Donald, that's your assignment. Harrison, check on the dates I asked for before."

Driscoll volunteered, "I'm having Masucchi and Cashiano picked up by our field offices."

"Have you located Silverman?" O'Brien asked the agent.

"Not yet, but we've got his office and home staked out."

The meeting was disbursing as O'Brien loudly cleared his throat to recapture their attention. He paused for effect. "One more thing. Other than the ID we found on the body of the recently deceased, how do we *know* the corpse was indeed the infamous Anthony Romano?"

Atkinson sat up straighter, Driscoll's jaw dropped.

O'Brien stated: "I saw the body. It had no *face*."

DAY TWO
TUESDAY, NOVEMBER 19 • 3:00 PM

"ROMANO MAY STILL be alive. Could he have the kids?" Atkinson asked, walking into the room.

Dr. Fred Wilkes dropped a file on O'Brien's desk. I printed our faceless corpse. Here's the autopsy report. Driscoll's running the prints though one of those high-tech computers now."

"Maybe, but where is he?" O'Brien asked. "Damn, good thing we're not playing the ponies, our luck is for shit."

"These guys are good, you have to give them that. Note in the newspaper. No one saw or heard anything."

"No one's that good. We've got to catch a break." O'Brien rubbed his neck, stretching. "It's a long day when it begins at three a.m."

Driscoll charged in, "You won't fucking believe it! We have *no* prints on record for Anthony Vincent Romano. *None.* All the agents tailing him and not a single fucking print on file!"

"He's never been arrested?" O'Brien asked incredulously.

"Never. One of those arm-length hoods; doesn't get his hands dirty, gives orders. No frigging prints! Can you believe it?"

"Wait," O'Brien jumped up. "He's got a condo downtown. Send the forensic people to print it. Maybe we can find it through the process of elimination."

Driscoll stood and stared at the Detective. "Good idea," he finally admitted.

Atkinson laughed out loud. "You are not winning friends and influencing people, O'Brien. You're a real smart ass, do you know that?"

"That's what they tell me," he admitted.

"Driscoll's men locate Silverman?" O'Brien pulled on his leather gloves.

"Not as far as I heard. Nothing new on Masucchi or Cashiano, either."

The chief was putting on his heavy jacket. "Let's take our own car, I don't want to be at the mercy of Driscoll."

"Was there a question?"

JONATHAN DIALED the number of Jack's Gym from his cell phone with a shaking hand and asked for Jack Handy.

"He's not in."

"Tell him it's the man with the money," Chamberlain ordered.

"Just a minute." Jonathan was getting nervous.

Finally. "Hello?"

"Handy, you got anything for me?"

"Uh, no. But I'm working on it. Call me tomorrow."

"You double-cross me, and I'll hand you over to the cops, asshole. Understand? My kids are missing, and, if anything happens to them, I'll see you fry for it."

"Sure, sure. Honest, I got people working on it. Call me tomorrow."

Handy hung up on him.

"Shit," Jonathan uttered to what he thought was an empty line.

"He called Handy," the FBI agent said as he pulled off the headset.

"Handy say anything?"

"What could he say? He knows nothing."

JONATHAN DID NOT want to go home. He drove along the lakefront and stopped at the Belmont Avenue beach. He parked and walked the deserted bluff, oblivious to the cold. He had to tell the police about Masucchi and Cashiano. He needed to find the kids, and nothing else mattered now. The tingling in his arm was returning. He hadn't eaten, and a sour, burning sensation was churning his gut. He thought of Hunter and Chelsea. The acid boiled into his chest, and he threw up in a clump of brown bushes.

He had to talk to someone. Maybe there was good news, he prayed.

DAY TWO
TUESDAY, NOVEMBER 19 • 4:50 PM

THE TOP FIVE FLOORS of Lake Point Towers were lost in fog. As the elevator doors opened to Tony's condo, Special Agent Driscoll stepped off first. The building engineer was right on his heels. "You guys sure this warrant covers me? I don't want Romano coming after me for letting you in." He turned and whispered, "Not the kind of guy you want as an enemy."

Driscoll ignored the man and shouted over his head. "No one touch anything until the print people have finished!" O'Brien, Atkinson and officers Harrison and O'Donald walked in behind him.

The contemporary furnishings were elegant and expensive. The room spoke volumes about the man who lived here: clean, uncluttered, tasteful and rich. "What was I saying earlier, about crime not paying?" O'Brien asked the chief.

"Don't get any ideas, O'Brien, I need you on my side until we've solved this," Atkinson suppressed a smirk.

Something is missing, O'Brien thought. No pictures, no notes, nothing to indicate a real person lived here. It looked like a model apartment.

For over an hour the FBI fingerprint team dusted every smooth surface, including glasses in the cabinets and bottles in the bathroom. The apartment looked like talc had exploded everywhere—white dust covered every surface.

"Damn," the team leader announced, shaking his head. "The place has been wiped clean! We found a few half-prints but not much to work with. I'm telling you, Agent Driscoll, it's as clean as a baby's butt. I can't guarantee anything."

"Fuck! Fuck! Fuck!" Driscoll was wired. "Either Romano's still alive, and we've been set up or he's dead, and somebody else wiped the place down."

O'Brien whispered to his chief, "What a conclusion—either he's dead or he's alive. Now I know why he's a federal dick, and I'm stuck out in the burbs."

"Okay, search it," Driscoll ordered, feeling in his element. The team pulled out drawers, tossed cushions, tore draperies, slit the back of paintings, and literally demolished the place. O'Brien tried to stay one step ahead of the disaster team. The den drew him in. Books. O'Brien took in the titles. Classical literature, novels, reference books, non-fiction bios, war stories. They all seemed well-read. Either that, or he bought them used, O'Brien thought, hating to give Romano credit.

A leather-bound set of the complete works of Shakespeare, Volumes I through VIII. Unconsciously, O'Brien counted, as he always did when something was numbered. Seven books. Strange. Before he could give any more thought to the missing volume, Driscoll's people charged in. They pulled the books from the shelves, held them by a corner and shook hard, then tossed them carelessly in a heap. The room turned to shambles before O'Brien's eyes.

O'Brien walked in to the master bedroom. The large bed was covered by a silk spread. The detective averted his eyes, hating where his thoughts were going. The bathroom was almost as large as the bedroom. Wow. He left, one step ahead of the disaster squad. "Let's go," he said to the chief, standing in the now-destroyed kitchen.

"The guy either had a cook or was something of a chef himself. Look at the equipment."

"Yeah, yeah, Romano's a real renaissance man. Come on, let's get back to the station, I can't think here."

DRIVING BACK TO WINNETKA, the chief asked O'Brien, "Do you think the body we found really was Romano?"

"I wish I knew. If not, maybe the stiff had some prints on record, and we'll at least find out who he was."

"And, if not? If the dead body *isn't* Romano, somebody planned this thing pretty good."

"Then we'll sit and wait for him to make a mistake. Only thing is, time is running out for the Congressman—and for the kids."

CONGRESSMAN Franklin Chamberlain boarded the private jet for Washington, escorted by

Agents Driscoll and Wornick, to talk to the President.

If the Chief Executive Officer of the United States could be persuaded to postpone the vote on the Organized Crime Bill, he would have the undying allegiance of the Congressman. And he could count on a substantial contribution to his reelection campaign.

If not, Franklin would have to call in every favor he held to defeat the bill.

Talking to the President about delay would be tricky. This was a campaign promise the President had made and was determined to see it through before the New Year. Congressman Chamberlain's power of persuasion would be sorely tested.

DAY TWO
TUESDAY, NOVEMBER 19 • 6:20 PM

CHIEF ATKINSON and Detective O'Brien walked into the station, dodging reporters and blazing camera lights.

"O'Brien, Jonathan Chamberlain has been waiting to see you. He's in your office," the dispatcher told him as he passed through the locked, outer doors.

Chamberlain rose as the detective entered. The man who faced O'Brien was the Dorian Gray image of the perfectly-creased man who had arrived just yesterday. He was now a crumpled facsimile, a broken older brother.

"May I help you, Mr. Chamberlain?" Jonathan futilely searched for words. "Would you like some coffee?" O'Brien offered.

"Thank you. And aspirin please."

"Would you like me to call your wife? Or perhaps your doctor?" O'Brien was remembering the recent heart attack.

"No. I need to talk to you first."

"Of course." O'Brien pressed a button. "We need coffee and aspirins. Now, what can I do for you?"

"Listen," Jonathan began, "I haven't been totally honest with you." His breathing was labored, and O'Brien was worried. The coffee came, courtesy of an officer, along with two tablets. Jonathan swallowed them, gulping the hot, bitter coffee.

"I'll be all right," he assured O'Brien. "Everything I told you is true. But what I didn't tell you is that two men came to see me when I was at my father's. I just found out who they were—Silvio Masucchi and a Dolf somebody. Masucchi is from New York, and this Dolf guy is from Las Vegas. They wanted a million dollars to knock off Tony Romano and my wife." Chamberlain's face was slack.

"Your wife! Is she in danger?"

"I don't know! I never gave them any money. I went to meet them later at a gym in Cicero, Jack's Gym. I told them to leave me alone. Next thing I know Romano is dead. In my house. I don't know if they have my kids or they'll hurt Meridith." He began to cry, "I just don't know."

"You do know that your wife's check for that amount *has* been cashed?"

"But that was for the loan—"

"Did you go to the gym this morning?"

Chamberlain looked at the detective curiously. He nodded, then hung his head.

"That's how I found out the names. I called the guy back, a Jack Handy, but he said he couldn't find anything out. Please, Detective, help me find my children." Chamberlain was pitiful. O'Brien wanted to feel sympathy for the man, but his actions were inexcusable, as far as O'Brien was concerned.

The detective admonished himself for allowing his feelings to get in the way.
"Look, Mr. Chamberlain, let me call your wife, tell her you're here, and have one of the officers drive you home. You're not well." Chamberlain said nothing. O'Brien called O'Donald. "Patty, take Mr. Chamberlain home, and see that his doctor is called." To avoid feeding the ravenous appetite of the waiting press, she gently escorted him into one of the police cars housed inside the station garage.

Meridith wanted Jonathan to return to Northwestern Hospital, but he refused. She gave him the medications he'd missed and put him in the master bedroom. It felt good to be back in this bed, he thought. He turned his face into the pillow and, breathing the fragrance of her hair, gave in to the sedative effect of the drugs.

"Please, God, I know I don't deserve any favors. But, if you bring my children home safe, you can do whatever you want with me. I know it's not a good trade, but it's the best I can do. They don't deserve to be hurt because of my mistakes. Please, God ..." he drifted off to a fitful sleep hoping God was listening.

DAY THREE
WEDNESDAY, NOVEMBER 20 • 6:00 AM

MERIDITH HAD SPENT the night in Chelsea's, raspberry-colored room. She felt closer to her daughter in there. What little sleep she managed was fitful, but she held on to a mother's faith. *If* something bad had happened to my child, I would *know*. She searched her spirit. That wrenching feeling in the womb, the spot beneath the heart that hurts when the child is in danger, that special place felt right. They were all right, they had to be.

She walked to Hunter's room, seeing it through her son's eyes: the posters on the wall, the stereo that played through the night, the model planes, monster figurines, an autographed baseball. Please let him return to this room to finish growing up, give him that chance. She implored the God she knew was listening.

•   •   •

O'BRIEN SPENT another restless night. Something was nagging him, and he couldn't put his finger on it. There had to be some way to find out whose body was lying in the morgue. There were no prints on file for the body or for Anthony Romano. The condo was wiped clean.

O'Brien dialed the station. "I'm on my way in. Has anyone claimed the body yet?" A pause. "Okay then. Find out where Romano's family lives, and get a search warrant for the house. Also, put out an APB for Romano's body guards." He checked his notes. "Frank Delvecchio and Jules Carboni."

He was going to have some answers today, he could feel it in his aching bones.

DAY THREE
WEDNESDAY, NOVEMBER 20 • 7:00 AM

BROOKE EASTON opened her front door to pick up the morning paper. Her brass mailbox was open, a small book holding the lid up. That's strange, she thought, the mail doesn't come until the afternoon.

She pulled the book out and examined it. It was a play. Clipped to the front page was a neatly hand-printed note: *Please deliver to Meri.* Someone must have dropped this off last night, she thought. Between the reporters and the police you couldn't get close to the Chamberlain house, so Brooke assumed that someone from the theatre left it for her to deliver.

"I can't believe anyone would think Meri would care about a play at a time like this," she told Chet as she tossed the small leather-bound book on the hall table. "Theatre people," she commented to the chocolate Labrador.

"Mommy, have they heard anything about Chelsea?" Elyse asked. The girl was having nightmares, and Brooke kept her home today.

"No, honey, but I'm sure Chelsea is going to be fine and home soon." Brooke wished she believed that. She worried about how Elyse would handle a tragedy and prayed her daughter wouldn't have to deal with one. At least not as a child.

The morning news program began with an update on the "Winnetka Kidnapping."

Walter Jackson was live from the police station, "We're here in the affluent village of Winnetka this morning. Police Chief Russell Atkinson still has no news on the missing children of prominent attorney, Jonathan Chamberlain, and his socialite wife, heiress Meridith Whitney Chamberlain. The children, Hunter, fourteen, and Chelsea, ten, have been missing since Monday morning.

"To further confound the already beleaguered law enforcement agencies, noted Chicago mobster, Tony Romano—" Brooke turned off the television as Elyse began to shudder. Elyse turned to her mother, tears in her eyes, "I'm so scared, Mommy." Brooke held her for dear life.

DAY THREE
WEDNESDAY, NOVEMBER 20 • 9:00 AM EST

THE PRESIDENT was seated behind his desk in the Oval Office when Congressman Chamberlain entered with FBI Agents Sam Driscoll and William Wornick.

"Congressman, I'm so sorry to hear of your misfortune," the President greeted Franklin, extending his hand.

"Thank you, sir. And, thank you for agreeing to meet with me."

"Agent Driscoll informed me of the circumstances. Please, sit down," he gestured to the Queen Anne chairs in front of his desk. Franklin took a chair, and the President sat back down. The two agents stood, several feet back, glancing at the Secret Service men standing along the wall.

"Mr. President, I know your time is valuable, so I'll get right to the point. Here is a photocopy of the note I received Sunday morning wrapped in my newspaper." He handed the paper to the President and waited while it was read.

"My God!" There was silence while the two men stared at the paper now lying on the desk blotter. "What can we do, Congressman?"

"Mr. President, I know how much this particular piece of legislation means to you. Is there any way we can postpone a vote until after the new year? It may mean the lives of my grandchildren."

The President sighed. "I'm a parent myself, and I can understand your feelings. However, you know my stand on terrorism and hostage situations. You must admit that this is a hostage situation. If organized crime, or anyone outside the law, realizes they can hold hostage the entire United States Judicial System, *no one* will be safe. I mean no one. That's exactly why the Crime Bill is so important."

"I understand. What if the press were told you sent the bill back to committee for review? Once my grandchildren are safe, then I will do everything in my power to assist its passage."

The President picked up a gold pen and twirled it between his fingers. "I'll have to talk it over with my people. Congressman Chamberlain, if my prayers are answered, and they sometimes are, your grandchildren will be found before Friday, and we'll pass this bill and stick it to Organized Crime." He stood, signaling the meeting was over.

"Thank you, for your time. And for your prayers, Mr. President."

"Goodbye and God bless."

When the door to the Oval Office was closed behind the departing Congressman, the President picked up his phone. "Get me the Director of the FBI, and send in Boyer."

"DAMN IT, Henry, I'd like to help the Chamberlains. Hell, they sure gave me enough money to warrant consideration. But, if it looks like we caved in, then no one's kids will be safe. Does that make sense?"

Henry Boyer, Vice President and dear friend, watched the world's most powerful man pace against the backdrop of the rose garden. The last of the autumn leaves were being raked.

"Let me talk to the Director and see what progress they've made and if we can't light a fire under their agents. If we're lucky, maybe they can find the kids, one way or another, and we won't have to make that decision."

"Sounds good to me, Henry. My lunch with the prime minister is at one. I'll hope to have some news after that."

"Yes, sir. Mr. President, may I have few more minutes of your time?"

Henry Boyer was often referred to as "dashing." He was charming, inoffensive, and highly intelligent. Originally from New York, Henry had polished the good ol' boy image to a gleaming perfection, hiding his cunning under a charismatic veneer.

"Certainly, Henry, what can I do for you?"

"I was thinking, sir, that maybe we should table this OCB thing until after the new session. Your public opinion is riding high, you don't need to worry about reelection. Maybe it's time to step back a little. The Chamberlain's have given quite a bit of money to the party."

"Thinking about running yourself next time?" he only half-joked.

"No, sir. Just thinking about the party. And about you."

"Well, that's mighty nice of you, Henry, but I promised the American people. And, I'll do everything in my power to keep that promise."

"Yes, sir. In the meantime, your wife is on your private line."

The President grimaced. "Tell her I just left." And to prove his point, he walked out the door, followed by the Secret Service men.

Henry paced the Oval Office, lovingly fingering the Presidential Seal engraved on the front of the rich, cherry desk. He lingered a moment, staring out the picture window. Independence Avenue was across the expanse of browning lawn. Sightseers cued up for the tour through the White House.

Boyer picked up the President's private phone and dialed. "It's me," he spoke. "We need to move quickly."

DAY THREE
WEDNESDAY, NOVEMBER 20 • 9 AM CST

"WE GOT THE prints back from the murder weapon. They definitely belong to one Silvio Masucchi. We've got an APB out, and the bureau in New York has been alerted. So far, no one's seen or heard of the guy." Agent Sanders was reporting to Chief Atkinson.

"How about Las Vegas? Any word there?"

"Nope. Nothing."

"The gun we found *was* the murder weapon?"

"Yeah, a .44. Awful big gun for a close-range shoot," Sanders added.

"You didn't see the mess left in its aftermath. Whoever the shooter was, he made certain he took the guy out fast. The bullet he used was illegal—not something you pickup at your local gun shop."

"It's hard to imagine that a pro like Masucchi would be so stupid as to leave the murder weapon lying beside the body *and* with his prints all over it." The chief puzzled over this.

"I'd like to release the photos of Masucchi and Cashiano to the press," Atkinson stated. "Should we clear it with Washington?"

"I don't see why there should be a problem, but getting Washington's cooperation never hurts," Sanders suggested. The man would be a diplomat, the chief silently predicted. Too bad Driscoll didn't have the man's tact.

"Chief, you've got a call from Special Agent Driscoll in Washington," the desk informed him on cue.

"Atkinson here."

"Chief? I just had a meeting with the Director," he paused for effect, " and he wanted me to inform you that you have the entire resources of the FBI. Do whatever it takes to bring this case to a resolution before Friday morning."

"That's great, Driscoll. Are you coming back to Winnetka?" the chief asked innocently.

"I'm accompanying the Congressman. I don't know his agenda at the moment. I'll be in touch."

"Great. Sanders is here with me. Any messages?"

"No, just tell him to hold the fort until I get there."

"Right. Roger and out." Sanders laughed with him.

"You didn't ask him about releasing the photos?" Sanders realized.

"I didn't, did I? Call O'Brien. We need to put together a press conference. I want those pictures in every paper and on every broadcast tonight. I'll find those two assholes if it's the last thing I do. And, I'll find those kids by Friday."

"Yes, sir!"

DAY THREE
WEDNESDAY, NOVEMBER 20 • 10:30 AM

O'BRIEN'S HEART SANK as the police cars pulled up in front of Mama Rosa Romano's house in River Forest. Two paneled, painting contractor's trucks sat in the driveway. The detective was the first one to the open front door. The furniture was piled in the center of the large living room and covered with heavy tarps. Four men stood on ladders painting the walls. "Where is Mrs. Romano?" Agent Sanders asked as O'Brien and Harrison ran through the rooms.

"How should I know?"

"How long have you been here?" O'Brien asked another painter.

"About a week, we're almost through. Painted everything in the house."

"Who packed it up?" Harrison's turn.

"A cleaning crew came in first." The man speaking seemed in charge. "Scrubbed the house down like it was an operating room or something. Never saw anything like it. I asked if maybe somebody was sick or died in the house, you know, like AIDS. I didn't want to work here if it was. But we was told 'no' the old woman has a cleaning fetish."

"And you have no idea where the owners are?"

"Nope. Ain't seen nobody the whole time we been here."

"Who paid you?" Sanders again.

"Got paid in advance. All cash."

"Chief, I checked inside the cabinets and the frige. Even the doorknobs. Everything is cleaner than the day it was installed. What do you want us to do?" Harrison asked.

"Let's pack it in. We aren't going to find anything worthwhile here."

"Wait, Chief, check the garage." O'Brien ran through the back door to the detached garage off the alley.

"No need," the painter called after him. "We painted it, too. The cars are gone."

"Damn," O'Brien hollered from the backyard.

"ANYBODY HUNGRY?" Harrison called out as he set a bag of hamburgers on the conference table. O'Brien looked at the bag, already greasy on the bottom, and walked away shaking his head.

"Why can't they come up with a burger that is good for you?" he asked O'Donald, who was already digging in.

"Aw, come on, O'Brien," she punched his belly, "one more ain't gonna make a big difference, and you know how crabby you get when you don't eat or sleep. We know you haven't been sleeping, so, please, for my sake, eat something!" He chuckled at the tall, slender woman. He was learning to respect the lady more each day, she had the instinct that makes a good cop great. She and Harrison made a super team.

Agent Sanders sat down with wrapped burger. "Phones are quiet. Nothing from your ends?"

O'Brien swallowed. "No word on any of the APBs, no match on the prints from the body. Nothing on the phones to either Chamberlain residence. I guess you could pretty much say we've got bubkis."

"*Bubkis.* Is that a Winnetka word?" Sanders asked mocking.

"Detective, there's a call for you on line three, they say it's urgent," the dispatcher yelled as he passed through to the bathroom.

"O'Brien."

The voice on the other end was garbled, obviously calling from an out-of-range cellular. "Detective O'Brien? I'm only going to say this once, so listen carefully. If you want to find the Chamberlain children before Friday, see Gino Sorrento and George Gravani in New York. They've got 'em. Hurry." The line went dead.

"Holy shit! Did you get that!" Sanders and O'Donald couldn't be contained.

"Play that back!" he ordered. The dispatcher quickly made a copy of the last call on another piece of tape and played it. They listened, mesmerized.

Agent Sanders was shaking. "Holy fuckin' shit! Dominick Sorrento is what they call the boss' boss. He's big. They say he runs the whole frigging country, even Sicily. Call the Director. We'll need help on this!"

DAY THREE
WEDNESDAY, NOVEMBER 20 • 2:00 PM

"MR. CHAMBERLAIN, we can't take you with us, you're a civilian." Chief Atkinson tried to reason with the distraught man. "Besides, your health precludes it. I can't be responsible for you."

"Screw that! These are my kids, damn it! I need to be there! And I am an officer of the court." They had already been arguing for over fifteen minutes, and time was precious.

"Swear to me you'll take orders and not try anything foolish, and I'll let you fly with us to New York. I can't promise anything beyond that. Understood?" The chief was firm.

"Thank you."

"They're waiting. Are we ready?" O'Brien asked, annoyed that the chief was capitulating. Chamberlain nodded.

"Promise to call the minute you hear anything?" Meri looked first at Jonathan then to O'Brien. "And, please, bring my children back with you."

O'Brien's belly screamed at him for scarfing the burger. "Officer O'Donald will be here with you, will you be all right?"

"Of course. Brooke is here, too. I'll be praying for you and for …" she trailed off. It went without saying.

The three men walked outside to a car where Agent Sanders and Officer Harrison were waiting. An FBI plane was flying them to New York. The director was already en route from Washington, with Special Agent Driscoll eagerly at his side. Meridith and Brooke watched the police car make its way through the amoeba-like mob of reporters then, with sirens wailing, disappear down Sheridan Road.

Meridith, Brooke and Patty O'Donald walked back through the house. "Can I get you anything, Meri?" Brooke asked. Meri shook her head and picked up one of Chelsea's books left on the counter. "Meri! That reminds me, I forgot to give you this," Brooke was trying to distract her friend. She went to her oversized bag. "Here it is," she said as she extracted the book.

"What is it?" Meri asked.

"I found this book in my mailbox this morning. Someone from the theatre must have left it there last night. I can't imagine why. Anyway, here it is." She handed her the small, red, leather-bound book.

Meri took it and saw the neatly printed note clipped inside the front cover. It was volume VII of the complete works of Shakespeare. She started to put it down when the title page fell open. *Romeo and Juliet*.

"Oh, my God!" She held it under the light.

"What is it?" Brooke's question hung in the air. Officer O'Donald repeated it. Meri looked at her friend, then at the police officer.

"Nothing. I just remembered that Hunter was reading this at school, that's all."

"Who would be so sick as to give you that book now?" Brooke shivered.

"It's all right, Brooke. Really." She stood up trying to conceal shaking knees and hands.

"Would you ladies excuse me for a minute?"

"Are you okay? Do you need help?" O'Donald was concerned.

"I'm fine. I'll be right back." She held the book and walked upstairs into her room, locking the door. Meri flipped through the book and noticed yellow highlighting. Carefully, she began at the beginning of the first highlighted section. Only a few lines on the pages bore the yellow accent:

Act III, Scene II.

Juliet's Nurse: *Ah, well-a-day! he's dead, he's dead, he's dead!*
We are undone, lady, we are undone!
Alack the day! he's gone, he's killed, he's dead!

Juliet: *Can Heaven be so envious?*
What devil art thou, that dost torment me thus?
This torture should be roared in dismal hell.

Nurse: *There's no trust, No faith, no honesty in men; all*
perjured ... Shame come to Romeo!

Juliet: *Blistered be thy tongue for such a wish. He was not*
born to shame.

At the end of the page:

Nurse: *I'll find Romeo to comfort you; I wot well where he is.*
Hark ye, your Romeo will be at night;

Juliet: *O, find him!*

Meridith's hand shook as she turned the page:

Act III, Scene III:

Friar Laurence: *Romeo, come forth; come forth, thou fearful man;*
Affliction is enamored of thy parts.
And thou art wedded to calamity..
Not body's death, but body's banishment.

Romeo: *Ha! banishment? be merciful, say—death;*
For exile hath more terror in his look,
Much more than death, do not say—banishment.
They may seize on the white wonder of dear Juliet's hand
And steal immortal blessings from her lips;
Who, even in pure and vestal modesty,

> *Still blush as thinking their own kisses sin;*
> *But Romeo may not; he is banished.*
> *Flies may do this, when I from this must fly;*
> *They are free men, but I am banished.*
> *And say'st thou yet, that **exile is not death**!*

The yellow highlighting stopped. Meridith held her breath as she read. Could this be wishful thinking? A bad, horribly coincidental joke? She reread the underlined passage, then flipped to the end of the play, and found one more passage marked for her eyes.

Act V. Scene I:

> Romeo:
> *If I may trust the flattering eye of sleep,*
> *My dreams presage some joyful news at hand.*
> *My bosom's lord sits lightly in his throne;*
> *And, all this day, an unaccustomed spirit*
> *Lifts me above the ground with cheerful thoughts.*
> *I dreamed my lady came and found me dead,*
> *(Strange dream! that gives a dead man leave to think,)*
> ***And breathed such life with in kisses my lips,***
> ***That I revived, and was an emperor.***
> *Ah me! how sweet is love itself possessed,*
> *When but love's shadows are so rich in joy!*

"Mrs. Chamberlain? Are you all right?" It was O'Donald. The voice startled her. She dropped the book.

"Meri? May I come in?" Brooke was with the officer.

"I'm fine. I just want a moment alone."

"Okay, but call if you need anything."

She listened and heard them walk away. When she retrieved the book her eye caught the fluttering of something falling from its pages. She stopped, bent back down and examined the object.

It was just a brown, weathered leaf. Her heart pounded! She picked it up and looked at it under the lamp. It was a small, four-leaf clover.

She looked at the handwriting on the note. *Please give this to Meri.* She tried to think—had she ever seen his handwriting? She couldn't remember. Her heart was pounding so hard; her throat was closing up, and she wanted to scream out. But she sat on the edge of her bed rereading the last passage: *"...And breathed such life with kisses in my lips, that I revived..."*

Tony was alive!

The children—could they be with Tony? The roller coaster careened downward. No, he would have sent that message as well. Where were they? She held tight to her faith. Tony was alive, and she instinctively knew they were, too.

"Meri, please let me in," Brooke begged. Meridith closed the book. After carefully placing the clover between the pages and setting it gently on the mantle, she opened the door.

"Meri, you had me so worried. Are you really all right, you look strange."

"I just needed a moment with my thoughts. And prayers."

"I understand," she told her dear friend as she hugged her tightly. "I have a good feeling everything is going to fine. And real soon." Brooke promised.

"Thank you, Brooke. So do I."

DAY THREE
WEDNESDAY, NOVEMBER 20 • 6:00 AM EST

"WHAT THE HELL'S he doing here?" Agent Driscoll demanded when he met them at the small, private Long Island airport.

"Look, I knew this might pose a problem, but he was insistent. How would you feel if they were your kids? And he is an attorney." The chief was apologetic and O'Brien squirmed. Driscoll mumbled but walked on ahead of them to the idling, government-issued car, an oversized dark limo, where FBI Assistant Director Richard Savage waited. Savage was known among the ranks as "blood and guts," due in part to the fact he ordered several raids that had ended in gunfire and death.

The ride along Long Island's Gold Coast was even more impressive than the one along Chicago's North Shore. Once, these American castles were the private dominion of wasp money, now they boasted the names of Chung, Greenberg and Giovani "Gino" Sorrento.

During the half-hour ride, Driscoll grilled Sanders trying to make points with Savage. As they pulled into the gated estate, a guard appeared on the locked side of the wrought-iron fence. The ten acre property was surrounded by a brick wall covered now by brown, withered ivy.

"Great place to hold the kids," Atkinson noted. "It's impenetrable."

The driver rolled down his window, "FBI to see Mr. Sorrento." He flipped his wallet to display his badge. A guard built like a body-builder came through the gate-house door and inspected it. He knocked on the back windows. "I need to see everyone's ID," he demanded. Each man searched under their coats. Chamberlain sat mute. After the guard examined five sets of ID, he looked at Jonathan. "Where's yours?"

"He's a civilian, he's with us," O'Brien told him.

"I still need to see who he is," the guarded insisted. Chamberlain took his billfold out and opened it. "Why are you with them?" he asked.

Before Jonathan could speak, O'Brien opened the door. "Look, he's here on official business. Open the damn gate, or we'll haul your ass in."

"You have no jurisdiction here, you fucking flatfoot. And, unless you have a warrant, I'm not opening the gate." The man folded his arms across his chest. Assistant Director Savage stepped out of the car and into the man's face. He pulled a paper from his jacket and shook it to release the folds.

"This do?" Savage asked with artificial courtesy. The guard stepped back, and the gates parted ceremoniously. Ahead they could see the white stucco and the red-tiled roof of a mansion built to impress the rich and intimidate the hell out of everyone else.

Savage spoke, "I'll do the talking. If anyone has questions when I'm finished, you can ask them. Chamberlain, say nothing or, I swear to God, I'll lock you up until this investigation is over. Understood?" The men nodded. Chamberlain looked sullen. "Okay, let's do it."

FOR OVER TWENTY, long minutes the group waited in the atrium foyer, built around a green marble fountain that spewed water at the feet of a nude woman. O'Brien really need to get off his aching feet. He hadn't slept much since Monday morning.

"I'ma so sorry to keep you gentlemen waiting. I was ina portant meeting and couldn't break away. Now, if I know you was coming, I woulda met you right away." The tall man who addressed them in broken English was elegantly dressed and sported a full head of wavy, white hair. His black eyes flashed when he spoke, contradicting the smile creasing his weathered face. He was accompanied by two men: Frances, balding, thin and worried-looking; the other, Vinnie, dark-complected, huge and angry-looking.

"Mr. Sorrento, I'm Assistant FBI Director Richard Savage." He then introduced the entourage. Sorrento seem uninterested.

"What may I do to help the Assistant FBI Director?" O'Brien detected a note of mockery in Sorrento's voice.

"Mr. Chamberlain's two children were kidnapped Monday morning in Winnetka, Illinois." Savage gestured towards Jonathan.

"I'ma so sorry," Sorrento turned to Jonathan. "Children," he clicked his tongue. "That's so sad. In the old days," he looked right at the Director, "no one woulda thought to involve a man's children. It'sa sad how the world has changed. What canna I do to help you?"

"We got an anonymous tip a few hours ago that they could be found here."

"Here! Who would say sucha thing? I wouldn't never hurt kids. Canna you believe that?" he asked his companions. They didn't answer.

"Then you wouldn't mind if we searched the premises?"

"Hey, I gotta nothin' to hide. Search away. Oh, by the way, it'sa big house. You wanna I should have coffee made for you. Or maybe lunch?"

"No, thank you," Savage stated. "Let's get started."

The FBI people started up the stairs, O'Brien and the chief began exploring the immense, first floor. The house was furnished in eclectic styles of heavy, baroque, Italian design; extravagant, French influence; and flamboyant, Chinese colors. Sorrento followed them, carrying a small china cup. "You sure you don't wanna espresso? I have the beans flown in personally."

"You're very generous, but, no, thank you," O'Brien really wanted a cup of the fragrant brew. Chamberlain followed the two policemen from room to room. The kitchen was practical and, obviously, well-used. There was a breakfast room that overlooked a beautifully manicured garden, now dormant. O'Brien could see the curve of Long Island Sound from the back of the house. Damn, he thought, remembering the view from the back of the Chamberlain's, maybe money couldn't buy everything, but it sure bought you a little piece of the world's better windows.

He was about ready to accept Sorrento's coffee when Savage's voice interrupted his thoughts. "We didn't find any sign of them. Let's go."

"Did he really think he'd find them sitting watching TV upstairs?" O'Brien whispered to the chief, who shrugged.

"Wait." O'Brien's voice stopped them.

"Mr. Sorrento, one more question on a local matter. Were you acquainted with Tony Romano?"

"Mr. Romano. I don't remember the name, it rings no bells. Do we know him, Frances?" The thin man thought, then shook his head.

"Why should I know this Tony Romano?" Sorrento asked, setting his cup on the marble counter.

"We found him dead in Winnetka." The chief took over. "He's supposedly connected to you, Mr. Sorrento. Are you sure you don't know him."

Sorrento contemplated the questions for a long minute. "No. No one by that name is known to me. 'Course lotsa people work on down the line for my businesses, maybe that's how. We look into it, huh, Frances? You check, and let me know, okay?" The thin man creased his brow further into his non-existent hairline.

"Thank you for your cooperation. If you should hear anything that may help us with either case, please, call me." Savage handed his card to the older man who took it and without reading handed it to Frances.

"There is a large reward, a million dollars, for the safe return of the children," O'Brien added. Chump change for the boss' boss, he thought, but it was worth mentioning to the two minions who stood at Sorrento's elbows. He did notice a slight change in the body-builders eyebrows.

"Thank you, again," the chief extended his hand. Sorrento shook it with both of his.

"It'sa nice to meet a real gentleman in the law enforcement business." That remark did not go unnoticed by the FBI agents who walked, without ceremony, to the car.

DAY THREE
WEDNESDAY, NOVEMBER 20 • 11:00 PM EST

JONATHAN STARED out the window of the New World Center Hotel. The city was wide awake. A jackhammer broke the pavement twelve stories below, taxis honked impatiently, and a river of people still streamed along the sidewalks.

Detective O'Brien was in the next room, God only knew where the FBI people went. Maybe they're like vampires, Jonathan thought, roaming the night for new blood. That would explain a lot.

He'd called Meridith and brought her up to date on the trip through Sorrento's estate. Talking to her made him feel more impotent. He couldn't just sit here and wait. Every minute that ticked by meant his children's lives were more and more in danger.

Impatient with himself and with the progress the so-called authorities were making, he picked up his coat and walked to the elevator. He had to feel like he was doing something. He walked through the lobby. The pulsating music from the bar beckoned him in. "Glenlivit, make it a double." Jonathan threw back the glass and felt the slow burn. He grabbed a glass of water to chase it. Although his stomach rebelled, the muscles in his neck relaxed.

Jonathan ordered another. The bartender looked like an amiable guy, ruddy face, bow tie, apron wrapped around a generous waist. He watched the barkeep pass an envelope to another patron then pocket a wad of bills.

Jonathan called the man over. "I take it you're a native New Yorker?" The man nodded. "Me? I'm from Chicago." Jonathan talked to a blank face but forged on. "Can you help me with a small problem?"

The bartender examined him. "Want another drink, buddy?" Jonathan nodded. When it was served, Jonathan smiled and asked, "Say, suppose a guy wanted to hook up with something. How would he go about it?" Jonathan pulled out his money clip and laid it on the counter.

The bartender appraised his customer. Guy didn't looked like a cop, clothes too expensive. Sounded more like he needed nose candy. "What kind of question is that? How the fuck should I know?" New Yorkers favorite utterance.

"As I said, I just got to town today. I'm carrying some—valuable merchandise. You know how the airlines are, couldn't bring my gun and I feel naked without it. I'm not looking for drugs or anything. I just need to know where I can buy a—piece, to protect my merchandise. I'm willing to pay. Can you help?"

Guns, huh, the bartender thought. No way the law could come back at me for that. "I maybe know of a place. It'll cost ya." Jonathan pulled a hundred dollar bill from the clip. The bartenders eyes lit up like the Fourth of July, and he reached out greedily.

"Wait. Your turn." Jonathan pulled the bill back. The man behind the bar grabbed a receipt from the register, scribbled on it, and handed it Jonathan. "This man, suppose he says he never heard of you? Can't help me?" Jonathan asked.

"That's the crap shoot you'll have to take, ain't it? Life in the Big Apple can be a real bitch." The bartender snatched the folded bill quickly and stuffed it in his pocket. Jonathan finished his drink and walked through the revolving doors into the drizzling night.

"I need to rent a car, can you help me?" he asked the doorman, bundled up in a mock palace-guard uniform.

"Not at this hour, man, 'fraid you're out a luck." Jonathan appraised the black man in the ridiculous garb.

"I got an idea that may help us both." Again he reached in his pocket. Pulling out two hundreds, he held them where the doorman could plainly see them. "How's about I rent your car for the night. I'm a guest here," he held up his key, "so you know I'm coming back. I just need to see a woman for a few hours." He winked at the man, who smiled broadly.

"Hey, man, I knows what you mean. But my car is bad, I mean it's a real piece of shit. Man like you wouldn't want to go driving around with a woman in an old, seventy-nine, deuce-and-a-quarter Buick."

"Sure I would. It'll get me there, won't it?"

"No problem, dude, I work on it myself. It's a classic now." Jonathan waved the bills closer. "You say you'll have it back by six, that's when my shift is over?"

"Sure, man, no problem," Jonathan echoed the man's words and handed the bills over. "I'm Chamberlain. Check it out, I'm in room twelve thirty-six."

The doorman's breath was visible in the cold, night air. He reached underneath the bulky coat and pulled out a set of keys. "Buick's blue, in the employees parking lot, underground, level five. Don't forget, six AM, or I'm in deep shit."

"Yes, sir, six o'clock."

•   •   •

THE PHONE brought O'Brien out of his stupor. "Hello?" he asked hoarsely as his brain begged his eyes to focus.

"O'Brien, it's Atkinson. We just got word. Chicago police found two bodies lying in a recycling dump next to railroad tracks. Forestview, just west out of the city off the Stevenson, between Harlem and Cicero."

O'Brien sucked in his breath, "Not the kids?"

"No, no. Sorry if I gave that impression. Two men, both very large. They're checking to verify the ID, but, according to the driver's licenses, it's Masucchi and Cashiano." O'Brien was simultaneously relieved and discouraged. If they didn't have the kids and couldn't be interrogated, where to now?

"Any word about the kids?" he asked the chief.

"No, it looks like somebody else is out there looking for the same guys we are, and we're a day late and a step behind. The men were shot, execution style, in the back of the head. They don't have much of a face left, either."

"I guess the killer didn't leave his calling card?"

"I don't have the whole story, yet, but they're checking it out now. In the meantime, the FBI is running everything through their fancy-schmancy computers. Now, we just hurry up and wait. Anything from Chamberlain?"

"Quiet next door. Keep me posted, Chief."

"Try to get some sleep. I'll see you downstairs at six?"

"Right, sleep. See you tomorrow."

DAY FOUR
THURSDAY, NOVEMBER 21 • 2:45 AM

JONATHAN CHAMBERLAIN retraced the drive to Long Island. The adrenalin neutralized the liquor he'd consumed, but his head was still reeling. Acquiring the gun had been easy, but not cheap. He felt its weight in his coat pocket. It reassured him, and it also scared the hell out of him. His hands sweated as they gripped the wheel.

The lights of the aging Buick spilled across the guard house outside Sorrento's. Instantly, a burly man clad in a bulky coat appeared brandishing an automatic weapon. He held the gun pointed directly at the windshield. Chamberlain carefully opened the car door.

"Tell Mr. Sorrento Jonathan Chamberlain needs to see him," he said slowly and loudly.

"Are you crazy? It's three o'clock in the morning! He'd kill both of us!" The man's breath hung in the frigid, black, night air.

"Either call him, or I'll shoot you," Jonathan calmly told the guard raising his own gun to eye level and steadying it with his left hand.

"You are fucking insane! You pull the trigger, and we'll both be dead!" The guard looked at the rusted-out car and the crazed man in the expensive overcoat. "Hey, Dominick, call the house. Ask for Frances. Tell him I've got a cocksucker out here who's asking to have his balls blown off. See what he wants me to do. Oh, the asshole's name is—"

"Chamberlain," Jonathan filled in.

"—Chamberlain. And he's got a gun." The two men stood at an impasse, each holding a gun barrel leveled at the other, for what seemed like much longer than five minutes in the cold air. Finally, the phone rang. The guard inside the house whispered something to the gunman who looked at Jonathan skeptically.

"I'm going to put my gun down. Get in your fuckin' car and drive in, very slowly. Frances will meet you. He says not to wake up the old man."

Jonathan's hand was frozen to the cold metal. He slid back behind the wheel and closed the door. A chill electrified his spine as he drove away from the man holding an automatic weapon pointed at his head. A lone figure was waiting on the front step—a menacing, black silhouette against the white house. From the darkness another figure appeared before the engine was turned off. Jonathan jumped as the car door was opened.

The voice, "Hand me your gun, and then get out very slowly." The gun was handed to the outstretched arm. "Now, get the fuck out of the car and turn around."

Chamberlain did as he was told. Funny, he thought, as the man patted him down, I'm not scared. His body was so numb he didn't feel the bitter cold.

"He's clean," the voice called to the form standing by the door. A strong hand vice-gripped his neck and pushed him towards the entrance. Jonathan stumbled through the front door, followed by the two men. Inside the familiar foyer, the lights blurred his vision. As his eyes adjusted, they focused on the two men who had accompanied Sorrento earlier.

"What the hell are you doing here?" Frances asked him.

"I need to know where my kids are." It was a statement. "It's over. I want my children back and I want them back now."

"Look, Chamberlain—"

Jonathan jumped to his feet and grabbed Frances around the throat. Before Frances could react, Chamberlain began to squeeze—hard. The tortured man tried to push Jonathan away, fighting for air. Jonathan's thumbs were pressing into the man's Adam's apple and his eyes were bulging. Frances was hitting Chamberlain—his back, his head, his arms—but Jonathan only squeezed harder. The numbness was spreading. He couldn't feel his hands but knew they continued to close around the dying man's throat. Suddenly, he was outside his body again, watching.

"*Enough!*"

Jonathan heard the voice from behind him, but his hands were no longer extensions of himself. He had no control over the vices that continued to squeeze the life out of the bastard who knew where his children were. Only when the man's tongue protruded from his mouth

187

and he went limp, did Jonathan let go. Frances' body fell slack on the floor.

"Is he dead?" the voice asked. Vinnie came over and felt his neck.

"I think so, maybe, maybe not." He held a gun on Jonathan. "You want I should shoot him?"

"No, take care of the body. Leave us alone." The big man threw the form over his shoulder and left the room.

"Did you mean to kill him or was it a spur of the moment thing?"

Jonathan turned and recognized the man behind the question.

"This has gone too far. I want my children, and I want them now. Tell me where they are, or I'll kill you, too, you bastard. I have nothing left to lose."

"Do you know this house is watched day and night by the fuckin' FBI? Videotaped, wiretapped, the whole friggin'ed nine yards. You could blow the whole thing!"

"I don't care, I'll go to them with the story, anyway, if I don't get my kids back tonight. Safe."

"Look, we've played this whole thing down to the last hand. Be patient. Things are going as planned."

"It's out of my father's hands now. There's nothing more we can do. Get my kids back, now."

"Unfortunately, Chamberlain, your father has made matters worse. The public is eager to see this legislation passed. They want to limit our power. We need to know the Congressman will lobby against it."

"There's more to it than that. I think, after everything you've put my family through, I'm entitled to know."

"Perhaps." The man behind the voice walked into the living room, and the indirect lights went on. "Modern technology," he remarked. "They're on sensors. They detect movement." Jonathan followed him in and watched as he poured Gragnano into two crystal glasses and handed one to him. "It'll help you relax," he told Jonathan.

"Cut the crap, you sonuvabitch. I said I'd kill you, too, and I will." Chamberlain's eyes were blazing.

"Calm down, Jonathan, you don't want to have another heart attack, do you? If your father agrees to step down, retire, after the vote tomorrow, we'll release the children unharmed. They're very safe now, believe me, having the time of their young lives."

Jonathan threw the glass at the wall and came towards the seated man. As he grabbed his silk jacket, a shot resounded throughout the quiet house. Chamberlain jumped back, his heart pounding.

"Sit down, Chamberlain, or you'll wind up another dead body they'll find floating in the East River tonight!" Vinnie had reappeared, holding a revolver pointed at Jonathan's head.

"Thanks, Vinnie," the voice said calmly. Adjusting his jacket, the voice worked to regain composure. "I suppose you have a right to know what our plans are—before you are eliminated." He took a slug of the liqueur. "You're a loose cannon, Chamberlain. You can't be trusted. You know too much."

Jonathan was sitting now, his knees shaking, feeling returning to his hands. "You could have been quite a valuable asset. We certainly tried to make you part of the operation. With Romano out of the picture, and Sorrento too old to make the right decisions, we need new people. Someone with your connections, your background and style, you could have been invaluable. But now—"

Jonathan eyed the gun aimed at his head. "What about my kids? What happens to them now?"

"It could have been so easy. All you had to do was wait. We would have contacted your father and asked him to step down and they would have been returned. Now, I don't know."

"You fucking bastard!" Jonathan was on his feet again. Vinnie pressed the gun up under his jaw, pushing it hard under his ear. He could feel the cold steel and smell Vinnie's breath, and almost hear the big man's heart beating.

"Sit down. This is exactly why we can't have you on board, Chamberlain. Like I said, you've got a wild hair up your ass. Not the kind of man we want around."

"Why would you want my father to step down?" Now he had to know.

"Because he stands in the way. Without your father to head up the House Ways and Means Committee, our man is next in line. And," he laughed, "we are very close to Presidency."

"Oh, my God!" The gun crushed harder and cut into his face.

Laughter. "We have before, and we will again—soon. We're just a heartbeat away. And accidents do happen."

"But you can't!"

"If the American people paid more attention to what was really going on in the hallowed halls than to the tabloid scandals or their wallets, you're right, we couldn't. But they do and we can. It's that simple." The voice was philosophic. "We promise them a better economy, put more people on the welfare rolls and scare the hell out of old folks with social security, and, like magic, we win the elections. It's so easy its almost scary. You'd think they'd catch on!"

"Please, my kids ..." Jonathan was pleading. His stomach was on fire and a sharp pain cut him in half.

"You want I should take him outside and do him now?" Vinnie asked.

"Any more questions, Mr. Chamberlain?"

"Yeah, did you kill Romano in my house?"

"As a matter of fact, no, we didn't. However, the killer did us quite a favor.

Unfortunately, he didn't have our permission, and that's a real shame. For a while, we thought you grew balls and did him. We suspect Mr. Masucchi and Mr. Cashiano. You have any ideas?"

"Look, I agreed to this kidnapping thing because I thought it would get me off the hook, get my father to stop the legislation. But I thought I would be able to see the kids, know they were all right. It wasn't supposed to go this far! I don't give a shit about myself anymore. Promise me you'll get the kids back to my wife. Do whatever you want with me just leave my family alone. Please." Hot tears streamed down his perspiring face.

The man was sickened by Jonathan. "Take him out now. I've had enough."

Vinnie picked up Jonathan by his coat and pushed him towards the foyer.

"What about the video camera?" Vinnie asked, without taking his eyes off his quarry.

"Not to worry, it's out of commission." Let the feds figure how out their computer remote became de-programmed, he thought, remembering those agency nerds acting so smug when they'd set up the operation outside the Sorrento Estate, bragging to the President.

With the gun stuck firmly at the back of Chamberlain's head, they walked outside. The man in the living room poured himself another drink and downed it as he heard the shot from outside.

He smiled and walked back to the kitchen. Coffee would be nice, he thought.

DAY FOUR
THURSDAY, NOVEMBER 21 • 6:00 AM EST

"OPEN THE DAMNED door!" O'Brien was talking to the maid.

"I'm sorry, sir, it's against the rules," she backed away.

"I'm a cop, and the man in this room may be in trouble. Please." He pulled his wallet out and flipped it to show her his ID.

"I—I don't know."

"Do it!" he ordered. Tentatively, she slid the master keycard along the panel, and the door unlocked. O'Brien pushed it open and surveyed the room. There was no sign of Chamberlain. "Fuck!" The maid escaped to the stairs as O'Brien picked up the phone. He dialed Atkinson's room.

"Chief, O'Brien here. Chamberlain's not in his room!" Pause. "I don't know! I called, and when there was no answer, I had the maid let me in. Doesn't look like he slept here. Call Mrs. Chamberlain, see if she heard anything. I'll see you downstairs."

The front desk had no record of Chamberlain leaving, and he had made one call to Winnetka.

O'Brien was trying to reach Driscoll when he saw the doorman gesturing frantically to the woman at the front desk. He walked closer until he could hear the conversation.

"Hell, he say he was a guest here. No, I just saw the key, I didn't check. He come down and say he needs a car bad. He looked real rich, white guy, expensive clothes. Wait, I wrote down his room. Here, I got it. Twelve thirty-six."

O'Brien snapped his fingers. Bingo, sometimes you just get lucky. "Fella! Hey, you. I'm Detective O'Brien," he flipped his ID, hoping no one looked too closely at his jurisdiction. "What's this about a man in twelve thirty-six?"

"Oh, shit! I give him my car. Don't tell me, man, that I'm not gonna get it back." The doorman was beside himself.

"You'll get it back, I'm sure. I'll find it myself. I just need to know a few things. Did this guy tell you where he was going?"

"Naw, said something about needin' a woman. I mean, man, he didn't seem like the type who would need to pay for it but ya never know. People done got their hangups, ya know?"

"Yeah, I know. Look, describe the car and give me your license number." O'Brien would call the FBI and get an APB immediately. "Here's a twenty. That'll get you home, and I'll find your car. I promise."

"You the strangest cop I ever met," the doorman assured him. "You *doin'* something' fo a change." O'Brien was on the phone.

"Anything?" O'Brien asked the chief after he'd briefed him about the doorman's missing car and the APB had gone out.

"Mrs. Chamberlain's heard nothing, and now she's worried, too."

"Hell. Anything new on the shooting?"

"The ID was positive for Masucchi and Cashiano. But no leads. It was as clean a shoot as you can have in garbage dump."

"Oh, by the way, did we find out who cashed Mrs. Chamberlain's check?"

"Yeah, it was deposited in a numbered account in the Cayman Islands. How about that? She says she has no idea who or why. Next question."

O'Brien took a deep breath and blew it out audibly. "Let's go see Sorrento."

"I'll stay here to man the phones, you take Driscoll and go."

DAY FOUR
THURSDAY, NOVEMBER 21 • 7:50 AM EST

SPECIAL AGENT DRISCOLL and Detective O'Brien drove an unmarked car up to the Sorrento estate and honked. No one came out of the gatehouse. O'Brien stepped out of the car. A light dusting of snow had fallen during the night, sugar-coating the grounds. Tire tracks led through the open gate down the driveway. The doorman's Buick waited for them with open doors at the entrance to the house

"Gate's open. Let's go," O'Brien told him as he jumped back in the car. O'Brien pulled his gun and released the safety. Driscoll gave him a side-long look but said nothing.

They peered into the empty, aging car then walked to the front porch and rang the chime. It echoed throughout the cavernous hall. Nothing. O'Brien knocked loudly. The two men exchanged another meaningful look, this time Agent Driscoll reached under his coat and unsnapped the shoulder holster, pulling out his own weapon. O'Brien tried the front door, and the brass knob turned in his hand. They walked carefully into the quiet house.

"Mr. Sorrento?" Driscoll called.

"I don't like it," O'Brien confided. With guns drawn, they walked into the living room. Giovonni Sorrento lay dead, sprawled across the bright red sofa. Blood puddled from his head to his outstretched hand, looking for all the world like the sofa had simply bled to death down the corpse's arm.

"Oh, my God!" Driscoll uttered simultaneously with O'Brien's "Holy Mother Mary!"

"Call headquarters!" Driscoll ordered.

"In case you have forgotten, there are just two of us here, and I'm not your man. I'll cover you while *you* call headquarters." O'Brien wasn't sure what they'd walked into—this could be an all-out mob war. Three men were very dead in Chicago. His heart was pounding so hard he could swear Driscoll heard it.

O'Brien stood in the arched doorway while Driscoll used his cell phone to call for help. "Now, call the local cops, they'll be here faster!" O'Brien ordered. "Forget protocol, we could be next!" Driscoll obeyed without any argument.

Where in the hell was Chamberlain, O'Brien asked himself. He didn't want to know the answer.

DAY FOUR
THURSDAY, NOVEMBER 21 • 8:30 AM EST

NEITHER AGENT DRISCOLL nor Detective O'Brien left the foyer to search the large estate until back-up arrived. They heard the wailing sirens before they saw the four squad cars pull into the long drive. O'Brien stood at the front door witnessing a surreal light show effected by the red and blue lights ricocheting off the new snow.

"This way," Driscoll shouted, escorting the uniformed men into the living room. O'Brien stayed on the porch, trying to make sense out of what was happening. He was standing there when he saw the two blue Chevys pull in, obviously FBI. Driscoll will be in Hoover heaven, O'Brien thought, as he watched the suited-and-sun-glassed men emerge.

"They're all in the living room," O'Brien pointed. He followed the entourage into the house in time to hear:

"Hey, up here, we've got another body!" A stream of uniforms and suits ran up the stairs. O'Brien braced himself.

Trying to make his way through the crowd, he called to Driscoll, "Is it Chamberlain?"

"No, I don't know who the hell it is, but it's definitely not Chamberlain." O'Brien parted the gawking masses to see for himself.

"This is one of the two men who stuck to Sorrento like gum yesterday." The body lay sprawled across the floor. O'Brien obligatorily felt for a pulse. The thin man had ugly, purple bruises around his neck but sported a large hole in the side his head for good measure. The deep scarlet wound looked back at O'Brien like a third eye.

"Small caliber bullet. Didn't leave us much of mess this time," O'Brien commented, trying to calm the quease in his stomach. "Looks like this one put up a fight first. Hell of a bruise around his neck." The FBI agents had to check for themselves. O'Brien noticed Driscoll mop his brow, looking slightly nauseous himself.

"Don't touch anything until the forensic people get here," O'Brien barked as he left the room. It never hurts to remind them of procedure. His knees were complaining as he walked back downstairs. "Anyone check the rest of the house?" he called up. "Where in god's name is Chamberlain?" O'Brien asked out loud.

"They found some people locked in the basement," Driscoll reported. "They're alive but scared shitless. Household help."

"Can they tell us what happened?" O'Brien was hopeful.

"Said last night they heard gunshots. Seems there is a wing where the help lives." Driscoll's eyebrows rose slightly as he continued, "Anyway, someone wearing a stocking mask broke in and herded them down to basement. They didn't hear anything else until we opened the door. They were pretty relieved to see the uniforms. One of our guys is taking names and statements now, but I don't think we'll get much more from them." Driscoll sat down across from O'Brien at the kitchen table.

"What now, J. Edgar?" O'Brien asked him after a few minutes of silence.

"Hey, you Agent Driscoll?" a uniform called to them.

"Yeah."

"Better see this," he told them, shaking his head and pointing to the guard house outside.

"Oh, God, here we go," O'Brien took a deep breath, gearing himself for another round of gruesome discoveries. Inside the guard house they found the bodies of two more men. Both of them employees of Sorrento, neither of them Chamberlain. One man wore a single, crimson, bullet wound on his head, like an Indian scarab. The other man's head was bloodied from a blunt object."

"The one with the bullet in his brain looks like the bodyguard we met yesterday," O'Brien stated. "Is the M.E. here yet?" he asked the uniform. "He's got his work cut out for him today. And if Long Island is anything like Winnetka, you guys ain't ready for what's about to hit the fan."

Two suited FBI agents stuck their face in the guard house and retreated quickly. "Agent Driscoll, we found something interesting out back. Could you come with us, please?"

Driscoll and O'Brien followed the others through the steadily falling snow. They walked through a breeze-way between the garage and the big house to the back lawn. The accumulating snow was obliterating footsteps from the entrance to the living quarters over the garage, but they could make out small gullies of tire tracks. It looked like a car had been driven around, picked up more than one person, and left through a hidden back entrance.

"You guys know there was an exit here?" Driscoll asked pointing to the back of the house.

"Yeah, our camera should have picked it up."

"You mean you had cameras trained on this place?" O'Brien shouted.

"Sure, this place has been under surveillance for years."

"Can we see the videos now?" O'Brien again had to contain his voice, his excitement was mounting. "What are we waiting for? Let's see the tape!" Driscoll shouted, running ahead of O'Brien as they raced for their car.

DAY FOUR
THURSDAY, NOVEMBER 21 • 10:15 AM EST

"WHAT THE FUCK?!" the Detective shouted. O'Brien was seated at a long, polished table in the Long Island Police Department watching last night's FBI video tapes. The tapes showed Jonathan Chamberlain drive up to the gate house at 3:20 AM according to the time code in the lower right of the tape. He got out of the borrowed car and pulled a gun on the guard. It was at this point that O'Brien uttered the expletive.

They watched, fascinated, as the car drove up to the front of the house and Chamberlain met a figure an agent identified as Francis Ambruzzi and was escorted at gunpoint into the house by Vince "Vinnie" Lazio. The video continued to roll for another ten minutes. People seated at the table began to squirm uncomfortably. It was too warm in the room, O'Brien thought, just as the video cut to black. The agent running the television playback hit the button to rewind. The tape went black again at the same point.

"Looks like the camera went out right then," he announced. "Or was put out of commission by somebody who knew how it operated."

"Shit!" Driscoll banged on the table. It was the first time O'Brien heard the agent use a four letter exclamation. "Holy shit sonovabitch fuck!" Driscoll made up for lost time.

Agent Wornick bolted into the room. "We may have finally gotten a break!" All the heads at the table swiveled in his direction. Wornick caught his breath and continued, "We've been interviewing the staff from Sorrento's. Seems that when the masked man escorted them down to the basement, he took them through the kitchen. One of Sorrento's guards, a Dominick—" he checked his notes, "—Sanangelo, aka Angel, was holding two other men at gunpoint. We've got a computer artist with them now, trying to put together some faces."

Driscoll jumped up. "Hot damn, we're cooking with gas, now." O'Brien marveled at the agent's colorful vocabulary.

"Hold on, Driscoll, there's more. When asked to describe the men, most of the people couldn't give us much. But one of them, the housekeeper, is a pretty savvy woman. She says she recognized the masked man's voice. He'd been at the house before, and she can describe him. She also said one of the men being held was very distinguished, with gray hair at the temples, well-dressed—" he waited for Driscoll to fill in the blank.

"—Chamberlain!" Driscoll obliged.

"Chamberlain," Wornick confirmed. "And the other was, and I quote, 'a very handsome man, black hair, blue eyes'—"

"—Oh God, Romano?" O'Brien couldn't wait for Driscoll.

"Bingo!" Wornick finished with a dramatic flourish.

"Were they in on it together?" Driscoll asked.

Wornick shrugged. "We don't know if it really was him or not, but at least, now, we have something more to go on."

"Speaking of going on, where are they?" O'Brien turned to the FBI men. "Would it be all right if I spoke with this housekeeper myself. I have a few unanswered questions. Like who was that masked man?"

Driscoll looked at Wornick. "Let's bring her in," Driscoll suggested. O'Brien knew Driscoll would follow this like a dog in heat, waiting to get lucky. It was a horse-race now, to find the kids before the guys that were one step ahead did.

DAY FOUR
THURSDAY, NOVEMBER 21 • 12:15 PM EST

THE PRESIDENT paced nervously outside the press room. "Has anyone heard from Boyer yet?"

"No, sir," the Secret Service agent replied.

"He's supposed to make that speech with me. I'm late for the noon briefing and the press is ready to riot if I don't show up soon. I'll have to wing his part." The President was addressing his Chief of Staff.

"He's never just disappeared," the Press Secretary stated as she came running in waving a paper.

"This isn't the one Boyer wrote, but I drafted it this morning when he didn't show." She crossed her fingers.

"Here goes," he whispered as he took the raised platform in the blue, press room. Cameras flashed and tapes rolled as he began to speak. "As you know, our Organized Crime Bill goes before the House and the Senate tomorrow for a vote. My fellow Americans, I promised you I would make crime my number one priority, and I am very proud of this legislation. A copy is being circulated."

The President took a moment to scan the speech in front of him. No new information. "I won't make this a long session. I still have a few more arms to twist before tomorrow." Polite laughter. "So, I'll entertain questions from the fourth estate."

"Mr. President, there have been rumors that Congressman Chamberlain's missing grandchildren are being held hostage until the bill is defeated. Can you comment?" The murmur rose to a rumble.

"I—I—" He looked to his Press Secretary. The Chief of Staff imperceptibly shook his head. "We have no knowledge of that. As a personal friend of the Chamberlain family, they have my prayers for the safe return of their children. That's all for today. I'll see you all tomorrow to celebrate the victory of our bill."

He whispered to his aide, "Find Boyer. He'd better have a damn good excuse, or I'll have the bastard's head on a platter."

DAY FOUR • EARLIER
THURSDAY, NOVEMBER 21 • 3:52 AM EST

JONATHAN TRIED to remember a prayer as he was walked outside the Sorrento Estate. All he could ask of God was the safe return of his children. He prayed they would never know he had been, in part, responsible for this. His beating heart was flooded by regret. The drizzle had turned to snow. He gazed up at the black sky, and it looked, for all the world like the stars were falling.

"Okay, Chamberlain, we'll make this fast," Vinnie promised. He heard the gun cock and the bullet fall into the chamber. He felt the sweat roll down his arms and tried to concentrate on Meridith's face, drawn in brilliant relief on the inside of his eyelids.

He heard the shot. The world went black.

WHEN JONATHAN opened his eyes he saw Romano's face. I must be dead, he thought, and my hell is to spend eternity with him. He felt cold. Then a sharp slap as Romano worked to revive him.

"Chamberlain, damn you, wake up, we've got to get out of here!"

"What the hell happened?" Jonathan tried to make sense out of what he remembered.

"You were about to die, you son-of-a-bitch. Vinnie's dead. First man I ever killed," he admitted to Jonathan. "We've got to get out of here before they come looking for him!" Jonathan stood on wobbly legs. Tony put his arm around Jonathan's back and hoisted him as they walked to a car waiting behind the house.

"How did you—I thought you were—dead." Jonathan looked at Tony when they were seated inside the idling car.

"No time now," Tony answered distractedly as he put the car in gear. Before either man had time to breathe, another shot erupted, sounding more like a thud in the silent night. They felt the car tire go flat.

"Sonofabitch!" Tony uttered.

"Get out of the car, or I'll blow you away where you sit!" The figure outside the window ordered. One of the guards had come to.

"Damn! I should have killed them, too." Tony blew out his breath between clenched teeth. He had stowed Vinnie's body in the gate house, trying to buy time, and knocked the two guard's unconscious.

"What now?" Jonathan asked.

"We get out of the car."

"In the house!" They walked in a back door ahead of the gunman, whose finger itched to blow away the bastard who gave him this throbbing head. "In the house, you fucker, before I have an accident!" Tony walked in first. The man in the silk jacket was sitting at the table, sipping coffee from a demitasse cup. A decanter of brandy sat beside him.

"I'll be damned!" Tony exclaimed under his breath. "It's you, Hank Boliano."

Sitting at Sorrento's table was the Vice President of the United States, Henry Boyer.

"Hello, Romano. I thought you were too smart to end up dead."

"And I thought you were too smart to end up here."

Boyer laughed wryly. "It seems everyone is returning from the dead." Boyer looked at Dominick, the man holding the gun. "I heard a shot."

"Yeah, Vinnie's dead. This guy," he pushed the gun at Tony, "broke into the gate house. Hit me and Ricky hard. I woke up." He looked like he really wanted to pull the trigger.

"So, who was it in the Chamberlain's house?" he looked to Tony.

"First, where are the kids?" Tony demanded.

"Still acting like the big boss, aren't you. *Il Duce*, the fuckin' Roman Rooster. I don't think you're in any position to be giving orders or making demands, Tony my man. Sit down." They remained standing. "I said, *sit down!*" The two men sat down at the round table.

"Let's share information here, shall we, Mr. Romano, after all, we're both on the same team. You first. Who's lying in the morgue with a toe tag that says *Anthony Romano*?"

Chamberlain was mesmerized. "Guy by the name of Dan Mason. He's the double we've been using to scam the feds when I need to be somewhere without them tagging along. Poor bastard, never knew what hit him. Masucchi did him, thinking he had me. Masucchi thought Frankie Delvecchio was with him, and he and Dolf Cashiano had Frankie set me—Dan—up. I was sorry to have to use him that way, but it was either him or me. Masucchi told Frankie to get rid of the gun, but Frankie left it, prints and all, on the desk. He took the file with the notes about your debt, Chamberlain, which Masucchi left for the cops."

"Why do him at the Chamberlains?" Boyer was interested. Not as interested as Jonathan.

"I didn't pick the house, Masucchi did. He wanted to send a message to Chamberlain. Masucchi, like you, thought he could have his own pipeline to Washington. Not to mention the money." Boyer thought about this as Tony continued, "You'd better watch your ass. Masucchi thinks he's going to be the boss soon."

Boyer's laugh was demonic. "Masucchi's no longer a problem. By now the Chicago police have found two big-assed goombas in a dump we own off the Stevenson Expressway, with the rest of the garbage."

"Why terminate them now?" Romano asked, playing, again, for time.

"Why not? As I was telling Mr. Chamberlain earlier, we can't have wildmen running around making their own rules, can we? They went to Chamberlain and to Delvecchio without talking to us. They knocked you, or the poor bastard they thought was you, off without permission. Masucchi thought he could gain control the old-fashioned way, with strong-arm techniques. Today, it takes more. But you know that, Tony. The Organization belongs to guys like us." Tony studied the face of the man who was next in line for the President's office, a heartbeat away.

"Speaking of doubles, how'd you evade the press, not to mention your Secret Service escorts?" Tony asked the smug Vice President.

"Everyone needs a few moments with a good woman," he laughed. "They think I'm shacked up in a little hide-away the President keeps for things like this. We had our own *exit* built in. When we're there, the SS guys turn a deaf ear.

Your turn, again. So where're your guys, Delvecchio and Julie? Boyer asked. "They're not tailing you, either."

When Tony hesitated, the gunman pushed the barrel of the automatic into the back of his head. "I gave Frankie my boat, I don't know where he went. I gave him and Julie some money to get lost. Told them I didn't want to know where."

"Where is your family?" Boyer continued to interrogate.

"Where you can't find them," Tony answered defiantly. "Look, we both know you're going to kill us anyway. Why should my family go down with me? Where are the kids?"

"Here." Boyer answered simply. Jonathan jumped up, and his chair tumbled noisily to the floor. The gunman shifted his aim. "Sit down, Chamberlain, it won't do you any good. You're not walking out of here alive. They'll find you both tomorrow. And I'll be far away. Still holding the Congressman's grandchildren until they find him—dead, victim of a heart attack. Stress, you know. The scandal of his son found in Sorrento's home. Oh, it'll all come out, Chamberlain, how you were responsible."

"You were in on it!" Romano's voice rose to a pitch that made even Boyer jump. Chamberlain said nothing. "You fucking bastard, I should of let them kill you!" His words echoed, and Jonathan hung his head.

Boyer was enjoying the moment. "When are you going to learn, Romano, that eventually, everything comes back to us. When we found out that Masucchi planned an end run around us, we contacted Chamberlain directly. Unfortunately, Masucchi and Cashiano won't be, shall we say, cashing in on their efforts." The intensity of Tony's hate increased as Boyer continued. "We offered Chamberlain a better deal: his life back in exchange for the death of that legislation. We felt holding the kids was the only way we could get his old man to cooperate. He even helped us arrange the details. Only trouble was, he had no patience. Didn't you trust us, Jonathan? By the way, you were the one who tipped the cops, right?" Before he could answer they were startled by another voice.

"Whatsa goin' on here?" Sorrento asked from the doorway.

"Go back to bed," Boyer ordered. "I've got it all under control."

"Looka you, I tol' you I didna want to be involved in somethin' where we use kids asa pawn. This hasa gone too far. Get outta my house." Boyer stood up and walked calmly over to Angel, the gunman. Without a word, he took the gun and, as they watched, Henry Boyer leveled it at Sorrento.

The shot sounded like thunder, the crescendo ricocheted through the stone mansion! Then silence. Sorrento fell in a crumpled heap at Boyer's feet. A fist captured Jonathan's heart and squeezed. Please, not now, he prayed.

"All right, pick him up, and get rid of the body," Boyer commanded.

"*Mi madonna!* What the fuckeryadoin'? Do you know what you just did? My god! Where—What should I do with him?" Angel stammered. His eyes popped. Drool fell from his open mouth. Boyer had just killed the boss' boss!

"Put him in the living room. We're out of here, anyway. Make it look like these guys did him." The henchman hoisted the old man's body gently, almost reverently, and took it away.

"You're going to kill all of us?" Romano asked calmly to mask his racing mind. Boyer turned and looked at him curiously.

"Do I have a choice?" Boyer's face had taken on a crazed expression.

"If you want to keep the kids alive, they can't see you." Tony reasoned. Boyer considered that. "Let Chamberlain and me bring them down, they'll trust us."

Tony continued, "What about the household staff? I'm sure Sorrento had help, other than these goons. What are you going to do with them?" Tony was stalling for time. He handed Boyer a black, knit ski mask. "Put this on, and we'll get the kids. Where did you plan to take them from here?"

"Back to Washington. Car's in the garage." Boyer held the mask. "Okay." He handed the gun back to the burly man who had deposited his former employer across the sofa. Blood stained the front of his down jacket. Jonathan looked away.

"Keep the gun on them while I get rid of the staff."

"You goin' kill 'em all?" Angel asked.

"No. Where can I stash them to keep them out of our way?"

"Wine cellar has a lock. There's more guns and ammo down there, too. Key's on the ring inside the door."

"Stay here, and watch them until I get back. If anyone moves, shoot 'em. I mean it." Boyer pulled the cap on and adjusted the mask. Tony saw a slight tremor in Angel's hand and realized he was as scared as they were. After several painful minutes, they heard the shuffle of feet as Boyer herded the group of three women and two men down the stairs, through the kitchen, where they tried not to establish eye-contact, and down the basement steps. Then Boyer reappeared and stuffed the knit object in his pocket.

"Okay, we're all going outside to the apartment over the garage." He returned from the basement with an additional automatic weapon. He held it with practiced authority. "Let's go. When we get there, bring the kids down, and go into the garage. I'll drive, Angel will sit in the back. I promise you, if you get any ideas, he won't have to kill you, I'll do it myself. In case your memory is going, remember this—I have nothing to lose."

The tingling returned as Jonathan walked behind Tony through the outside door and up the stairs that connected the apartment. The gun was pointed at the back of Romano's head while Boyer fumbled with the keys. Jonathan felt his shirt grow wet under his heavy coat. The door finally unlocked and opened into a small living area. Angel pushed Tony into the room first. Jonathan stepped in, his eyes searching for a sign of the children.

"Hunter? Chelsea?" he called out. Boyer was pulling the ski mask down his face. "It's Dad, are you here?" A single light came on, spilling out from an adjoining room. Jonathan followed the beacon, calling their names. He felt them before he saw them, grabbing onto him and holding tight.

"Dad! I knew you'd come," Hunter was crying hoarsely.

"Daddy, Daddy, we were so scared!" Chelsea had her arms around his waist like a small vice. His tears came hot and furiously. He couldn't hold them close enough. For a split second he forgot where and who he was.

Then, "Dad, who's that man? What's going to happen now?" Hunter broke the reverie.

"It's okay, Hunter. Don't cry, Chel, don't cry. Dad's here now," Jonathan tried to console them. Tony watched, his emotions doing a tailspin. How could Chamberlain have gotten into this, Romano wondered. Damn him to hell!

"Okay, let's get going," Boyer ordered, his words muffled through the woolen guise. He held his gun leveled at the Chamberlains, Angel continued to keep the barrel of his weapon close to Tony's head. They walked single file down the stairs to the garage. Jonathan recognized a government limo by the plates. Boyer opened the back door. The children turned to Jonathan with a questioning look.

"You first, Chamberlain, then the kids. Then Romano. Angel, remember what I said about shooting them. You fuck this up, and you're a dead soldier." They stepped into the car as directed. Both Jonathan and Tony had ridden in enough limousines to know the locks were controlled from the driver's seat.

When the doors were secured, Boyer disappeared into the darkness. The children burrowed into Jonathan's wool coat. Their sweatsuits weren't warm enough for the weather, despite their own jackets. Silent snow fell against the dark windows. Two shots split the serenity of the dark night, like the pop of two firecrackers. The children jumped, Jonathan held them tighter, perspiration pouring under the coat. Tony reached over and patted Chelsea assuredly. Jonathan couldn't meet his eyes. Boyer returned, sat down behind the wheel and raised the glass partition. Tony watched Boyer through the murky glass as his silhouette pulled off the ski mask.

"What's going to happen now, Daddy?" Chelsea asked. Hunter stared at the gun pointed at them.

"It's okay, honey. It's going to be okay." He held her tight.

"What're *you* doing here, Mr. Romano?" Jonathan sat up straighter.

"Trying to help your father, Hunter, he's been searching for you."

"Oh." Hunter looked at his father like he'd just made the winning goal.

"How long's the drive to Washington?" Tony asked Angel, trying to engage him in conversation. Angel sat stone-faced. "You know he can't let you live, don't you? You heard the shots. All the other witnesses are dead."

"Shut up."

"It's about five or six hours," Jonathan answered, trying to distract the children from

Romano's comment. Tony checked his watch. Six forty-three. They'd be in Washington around one.

DAY FOUR
THURSDAY, NOVEMBER 21 • 12:35 PM EST

"GOOD-LOOKIN' GUY," O'Brien commented passing the composite around the Long Island Police Station. "It's Anthony Romano, the Chicago Boss."

"Then who's body is in the morgue?" Agent Wornick asked.

"Beats the hell out of me," O'Brien answered. "Guy must have a double." The FBI people looked at one another, embarrassed. "And this, my friends, is Jonathan Chamberlain." He passed another computer sketch around.

"Do we know who the masked man was?" Nervous laughter.

O'Brien couldn't help himself. "No, Kimo sabe, but we know it ain't the Lone Ranger. The housekeeper is pretty vague but says she recognized the voice and can put it together with a face."

"But, now, it gets interesting," Driscoll took over. "She knows the masked man came in to see the *guests* being kept in the apartment over the garage—the room we missed during our search." He looked pointedly at Wornick. "Anyway, she says she never saw them but assumed it was children from the food she sent up: peanut butter, cookies, milk. Not your usual *paesan* pasta. Anyway she's working with an artist to give the voice a face."

"So we assume the kids were there and Chamberlain and Romano tracked them down. Now where are they?" O'Brien netted it down. "I'll call Mrs. Chamberlain and bring her up to speed."

"Go ahead," Driscoll told him. "I'm going to call Savage. He's keeping the President abreast."

"We've got a rough idea of the masked man," the artist announced. "Look familiar?"

"Driscoll's on the phone," O'Brien told him. "Lemme see." The Detective shrugged. "Sort of. Looks like someone I should know, but I can't put my finger on it."

"We're running it through the computer, but, if the guy doesn't have a record, we'll get *nada*," the artist told him.

O'Brien found an unoccupied office and called the Winnetka number. He knew the FBI was listening and recording. "Mrs. Chamberlain, O'Brien. I'm at the Long Island Police Station."

"Yes, Detective," she said anxiously. "Anything?"

"Yes m'am. We think your children were being held at the home of a man named Giovonni Sorrento."

"Who? Are they all right?" She held her breath.

"We think so, Mrs. Chamberlain. The housekeeper thinks your husband was also at the house early this morning. Along with another man she described—who could be Tony Romano." Meri's heart stopped.

"Detective O'Brien, what does that mean?"

"The housekeeper told us that she, along with the household staff, were taken down to the basement of the estate by a man in a ski mask. As they walked through the kitchen, she saw two men being held at gunpoint. Right now, we think one was your husband, and the other, as I said, sounds like Romano. There is no one at the house now." O'Brien refrained from telling her about the four dead bodies. O'Brien prayed they could find the missing party before the press got word of the massacre at the Mafia mansion. O'Brien the headline writer.

"You have no idea where they were taken?"

"No, ma'am, but they left in one of the cars. We're checking all the leads now. I'll call you the minute we hear anything."

"Thank you so much for calling, Detective O'Brien. I really appreciate your kindness." Suddenly Meridith remembered Blanche DuBois' line at the close of the play: "I have always depended on the kindness of strangers." Life imitating art again.

"We'll all be praying together, Mrs. Chamberlain. Good bye."

"OmyGod! I can't fucking believe it!" O'Brien could hear Driscoll from the conference room. He ran to where bedlam had just broken loose.

"What's up?" he asked Wornick.

Wornick's bottom lip protruded out, making his face appear cartoonish, his eyebrows surprised. "Damned if I know," he answered shrugging.

Special Agent Driscoll's eyes bugged out, he was gasping for air. "Do you know who this is?" he asked the room. Without waiting for an answer he announced, "This, my friends, is the Vice President of the United States, Henry Boyer!" He held the artist's computer drawing over his head. "This is the man Giovonni Sorrento's housekeeper claims came to the estate yesterday, spent the night, and, now, has disappeared! This is the man who's voice she heard inside the black ski mask!"

Special Agent Driscoll was doing the Snoopy Dance around the conference table. "Call the Director. Tell him to meet us at National Airport. Wornick, get a helicopter here, and have the Bureau's plane ready. We're going to Washington to catch ourselves the biggest fish ever. Hot damn! What a story this'll make!"

WITH ONLY ONE STOP to accommodate the children, the limo drove straight through, arriving in Washington in a little under six hours. Boyer was careful of the speed limit. A ticket now would spoil everything. Planning was in the details.

No on spoke during the long drive. The children dozed, huddled close to their father. Jonathan's eyes closed, lulled by the quiet purring of the engine and the warmth of his son and daughter. Tony saw Angel's eyes droop, and he remained motionless, waiting for the man to nod off.

When Tony saw the green highway sign announcing D.C., he realized his window of opportunity was closing. He feigned sleep and allowed his body to slump against the window. Angel sat directly across from him in the limo's jump seat. Through a squint, Tony saw Angel's head drop. His hand inched slowly down his leg until he felt the hard steel of the knife taped inside his long sock. He pulled at the handle, allowing the blade to cut itself free from the tape.

Angel flinched, Tony's heart stopped. Angel's face dropped forward as the car crossed the Veteran's Bridge across the Potomac into Virginia. The knife was free. Tony tried to catch Jonathan's eye. Failing, he turned Chelsea's face toward her father's chest with one hand. He quickly lifted the knife and lunged at Angel, plunging the blade deep into the man's neck.

Angel's eyes opened to round, white circles. He tried to wrest the carved handle out of his body and cry out—but the knife cut through his vocal cords. The only sound that escaped was gurgled and choked in blood.

The commotion woke the children. Tony reached across Jonathan and held his hand across Hunter's mouth. Releasing his grip he put his finger to his lips, signaling silence. Chelsea buried her head against her father. Jonathan's color faded from his face as Angel's blood bubbled down his chest, and his head again fell back against the seat.

"Don't say a word!" he warned as he lifted the weapon from Angel's still form. Hunter stared at Tony then at the dead man. "Don't worry, Hunter, it'll all be over soon, and you'll be back home with your mother." For the first time, even Tony believed that.

The car pulled into the underground garage of Henry Boyer's condominium in Arlington, Virginia. Tony's hand shook as Boyer, mask in place, came around to open the back, car door. Before Boyer could react, Tony leapt from the seat and knocked him to the ground. He kicked the gun out of Boyer's grasp then kicked the man—hard—in the gut. Boyer moaned.

"Chamberlain, pick up the gun!" he commanded. Jonathan was out of the car and grabbed the weapon. His left arm wasn't cooperating. "Keep the gun trained on the bastard," Romano warned. "Okay, kids let's get you out of here."

Boyer laid on the floor of the underground garage, watching Romano come towards him. He scrambled to his feet. "Give me the keys," Romano demanded. Boyer reached into his pocket and pulled out the ring. "Okay, throw them over here." Boyer did as he was told. Tony reached down, never taking his eyes of his quarry and picked up the keys.

"Chamberlain, take the kids and drive until you find the nearest police station or phone. If the car phone works, use it. You're on your own."

"What about you?" Jonathan asked.

"You never saw me, you understand? You have to make the kids understand. As far as anyone knows, I'm dead. My only way out is to disappear." Tony took his eyes off Boyer only long enough to look into Jonathan's face. "You have to do this for me."

"I know," he looked at Tony now. "What about Meridith?" He asked, afraid of the answer.

"You'll work it out. Tell her I had to leave, she'll understand. And Chamberlain," his voice came from deep in his psyche, "if you ever hurt her again, I'll know, and," he lowered his voice, "I'll kill you."

"God, Tony, believe me, I'll spend the rest of my life making it up to her and to the kids."

"Get out of here," he tossed Jonathan the keys.

"Tony, thanks." Boyer started to move but Tony cocked the gun in his direction. Romano waited until he heard the ignition fire before pushing the gun into Boyer's back.

"No one will believe this, you know that." Boyer was almost laughing. The Vice President of the United States and the Mafia. Come on, it's almost cliche."

"Maybe no one will have to believe it. They'll just find you dead." Now Boyer was seriously quiet. "Get up, slowly." He followed behind Boyer, holding the gun leveled at the man's head. "What floor are we going to?" he asked his hostage.

"Seven." They walked towards the elevator, but the car continued to idle, never leaving the parking space.

"Hey, Chamberlain, get the hell out of here!" Tony shouted. They waited at the elevator doors. The car continued to idle.

Suddenly, the back door opened, and Hunter cried out, "Mr. Romano, it's my dad! I think it's his heart!" Boyer took advantage of Tony's distraction and threw himself at the gun. They fell to the cold, cement floor, wrestling for control of the weapon. Hunter yelled, "Dad! No!" Tony could hear Chelsea scream as a burst of gunfire swept across the floor, shattering concrete and leaving Tony's leg spurting blood. Boyer picked up the gun, the victor.

"Okay, walk over to the car, and see what the fuck is going on." Boyer now pushed the gun into Tony's face. Tony tried to stand on his wounded leg, but the pain seared through his body. His eyes teared, and he bit down on his lip as he hobbled to the car.

Hunter had opened the driver's door and was shaking Jonathan, trying desperately to revive him. He stood back when he saw the trail of blood. Tony pulled Jonathan's face off the steering wheel. It must have been sudden—his heart just stopped. His face was ashen, his eyes stared blindly, his mouth slack. Tony searched for a pulse.

"Call 911. Do something!" Hunter pleaded.

"I can't, Hunter. He's gone." The boy looked at Tony in disbelief. Chelsea began to cry. She was huddled in a ball, her hands across her eyes.

"We have to get out of here," Boyer ordered. "Okay, both of you, get over here."

"You can't leave him here like that!" Hunter shouted at Boyer. "Mr. Romano, do something!"

"Hunter, listen to me," Tony kept his voice as even as he could with the pain wracking his body. "You've got to think about your sister—and your mother. They're both going to need you now more than ever. Be a man, Hunter. Get Chelsea, and come with me." Hunter turned his face away from his father's body to look at Tony. "Okay," he answered. "Chel, it's okay. Come here." Chelsea, still shaking with sobs, slid across the wide seat and held her hand out to her older brother who took it gently.

"Okay, kids, let's go." Tony placed his hand on Hunter's back and Boyer herded them towards the elevator.

"Don't try anything, Romano. Right now I'd just as soon shoot all of you."

They reached the seventh floor, and the doors opened. Boyer used the gun barrel to prod Tony out first. He stepped out of a puddle of blood, leaving crimson footprints behind him. Hunter and Chelsea, holding hands, walked with him. Boyer fumbled in his pocket for the door key, Tony caught Hunter's eye and the young man instantly understood.

Using his best soccer kick, he caught Boyer between the legs. Startled and in great pain, Boyer fell to ground for the second time. Tony grabbed the gun and placed it squarely on the spot Hunter had kicked moments before.

"Don't even think about it," he told the whimpering man. "Hunter, take the key, carefully, and open the door." Chelsea picked it up off the carpeted floor and handed it to her brother.

"Okay, open it," Tony prompted. The door swung open, and the children walked in. "Don't even get up," Tony cautioned, "just crawl, like the viper you are." Still writhing in pain, Boyer made his way across the threshold into his apartment.

Once inside, Tony walked to the large, picture window. The east wall of the building overlooked the Potomac River and the spire of the Washington Monument. Tony pulled the drawstring off the curtain rod with a quick jerk. Then he rolled Boyer on his stomach and wrapped the cord first around the man's hands, then his feet, lashing them all together behind his back like a rodeo calf.

Convinced he'd incapacitated his enemy, he turned to the two terrified children. "Listen to me carefully. I'm going to tell you a story. It's very important, so listen closely, we don't have much time. Your father was a very brave man. He risked everything to find you, and it cost him his life. His heart wasn't strong enough for the shock." Chelsea began to cry again. Hunter bit his cheek to keep the tears from emasculating him.

"I'm a good friend of your family's, but I have a problem. I belong to an Organization made up of some very bad people. I wanted out, and they wouldn't let me. They found a man in your house who they think is me—I didn't kill him." Tony was quick to add. "We need to let them continue to think it was me so I can get away. Do you understand? Does this make sense to you?"

Hunter's eyes questioned, but he nodded. Chelsea stared, first at Tony then her brother. Tears streamed down her swollen face. "Okay, then, here's what we're going to do. I'm going downstairs and bring your father back up here. Then I'm going to call the police. When they come, you tell them your *father* captured Henry Boyer, this man here—" Tony kicked Boyer's ribs and he moaned through's Tony's instructions, "—before he died. Your father deserves to be the hero. And you, too, Hunter. You've been very courageous, your mother will be very proud." He thought of Meri and wished he could be there for her.

"But what about you? Your leg?" Chelsea asked through hiccupping sobs.

"I'll be fine. But you can't tell them about me," Tony warned. "We do need to explain the blood, though." He thought about that for a minute. "Boliano, or whatever you call yourself now, you had it all. Why get mixed up in this?"

Henry Boyer looked at Romano with indescribable hate. "You fuckin' piece of shit. You could have been right there at the top with me. I was this close to that desk in the Oval Office." His tone changed from loathing to pleading in an instant. "We could still have it all, Tony, just untie me. We could still do it."

"Kids, go in the bedroom. Don't come out until the police arrive. Promise? You may hear some noise, don't be afraid." They stared at Tony. "You've got to promise me!" His voice was rising. Time was running out. His leg throbbed and he had to stop the bleeding.

Hunter spoke, "We promise."

"Go in the bedroom, and close the door. Lock it behind you." He held the gun on Boyer until he heard the lock turn. He grabbed a towel from the kitchen and tied it tightly around his wounded leg. Then he tested the binding again. "Don't go anywhere," he taunted Boyer, "I'll be right back."

IT TOOK a monumental effort for Tony to lift Jonathan's body and heft it onto his back. Panting and sweating, he managed to carry it over to the elevator and into the apartment. He could hear Boyer yelling before the door opened. Tony prayed the neighbors worked during the day. He dragged the body to the sofa and placed the gun in Jonathan's wooden fingers, insuring the dead man's prints on the grip.

"Okay, kids," he yelled to the closed door, " you'll hear a gun, don't be frightened. After the noise, I'll be gone. Wait in there for the police."

Tony released the safety and aimed it. "What the hell are you doing?" Boyer screamed at him.

"Don't worry, I'm not going to kill you, that would be too easy. I'd rather you live with the shame you'll face when the media does it's number on the *Mobster Vice President*." Tony laughed. "Gangster or politician, sometimes there's no difference, huh? One last thing, Boliano, why?"

"Why? Tony, think! Power! Do you know how close I was to the most powerful seat in the world? The Organization's force combined with the prestige of The White House. Think of the control, the money, the *real power!*" He searched for the words to convince Romano. "Can you begin to comprehend what we could do with that kind of power? Tony, we could still do it. Think what you're throwing away."

"Look, Boyer, a few months ago I spouted that propaganda, too. And, like you, I believed it." He was remembering his talks with Meridith. *Meri.* "Suddenly that kind of power doesn't seem important, *Boliano.*"

"What the fuck kind of talk is that? Power is everything." He looked at Romano and sighed. "Love does strange things, Romano. Think with your head, not your prick. We're talking *world* domination. The time is so right. We're the only country with a stable economy right now. With the rest of the planet in turmoil, they're ripe for takeover. Hungry people don't give a fuck where the food comes from. Think! It would be the first time in history we could have domination and control without *war!* We could stop all the fighting *everywhere* and just move our people in! What the hell is this bullshit?"

The gun twitched in Tony's hand as Boyer tried another tact. "You'll never get away with this, you know that?"

"Probably not. But I'm dead, either way, so what's the difference?" For the first time Boyer noticed the sleek, black leather gloves Tony was wearing. No finger prints. The restrained man stalled for time. "Tony, Tony, I have the power to get you out of this."

"Freedom, that's the real power. I'm trading *everything* for my freedom." Pause. "Maybe we should give it back to the people, where it belongs."

"Hell, people traded their freedom for security a long time ago. The kind of freedom you're spouting comes with too much responsibility for *the people*. Tony, you and I, we can rule the whole damned country, hell, we can rule the fuckin' *world!* The *universe*, Tony!" Boyer's eyes glistened.

"How much does one man really want?" Tony asked the rhetorical question to a man roped on the floor, begging for his life. "I'm remembering another little man in the footnotes of history." He thought about being the *boss* and about all the men throughout history who lost it with one last roll of the dice. An endless list of greedy, failed power-hungry men. "Napoleon once said, *'Power is my only mistress.'* And we know how he ended up ...Tony sighed and shook his head; Boyer writhed as much from the pain of frustration as physical injury.

Tony aimed the weapon and lowered his voice, "What the hell would you do with it all, anyway?" Laughing, his eyes glazed over and he shouted, "I've got the power, now. Isn't that what a person holding a gun thinks? But it doesn't matter, anymore. You're about to lose it all, Hank, old man!" His finger squeezed the trigger. "Sorry. I hate to do this, but—I have to explain the blood."

The gun sounded like fire-crackers, sending sparks across the living room. One of three bullets scored Boyer's leg just enough to leave a splatter across the carpet. The wounded man cried out! Chelsea screamed from the bedroom.

"It's okay, Chelsea," Tony reassured her. "I said there'd be a noise, it's all over now. Remember what I told you. And, be strong for your mother, she'll need you now. Tell her—" Tony hesitated. "Tell her I'll be thinking about all of you."

With that he put the gun in Jonathan's lap, grabbed another towel from the kitchen and limped out. He could hear Boyer moaning through the closed door.

DAY FOUR
THURSDAY, NOVEMBER 21 • 2:00 PM EST

NOTHING SEEMED to be moving fast enough for the men disembarking from the Bureau's jet. O'Brien joined the agents in the race to the waiting cars.

Reagan National Airport is located across the Potomac River, less than a five minute ride to Boyer's apartment with sirens wailing. A small group standing outside the building stood back as the agents stampeded through the revolving doors. The astounded doorman was silent as the agents flashed badges across the marble lobby. "Boyer! What floor?"

"Mr. Boyer's on seven, but you can't go up there." He started to pick up the phone.

"Call him and you're under arrest for obstruction," Driscoll warned. "What's the number on seven?"

"Seven oh three, but—"

"Stay with him," Driscoll ordered another agent.

O'Brien took the stairs, impatient with the elevator. He heard footsteps behind him and turned to find Driscoll on his tail. They reached seven, breathless and sweating. O'Brien pulled open the fire door to the hall with his gun drawn. The two were met in the hall by the FBI contingent.

"Driscoll, check the floor," one pointed out. Blood. From the elevator doors to the entrance to seven oh three. "It's in the elevator, too."

"Shit!" Driscoll muttered.

"God, I hope we're not too late again." O'Brien said to the agent, "You or me?" Without a word they both banged on the door.

"FBI, open up!" Driscoll shouted. They heard a moan behind the door.

"Get away from the door, we're going to shoot the lock!" O'Brien yelled.

"Wait!" a small voice screamed. The men in the hall all froze in place as the door slowly opened. Hunter held it open for his sister, and the two children walked into the hallway.

"Oh, thank you, God!" O'Brien crossed himself and grabbed each of the children in his big arms, hugging them together. Driscoll walked around them into the condo.

"Jesus Christ!" As the agents entered they were all struck speechless by the macabre scene. The Vice President of the United States was trussed like a Thanksgiving turkey, wounded, bleeding profusely. Jonathan Chamberlain was dead on the sofa with a gun in his lap. Driscoll checked his pulse then shook his head to O'Brien.

"Can we go home now?" Chelsea asked the Detective.

"Of course you can, sweetheart. Let's call your mother first." He turned to Driscoll, "Call the Congressman. Tell him we'll bring the kids there until Mrs. Chamberlain can get here."

"We'll need to know what happened. Hunter can you tell us?" O'Brien was quiet while Hunter relayed the story of their abduction from school and the plane trip to Long Island.

"The people treated us nice, but we were scared. We were brought to a big house, and a nice old man spent the day with us watching TV and eating whatever we asked for. Then, last night, while it was still dark, a man in a mask," he pointed to Boyer, "came to the room with our dad and got us. We all drove in a limo to Washington. When we got out of the car my father got the gun from that man, and brought us up here where he tied up the man on the floor, and shot him when he tried to get away."

"What happened to your father then," O'Brien prodded.

"Then his heart attacked him, again, but this time he died," Chelsea finished, tears streaming down her tiny face. O'Brien knelt down and put his arms around her. She allowed him to hold her until the shaking subsided.

The paramedics arrived. Boyer listened to the boy's narrative but remained silent, locked in his own pain. "You have anything you want to add?" the agent asked him.

"I want to see my lawyer," Boyer answered as the paramedics began cutting the cording holding him in bondage.

"Who tied him up like this?" the medic asked Hunter.

"My father," Hunter lied.

"He must be one hell of a sailor. These knots are killers." Then he realized the impact of the word he used and turned red with embarrassment.

"Was your father a sailor, Chelsea?" O'Brien asked the little girl.

"No." Hunter shot her a side-long glance. "I think so," she corrected.

"Tell me, Chelsea, was there anyone else here with your father. Anyone who could have helped him?" Chelsea looked to Hunter. O'Brien saw the look pass between the children.

"No." As the paramedics placed Boyer on a gurney, O'Brien stood up and looked at the bottom of the wounded man's shoes. No blood. He lifted Jonathan's foot off the ground. No blood. He walked back into the hall and bent over to inspect the bloody footprints.

"Agent, could you keep an eye on the kids for a minute? I want to check something." This time O'Brien waited for elevator, and saw the bloody prints on the tiled floor of the elevator car. He took it down to the garage. Hunter told him they rode in a limo. The footprints led him to an empty space.

"Damn!" O'Brien expressed his frustration by banging his fist against one of the columns. Then he saw the puddle of blood on the garage floor. "Somebody's hurt bad." His voice echoed in the deserted chamber. "And my money is on Romano. But why would the kids lie for him?" The man was like a splinter under the detective's nail. He had to find out for sure. What was the power Romano wielded over people? He had to solve the mystery.

DAY FOUR
THURSDAY, NOVEMBER 21 • 3:12 PM EST

"MOM? OH, MOM, Dad's dead!" Hunter blurted into the phone when he heard his mother's voice. Meri was stunned. Her children were safe, but Jonathan was gone. O'Brien had given her an abbreviated version before putting the boy on the phone.

"I'm sorry, Hunter. I'm so sorry you had to go through this and you and Chelsea had to be alone when it happened." She needed to know the whole story, but, for now, Hunter and Chelsea needed her reassurance.

"Mommy? It's so awful here, I want to come home. I miss you," Chelsea sobbed into the receiver.

"I know, honey," Meri began to cry. "I'll be there in a few hours. Grandpa will be with you until I get there. Will you be all right until then?" Chelsea nodded at the phone.

"Mrs. Chamberlain, this is Detective O'Brien. Agent Driscoll told you what happened. I'm so sorry. But the children are okay, they're here with me. I'm taking them over to the Congressman's house now. We didn't think he should come here and see his son like this. I'll stay with them until you get here."

"Did—Jonathan suffer? Do you know?" she asked tentatively.

"We don't think so. Right now it looks as though he rescued the kids and turned the tables on their abductor—tied him up and kept a gun on him while he called the local police. Then, his heart just gave up. Too much for him, I guess. Mrs. Chamberlain, your husband was a brave man."

"He did this all alone?" Meridith asked. O'Brien, the Detective, heard the dismay in her voice. She knew, too.

"It looks that way at the moment. No one here but your children and the kidnapper, trussed up like a goose. Your husband must have been a hell of a sailor from the look of the knots." He waited for her response. A pause.

"Thank you, again. I always seem to be thanking you," she was crying harder. "Please, Detective O'Brien keep them safe until I get there." She hung up.

"Oh, Brooke, the kids are okay. But he's dead, Jonathan's dead." Brooke held her until the tears stopped.

"What about Tony?" Brooke finally asked.

"Tony? You knew he was alive?" Meri was shaken.

"After I gave you the book and you went upstairs with it, you've been different. I picked it up and read the highlighted passages. What else could it have meant? Is he there with the children?"

"I don't know. No one said anything, and I'm afraid to ask."

"Let's go get the children, they need you now, and you need them."

"You'll go with me?"

"You're not in any shape to go alone and make the arrangements that need to be made. Let me call Chester while you get us on a plane."

"The Whitney Foods jet is at Palwaukee. I'll call and have it ready."

"Meri, you'll have your children back here tomorrow!" Brooke hugged Meridith again. Meridith Whitney Chamberlain set her jaw. "Yes, and, somehow, I'll make this up to them." And to all of us, she promised.

"I'm taking the kids to the Congressman's," O'Brien announced to one of the local officers who swarmed the condo. "Can you give us a ride?"

"Sure thing! You FBI?"

"No, Winnetka police."

"Winnetka? Where's Winnetka?" he asked.

"Too long a story," O'Brien smiled at him. "It's where the kids are from."

O'Brien found Hunter and Chelsea huddled in the bedroom, waiting for him. Chelsea's face broke into a sad smile when she saw him.

"Can we go now?" she asked. O'Brien could see a childhood version of Meridith.

"Let's blow this pop stand," he told the kids.

"What does that mean?" Hunter looked skeptical.

"I'm old," he explained. To children, that went without saying. O'Brien took their hands and led them through the maze of uniforms and the photographer's flashes. "Don't look back," he said as they left the condo.

DAY FOUR
THURSDAY, NOVEMBER 21 • 7:45 PM EST

WHEN THE POLICE car delivered Meri to the Congressman's Georgetown home, Chelsea and her brother met her halfway down the sidewalk. Meridith Chamberlain couldn't hold her children tight enough! O'Brien's throat constricted, fighting tears.

Passers-by stopped to witness the strange scene. O'Brien gently escorted them back into the house. It wouldn't be much longer before the press descended on them, again, here. Damn, sometimes he really hated their draconian ways.

"Mommy, it was awful!" Chelsea told Meri as they sat on the floor hugging.

"I know, honey, I know." The tears continued as Franklin knelt down and placed his arms around the two, holding them tight. Hunter swallowed hard and finally gave in to deep, racking sobs, becoming part of the family huddle. Detective Charles O'Brien stood by helplessly, wiping the tears off his chin. Brooke stood back, too, her heart hurting for the family she loved like her own.

Chelsea hiccupped loudly, and this caused Hunter to laugh. Franklin stood up and took his handkerchief from his pocket and handed it to Meri. He looked at the detective, "How can I ever thank you?"

"I'd like to take the credit, sir, but your son was the real hero here." O'Brien watched Hunter and Chelsea steal a look.

Franklin held his head higher. "That makes it easier, somehow. Thank you." The Congressman walked into the kitchen to dry his tears.

"Mrs. Chamberlain, I appreciate what you and your family are going through, really I do. But I must speak with you privately."

"Yes, of course. But not right now, Detective." She was holding a cold cloth on her daughter's swollen face.

"Mrs. Chamberlain, could I ask you to call me Charlie?"

She smiled, a sad half-smile. "Of course, Charlie. And you were supposed to call me Meridith."

"Detective, I mean, Charles," Meri addressed him. No one but his mother ever called him that, but, coming from her, he liked it. "You'll have to excuse us. I'd like to have a few minutes to clean up and get the children some fresh clothes. Please make yourself at home."

She picked up the bags the police woman brought in earlier.

"Here, let me," he offered, taking them up the stairs.

MERI RAN THE bath for Chelsea while Hunter showered in the second bathroom. Once her daughter was emersed in bubbles she sat on the tub and looked into her face. "Okay, tell Mother exactly what happened. And don't leave anything out."

Chelsea thought for a moment, took a deep breath, and recited the story. From the woman in the school turnaround to Tony's admonition about keeping his secret, it unfolded. Meri wasn't sure what she was feeling, other than numbness. The flood of emotions was causing her to go into overload and shutdown.

"Thank you for trusting me, Chelsea. I'm so proud of you and Hunter for being so brave and being there with Daddy. He loved you very much."

"He really was brave, Mom. He and Mr. Romano saved us."

"And for that I will be forever grateful. And we will keep his secret, Chelsea." She kissed her daughter's slippery cheek.

"Don't cry, Mommy, it makes me cry." The tears returned quickly.

"It's okay to cry, Chel. We're sad for Daddy and for us. Soon, it won't hurt so much. We'll all be okay because we have each other."

Now, she needed to reassure Hunter.

DAY FOUR
THURSDAY, NOVEMBER 21 • 8:25 PM EST

MERI AND THE CHILDREN returned downstairs feeling a little better. Franklin's housekeeper, Mrs. Tole, set out hot chocolate, and O'Brien lit the fire. Just like he'd foreseen, the press was gathered, and their din grew louder. Brooke had pulled the draperies but the flashes and the video lights broke through at regular intervals. No one turned on the television.

The family tried to eat the dinner that was set out for them, but fatigue overcame hunger. They sat huddled together on the sofa trying to make sense out of their ordeal.

Mrs. Tole tried to tempt the children with cookies, but even that offer was met with a shrug. "Oh, Mrs. Chamberlain, I almost forgot. I picked up the mail as I came in, and this was in the letterbox for you." Meri's heart pumped harder. Mrs. Tole handed her an innocent-looking, white envelope.

"Thank you," was all he could manage. With a shaking hand, she took it and walked quietly upstairs to the guest room. She sat down on the bed and began to read:

My darling Meri,

I'm so sorry for your anguish. Please find it in your heart to forgive me—and to forgive Jonathan. In the end, he did what was right. In his own way, he loved you and his children. Hunter and Chelsea are safe, and that's all that matters. They are wonderful, brave children. You can be very proud. I am. Mama Rosa and the family are safe, too, and send their love.

God gave me the precious gift of your love, but we both knew it could never last. The gifts we exchange are priceless. I give you back your children, and you've given me freedom. Trading your love isn't a good deal, but its the best one a guy like me could ask for. You deserve the moon and the stars, and I can only give you more heartache.

Shakespeare tried to teach us that all lovers are not kissed by destiny, and Tennessee's dramas all don't end happily. We all have lessons to learn in this lifetime, but you, my lovely lady, taught me mine—the only real power is love. I will always love you.

The handwritten note was unsigned. Meri reread it several times before carefully folding it and placing it back inside the envelope. As she did, she noticed something else—an oblong bank receipt. She looked at it curiously. It was a copy of a deposit slip made to the Cayman Island Trust Company, Ltd. The name on the account was *Meridith Whitney.* The amount was a million dollars. Handwritten across the back of the slip was a note: *I attempted to negotiate for the children's safe return. When I failed, I prayed for a Guardian Angel. Mama Rosa says we all have one and Mama's always right.*

Meridith put the receipt in her wallet and the letter in her handbag. She was trying to cool her burning eyes when there was a knock. "Mrs. Chamberlain? Meridith?" It was O'Brien.

"Yes?" She put her purse in the dresser.

"I'm sorry to bother you, but we need to talk. Can I come in?"

Meri opened the door. "Please." He walked into the guest room and took a chair.

"I don't know how to begin, so, in my usual clumsy way, I'll just jump in. We know there was someone else with your husband and children. There were bloodstains we can't account for. Have they told you anything they didn't share with me?" Meri appraised the detective for a long while, saying nothing. "I must know, Meridith. I promise you can trust me." He had earned her respect.

"Okay. I'll trust you to do what you have to with what I'm going to tell you. But I'd like to ask you to remember my children's lives may still be in danger." He nodded. She took a deep breath.

"Chelsea and Hunter told me that Tony Romano was with Jonathan at the house. He tied up Henry Boyer and carried their father up to the apartment after Jonathan died in the car. Tony killed the guard that was holding a gun on them in the car. I have no idea what he did with the body." The Washington police will find it floating, O'Brien was sure. "There's one thing I can't understand. Why would a man like Henry Boyer want to kidnap my children?"

"That's something that's bothering everyone, especially me. Meridith, I never had much in life, but what I have had, I hope I appreciated. Some men, no matter how much they have ..." he trailed off thinking of Jonathan as well as Boyer.

Meridith shook her head sadly. "Don't you think that at some time ego takes over? Ambition becomes almost narcotic. Don't you agree?"

"Ego, huh? Well, I never had much of that. Guess that explains why I'm not in their league." Suddenly, Charlie O'Brien was feeling very old and very tired.

"Detective, I'm sure Tony saved all their lives. Charles," she was trying to appeal not to the officer but to the man, "Jonathan was not courageous by any means. Tony left my children with a legacy from their father. If they had to lose him, at least they'll remember him as a hero. Don't take that away." Meri paced, measuring her words now. "Tony wanted out of the Organization. Let him disappear. You have a body, can't we call it Tony Romano? Who knows what the men in the Organization will do if they discover my children have information on the man they think they killed? Let me put it to you this way—Tony's life in exchange for Hunter's and Chelsea's?" She sat across from him and looked deep into his eyes, silently pleading.

"Mrs. Chamberlain, you're asking me to go against everything I've stood for. I've always been just a good cop, that's all I am. Now you want me to forget I know that one of Chicago's biggest hoodlums is still alive? Even if I agreed, we still have the FBI to contend with."

"Is there any real proof he was there?" she asked, honestly wanting to know."Not really." He was thinking of the footprints they missed. "But what if he was lying to you? To save his own skin? Did it ever occur to you that this is a man capable of deception?" O'Brien was on his feet.

Meridith walked to the dresser and took out her purse. She retrieved the letter and handed it to O'Brien. "Read this, and if you still believe the man who wrote this is capable of that kind of duplicity, then do what you have to do."

Charlie O'Brien read the letter. The ink had blurred slightly over a few tear-stained lines. When he finished, he carefully folded it and handed it back.

"Meridith, we'll do it your way. For now. Somehow, I'll have to convince the FBI. Of course, they'd like to close the books on this one, too. And it wouldn't be the first time the books were *edited* before publication." He laughed softly to himself, and left the room without another word.

By the time Meri composed herself and walked downstairs, Detective O'Brien was gone. The children were asleep on the sofa, Chelsea's head on her brother's lap. Franklin was close by, staring at the fire reflected on their faces.

Brooke looked up. "Okay?" she asked in feminine shorthand.

"Tomorrow we'll talk," Meri told her friend as she lifted her daughter and carried her upstairs to bed.

"I'll get Hunter," Franklin offered. By nine forty-five the long day ended the even longer week for the people in the townhouse on Congressional Avenue, a long way from Winnetka.

JANUARY 12 • THE NEW YEAR

FROM THE FRONT PAGE of the Washington Post:

FORMER VICE PRESIDENT FOUND DEAD

Henry Boyer, 52, once the country's second most powerful man was found dead of an apparent suicide early this morning in Rock Creek Parkway.

A passing motorist spotted the body from the highway. A single gunshot to the right temple was the cause of death. The weapon was still in Boyer's right hand.

Boyer was alleged to have been the mastermind behind the kidnapping of Illinois Congressman Franklin Chamberlain's two grandchildren in November from the affluent suburb of Winnetka. The children's father, Jonathan Chamberlain, a noted Chicago attorney, died of a heart attack during their rescue. The two Chamberlain children, Hunter, 14, and Chelsea, 10, were returned to their mother, socialite and Whitney Food heiress, Meridith, unharmed.

The State of New York was attempting to extradite Henry Boyer on four counts of murder. Reputed Organization Boss, Giovonni Sorrento, and three of his associates were killed in his Long Island Estate during the aborted kidnapping.

Reputed Chicago kingpin, Tony Romano, was found dead in the Chamberlain estate prior to the kidnapping. Police and FBI officials were never able to uncover the motive for his murder, and no one has been charged with the crime, although authorities suspect a link with the kidnapping.

Henry Boyer, in an unprecedented ruling by Federal Judge Richard Nevers, was out on bail when the suicide occurred. The Judge had no comment when contacted. According to the FBI, Boyer was trying to workout a plea-bargain in exchange for information on organized crime.

The President released a statement conveying his sympathy to Boyer's family but offered no explanation as to why he felt the Vice President had become involved with the crimes. Boyer's father, the late Marco Boliano, was reputed to have had mob connections but never convicted. Boyer is survived by his mother, Josephine Boliano, and a sister, Helen Boliano Marcelli, both of New York.

The White House had no comment as to how they felt this would effect the President and his current agenda. In an ironic twist, it was Vice President Henry Boyer who was instrumental in the passage of the President's Organized Crime Bill.

GEORGE GRAVANI, the reputed new Boss' Boss, read the article and tossed it across the table where he was enjoying breakfast. "Poor bastard," he commented to his body guard, Jake, as he bit into a hot muffin. "Funny thing though, I always thought Hank Boliano was left handed."

AN ITEM appeared in Irv Kupcinet's column in the Chicago Sun-Times:

Our sympathies go out to the beautiful Winnetka philanthropist and talented actress, Meridith Chamberlain. She lost her courageous husband, Jonathan, just before Thanksgiving. Essee and I were happy to see her, accompanied by her charming children, Hunter and Chelsea, enjoying the holidays in the Cayman Islands. Best wishes to you all for a better New Year.

AND in the local Pioneer Press papers, under *"Promotions:"*

LOCAL HERO RETIRES FROM FORCE

Detective Charles O'Brien announced his resignation from the Winnetka Police Force. O'Brien will assume the position as Chief Security Officer for the Whitney Foods Corporation, a division of Carolina Tobacco.

Hailed as the hero behind the rescue of Congressman Franklin Chamberlain's grandchildren, O'Brien said he is looking forward to enjoying a quiet life in the private sector.